ALSO AVAILABLE FROM
KELSIE LEVERICH

The Valentine's Arrangement: A Hard Feelings Novel
Pretending She's His: A Penguin Special Novella
Feel the Rush: A Hard Feelings Novel

A BEAUTIFUL Distraction

A Hard Feelings Novel

KELSIE LEVERICH

A SIGNET ECLIPSE BOOK

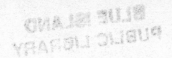

SIGNET ECLIPSE
Published by the Penguin Group
Penguin Group (USA) LLC, 375 Hudson Street,
New York, New York 10014

USA | Canada | UK | Ireland | Australia | New Zealand | India | South Africa | China
penguin.com
A Penguin Random House Company

First published by Signet Eclipse, an imprint of New American Library,
a division of Penguin Group (USA) LLC.

First Signet Eclipse Printing, May 2014

LIBRARY OF CONGRESS CATALOGING-IN-PUBLICATION DATA:
Leverich, Kelsie.
A beautiful distraction: a hard feelings novel/Kelsie Leverich.
p. cm.
ISBN 978-0-451-46894-9 (pbk.)
1. Man-woman relationships—Fiction. I. Title.
PS3612.E923455B43 2014
813'.6—dc23   2013048584

Printed in the United States of America
10 9 8 7 6 5 4 3 2 1

Set in New Caledonia
Designed by Spring Hoteling

To my ladies.

May your hearts swell and your toes curl. Always.

ACKNOWLEDGMENTS

The list of bloggers and readers who have helped promote my novels is endless. To every single person who posted and shared and pimped and promoted, thank you. Please know that I could not reach the readers I reach without the continued support from you all. The reading/writing community is beyond amazing with everyone's eagerness and willingness to support one another. The bloggers who take time away from family to support us writers simply out of the joy of reading will never fail to astound me. I'm humbled and honored to have the encouragement and love from all of you. I appreciate you more than words can express.

My family never ceases to amaze me, continuously encouraging me—even when the house is a mess and we order pizza once a week—and supporting my dreams. Especially my six-year-old son, who lights up even more than I do when I get exciting news about my novels. It makes all the late nights worth it.

My friend Heather, I couldn't write anything without you. You are my go-to girl when I need to bounce an idea around, and I couldn't love you more for always being ready and willing to have a beer with me and plot.

Kim Karr, I'm so happy to have formed a friendship with you. You're an amazing author whom I adore and an even more amazing woman. Thank you for the hours of phone calls when I needed to

ACKNOWLEDGMENTS

plot, or vent, or just chat. It's been so fun going through this journey with you.

It has been such a pleasure working with my editor, Danielle Perez, on this novel. Danielle, I can't thank you enough for all the time you have invested in me and this story. Your guidance has been invaluable.

My agent/critique partner/proofreader/advice giver, Jill Marsal, you're amazing! Seriously couldn't have walked this road without you. Thank you!

And from the bottom of my heart, thank you to our military. Your world has inspired me and humbled me, and I am grateful to you and your families each and every day.

A BEAUTIFUL Distraction

PROLOGUE

*F*allon Kelly walked slowly out to the middle of the stage. It was dark. She could see them—they just couldn't see her.

Not yet, at least.

Looking around the club, Fallon listened as the voices hushed and she watched as the mingling, exuberant eyes shifted their focus to the stage—to her. She always loved that part, commanding a room like this. Sure, her lady goods on display were an enticing incentive for their attention. But even then, the dominance she wielded while on that stage was worth it—breasts out and all. She didn't doubt for one second that if she said "Jump," the room would shake with the vibrations of shoes landing back on concrete.

She'd been dancing at Velour for the last six years, and even now the terrifying feeling of being on that stage still rang through her body the way it did the very first night she danced there. She didn't know how to describe it. It was a complicated contradiction of emotions, but they went together hand in hand—one not complete without its counterpart. Nervous yet satisfied, powerful yet scared, confident yet with a tinge of diffidence. It pulled and pushed her in every single direction. Her skin felt sensitive under the lights; her stomach fluttered and rolled. But at the same time she was hyperaware of every pulse of her heartbeat as a warm feeling of contentment spread through her veins.

Fallon adjusted her weight on her feet, the tulle from her tutu brushing against the bare flesh of her upper thigh that was exposed between her white lace thigh-highs and her briefs. This wasn't the typical dance for the club. Pointe shoes and tutus weren't characteristically burlesque attire. But this was *her* dance. She danced this routine for herself—no one else. Even if she did get a high from the crowd's admiration, the high she felt when she slipped back into those pointe shoes was even better.

The music started to play, and the dim spotlight flicked on and hit her face.

Now they could see her.

This routine was her signature. Yet she didn't do it often. It was too real, too intimate for an audience. But every now and then she needed it.

Growing up, Fallon had excelled at ballet. She'd been her mother's shining star, her prima ballerina—an additional step to her mother's climb on the social ladder to hell. And Fallon loved to dance, which made her resent the appalling little fact that her mother loved her dancing too—she just loved it for the wrong reasons. Fallon hated that she enjoyed something that played into her mother's flagrant quest for prestige. She was merely an aesthetically valuable pawn in her mother's game.

After she'd lost her burlesque virginity to the stage at Velour six long years before, she'd gone to the basement studio, where the dancers choreographed and practiced their routines. And she'd bawled her eyes out. For the first time in two years, she'd cried. She'd cried for what she had done in her past, and she'd cried for what she had done on that stage. Baring her body to a roomful of strangers for the first time almost made her feel as if she'd debased her value as a woman.

Almost.

But the reason her tears had fallen that night wasn't because she felt ashamed, but because it felt liberating.

So she'd stood up and danced. She'd moved to silence for hours, well into the early morning, staring at herself in the mirror—watching her body move like she hadn't seen it move in a long time. She'd danced every torturous emotion that was suffocating under the thick skin she'd grown, and it was powerful. It was freeing. And she loved it.

As the music ended its angelic melody, preparing to break into the passionate, quick-beat tempo, Fallon refocused her mind from the past, closed her eyes, and carefully rose onto pointe. The club was crammed near capacity, but not a single noise could be heard above the music—and Fallon knew, without needing visual validation, that everyone was fixated on her.

Her hands fluttered to the bodice of her costume. It was cut low and allowed her breasts to spill over the top, accentuating the perfect amount of cleavage. Sensually skimming her fingertips down her sides, she pulled the tulle of her skirt between her fingers. The volume of the music rose and drummed through her body and she raised her arms and lifted her leg into arabesque. As she held her position, the music started to pick up and she spun around; throwing her body into the air, she leaped across the stage. The audience hollered out, their appraisal for the beauty of ballet surprising her as always. She loved the little shock factor she received when the club's patrons animated over a grand jeté and a few pirouettes.

Her body began to feel the familiar comforting pull in her muscles. The vibrations against the stage from the music ricocheted through her bones as the speed held a steady tempo—the instrumental sounds were intense, seductive, almost scary. Her hands found the clasp of her skirt as she pushed off into a sequence of fouetté turns and with every turn her skirt spun off her body until she was covered in only her corset bodice and briefs.

The crowd cheered as the layer fell to the stage the moment her feet left the ground. Slowly, knowing that the act of undressing was more arousing than the result, she easily and deliberately untied the ribbon attached to the back of her corset, all the while circling the stage in pique turns. She looped the ribbon around her wrists and unsnapped the hooks down the front of her corset as she stood with her leg extended in the air. Then she let it fall to the ground, exposing her breasts, covered in a scanty leather bra. The crowd praised her again as she used the movement of her body paired with the beat of the music to slip her briefs to the ground, exposing matching panties that covered little of her bottom.

Then, as if he had spoken her name aloud, her attention was drawn to an unfamiliar man sitting at a table close to the back of the club. Even from a distance she could see the rich, luxurious softness inked into his dark stone irises. He returned her stare, holding her captive in his trance. His posture was lax, his thumb running across the rim of his glass, his breathing controlled. Yet she knew she was affecting him. Not in the movements of his body, but in the way he was commanding her attention, refusing to release his eye contact. She felt the even, steady beat of her heart jerk into a jagged rhythm, her body melting under the smoldering heat of his gaze. Apparently, he was affecting her equally as much.

His eyebrow cocked and a slow, intentional smile pulled unevenly across his face as if he could see the increase in her pulse and feel the flutter in her stomach.

His lips staggered upward a little higher, impishly lifting, as he continued to watch her. It was different from the other attentive eyes on her.

It was distracting.

A familiar rattling along with a swooshing sound blended with the music, breaking the visual spell she was under. She knew the curtain was pulling open, cuing her to the final part of her dance.

A gold pole was revealed in the middle of the stage. No one else used this pole but her. Their routines weren't based on the stereotypes of strippers and poles. But the pole—she loved it. The power and strength it took to maneuver her body up and down the pole, spinning and gliding with only her hands and thighs as support, was, for lack of a better word, addictive.

Wrapping her hands around the cool metal, she leaped into the air, using her upper-body strength to keep herself gracefully spinning. She slowly flipped and rolled her body into an arabesque, using only her thighs to keep her in position high up on the pole while she extended her arms and leg. The lithe way she could elongate her body while holding on to the metal and elegantly pose made her feel like she was a prima ballerina with wings.

Only she gave the prima ballerina over to seduction.

And it felt powerful.

CHAPTER ONE

The previous night

Rafe Murano's boot slipped from the bottom of the barstool, landing with a thump on the grimy concrete floor of the dive bar he'd been frequenting the last few weeks more often than he was proud to admit. His body swayed unsteadily at the unintentional shift in his weight.

"Easy, killer," Trish said from behind the bar, where she was wiping the slick remnants of beer and liquor clean with a rag.

Rafe lifted his head from where he sat studying the slow burn of paper from the cherry of his Marlboro. He watched as Trish shook her head at him, attempting the illusion of disappointment when he lifted his lips and flashed his teeth.

"You know that shit doesn't work on me. A pretty smile from a sexy man does nothing for a woman when she's repulsed by penises. Now put that smile on a blonde with a nice pair of tits, and I'm putty."

"I get a blonde with a nice pair of tits tonight, and I'll share her with ya. How does that sound?"

Trish smiled, then squatted down to the floor, out of Rafe's line of vision. He could hear her fumbling around, then the distinct sound of glasses clinking together. When she rose, she had two glasses in one hand and a bottle of Angel's Envy in the other. Trish not only shared Rafe's love for women, but also his love for whiskey. And Angel's Envy was like drinking nectar from the gods.

Silently watching her, Rafe sealed his lips around the filter of his cigarette and pulled the smoke into his lungs.

"Rafe, baby, I love you. But I don't share my women. And you—you don't strike me as a man who likes to share either," she probed. She poured the golden liquid into the glasses and slid one over to Rafe.

He wrapped his hand around the glass and pulled it in front of him.

"I take it by your silence that I hit the nail on the head?" Trish pried, cocking one of her thick brows, then lifted her glass to her mouth and took a leisurely sip.

Putting his cigarette back to his lips, he took another long drag, then stubbed it out in the ashtray next to him, releasing a cloud of smoke from his lungs. Picking up his glass, he met Trish's eyes and held them stolidly. "I don't share what's mine."

Her other eyebrow darted up as well. "And if it's not yours?" she asked cautiously.

"Then it's not mine to share in the first place so it doesn't really fucking matter then, does it?" he barked.

"Watch it," Trish admonished. "I see that I struck a chord, but I don't put up with drunk, asshat soldiers. I'm warning you now."

Rafe could feel the tension in his body as if it were a visible limb attached from the inside out. He emptied the contents of his glass into his mouth and swallowed, then slid it back to Trish. She absentmindedly refilled it with more whiskey, never taking her eyes off him, waiting for a verbal strike, then slid it back across the worn wooden counter.

"I'm good, Trish," Rafe assured, running his thumb over the rim of his glass. He propped his black boot back up on the bottom leg of the barstool next to him. This had seemed to be his nightly routine as of late. What the fuck else was there to do now that he was back? After being deployed for the last twelve months—living every minute of every day on mission, serving his country—the normalcy of civilian life wasn't so normal anymore. He went through this every time he came off deployment, though: attempting to adapt back to life without carrying his M-16 over his shoulder or transporting in armored vehicles or sweating his balls off in hundred-degree heat in full battle rattle. It made most men appreciate the ease of civilian life, and it sure as hell made Rafe appreciate it too. But there was always a part of him that missed it. Missed the constant missions, the uncertainty of every second. The way it took him over. He was fully focused and committed to his squad, and he didn't have time to dwell on anything other than his job and the safety of his men.

"You better be. I wouldn't want to have to kick my favorite customer out of my bar. Plus, our big-boobed blonde is heading this way. I may be calling dibs on this one, big guy. She looks sweet enough to savor."

Rafe smiled, grateful for the mood-lifting ability that

Trish possessed. He looked over his shoulder to the short blonde who was meekly approaching the bar. Then, almost as quickly, he turned back around.

Innocence.

It basically encased her in an invisible protection shield. Rafe didn't fuck with those ones—in every sense of the word. The sweet ones had a tendency to slip under the radar and find a way to screw with his mind. These days he kept his dick on the straight and narrow as long as that straight and narrow led to the pussy of some chick who neither wanted nor expected anything other than a good time— and one time only. No repeat offenders for him.

Rafe pulled the last cigarette from his pack and lit the end, inhaling deeply. His focus returned to Trish, who was close to salivating. And goddammit, seeing Trish get hot over a woman sent the alcohol-infused blood in Rafe's body rushing toward his dick. Trish was a knockout. Long, lean legs covered in black pants that adhered to every inch of her from hip to ankle, her hair jet-black with streaks of blond flashing around her face as she moved.

Rafe followed Trish's gaze back to the blonde behind him. Her hips and thighs were curvy with a little additional padding, but her waist was small. Her jeans were snug and hung low on the flair of her hips. The purple shirt she wore clung to her body like a second skin, showcasing a flat stomach and an incredible pair of tits with a generous amount of cleavage peeking over the deep V-neck. Her long hair was tied back away from her round face, and a soft blush spread across her neck when she noticed Rafe watching her.

"I'll have a Bud Light," she told Trish as she stepped up to the bar and leaned her forearms over the counter. He knew Trish was getting an eyeful and he knew she was loving it. Trish may not be into sharing, but maybe he could talk her into letting him watch . . .

"I knew your sorry ass would be here."

Rafe resisted the urge to roll his head back on his neck and groan. He didn't bother to look at who had suddenly taken up residence on the stool next to him. The irritating tone to his voice, warning of an impending lecture lingering on the surface, told him exactly who had made an appearance.

"What's up, Carter?" Rafe asked, exasperated. He noticed the slight lag in his words and looked down for confirmation at his near empty glass before taking another hit from his cigarette.

His focus turned to the rows of liquor shelved in front of him. Carter was a good guy, but a little over-the-edge eager to be the one who jumped on the moral high horse. Not particularly a guy Rafe was interested in throwing a few back with. Rafe's moral sensibilities were somewhat unbalanced at the present.

"Saw your car here—*again*," Carter stated with an undertone of accusation.

Rafe's head turned to the side and he glared at Carter from the corner of his eye.

Carter's eyes darted past Rafe behind the bar and he nodded, indicating to Trish he wanted a drink, which meant he was sticking around. Son of a bitch.

"Look, man," Carter started, and the subtle uncertainty in his voice drew Rafe's attention away from the order of the liquor bottles he was memorizing back to Carter. He looked him in the eyes.

"I'm not trying to interfere with the apparent binge you've been on for the last few weeks—to each his own—but if you need to talk to someone . . . I'm . . . Shit, Murano . . . if you're not dealing with—"

"What are you trying to say, Carter?" Rafe questioned, having a pretty good idea as to where Carter was going with his current lecture.

Rafe had been deployed four times since 9/11 and he'd easily seen his share of fucked up and could add a list of things that he'd done overseas that exceeded the definition of fucked up, but he compartmentalized it all in the recesses of his mind and dealt with it. Rafe's rampant bender had nothing to do with his job, his duty as a soldier.

If anything, he wanted to go back, to use his missions to fill the void and distract him from his fucking ravaged heart. He yearned for the fight, the constant sharp edge of war, the adrenaline that would invade the vacancy in his heart as it surged through his veins. He needed it. Without the distraction to ferment his heartache, it swelled, and the whiskey kept his shameful pang muted down to a simple, dull throb. So yeah, he'd been milking this shithole of a bar for every drop of liquid oblivion Trish would serve him, and he had no intention of stopping just because Carter felt the need to intervene.

"All I'm saying is . . ." Carter trailed off, sitting up straight as he met Rafe's challenging stare.

Deep down Rafe could appreciate Carter's concern, but Rafe was three sheets to the wind and Carter didn't know the first damn thing about what was going on in his head. And it lit a fuse.

His fingers parted over the ashtray and his cigarette landed in the accumulating ashes. "You wanna play Dr. Phil, go elsewhere. You're trotting way off course here," he said, his voice low and menacing.

"You need to calm the fuck down."

Wrong move. Rafe could feel his impending outburst lick up his spine, working its way to the surface as Carter's words rang through his mind and triggered his adrenaline to start pumping. Alcohol was like gasoline in Rafe's veins. All he needed was a little spark and he would catch fire.

Standing up and latching onto the edge of the table for support, Rafe leaned in closer. "One thing you should have already learned about me, Carter, is that I don't take orders, and you're walking a thin fuckin' line, my friend."

"Yeah, well, we're not in Afghanistan right now, *Sergeant*," he said mockingly, apparently not giving a shit about his chain of command. "And I'm not putting up with your bullshit, man. You're piss-ass drunk. You seriously want to fuckin' do this, Murano?" he hissed between clenched teeth. "I have no problem laying your ass out right now."

"Whoa, boys," Trish said, appearing next to Rafe. She stepped in front of him and pressed her palm to his chest. "Look at me," she commanded. Rafe slowly lowered his gaze until he was looking at the hauntingly dark irises staring back at him. "You're drunk, and whatever the hell made you snap, you need to rein it in and get ahold of it because I'm about two seconds away from using your balls as a bottle opener." Her hands moved to his shoulders and she gave him a gentle squeeze and smiled.

There she went again, shifting his mood with the snap of her finger.

Rafe sat down and blew out the air that had collected in his lungs. "You need another?" he asked Carter, who was watching him.

"Dammit, Rafe," he sputtered, sitting back down on the barstool next to Rafe. "You're fucking bipolar, you know that?"

"I never claimed to be sane, that's for damn sure."

"Guess I'll leave your dumb ass to your own devices then."

Rafe looked at him, watched as he took a long pull from his beer while his eyes focused straight ahead. "Yeah, I'd say that's a pretty good decision," Rafe finally replied.

Carter shook his head. Rafe knew better than to think he was in the clear from Carter's meddling. "Look," Carter pressed, shrugging his shoulders. "We may not know each other that well apart from our deployment, but I recognize that look in your eyes, man. I've been there. Women got a way of sucking the life from us."

An exasperated sigh heaved from Rafe's chest. Sucking the life out of him was one thing—he could handle that. It was the constant battle of missing her and hating her and wanting her that engulfed him, confining him within the depths of his depravity.

Nodding, Rafe drained his glass, enjoying the smooth, cathartic burn as the alcohol coated his throat. "I get that you're trying to help. I do. But the whole point of this"—he raised his empty glass—"is so I don't have to think about the woman who broke my goddamn heart," he admitted, flagging Trish down with a tilt of his head.

Rafe didn't want to think about Bridgette. He didn't want to think about the way his body craved her, or the way her taste would assault him, deluding his senses at the simple thought of her mouth on his. And he definitely didn't want to think about the way she'd eviscerated him from the inside out until he no longer recognized the man he used to be. No, all thinking about her did was piss him the fuck off.

Picking up his beer bottle, Carter stood and gripped Rafe tightly on the shoulder. "All right, man." He gave Rafe's shoulder a squeeze, then drifted toward the pool tables, leaving Rafe to refocus on his attempt at becoming numb. At this point, the amount of alcohol infusing his blood would have him detached from his self-inflicted torment in no time . . .

A couple of minutes of silence later, the blonde who had caught his attention when he'd first got to the bar a few hours earlier somehow found her way onto his knee. He wasn't going to protest. The alcohol had taken care of his mind, and if he played his cards right, this woman would take care of everything else. He'd found that the best way to smother that damn ceaseless pang in his chest was to bury himself inside a warm, eager pussy.

He slinked his arm around her waist, his fingers brushing across the small amount of flesh that was exposed between her jeans and her shirt. Smooth. He liked that.

"What's your name?" he asked as his fingers toyed with the top of her jeans.

She tilted her head over her shoulder to look at him. "Amber," she said nervously, which shocked him, considering she'd hopped up on his lap like he was Santa Claus.

"You want to get out of here, Amber?"

A faint smile tugged on her glossed lips. "Can I bring my friend?" She nodded her head to the side where the curvy blonde was sitting, flirting with Trish. Rafe laughed. Trish was going to be pissed as hell when he took that little bombshell away from her.

Grabbing on to her hips, he lifted her off his lap and stood up. "You can *absolutely* bring your friend," he replied.

Amber's smile widened and he watched as her shy, nervous persona shifted. Her lids lowered slightly, her brows arched, and her shoulders straightened. He liked this game.

K*nock-knock.*

Setting the stack of papers back down on her desk, Fallon uncrossed her legs and swiveled her plush office chair around to face the door. The chrome clock on the wall read three in the morning and it was as if the visual time triggered her internal clock, making her yawn with exhaustion. Sleep was something Fallon got little of, and she welcomed the ache of fatigue like an old friend. Sleep meant dreaming, and the dreams that seemed to follow Fallon around weren't filled with fluffy bunnies and cotton candy the way they had been when she was a child.

"Come in," she hollered.

The heavy metal door pushed open and a dark head of hair popped into her office. Jade's short brown hair waved around her face, and her round, blue eyes were lined black on her top lid and ringed with long, dark lashes. She was stunning. A subtle, innocent beauty. But she only looked innocent. That was the thing that was most appealing about Jade: her innocence was alluring, but her experience was enthralling.

"Hey. I'm heading up. Everything's locked up and George is getting ready to head out. He wanted me to see if you were ready for him to walk you to your car?" she asked.

Fallon stretched her arms out in front of her as another yawn filled her lungs and escaped in a long sigh. "No, tell him I'm gonna crash here tonight."

Jade eyed the crushed-velvet vintage sofa that was pressed against the back wall of the office. Fallon could see the protest on her face before her mouth even opened to speak. "Fallon, this makes the third night this week you've stayed here. Get your ass home and crawl in an actual bed."

Fallon loved her house. She'd bought it three years ago, the first home she had ever purchased. And it was magnificent. Large and spacious, with an open kitchen and a wraparound porch. It was her sanctuary. But some nights, the small confines of her office comforted her more than the familiarity of her own bed.

Her office wasn't a typical office to begin with. It could

easily classify as a loft apartment for most. It had a sitting area carved out in a little nook in the back wall of the room. She had a full bathroom with a vintage bronze pedestal sink, complete with a deep claw-foot tub. A vanity sat opposite her desk, in deep mahogany wood.

There was a small round table the height of a bar that sat in the back corner with two barstools, and next to it was a mini fridge and a fully stocked built-in floor-to-ceiling wine rack. Since Fallon rarely ever drank, the wine went virtually untouched.

She had everything she could need right here in this one room, and the simplicity of that was hard to resist. That, along with the ability to drown herself in busywork.

"I have to go over a few inventory shipments and look through some things for my accountant and then I'm going to make myself comfortable on the couch and pass the hell out."

Jade rolled her eyes and made sure to overdramatize the heavy sigh that released from her chest. "Fine. I'll be upstairs if you need me," she offered.

Fallon not only owned Velour, she owned the entire building, and when Jade had nowhere else to go, Fallon insisted she move into the loft apartment above the office. She'd been living there for almost two years now. Lord knew nowadays Jade could afford any swanky condo she could get her paws on. But Fallon had grown accustomed to having Jade so close, and she was pretty sure Jade felt the same way. It was especially nice to have her around on nights like tonight when she had a mound of disorganized paperwork on her desk to shuffle through. Jade was always willing to take her place and help George close up. Maybe she would drive to that little boutique downtown tomorrow and buy her that new Gucci handbag Jade had her eye on.

Fallon smiled. "I know. Thanks."

Jade flattened her palm against the door and gave it a few pats. "Get some sleep, princess. Tomorrow night is going to be packed."

"Friday nights are always packed."

"Yes, but tomorrow night our VIP will be full of those dirty little politicians. I hate when they come."

Fallon groaned at the realization and leaned back in her chair. "Shit. You're right."

Every other month a handful of the state's top dogs would show their faces and sleaze up her VIP with their holier-than-thou attitudes and their overflowing wallets. It wasn't uncommon to find a few "headliners," as they liked to call them—athletes, politicians, the occasional celebrity—on any given weekend. Fallon's club was the most exclusive, luxurious club in Denver. Its reputation spanned far and wide across the States and she had even hosted a few elite private parties—for the right people and the right dollar amount, of course.

But tomorrow's headliners were a group of crooked bastards who wore their political status in their pants. She hated them the most.

"Thanks for reminding me. I will call George and have him pull a few extra guys to work security and we'll bring Ace in as another bouncer."

Jade yawned and nodded. "All right. I'm going to bed. Good night. Oh, and by the way, Dex is coming tomorrow night," she said quickly as she started to shut the door.

"What?" Fallon replied before Jade had a chance to escape.

Pushing the door open, Jade stepped one foot in. "He and a few of his friends are coming to Denver for the night and are gonna swing by the club." Jade's head lowered infinitesimally. She knew this little tidbit of information would not make Fallon happy. At. All.

"You know the rules," she stated calmly, needing no other explanation. The tension radiating between them was explanation enough.

Lifting her head so she could see into Fallon's eyes, Jade frowned. *Ah, great.* She was going to try to win over the friend side of Fallon that was lurking around somewhere. Somewhere that was usually unattainable when her club was involved. *It's not going to work,* she thought when she saw Jade's eyes soften around the edges.

"Come on," Jade pleaded, and Fallon was pretty sure she saw her bottom lip pucker out a little bit.

"You know I don't allow boyfriends in my club, Jade. Ever. No exceptions. If I let you, I would have to let all the other girls, and I'm not doing it. I'm sorry. Those have been the rules long before I enforced them."

Jade leaned her back against the door frame and she sighed. "Take me off the lineup tomorrow," she proposed. "I'll work tables."

"The headliners love you. I'm not taking you off the

lineup so you can play footsie under the table with your boy-friend." Fallon hated being the bitch, but rules were there for a reason.

"Please."

"No."

Fallon watched as the wheels started spinning in Jade's eyes while she shifted through her schemes to get off the lineup. She would give her credit for trying.

"Take my place? You know the headliners would rather see you than me anyway." She stepped all the way inside and shut the door behind her. "If you would actually let yourself have a man in your life, I would do it for you. No questions asked."

"I would never allow my boyfriend to come to my club knowing the rules in the first place," she retorted.

"Dammit, Fallon. Quit being such a hard-ass and let me off the damn lineup."

Fallon inhaled a deep breath and closed her eyes, ac-cepting defeat. "Fine," she started, and Jade's eyes widened and a smile broke out on her ivory face. "*But*—as far as the other girls are concerned, I did *not* give you permission. And I took you off the lineup as punishment and docked your pay for the evening."

"Deal." She beamed and opened the door.

"And, Jade," Fallon said before she stepped out. "You know that if there are any problems—any—I will instruct George to haul their asses out of here by their shirttails, right?"

She smiled. "I wouldn't expect anything other than that from you, babe. But there won't be a problem. I promise."

"I hope you're right."

Jade rolled her eyes and started pulling the door closed. "Night," she sang.

Sighing, Fallon shook her head, hoping to god she hadn't just made a huge mistake. "Night," she replied, watching the door click closed.

Fallon slipped her Mary Jane peep-toe stilettos from her feet and curled her toes. She had just purchased the sexy deep purple Prada pumps a few days before and the arches of her soles ached. A few more times around the block and those puppies would be good and broken in. She stood up and made her way barefoot to the wrought-iron wardrobe next to her vanity and pulled a satin slip from the lingerie drawer.

She had on one of her favorite wrap dresses. It cut low on her chest and the tie cinched at her waist, leaving the skirt of the dress to flow easily above her knee.

She pulled on the tie and the dress fell open, allowing her to slide her arms out. It gathered at her feet and she slinked into the satin slip before stepping out of her dress and kicking it to the side.

Sitting down at her vanity, Fallon reached behind her neck and unclasped the thin gold chain that rested along her collarbone. She dropped the necklace in her palm, the small, delicate pendant heavy in her hand as she brushed her finger over it before placing it in its designated spot in her vanity.

Her lids began to feel heavy, weighted down. She had a bit more work to finish, especially now that she needed to make sure everything was in order for her headliners tomorrow, but instead of sitting herself down at her desk, she fell onto the sofa and curled her legs up on the soft velvet.

She pulled the throw blanket from the back of the sofa down over her and wedged herself deep into the back cushions. Hopefully sleep would find her tonight.

CHAPTER TWO

Fallon's eyes fluttered open to the sound of a knock on her door. She sat up and gathered her surroundings, her eyes shifting to the side and focusing in on the disheveled stack of papers cluttering her desk. That's right—she was in her office.

Standing up, Fallon groggily crossed the short distance to the door, and the thick, plush carpet felt warm under her cold toes, only adding to her desire to curl back up on the couch. Her eyes were heavy from sleep, and she blinked a few times in an attempt to clear her vision.

Stifling a yawn, she pulled the door open. "Naomi?" she asked when she saw the door-knocking culprit.

Naomi shouldered the door open a little more and walked in. "Hey, boss."

Sure, come on in, Fallon thought, slightly annoyed, as she pushed the heavy door closed behind her.

"Is there a reason you're here at the ass crack of dawn?" She walked back to the sofa and plopped down, tucking her legs up underneath her. By the way her lids almost refused to stay open, she couldn't have been asleep more than a few hours.

"I was at the gym—you know how I teach the early-morning kickboxing class on Fridays. Anyway, I was driving home and I saw your car." She raised her brows and cocked her head accusingly. "Girl, did you sleep here?"

"What gave it away? The nightgown or the bed head?" Fallon grumbled, pulling the throw blanket up over her bare legs. Mornings had become her worst nightmare ever since she took over the club after Frank, the former owner, died. That crazy old man had left her the club, probably knowing she had nothing else of any importance in her life. If anyone understood and appreciated how much Velour meant to Fallon, it was Frank. He might have been an old pervert who loved his beautiful young women as much as he loved his liquor, but he ran one hell of a club.

She yawned again. Late nights and early mornings didn't go well together.

Naomi laughed. "Yeah, you're lookin' rough. Come on. Get dressed. Let's grab some food."

Fallon groaned. Naomi was way too perky for her liking. Women who walked with a pep in their step gave her visions of shoving her five-inch Prada heel up their asses. She'd love to see that pep in their step with a stiletto between their cheeks.

She rubbed her hands over the blanket, pushing the warm fabric against her chilled legs. "It's too early," she stated, letting the obvious conclusion go unsaid.

Pulling the headband from her head and readjusting it

back in place, Naomi sighed. "Come on. You ain't gotta look all pretty. Just throw that hair up in a ponytail and pull on some jeans and let's go. I'm hungry and Lord knows you need to eat."

As if Naomi needed further incentive to persuade Fallon to go with her, her stomach rumbled loudly. Naomi was right: she needed to eat. She hadn't eaten dinner the night before and her stomach had taken a cacophonous lashing as punishment.

"I want Chinese." She groaned, scooting down so her head was resting on the armrest of the sofa and pulling the blanket up a little higher. Fallon's choice of breakfast cuisine never included actual breakfast food. She was more of a cold pizza and leftover Chinese kind of girl, and Chinese sounded delicious. Still, falling back into dreamless sleep sounded much better.

"I will kick your skinny rear if you dare try to eat that garbage in front of me. Come on. We can stop by the farmers' market and get some fresh fruit." There Naomi went again with her health tirade. That woman was bound and determined to turn everyone at the club into a vegan.

Lifting her eyes in the most effective glare she could produce for holy-shit-it's-early, Fallon snorted. "No, thank you." Naomi was about two very real seconds away from becoming better acquainted with Prada.

Naomi's butt found its way onto Fallon's desk chair and she swiveled it around to face her. "You're a grouch, you know that?"

If Fallon had had something hard, and preferably sharp,

within reach, she would have thrown it at Perky Miss Perkster's head. "Have you considered that this might be the norm for people who were rudely awakened before the sun was up?"

Naomi's eyes shifted to the ceiling and her mouth puckered to the side as if she was actually pondering that very scenario. *Smart-ass.* "No, I haven't," she answered matter-of-factly. "But I have considered that it's the norm for overworked skinny white females with no active social life—or sex life for that matter."

The skin around Fallon's eyes tightened as they bulged from her head. "Excuse me," she snapped.

"I don't believe I need to reiterate, but I will. You're a grouch because you practically live in this damn office. You probably barely see the light of day if it's before noon, and I have never—I repeat, never—seen you with a man. Or a woman for that matter."

Fallon narrowed her eyes and frowned in confusion.

"Hey, I don't know what your preferences are. All I'm sayin' is, no lovin' is the main ingredient in bitch moods."

For owning a burlesque club where inhibitions were checked at the door, Fallon was pretty reserved when it came to her personal life. It was just easier that way. It was her coping mechanism, her life preserver, her safety net. Keeping everyone around her at a safe distance from her heart was the only way she knew how to protect it from herself.

"I'm not going to divulge the private details of who I sleep with to you, Na," she snapped. And the truth of the matter was, Fallon had an extremely healthy sex life. Maybe not the most adventurous social life outside the mingling required in her club, but that's how she preferred it. She had a few men—and by "a few" she meant two—who were delighted to come to her house at any given time—just not at the same time; she hadn't quite figured that one out yet—and fulfill her need for a warm body when she saw fit. But it was always prearranged, always on her terms, and never lasted more than a few hours. So there was no need to fill anyone in on the intimate details. She wanted to keep the men in the positions she designated for them. Including them in any other facet of her life, emotionally or physically—or even verbally—would just shift them away from their secured space. It was too risky.

Arm's length. That's how she liked to keep her relationships, intimate and platonic alike. That was her motto.

Hell, it should be a bumper sticker.

Crossing her arms over her chest and pursing her lips, Naomi proceeded to roll her eyes. "Mmm-hmm," she hummed between tight lips. She had this doubtful expression thing down pat.

Bounding out of the chair as if it were a track meet event, Naomi stood up and skipped toward the door. Literally skipped like a schoolgirl. "All right, girl. I can tell when I'm not wanted."

Yeah, right.

"I will let you get back to snoring."

"I don't snore."

Opening the door, Naomi laughed, turning her head

over her shoulder to send Fallon a quick glance. "For being such a lady, you snore like a three-hundred-pound man with sleep apnea," she accused. "I could hear you through the door."

"Seriously?" Fallon complained.

"Seriously."

Huffing, Fallon pulled her thighs up against her chest and cuddled into the couch. "Well, it could be worse. I could drool and snore at the same time."

"Hate to point out the obvious, but you sleep alone, girl. In your office. I don't think whether or not you drool or snore is the issue here." She offered what looked like a try at a partial grin and partial frown, and it was probably the most pathetic effort of comfort Fallon had witnessed to date. Then Naomi stepped out and shut the door behind her.

Much to Fallon's annoyance, she wasn't able to fall back asleep.

The shrill sound of the alarm sent a signal to Rafe's muscles and his body was up and out of the bed before his mind had a chance to wake up. Then disappointment set it. He wasn't in his room on the FOB in Afghanistan getting ready to head out for his next mission. He wasn't about to give orders, or load his weapon. He wasn't about to get back to the thing he loved—fighting for his country—the one thing that seemed to distract the clusterfuck in his mind from taking him over.

No. He was in his room back in his house in Colorado Springs, just outside Fort Carson. Rafe's vision started to clear as he regained consciousness. He dropped his back onto the bed and heard a soft moan next to him as the mattress shook from his body weight.

"Dammit," he mumbled, remembering that he wasn't alone in his bed. The night before consisted of one too many glasses of whiskey and . . . a blonde? Murano leisurely lifted the sheet that was covering the woman next to him. Yep, she was a blonde.

He grinned.

And so was her friend.

The bits and pieces from last night started fitting together in his mind, making one hell of a slide show of nude images.

He looked down at the naked women and tried like hell to remember their names. One was Amber? Or was it April? What in the hell was the other chick's name?

"Hey," he said gently.

They didn't even stir.

"Hey, I've got to get ready for work," he tried again, only this time he let his voice carry a little louder.

They still didn't budge.

With a heavy sigh he threw his legs over the edge of the bed and stood up, stretching his arms above his head.

"Now that's a view to wake up to," a soft, sleep-induced voice said from behind him.

Turning around, he was greeted with a smile that was equal parts shy and coquettish. Ah, yes, Trish's blonde from the bar. Damn, he'd been wrong about this one. Her smile was sweet, and the easy blush that spread across her cheeks made her round eyes soften even more. But that force field of innocence he'd thought he'd been privy to turned out to be one hell of an illusion. This woman didn't delineate innocence in any shape or form. And she definitely didn't lack in experience or skill.

Her ravenous eyes skimmed across his exposed body and honed in on his morning hard-on. "Why don't you climb back in bed and let me take care of that for you?"

The idea appealed to him in more ways than one. This chick was hot, willing, and already naked in his bed. But she'd served her purpose to him and he wasn't interested in round two. And yes, he realized that made him a complete asshole. Not that he would actually tell her that, though.

Pleasing a woman was beyond gratifying for him. He loved to make a woman scream out his name by the mere power of his tongue between her thighs. Goddamn, he loved to feel a woman's body squirm beneath him by the pressure of his fingertips, the blissful enjoyment of feeling the softness of a woman quivering as his body pressed into her.

But it hadn't been that way for him in a while. Not since Bridgette. Now when he was with a woman she was just someone to fuck in an attempt to fulfill that one need that his body was craving. And it never worked. It would take the edge off, but fucking just to fuck was never completely satisfying. Sure, he'd get off, and he made sure to get whatever woman, or women, under him to come too, in the hopes of preventing that asshole feeling from returning, but it never worked that way. He still felt like the prick he knew he was.

"Come on," she coaxed soothingly, and the woman next to her stirred awake. "Don't get shy on me now." She glanced at her friend, who was now sitting up beside her, and offered her a roguish smile. "Morning, Amber," she hummed. *Amber—that's right.*

Amber's hand snaked out from under the sheet and found its way to the blonde's tit, all the while directing her "fuck me" eyes at Rafe. They knew what the hell they were doing. And it worked.

Rafe grinned and walked to the edge of the bed. He wasn't going to walk away from watching them please each other.

The blonde reached out and wrapped her fingers around his erection and his hips instinctively rocked forward and he groaned.

"You like that?" she asked, readjusting herself onto her knees and lifting her mouth to reach him. He didn't give her the satisfaction of a response—that would require more effort than he was up for right then. Instead he just looked at Amber. "Touch her," he instructed, and the delighted look that fanned her face told him she was more than grateful to be included.

He enjoyed both views the women were giving him until he felt the need to roll his eyes to the back of his head. "You better stop or I'm going to come in your mouth," he warned with a deep growl.

A breathy giggle caused his eyes to open. "She won't stop," Amber informed him, grinning. And she was right. The blonde's grip only tightened and her mouth moved more hurriedly, pulling him in deep.

Then he came.

His release hit him hard, but it didn't linger or last and it lacked the delicious wave of aftershocks that accompanied a great orgasm.

He hadn't felt aftershocks since he'd severed the link between his heart and his sex drive.

Rafe pulled himself from the blonde's mouth and ran his fingers through her hair. "Thanks," he praised as warmly as he could. "Now, as much as I hate to leave you ladies alone in my bed," he said, feigning disappointment, "I need to get in the shower and get ready for work."

They both sighed and whined in frustration, pouting, and it annoyed the hell out of him. "You two finish without me," he retorted, hoping to shut them up as he headed for his bathroom. Another round of whining met his ears and caused him to cringe inwardly until the noise was muffled through the closed bathroom door.

He turned the water to hot, the spray pelting the tile wall as he waited for it to heat up. Latching onto the sink, Rafe lowered his head between his shoulders and groaned as the first wave of a hangover slinked through his head, thrashing him with a dull, steady ache behind his eyes.

He opened his bottle of aspirin that was conveniently next to the sink and popped a few pills in his mouth, the chalky coating churning his stomach. Turning the faucet on, he leaned over and sucked water between his lips and swallowed the pills.

Stepping into the shower, he hoped the water would wake him up and lessen the pounding in his head, but past experiences had told him that was a long shot. And within ten minutes he was walking back into his bedroom with a towel hanging on his hips—still tired as hell and feeling like ass. He paused as he glanced across the room.

His bed was empty.

Curious, he padded into the living room, only to find it empty as well. So was the kitchen.

Walking back into his room, he scanned the foot of his bed, no longer seeing bras or panties littering his floor. They were gone. And thank god. It was always nice when they took it upon themselves to leave.

After putting on a clean pair of ACUs, Rafe pulled on his boots, grunting when the pounding in his head amplified as he leaned over to tuck his pants into his blousing rubbers. Then he grabbed his keys from the coffee table in the living room and left the house.

The cool air soothed his still throbbing head as he made his way to his Jeep. It was an old Jeep Wrangler, but he loved it. Four doors, lift kit, thirty-six-inch tires—it was sexy. His prissy-ass brother thought differently, though—not that Rafe particularly cared what his suit of a brother thought about his mode of transportation. But it made him smile thinking about his brother ribbing him about it. He missed that fucker. His wife was pregnant and Rafe hoped like hell Luca was forced to trade in his vintage sports car for a minivan. He would love to see the day his top-dog, all-business brother got behind the wheel of a soccer van. Rafe knew it was only a matter of time. His sister-in-law had a tendency to get her way—from all of the Murano men. He still hadn't figured out how in the hell she'd gotten him to take her to see that damn musical in the city a few years back. He was home visiting and by the time they had finished dinner she not only had him agreeing to take her to the musical, but she had him believing it was his idea.

His eyes did an automatic roll as he grinned at the memory.

Rafe grabbed his ID out of his wallet and handed it to the guard as he pulled up to the main gate that led in to Fort Carson. The overweight, balding man glanced quickly at his ID, then flicked it out between his two fingers, handing it back to Rafe. He nodded, then pulled forward onto post.

CHAPTER THREE

Smoothing the fabric of her red dress over her legs and making sure the girls were in their correct positions, Fallon left backstage and walked into the main level of the club. The bodies were packed in tight tonight. All the men were in suits and blazers and the few women who dawdled around the tables were in little cocktail dresses.

Fallon was unforgivingly particular with the visual quality her club maintained, and that included the appearance of her clientele. She made sure her men at the door enforced her strict dress code. She didn't want any Joe Blow off the street to meander into her club with his jeans around his ass and his shirt sloppy, and more than likely smelly, looking to get his rocks off. Seriously. It wasn't that type of club. She had standards. Sure, it was uptight and some presumed her to be a royal bitch, but it was her club after all. And it's what allowed her club to stand out among the rest. It's what made hers so successful. It wasn't prestigious and exclusive by accident.

Among the top-shelf favorites, her bars were also

stocked with premium wines and liquors and delicious imported beers. The atmosphere was luxurious and seductive, her women sensual and glamorous. They were sexy in a way that ignited uninhibited fantasies while exuding a feminine poise and allure that was provocative and inviting, yet just out of reach.

Fallon worked her ass off to ensure that her club maintained its reputation. Anyone could come to Velour—as long as you played the part—and *everyone* wanted to.

Illusion was a damn good seduction.

Fallon had been around the block a time or two in her short twenty-five years and had quickly learned that if she wanted to get anywhere in this cutthroat society everyone lived in, she was going to have to grab society by the balls and tell it to go to hell. Fallon did things her own way and she wasn't going to apologize for it. She'd been at the top of the totem pole, all the way down to the bottom of the barrel, and everywhere in between. Acceptance wasn't something she needed nor wanted from anyone—anyone other than herself, that is. And from where she stood in her Giuseppe Zanotti–sculpted wedges, she was doing pretty damn well.

Growing up in a family where social status and your ability to eat your way through the social food chain were of utmost importance, she was aware that she was creating this too-good-for-you image with her elite invitations, strict dress policy, and selective staff. She'd been bred with that image ingrained in her mind, imprinted in her genes, and just to top it off, it was shoved down her throat with a golden spoon. She'd hated the pressure and conformity that her parents had inflicted on her. Pressure to live up to their "standards." Yet here she was, setting the bar so damn high it was near impossible to reach without stepping on a few backs to get there.

But the only back she stepped on was her own.

And she wore stilettos.

One act of rebellion and her family threw her out on her ass without so much as a "It's been a fun seventeen years; have a great life." Or hell, she would have even settled for "Good luck out in the big bad world with nothing but the hundred bucks in your pocket and the clothes in your duffel." But they had just stared at her with narrowed eyes and tight lips as they simply confiscated everything they had ever provided her with and slammed the door in her face.

She grinned.

If only they could see her now. They wouldn't know whether to die from mortification at her career choice or drop to their knees and kiss her designer shoes and perfectly pedicured toes. But she had absolutely no plan on traversing down that little scenario. Point-blank, her family was dead to her. Nothing more than the hatred in her veins and the example of what kind of person she would never become locked into her memory. She may manifest the same aspiration for luxury as her parents, but it didn't consume her. It *did not* define her.

She'd concede she mirrored them on the outside, but she would never be them on the inside.

Not if she could help it.

Stepping gracefully between tables of chatting patrons,

Fallon made her way to the front of the club, where a spiral staircase led to the second-floor VIP area. Inhaling a serene breath into her lungs, she climbed the black marble staircase. The tables at the top of the VIP landing were occupied to capacity, and a thick aroma of sleaze saturated the previously healthy quality of oxygen. She was grateful for that breath she'd taken.

Commanding her body to conceal her disgust, she pulled her shoulders back and added a little extra sway into her step.

"Well, if it isn't my favorite lady," a tall, lean man said from the table situated in the middle of the landing.

Reaching into the stockpile she had stowed away in her mind, she easily pulled out her smile. The one that took years to perfect. This smile had several variations that she had learned were key to securing her control. She just needed to observe and learn which smile to use when.

"Hello, Senator," she replied warmly as she rounded his table and paused elegantly in front of him. "You gentlemen enjoying yourselves? Are my girls taking good care of you?" she asked, smiling at Amelia, who had just appeared at the table with another round of specialty drinks for the men. Amelia was one of her best waitresses, and she also was the most brazenly flirtatious. Typically, Fallon disapproved of the blatant, aggressive flirting and touching of her customers. Her girls were sensual and alluring—and they were for eyes only. But Amelia liked to push the limitations. She cooed and sighed and swooned at all the opportune times to receive a fat tip at the end of the night, but she also brushed hands, rubbed thighs, and any and all other forms of subtle physical contact.

So, yep, Amelia was a little slutty. No harm in a woman knowing what she wanted and when she wanted it. Besides, Fallon kept a tight rein on her, and Amelia knew better than to cross her.

The senator cocked his head to the side and Fallon watched as his retinas singed Amelia's clothing as if he had heat vision, looking at her as if every article of clothing had been seared from her body and she was standing naked in front of him. Subtlety obviously wasn't something he practiced, and he apparently had a Superman complex.

"Yes," he said, licking his lips, causing Fallon to force away the shudder that formed in her muscles. "She's doing a great job."

Amelia's hand darted out and rested on the senator's bicep and she giggled softly as if rehearsed—which it totally was.

"So, Miss Kelly, are you going to grace us with your talent tonight?" the short, bald man who was sitting next to the senator asked. She thought he was his attorney, but she couldn't remember for sure. They all started blending together after a while. Plain. Arrogant. Perverted.

And this was coming from a woman who owned a burlesque club. Perversion was her specialty.

A cluster of disappointed sighs rang through the space around the table when Fallon cast her eyes to the ground and let loose a timid smile. She wasn't the least bit modest, but men like this enjoyed watching a woman shrink in their presence. They were vultures. They fed off intimidation and insecurities. And they were playing right into Fallon's hand. She knew how to work this group. They thought they held the power. They were wrong.

Her long, thick lashes brushed beneath her sculpted eyebrows as she meekly lifted her eyes back to them and pulled yet another smile from her stockpile—only this one was tauntingly sensual and just a little bit shy.

"Oh, come on now, Miss Kelly," the senator implored.

Fallon winked and allowed her smile to ascend the rest of the way up until she was all teeth. "Well, Senator," she started, coaxing just the right amount of confidence into her tone but not enough to shadow her false timidities. "It just so happens that I *am* on the lineup tonight."

"That's what I like to hear," the bald man replied. He was beginning to resemble one of those inflatable clown punching bags. He was just so round and short that she couldn't help but want to see whether he'd bounce back up if she knocked him over.

"What a treat," chimed in another man, who was just as pompously couth as the rest, bringing Fallon's mind away from the visual image of baldy swaying side to side with a giant red nose.

"Thank you." She stepped away from the table. "Now, gentlemen, if you'll excuse me, I need to get back to work. It was great to see you all again. Please, don't hesitate to ask Amelia if you need anything," she said.

The men smiled and nodded and said their good-byes; then Fallon easily and happily clicked down the stairs. She was grateful to be out of the presence of deceitful political predators who enjoyed the visual offerings of her employees and then turned around and picked up the woman on the corner to enjoy her physical willingness. Then ending the evening by going home to their social-piranha wives.

She knew when to bite her tongue. And when it came to those men, she bit hard. Courtesy of her parents, who fit the pompous couth and social-piranha mold, she'd been subject to men like them her entire life, so often that her tongue was now numb. It wasn't backing down or cowering. It was prevention. If she opened her mouth and started in on exactly how she felt about men like them—men with no regard for anything or anyone other than themselves and their rise to success—then she wouldn't be able to stop.

Fallon paused a few times along the way back to her office to greet familiar customers, and when she was finally able to make it backstage and through the long hallway to her room, she stepped inside and shut the door behind her, twisting the lock. Then, grabbing the hem of her dress, she lifted it above her head and peeled out of her clothes.

Rafe parked his Jeep in the parking garage down the street from Velour and started making his way in that direction along the sidewalk. He could see the club up ahead; it almost looked out of place resting alongside the road. The building was a large, modern two-story structure with big windows lining the entire second level. The main level was gray brick with steps that led to the small landing outside a large metal door. A line of bodies trailed from the landing and wrapped around the sidewalk and to the back of the building. There was no way they were getting in this club tonight. And there was no chance in hell he was waiting in that line either.

Pulling out his phone, Rafe stopped midstep and sent a quick text to Graham.

I'm here. Pick another club. Not getting in this one.

A text came back almost immediately.

Already here. Go around back. Tell my man George you're with me.

Shoving his phone into his back pocket, Rafe waited for a break in traffic, then jogged across the street. How in the hell had Graham gotten into this place? Rafe had heard of Velour, knew of its reputation, but he'd never been here before. He was surprised Graham would even consider dressing up and coming to a place like this, let alone actually do it. And have connections. It was a place hoity-toity assholes with thick wallets went to watch women dance around half naked. If Rafe wanted to pay to watch some chick take off her clothes, he could go to the strip club down the street, get in for twenty bucks, and probably leave with a blow job. Unless they were in your hands, tits were tits. And watching a chick's ass bounce around on your lap was going to be the same no matter where the fuck you were doing it.

But he'd admit, he was definitely curious as to what all the damn fuss was about.

Walking past a slew of men and a few women creeping slowly through the crammed line, he passed the stairs that led to the main entrance and went around to the side of the building where an identical staircase and landing were housing a line of about seven men.

Rafe stepped up onto the steps and climbed the short distance to a man who looked like he'd be a better fit for the ticket counter on Broadway rather than at the door to some exclusive titty club. His styled hair and lean body lacked the intimidation factor Rafe assumed this George character would have.

But when Rafe stepped in front of him, his eyes hardened and his jaw set tight—and Rafe knew this guy was someone you didn't want to fuck with. Rafe knew the look—he mirrored that look more often than he was proud to admit.

Rafe nodded. "George, right? I'm a friend of Graham's," he stated, hoping that was all the information he needed to present.

The bouncer nodded back his reply and stepped aside to allow Rafe in.

Okay. Easy enough.

The first thing Rafe noticed when he walked in the club was that it looked nothing like he'd expected. Judging from the clean lines of the exterior architecture, he thought inside he would see sleek white leather couches, contemporary furnishings and accents, solid primary colors.

But instead, he walked into a room that was saturated in warmth and luxury. The concrete floor was stained a crisp cream with deep, rich mahogany faded throughout. The bar that was directly to his right was placed in front of a mirrored backdrop, the entire wall a solid mirror sheet. The bar itself was tall and thick, with a gold trim engraved with intricate patterns. And the deep cherrywood of the counter was sheened with a glaze and aged beautifully.

Rafe's parents owned a bakery in Philly. He'd been just a kid when his mom opened the bakery, but he noticed, even at such a young age, her eye for detail—her love of the little things that made up the bigger picture. And Rafe paid attention. He took notice. He digested the little details. She'd taught him to appreciate the small beauties—whether the shape of the almonds in her biscotti, the fresh-cut peonies she put in the vase on the counter, or the wrinkles around her eyes when she smiled at him, he'd learned to notice.

And so he discerned the elegant beauty in this place. The deep plum of the sofas that gathered in the center of the club. The tall, thick tables that scattered around the floor. And the stage. There was only one. It was elaborate and large, rimmed with the same intricate gold trimming that was on the bar. A beautiful cedar-colored hardwood floor covered the platform and a thick gray curtain draped across the back. Had he known any better, he would have thought he was at a theater.

The strip clubs he frequented consisted of a few long tablelike stages that made runways throughout the room, and at any given time there were nearly naked women slinking around.

Only one stage here, and he didn't see one stripper.

Glancing around, it didn't him take long to spot Graham. Although he was dressed to standards, Graham stuck out among the rest of the men. But then again, Rafe probably did too.

"Hey," he said as he pulled out a barstool from beneath the table and sat down.

"You find the place okay?" Graham asked, looking around.

Rafe followed his gaze but couldn't see anything worth searching for, so he refocused his attention back to Graham. "Yeah," he answered. "And how the hell do you know the bouncer?"

Finally Graham peeled his eyes away from where they were sweeping the room and looked at him. "Oh, my buddy Dexter—I don't think you've meet him. He's in Iron Brigade. His girlfriend works here so he brought me with him quite a bit before we deployed. George is good people."

Rafe's head flinched back slightly as Graham's explanation registered. "So we're here to watch some dude's girlfriend get naked?" There is no way in hell that shit would fly if it were him.

Rafe thought he just witnessed a flash of guilt cross over Graham's face, but it was quickly replaced with a toothy grin. "They don't get naked—not completely, unfortunately. They dance. They call it burlesque or some shit . . . I think. And, hell yes, we're watchin'. She's fuckin' hot."

Crossing his arms over his chest, Rafe narrowed his eyes at Graham. "That's all good and well, brother. But where's this friend of yours? He's fine with us watching his woman's tits bounce around onstage?"

Graham laughed. "He's not coming now, didn't say why. He's never seemed to care about other men watching Jade, though. Dexter was the one who suggested we come here tonight in the first place. Who do you think brought me here all those times before he started dating one of the dancers?"

Rafe shook his head. "Fuck that. I'm telling you, I could never let my girl get naked for other guys."

"They don't get fully naked."

"I don't give a shit if they wear granny panties. No woman of mine would take off her clothes and dance around onstage for fuckers like you. Period."

"Fuckers like me? Shit, I'm their favorite customer." Graham laughed, glancing around the room again. "The women here love me, man. I'll introduce you to them."

"Who are you looking for?" Rafe finally asked when Graham continued eyeing the club like a Secret Service agent.

He snapped his head back to Rafe. "Huh? Nobody."

Rafe nodded at the waitress as she finished dropping off drinks at the neighboring table. She walked to Rafe, popped her hip to the side, and winked. One look at her and it was obvious he wouldn't have to put forth any effort into finding pussy tonight should he decide to go looking.

"My name's Amelia. I'll be taking care of you fine gentlemen tonight," she purred, and Rafe could basically see the innuendo written out on her forehead. "What can I get ya, handsome?"

He smiled but was already bored with her provocative alacrity. "Whiskey."

Fallon's fingers caught in the small tangle that twisted in her golden brown hair as she raked them through the soft curls, loosening them a little around her face. Her makeup was scattered over the top of her vanity and her ivory robe, which had hung on its prized hook on the inside of her wardrobe door, was now covering her slender body.

Looking into the oblong mirror, she lined her lids and pressed her false lashes into place. She never particularly liked the lashes, but when you were onstage, it was important to make your features stand out—expression was half the fantasy. Finishing her face, she smoothed crimson lipstick across her full lips and blotted them gently with a tissue.

It had been a long time since she'd gotten up on that stage. Running a business had taken priority over the fulfillment the stage held, and she'd be lying if she said she didn't miss it. This was her life, and even if it wasn't the one she had dreamed of, she loved it. There was something that coursed through her veins when she was up there. There were nerves, always nerves, and anyone else who said otherwise was lying through their teeth. A woman didn't take her clothes off and expose her insecurities without getting a little woozy at the thought.

Yet at the same time, the nerves were what made her crave the stage. The power she felt from fear was compelling, and the power she felt from overcoming those fears was addictive. But there was something else that tangled around the myriad cluster of emotions: desire.

She leaned over and slowly pulled her worn black pointe shoes onto her feet, lacing the gray ribbon up her ankles.

Fallon heard a very distinct, unhappy voice mutter, "What an asshole," a second before she heard her heavy metal door close with a loud thump.

Fallon looked up, already aware that the look on Jade's face was going to be screwed up tight, but she didn't expect to see the tears sheening across her eyes as well. Leaning back into her chair, she crossed her legs and frowned sympathetically at Jade, waiting for the onslaught of the mother of all rants to hit her.

"Put me back on the lineup," Jade spat as she flung herself down on the velvet couch. The first tear fell from her eye but clung to her bottom lashes as if she were willing it not to fall.

Fallon didn't need confirmation from Jade to know that Dexter was no longer coming tonight. The fact that she was crying said it all. Jade liked to hide her emotions—she and Fallon were the same in that aspect, always trying to desperately ward off the crippling feelings that somehow continually found a way to resurface. Besides, she would never ask Fallon to go back on the lineup if Dex were here.

"Why don't you just go on home?" she suggested. "Or go

sit at the bar and have Simone fix you one of her martinis that you love. Take the night off."

Jade's finger reached up and brushed underneath her eye and she sat up a little straighter. "No, I want to work," she stated definitively. Fallon could understand that—the need to keep your mind off the ominous cloud that had enveloped your thoughts was alluring.

"All right," she agreed. "I will put you in the closing routine and take Naomi out. For now, rotate with Amelia. She's got a few tables in the back plus VIP, and I'm sure she needs a break from those men."

Jade's small feet were covered in a hot little pair of charcoal gray satin stiletto pumps, and the thin heels sunk into the plush carpet as she stood. A wicked smile started to find its way onto her sullen expression and she cleared her throat as she pulled the hem of her black dress slightly lower on her thighs. "Are you sure you want to unleash me on the headliners? I'm not in the best mood," she advised. "I can't play the game tonight, babe."

Fallon laughed. Jade may be a little sour at the moment, but the headliners loved to watch her almost as much as they loved to watch Amelia. She never worked the tables, so not only would it be a nice change, but those men could definitely use a little shock factor. They're the type of men who always get what they want, no questions asked. Bring in sweet little Jade with her innocent eyes and delightful smile, and they would be foaming at the mouth. Then wait till they learned that sweet little Jade isn't so sweet tonight. Fallon grinned at the very thought.

"I'm not asking you to," she finally replied.

Jade lifted an eyebrow skeptically and walked to the door.

"All right," she said, but it sounded more like a question.

Fallon winked and Jade just smiled.

Then Fallon dropped her robe. Showtime.

CHAPTER FOUR

"Who was that?" Rafe asked before he had a chance to get the image of the woman he had just watched onstage out of his vision.

"I'm not sure. I've never seen her dance before," Graham replied.

Wrapping his lips around the end of his cigarette, he lifted his lighter and inhaled as the flame singed the paper and lit his cigarette. That wasn't like anything Rafe had ever seen, but he knew he wanted to see it again. There was something desperate on that woman's face that sent a desire through him beyond the reaction of seeing her bare tits or her round ass. She was fucking beautiful. And the way her body moved caused his eyes to lock on her even before she removed her clothes. She was elegant and strong. Nothing about the way she danced was intended to arouse the men in the crowd. No, she moved like she was trying to seduce herself. Like she was the only person she was dancing for. It was sexy as hell.

Graham nudged him on the arm with the side of his

beer bottle. "Dude," he questioned, his brows bunching between his eyes.

"What?"

Lifting his beer, he took a few pulls from it while continuing to stare mockingly at Rafe. The bottle hit the wood table with a hollow clank as he set it back down once it was empty. "See something you want?"

"I can always find something I want."

Graham leaned against the back of his barstool, the front two legs slightly rising from the concrete floor. "Rafe Murano has been here a grand total of twenty minutes and already has his sights set." He sounded like a proud father announcing football stats or some shit.

"Here ya go, handsome." Amelia stood in front of their table again, voluntarily restocking their drinks. Rafe loved when a waitress was on her game and didn't make him ask or keep him waiting.

The music blared and a line of girls walked onstage, all wearing matching costumes covered in different colors of beads. They looked nothing like the last woman. They danced seductively, provocatively, and their movements and facial expressions better represented how he pictured a stripper—burlesque dancer, whatever—to look like.

They were hot. No getting around that. Especially the tall mocha woman in the center. She led the women and was the focal point of their dance. No matter what the others were doing, Rafe's eyes kept navigating back to her.

"That's Naomi," Graham interjected, raising the volume of his voice so he could be heard over the loud beat of the music. His head rocked back in an approving nod and he smiled like he was entertaining some private joke. "Hot, isn't she?" he asked, then refocused his eyes back on her and took a drink from the beer Amelia had just brought him. "She's a good girl. Sweet."

"That your friend's girl?" Rafe asked.

"No. I love Na, but if Jade was onstage we wouldn't even be discussing Naomi."

Raising his brows, he decided against asking for elaboration. Rafe was still positive that the angel he first saw on the stage was beyond comparison.

Amelia returned with two more shots of whiskey—at this rate he was going to be tanked in no time. She didn't greet him—well, not with words. She preferred to use her body to show her hospitality, taking it upon herself to smoothly glide onto his lap. Not that he was protesting, but it took him by surprise.

Apparently she wasn't interested in conversation. Instead, she crossed her legs, her tight green dress showing off more thigh than was publicly decent—again he wasn't protesting—and wound her arm around the back of his shoulders. She glanced once at the shot glasses she had set on the table, then returned her sultry "come and get it" eyes back to him. She picked up one of the shots and rolled it between her fingers.

"All right, handsome, open up," she instructed, her tone shifting from friendly to suggestive as it unfurled from her lips. She readjusted on his lap, her dress moving even farther up her thigh, and pressed her chest against his. Keeping his eyes on her, he joined in on her little game, moving his hand to her hip, his fingers shamelessly applying pressure to the smooth curve where her ass met her thigh. Her smile widened.

She lifted the edge of the glass to his bottom lip and he opened his mouth for her and tilted back, guiding the liquid into his mouth and down his throat.

Her smile lifted slowly while her eyes fixated on his lips. He mindlessly ran his tongue over the deep scar that sliced through his bottom lip. He was usually unaware of the hideous slash that extended from his mouth down to his neck, but when he happened to catch the scrutiny of someone's stare, it was as if the scar became hypersensitive.

She pressed her mouth to his ear. "Come and find me after we close," she whispered.

Rafe nodded.

"Graham, I'll go grab you another beer," she said, standing up and readjusting her dress.

"Thanks, sweetheart," Graham replied. And she winked.

Rafe watched her as she walked back toward the bar, enjoying her ass in her tight dress. "She always like that?"

Graham's eyes were secured on something behind Rafe and an odd sound escaped his mouth. Turning his head, Rafe looked for who or what had suddenly distracted him, but he came up short.

The wooden legs scraped against the concrete as Graham pushed away from the table and stood up. "I'll be back," he muttered, then rushed toward the door.

Rafe turned back around and caught Amelia's stare as

she looked over her shoulder and smiled at him. She was all too easy. He knew he would barely have to try for it, and he was fully confident that if he pulled her into the restroom right now, she'd let him fuck her on the sink. And she'd be sweet, attentive. And she'd like it.

He stood up, deciding to put his plan in action, and followed her as she made her way to a spiral staircase at the back of the club, weaving in and out of tables of men, all dressed in their fucking suits.

A guy, probably around Rafe's age, stepped from the stairs as Amelia approached. He was wearing a tailored suit, his jacket open and the top buttons of his shirt undone, and had a prissy-ass flip to the front of his hair that aided his already pretty-boy image. Rafe could see her smile from the side, and it was forced—not the easy smile she presented him and Graham with. And in the matter of a heartbeat, the air around him shifted as he watched Pretty Boy grasp ahold of Amelia's arm and pull her body against his.

Rafe didn't know this chick other than the feel of her ass, and she was apparently sexually unabashed, but the way her petite body straightened and stiffened at Pretty Boy's touch made his hackles rise.

His feet stalled, pausing in between a cluster of crowded tables, while he watched the interaction between the two of them. Rafe had a known tendency to overreact, especially when he'd been drinking.

He was working on it.

But then his gaze dropped from Amelia's mock smile and down to her hands, pressed firmly to Pretty Boy's chest, struggling to push away while his grip on her arms remained.

Rafe didn't need any further confirmation.

He was fully aware that his physical need for women as of late was dancing along the line of immoral. But he never once treated them with disrespect. Regardless of his emotional detachment, that was one line he never fucking crossed.

And Pretty Boy had crossed the line.

Amelia's expression morphed, pain screwing her eyes tight while fear labored her breath. Rafe's nostrils flared and he ground his teeth together as his skin reddened in anger. The soles of his leather shoes thudded as he stalked toward them, his fingers flexing at his sides.

The willpower he was currently experiencing should earn him a pat on the back because all he wanted to do was rip the fucker's arms from his sockets and slam his head against the wall. He'd seen what pricks like Pretty Boy could do when they thought they were invincible. This guy was in for a rude awakening.

Gently, so he didn't startle her, Rafe lifted his hands to Amelia's waist from behind her and leveled his eyes on the man who was forcefully holding on to her.

"Let go." His voice was controlled, even—but deadly.

He felt more than heard Amelia's sharp intake of air as his words flooded over her to the man in front of her.

Pretty Boy let go of her arms, his palms still in the air. Rafe's blood ran hot as he looked at the blanched imprint of douche bag's fingers on her skin. He softly shifted Amelia to the side and squared himself in front of the son of a bitch. The muscles beneath his jaw tightened and his breathing quickened. Restraint was a thing Rafe had always struggled with and he found his current struggle waning as he watched Pretty Boy's mouth stretch into a smirk. A smirk that said he didn't give a flying fuck about cause and effect, a smirk that said he thought he was invincible.

Rafe's fingers curled into a fist and the muscles of his bicep stiffened as he stretched his neck to the side. Knock his sorry ass out in one hit? Or spread the pain, enjoy the fight? He cracked his neck to the other side. No way in hell was this asshole getting lucky with one hit to the dome. He'd make him hurt all over before he'd be done with him.

Just as Rafe pulled his arm back, he felt a shaky hand land desperately on his forearm. Even then he was unable to pull his eyes away from that fucking smirk. "Come on, he's drunk and not worth it," Amelia said quietly, gently tugging on his arm.

Taking a deep breath, Rafe slowly turned and stepped away. Had he not been so worked up, he would have been proud of leaving Pretty Boy's face devoid of blood. But instead, he was disappointed.

But then a chuckle reached his ears, and the unmistakable arrogance it held sent a hot burn coursing along Rafe's nerves. The asshole didn't have an ounce of remorse for putting his hands on a woman like that. He had balls, Rafe would give him that.

"Piece of advice," Pretty Boy called out from behind, his words at the beginning stage of slurring. "I wouldn't waste your time with that one. I've had her. And she's not that good. Easy, but lousy."

Restraint was over-fuckin'-rated.

Rafe spun and took one long stride the second before his fist connected with Pretty Boy's jaw, sending him staggering backward. Was he satisfied? Hell no. So when Pretty Boy regained his footing and straightened his body, Rafe looked him in the eye—giving him a wordless heads-up—then went back in.

He needed to hear the crack of bone meeting bone; he needed to see flesh bruise and bleed. And he needed the fight.

This time Pretty Boy dodged his advance and a slow smile trickled onto Rafe's face. *Yes. Fight me back, you son of a bitch,* he thought as Pretty Boy lowered his upper body and charged him, wrapping his arms around Rafe's stomach, sending them both crashing backward into a table behind them. The seconds following blurred as the adrenaline took over Rafe's body. Blood trickled from the corner of his eye after Pretty Boy landed a few lucky blows to his face, but each one only intensified the force of his own fist when it connected with Pretty Boy's body.

A part of him—a large part of him—craved this. Always had. Passion of every form had always coursed through his veins. Whether love or hate, good or bad, it ran deep. So deep that its strength consumed him. Sometimes it was a curse, harboring a blazing intensity inside him. Especially when that blaze had formed an inferno, turning his control to ash.

Pearls of sweat beaded his forehead. He ducked, missing Pretty Boy's weak right hook, and landed a fist to his stomach. Several pairs of hands tore at his shirt and gripped on to his shoulders, attempting to pull the two of them apart. He was acutely aware of the voices around him, some encouraging and others disapproving, but the sound of his blood rushing through his ears muffled the noise.

It wasn't until he heard a voice telling him to stop—no, *commanding* him with that one single word—that his body finally stilled. Her soft, gentle voice eased over him until the essence of her intonation saturated his tense muscles. But it wasn't just the melodic sound that caught his attention in the midst of his aggression. It was the threatening demand in her voice that snapped his mind from whatever plane it was floating on and brought him back to the present.

In a single instant, all the oxygen heaved from Rafe's lungs as his body caught up from the fight. He looked down at the man beneath him covered in blood staring back at him with a fear in his eyes that almost made Rafe feel sorry for him. Almost. But then he remembered the fucker put his hands on a woman when she clearly didn't want him to, then proceeded to defame her, and he was tempted to beat his sorry ass all over again.

The silence was deafening, suffocating. He searched for Amelia and found her across from him, leaning her weight against a table for support. Her hand was covering her mouth and her eyes flashed with worry and shock, but when she met his gaze, he saw her gratitude. And that was all the reassurance he needed to know that he hadn't just lost his damn mind.

A light touch skimmed across the top of his ridged shoulder, over his tense back, and then slipped onto the other shoulder. Without delay, the heat simmering inside him started to intensify again. His body fired back to life at the same moment it went slack. He didn't need to turn around to know the beauty that stood behind him. She had already captivated his vision when he'd first seen her on that stage. And now, with her dexterous fingers pressing into his shoulders, she enamored his body as well. It was *her*. The angel.

Her featherlight touch drifted down his arm, her fingertips grazing his hot flesh with a tenderness he hadn't felt in a long time. "Come with me," she cajoled. And again, she wasn't asking.

CHAPTER FIVE

$\mathcal{S}$he'd seen the whole thing happen. She'd seen that
sleazebag headliner put his hands on her girl as if she
were a walking sex toy, and if that man hadn't intervened,
George sure as hell would have. But what had made *her*
intervene was the look on the man's face when he pulled
Amelia away. It wasn't a territorial possession. It was a protectiveness masked with anger. He hadn't been staking his
claim; he'd been defending her.

Fallon had watched numerous fights break out in her
club over the years, and she'd seen other assholes touch her
girls as if they had claim to do so. But she'd never witnessed
the expression that she saw on his face before. It was foreign
to her, seeing a stranger possess such selfless concern for a
woman. A concern that stemmed from somewhere genuine
and then manifested into unrelenting anger.

It was a rarity, that kind of passion, that protectiveness.
And she was uncontrollably drawn to it—to him.

But Fallon didn't need to observe the raw emotion that

seeped from his movements to feel the pull to him. His eyes alone had already done that.

She didn't pay attention to the men in the crowd while she danced. She slipped away, engulfed in the high her body provided her as she moved to the music. But she'd seen him. She'd felt his eyes whisper over her body. It was unfamiliar and magnetic and it rolled waves of unexpected sensations through her. She was unexplainably drawn to him—a man she'd never met or seen before. And it terrified her, because in that small moment she'd felt powerless.

She'd stood by the stage and watched him after she'd changed. Fallon wasn't taken aback by men; she didn't get that giddy feeling of lust most women strive for. But it wasn't lust that nuzzled an awakening inside. It was curiosity. And any man who had the ability to steal her attention and deprive her thoughts while she was dancing was worth a closer look.

She'd been out of view, tucked away at her observation post next to the stage. Her eyes followed his as he'd watched Naomi onstage. Na was always a crowd favorite. Tall and dark and lean and just completely beautiful. But he still didn't give her the attention the majority of the men in the club had. He'd just sat nearly motionless, his face construed as if he was deep in thought while he occasionally glanced at the stage, emptying glass after glass of liquor.

An incomprehensible burn tightened her stomach as a subtle spark lit in his eyes when Amelia had taken a seat on his lap. She'd watched as Amelia pressed the glass to his lips and she'd watched his throat as he swallowed. She'd had a moment's thought to look away, that she was being ridiculous watching this man, that whatever magnetism she'd experienced while she was dancing was completely ridiculous. But then the look in his eyes hardened. And she was sucked right back in.

Fallon had zero tolerance in her club for fighting. You fight, you're thrown out on your ass without so much as an explanation. And you can never come back. Period. Had Fallon not been so enthralled with this man, she would have had no problem letting George haul them both to the curb for the police to pick up.

But that wasn't the case.

She was surprised at how quickly she'd been able to grab his attention. He'd snapped his head to her as if her voice had physically pulled him away. Then his eyes had locked with hers—they were intense and raw, mixed with pain and a passion that sent chills through her entire body. And it was there, that pull. That unfamiliar trance washing over her as the ink in his eyes marked her.

"Fallon!" George called out from somewhere in the tight bodies of bystanders.

She blinked and refocused. "We need to hurry," she stated calmly, still holding on to the hand of the man who had just beaten the living snot out of one of her headliners.

He didn't respond, but she was severely aware of the small space between them that he closed. She could feel his body brush against hers as his steps coincided with her own, their pace quickening as they rushed through the club and climbed the stairs that went backstage.

His hand held hers firmly as she led him down the long hall and to her office. "Wait here," she instructed. She unlocked her door and hurried inside. Her peripheral vision allowed her to see him as he stepped into the doorway while she grabbed her purse from the sofa.

His dark dress jeans fit him perfectly, pulling just the right amount over his thighs and hanging slack and straight to his ankles. The coral color of his shirt was not one every man could pull off masculinely. But god, did he. The soft coastal color accentuated his dark olive skin and warmed his deep sable eyes. One side had pulled loose from his jeans during the fight, and as much as she loved and appreciated a well-dressed man, she wanted to slip the other side of his shirt from his waist and marvel in the way she knew it would drape from his body.

The tie around this man's neck made him look lethally delicious. *Delicious?* Yes, apparently he now looked edible. The kind of edible that looked so good but she knew it would be so bad . . . only bad in a way that was so good . . .

Oh god.

She cleared her throat, slid her purse onto her forearm, and squared her body back to face him. Which was probably a wrong move, because now she was looking right into his eyes—eyes that were just watching her. Not judging or appraising, just watching: watching her in a way that softened her slightly.

A tangible current charged between them. It was heady and carnal. She swallowed. She didn't lust. She *didn't*. Yet her body begged to differ. Her pulse accelerated and a twisting started in her chest and worked its way into her stomach, spreading a warmth she never expected.

His eyes seemed to have that effect on her, though. There was a depth to them, like a secret or a promise or maybe even a threat, and it compelled her, confined her.

Forcing herself to desert the embrace his eyes had hers in, she lowered her gaze. She had to. His eyes were like quicksand.

His jaw was relaxed, his mouth parted, and his breathing still labored. There was a scar on his bottom lip. Deep, as if a slice of his beautifully crafted mouth had been removed. It continued down the side of his chin, down his neck, and disappeared beneath the buttoned collar of his shirt.

One shoulder blade was resting against the doorframe and his arms were folded across his chest. The intensity of his posture had eased some, no longer ridged and tense. He looked, unaffected, approachable.

Touchable.

Dropping his arms to his sides, he pushed off the door and took a cautious step toward her. "You okay?" he asked. His misplaced concern confused her. Why was he asking if she was okay?

"Me? I'm not the one who's got blood dripping down my face." As the words left her mouth she understood his worry. There was a quake to her voice, an uncertainty that apparently mirrored her expression, and she hated it.

She didn't understand her body's response to him. The confidence and control she survived on was faltering under his very presence—so, no, she wasn't exactly okay.

Frowning, he moved closer. A faint heat flushed her neck and her mouth parted. She had the desire to retreat, but an undeniable need to remain where she was won out. He was overwhelming, tall and broad, and his nearness swallowed her completely.

She was a woman, raised to be poised and graceful, to exude femininity. Yet she had never in her entire life felt more feminine than she did at this very moment.

He was nothing but pure man, rough and masculine. His physique was raw and intimidating, confident in his movements—completely sexy. And there was a danger to him, a darkness. It was as if he was layered in pain, contoured in aggression. Yet she didn't fear him in the least. As he remained focused on her, his mouth slack, his eyes sharp, she saw reassurance, tenderness.

It was a wanton urge, an electric physical attraction, and she felt it from her scalp to her toes. She didn't think any woman would be capable of feeling anything less than attraction to him.

He lifted his arm and Fallon's eyes flitted to the sleeves of his shirt, where red drops were splattered. His hand moved toward her as if he was going to wrap it around her nape or run it through her hair. But he stopped, his eyes darting to his knuckles, where crimson cracks of dried blood were already forming.

His brows pulled in and he turned from her, rubbing

the back of his neck. He was struggling with his apparent need to comfort her—however unnecessary it was—and with his reluctance to touch her. Releasing a low, quiet grunt, he balled his fists and dropped them back to his sides.

"Dammit, look—"

"It's fine," she assured him. Rushing to the bathroom, she snatched the towel she had draped over her tub after her bath that afternoon. Good—it was still a little damp.

Latching onto the sides of the pedestal sink, she paused in front of the mirror and pulled in a deep gulp of air. A soft blush fanned across her cheeks, and her chest rose and fell with long breaths. She looked . . . not like herself. Straightening, she sucked in one last breath. Whatever hypnotic effect this man had on her was ending . . . now.

Once she was a little more composed, she strutted back into the office. She wouldn't allow herself any more weakness. "Here," she said, tossing the towel against his chest as she stepped back in front of him.

"Thanks," he replied, already wiping the drying blood from his knuckles.

She rested her hand on his forearm and gave him a gentle shove so she could move him out of her doorway and get him the hell out of there. Controlling the situation—that was what she needed to do. She'd stood solid for far too long to get weak in the knees over a bad boy with addictive eyes.

"You can wash up in a few minutes but right now we need to leave." Quickly, she locked up behind her. "Let's go. I can guarantee my bartender has already called the cops, and if we're lucky we'll get you out of here before they show up."

Simone, her bartender, didn't put up with any man's shit and she didn't care about the who, the what, or the why—which was one reason Fallon liked to keep her around. So she knew that this knight in shining armor didn't have much time to get out of there. Not to mention her VIP section was chock-full of influential men who could easily have him thrown behind bars in the blink of an eye.

A few of her girls were getting dressed for the next number as Fallon left the hallway and entered into the backstage dressing area. They regarded her with wary eyes as she passed them, her follower close behind. Yes, this was completely out of her character—*everything* was completely out of her character tonight. But her girls knew her. She didn't allow random men—or any men for that matter, aside from George—backstage. It was another one of her strictly enforced rules, and another one that she was breaking for this man.

She paused in front of Naomi. "Finish the lineup. I'm leaving for the night."

"What? Are you okay? Who's he and—?"

"I'm fine. Tell Jade to close up with George."

Naomi glanced around, then narrowed her eyes at the man who was standing behind Fallon. "Okay, boss."

Shoving the sturdy door open, Fallon stepped outside, the cool air nipping her exposed skin. Her gaze caught his as he narrowed the space between them. She didn't get distracted while she danced; she didn't break up fights or bring men backstage. And she sure as hell didn't lead them out the back door to her car.

*R*afe followed behind this woman, who was moving faster in a pair of heels than he thought physically possible as she clicked down the steps that led to the back parking lot. She fumbled around in her purse, then brought out a set of keys, pushing the unlock button as she circled around a sexy little sports car.

She gracefully slid into the car, her body slinking down into the seat before she shut the door. Rafe stood next to the passenger-side door, looking at his reflection in the tinted window. He looked like complete shit. His shirt was a mess, his hands still scattered with blood. His tie was hanging loosely around his neck and the small cut on the corner of his eye was making a trail of fresh blood down his cheek.

He could only imagine what was going through her mind when she looked at him. Reading her was difficult. One moment she looked like she would convulse on the spot if he even brushed against her; the next she was shoving him out her office door like she couldn't stand to be in the very room with him.

And he didn't blame her.

He'd seen the look in a woman's eyes before when she was afraid of him. He'd heard horror seep from a woman's mouth in a pleading scream while she witnessed his body giving in to the rage inside him.

That's why his missions fed him, why combat distracted

him. When it came down to it, fighting for someone, including his country, led him down a one-way road with no deviation.

Until her.

Standing there, looking at the dried blood on his hands, he cringed. Not because he regretted it; he never did. But because, for once, someone was able to shift through the debris around him.

Groaning, he balled the towel in his hand and opened the door, throwing his large body into the tight confinements of the passenger seat. He heard her breath catch in her throat. It was subtle, but he heard it.

His eyes shot to hers. She was looking back at him, her brows pulled in tightly, wrinkling the skin between her beautiful champagne-colored eyes.

"You don't need to be afraid of me," he said, almost pleading.

"Who said I was scared of you?" she asked, and her voice was firm, confident. He waited for it, for her shield to lower. But it didn't.

"What's your name?" she asked, breaking the silence that had begun to stretch between them.

"Rafe."

"Rafe? Like 'safe' with an 'R'?"

His head cocked to the side as he looked at her, confused. "Yeah?"

She laughed once. Just one soft little laugh, a giggle almost, and it relaxed him. A fucking giggle relaxed him.

"Safe. Kind of ironic, isn't it, Rafe?" she asked, starting the car, the engine roaring to life beneath them.

"And your name?"

"Fallon."

"Well, thank you, Fallon."

She looked at him, her eyes reflecting tiny little bursts of light from the lamppost in front of them. "For what?"

"For stopping me." That prick had every ounce of pain coming to him, and Rafe hoped like hell the pain he'd inflicted penetrated deep enough that the man would never put his hands on a woman again. But Rafe was glad she'd stopped him—he'd already experienced what could happen if he didn't stop.

She smiled a soft, knowing smile and shifted her eyes back to the parking lot in front of her. "You needed a distraction," she explained. "It's what I do. Distractions are kind of my specialty. They're part of the job description." Her head shifted toward him for a brief moment and she extended her smile a little more. "They just usually don't include an exit strategy."

Rafe nodded, then leaned his head back against the seat as Fallon pulled out of the parking lot right as the police sirens came into earshot.

She didn't know how true her words were. He needed a distraction in every sense.

As the sirens rang closer, Fallon breathed a sigh of relief that they'd left before the police arrived. Leaving her club unannounced after a fight—not to mention a fight with a headliner—would cause one giant headache in the morning, but she also knew Simone would step up and take care of it for her. She was gonna owe her big time.

The following ten minutes they sat in silence as her tires spun across the black asphalt. Fallon kept her eyes on the road in front of her, but she could feel Rafe's gaze shift over to her every now and again. And it was strange the way those little looks made her feel. Excited? Nervous? Neither one was an emotion Fallon was familiar with. *Arm's length, remember?*

Pulling into a small parking lot, Fallon parked her car away from the few others and killed the engine.

The silence between them was growing—and it wasn't growing roses, that's for damn sure. It was tense and unsettling. Brooding . . .

Fallon shifted in her seat, facing Rafe. He remained silent, looking at her with an expression that pricked a tiny little ache beneath her collarbone. She was used to men looking at her—it was her job. She was used to seeing desire and need in men's eyes as they watched her. But there was something so different in the way Rafe was regarding her in that moment. He wasn't looking at her like he was ready to undress her. Instead, he looked at her with a curious hunger that matched her own. A desperation that she was all too familiar with.

"Why'd you do it?" he asked.

"Do what? Stop you from fighting in my club?"

"Why'd you get me out of there? Why didn't you just let the cops arrest me?"

She inhaled a breath, slushing through her different answers, and opted for telling him the truth. "Because you were defending one of my girls. And because I was watching you."

His brows darted up in a cocky way that suited him a little too well. "You were?"

"Yes," she replied. Her confidence reached up and found its role in her voice, and she let it carry her. "I watched you watch me." She paused, then shook her head. "That doesn't happen."

"What doesn't happen?" he asked, his voice still even, but she could tell his curiosity had spiked.

"I'm not easily distracted."

His head moved back just the tiniest amount. Not enough to call it a nod, and not enough that she should have noticed, but she did. And she also noticed the subtle pull in the muscles on the corner of his beautiful mouth—the warning sign of an imminent smug grin. To her appreciation, he was fighting it.

Then the complacent expression in his eyes vanished as he blinked, and when he set those smooth, sable eyes on her again, she lost her breath.

Literally lost it. She couldn't remember how to inhale to fill her lungs with much-needed oxygen. She was too trapped. Too entranced by the way he looked at her. She couldn't remember the last time a man could draw such a strong physical reaction from her with just a look. That look could make her beg, and Fallon didn't beg.

Anyone. Ever.

But she'd admitted it and accepted it. The way he held her captive with his eyes felt like he was truly touching her, containing her—holding her. And if he looked away, she was afraid she would beg him to look back.

"Looks like we've both got a talent for distracting the other when no one else can," he commented.

The balmy air in the car morphed thick and hot, a tangible tension clinging to them. What was it about him that did this to her? She didn't know how long she just sat there watching the twitch of his chiseled jaw beneath a few days of stubble, imagining the feel of his buzzed head beneath her fingers, captured in his controlling eyes. Surely minutes had passed, many minutes.

A hum sliced through the silence in the car, and Fallon turned away from him, focusing out the windshield. She felt the moment his eyes moved from her body and she sighed inwardly.

She faintly heard his voice as he answered his phone, but it was muffled by the volume of her rambling mind. Taking back her body's control was imperative. She wasn't this woman; she'd never been this woman.

"Sorry about that," Rafe said a few moments later, pushing the phone back into his pocket.

"Lose the tie."

His eyes widened at her sudden command. Then, cracking a smile, he pulled on his tie, loosening it a little more so he could lift it from his neck.

"Come here." The breathiness she was prepared for never coasted from her lips. Relieved, she lifted her hands to his collar, fumbling with the cream buttons, sliding them through the small slits.

"What are you doing?"

She peered up at him through her lashes, fingers stalled on his collar. Trademark move right there. Every woman should learn and master the lash-look. Drove men crazy. More than likely because it reminded them of the way women looked at them when their jeans were around their ankles. Sometimes they were such predictable creatures. And if she wanted to gain the upper hand, she had to go all or nothing. "This isn't a tie atmosphere."

Nodding his response, he continued to watch her as she returned her attention to his shirt.

After she unbuttoned the top three buttons, slightly revealing his chest, she went to his wrists, unbuttoning his sleeves and rolling each one up to his elbows.

Her eyes immediately lifted to find his. "Hmm."

"What's your 'hmm' for?" he questioned, studying her carefully.

She simply shrugged; however she assumed he deduced her reason from the cocky glint that flashed in his eyes.

Both his arms were covered in ink that began at his wrists and disappeared beneath his shirt. And she imagined if she unbuttoned it the remainder of the way and pushed it from his arms, she would find that the tattoos covered them completely.

What was it about a man with sleeves of tattoos? Was it the ink itself that detonated a physical reaction from women, or was it the assumption of what was behind the ink? What the tattoos portrayed?

It gave off the stereotypical impression of a bad boy, a man with edge, a glimpse of danger.

But even before she saw the ink on his arms, she knew. She saw the flash of danger flecked in his eyes. He was a sexy bad boy in a tie. Now, with the tie gone and his tattoos on display, he became lethal.

Gone was the bad boy, replaced by a man who threatened her resolve.

"There," she said, inspecting her quick moderations. Fallon seemed to be attracted to men who were put together—well dressed, well groomed. Blame it on her shallow upbringing. But now, sitting next to a man who couldn't possibly look more unkempt if he did it deliberately, she found herself second-guessing her typical type.

"Let's go, tough guy." She opened the door and gracefully stepped out of her car. Rafe met her around the front and placed his hand on the small of her back—and she flinched.

A deep groan hummed in his chest, barely audible, but they were so close she heard him. "Don't be scared of me. I know I lost my control back there, but I'd never hurt a woman."

The rough texture of the asphalt beneath her stilettos complicated her turn as she spun to the side to face him. "You didn't—*and you don't*—scare me," she said, trying to remove some of the anguish she felt in his words. "I've got enough sense not to take a man on a joyride if I think he'll hurt me. So stop worrying that pretty little head of yours. You just startled me," she admitted, once again facing the bar in front of them.

Her steps echoed through the nearly empty parking lot, but the second Rafe's hand swept along the small of her back again, the sound stopped. She stopped.

"I believe I can walk without your assistance, thank you," she muttered, irritated with the way his touch seemed to scorch her skin.

"I'm sure you could." He didn't move his hand from her; instead, he only pressed it against her more firmly. The heat from his palm felt as if it was singeing the fabric of her dress, smoldering the remains onto her flesh, heating her from the outside in. "Correct me if I'm wrong, but we're not in Kansas anymore, Toto."

So they'd crossed over to the rough part of town. Little did he know she lived alone on this side of the economical line not too many years ago. They might not be in Kansas anymore, but she was well acquainted with this half of the yellow brick road.

"So, what, you feel the need to protect me?" she asked, slightly annoyed, slightly intrigued.

"You're with me tonight," he stated, urging her forward with his hand, forcing her feet to move one in front of the other. She was rummaging through her stockpile of witty comebacks when she felt warm breath on her ear. "You okay with that?" he whispered.

She didn't like this. He was trampling on her control and she felt defenseless. But was she okay with the way it felt to have his lips so close to her skin? Surprisingly, yes.

"I'm a little conflicted at the moment, so I don't have a logical response to that question," she replied honestly, willing her confidence to command her words.

"Well, let me simplify it for you," he whispered, shifting behind her. His free hand swept her hair from her back, pushing it over her shoulder. Then he leaned his mouth to her ear again. If he wanted to simplify things, he wasn't doing the best job, because now she was even more conflicted than before.

"We're in a rough neighborhood, and you look like Daddy's trust fund wrapped up in a sexy little bow just ready for some fucking douche bag to try to unwrap. You're with me tonight. And I'll let everyone know it."

She snapped from his touch and stepped back. The lids of her eyes dropped into slits. "Daddy's trust fund?" A menacing laugh swayed across her lips from deep in her chest. "My 'Daddy' threw me out on my ass when I was seventeen years old with no more than the hundred bucks I had in my back pocket. I was completely cut off, left to fend for myself, with no one to turn to. Just so happens, this pretty little bow I'm wrapped up in I tied myself." Spinning around yet again, she stomped off toward the bar, determined to reach it without any more interruptions from Rafe.

How dare he! Her blood grew hot, flushing her skin with anger. The success she'd achieved would never be credited to them.

She'd hated her old life, the life she lived under Daddy's roof. It was a lonely existence in that house. And it was a hell of a lot worse when she was living under the roof of a rotten apartment, cold and empty.

An unwelcome heat seared the backs of her eyes. It was horrible being raised under the microscope, forbidden to experience the joys childhood and youth had to offer. But it was a nightmare, a living, suffering, horrifying nightmare, living in a cesspool of nothing. Staying awake till nearly dawn so she wouldn't have to sleep at night, in the dark, vulnerable to the scum the shadows held outside her door, and vulnerable to the dreams that awaited her while she slept.

And they'd thrust her into that nightmare. Her family, her parents, cloaked with their own aspirations, tossed her on her ass. All because she'd developed her own ambitions outside the structured interior of their rules. She'd snapped under the weight of their expectations and dared to spread her wings. She'd wanted to find a small taste of life beyond her family's impostrous world.

She'd been seventeen, primed for new experiences, craving chaos—thirsting for freedom from her isolation. Needing passion and abandon. She had wanted to feel. Something. Anything.

But promiscuity and impulse and lack of inhibitions didn't portray the facade her parents had contrived. She'd become nothing more than a hindrance to their reputation. They didn't allow room for mistakes, didn't offer second chances.

It was hell. Being completely, absolutely alone in the world. It had ripped her open, branded her with a pain and anger so vehement there was no differentiating them.

But she would relive that hell, even knowing how scary and heartbreaking it was—she would relive it all over again just to save herself from turning out like them.

The distinctive clunk of shoes meeting pavement thumped from behind as Rafe strode quickly to catch up with her.

His arrogant mood swing took her by surprise, though really it shouldn't have surprised her. He embodied the exact characteristics that made up the type. Aggressive, intimidating, unlawfully sexy. Add a touch of asshole to the mix and you've got an arrogant wrapped up in a pretty little fucking bow.

Asshole.

"Fuck," she heard him mumble from behind her. "Fallon, stop."

She didn't take orders from men. She gave them. But the mix of power and concern in his voice swayed her. She stopped.

"Dammit. I'm sorry. That was an asshole thing for me to say."

"Coming from the asshole himself," she whipped. "You know jack shit about me."

"Look," he started, his long fingers wrapping around her wrist, spinning her around to face him. "All I meant was that you're gorgeous, sexy as fuckin' sin, and any man within reaching distance will be looking for a grab. That shit doesn't sit well with me, if you didn't notice earlier."

Gently and slowly, he settled his hand back onto the small of her back and stepped into her, positioning her against his body. Hard muscle collided with her stomach, and breasts, and thighs, as he urged her body to contour along his.

Her knees nearly buckled on the spot, but, always a pro at keeping face, she recovered quickly. Yet her skin still felt charged with an electric current. Every inch of her ran along him and she was forced to tilt her head back to see him.

Simmering anger dissipated as she stared at the raw power in his eyes. She felt the same compelling need that she'd felt earlier when she saw him fight. Only this time, instead of distracting him, she wanted to mollify his guilt. Maybe it was his genuineness or maybe she was just out of her mind, but she eased up on the bitchy attitude. At least for the time being. "Apology accepted. Horrible apology, but you call a girl gorgeous and it lets you off the hook a little bit."

His shoulders rolled forward as he sighed, and that damaged mouth of his desperately avoided curving into a devilish smile. Two things crossed her mind at that point. One was that her body seemed content with the feel of his lining hers. And the other was that she actually appreciated his concern, his protectiveness. She couldn't pinpoint a moment in her life when a simple touch made her feel secure. And even though his gesture was hardly necessary, she allowed herself to welcome the sensation.

Fallon leaned against the glass door smudged with layers of fingerprints and walked inside. As usual, it was occupied by its regulars and she could count them all on her fingers and toes.

"Well, look who has graced us with her presence," a rough voice, well attained by years of cigarette smoke, belted as Fallon made her way through the small bar with Rafe close behind her. His hand was still resting on her back and she could feel the eyes of the men watching her. But not for reasons Rafe would have assumed.

"Good to see you too, Pete," she greeted. Her shoes peeled from the sticky floor as she crossed to the bar. Sitting down on the barstool, she leaned over and gave Pete a one-armed hug.

"Who in the hell's he?" Pete pinned his stare to Rafe. He was standing next to her, hand no longer on her back.

Rafe's arm darted out in front of him, offering his hand to Pete. "Rafe."

Pete studied Rafe's swollen and cracked knuckles while his hand hung in the air between them. Disapproval was evident on his aged face. Looking to Rafe, he clamped his hand to his and shook it with one firm jerk.

Nodding, Pete dropped Rafe's hand with a silent understanding, or maybe defeat—Fallon wasn't sure—then turned his scrutiny to her. She'd accept the ass chewing she was bound to get. She hadn't visited in more than a year.

"Nice seeing your pretty face again," he lilted, lifting a glass from beneath the bar and wiping it clean with a rag. "You ain't bringing trouble to my bar, are you, girl?"

Pete pulled a narrow glass bottle from the shelf behind him and flooded the tumbler with its golden liquid.

Fallon crossed her legs underneath the ledge of the bar. "You should know me better than that, Pete."

"I know you better, but I ain't know this man"—he tilted the liquor bottle toward Rafe—"and he's got trouble dripping down the side of his face."

Fallon looked to Rafe, who had taken a casual stance against the bar, leaning his side into the old, gritty wood. He seemed relatively amused by Pete, his arms hanging loosely at his sides. Fallon took a moment to appreciate the artwork that covered every inch of flesh on his muscular forearms. The dim light of the bar made them look different than when she first saw them in the dark parking lot. They were beautiful, intricate, a complementary mix of blacks and grays woven around vivacious colors.

Coasting her eyes to his face, she saw that the small cut on the corner of his eye was bleeding again. It must have been deeper than she'd originally thought.

Pete slid the glass he'd just filled to Rafe.

"Thanks," he said, picking up the glass and pressing it to his lips. Watching him drink was a form of hypnotism. His mouth and his throat—they both made her feel as if she were in a trance.

"How'd you know what I'd like?" he asked as he set the empty glass back down on the bar.

"Lucky guess," Pete answered, handing Fallon a glass of Diet Coke.

"I don't drink," she said, answering Rafe's unspoken question. Swiveling off her stool, she went behind the bar, lifting a small container from beneath the counter. "Now come on. Let's get you cleaned up."

CHAPTER SIX

Once again Rafe was amazed at the speed that woman could attain in a pair of heels. Her hips rocked back and forth harmoniously to the sound of her gentle clicking as he followed her to the back of the bar, completely enjoying his view.

"In here," she instructed, pushing the bathroom door open.

"Kinky. I didn't know bathrooms were your thing," he quipped, stepping next to her in the doorway. His body was crammed against hers in the tight confines. Sleek, soft curves lined his firm frame. The top of her head reached his chest, his height towering over her.

Silky brown hair tumbled over her shoulder as she tilted her head to the side. "Huh." She chortled, amusement lining her lips. "I didn't realize sarcastic wit was your thing. Unfortunate."

Her hand levered against his stomach as she squeezed past him. He remained in the doorway, watching her reflection in the mirror as she stood at the porcelain sink wetting a couple of paper towels.

"Come here," she said, spinning around to face him.

One stride closed the distance between them and he stepped into her, his thigh brushing between hers as he tilted his head down so she could reach him. Grabbing his chin in her hands, she turned his face to the side and gently wiped his eye. Water from the paper towel dripped down the side of his face and her thumb brushed across his cheek, catching the drop.

"So I'm a little confused as to why a woman like you, who doesn't drink alcohol, is buddy-buddy with the bartender at a place like this," he asked as she continued her cleanup.

He felt the paper towel press against his skin a little harder as she cleaned dried blood from his temple. "I used to work here a few nights a week."

He tried to move his head to face her, but her grip on his chin tightened. "You used to work here?"

"Yeah, for about a year when I was eighteen. Like I said, I've been on my own for a long time."

Releasing his chin, she threw the paper towel away and stepped to the side. Rafe turned the water back on and ran his hands underneath, washing away the blood he had been unable to remove earlier.

"And how did you end up at the club?" He turned from the sink to face her, and an elated smile spanned across her face.

"I met a woman—"

"Best way to start a story," he interrupted, resting on the edge of the sink. He folded his arms over his chest and nodded for Fallon to continue.

"She came into the bar looking for Pete, her uncle. She was graceful and elegant. Only a few years older than me and sexy in the most sophisticated way. I was immediately jealous."

"Jealous? You just described yourself, sweetheart."

Lifting her brows, she fastened her eyes on his. "Camille was everything my old life represented. She'd looked like she'd just come from one of my mother's weekly dinner parties. She looked like everything I was raised to be. And the way she claimed a room, demanded respect, and exuded gentle confidence—I wanted that. But there I stood in worn jeans, a tank top, and scuffed patent leather pumps, and I was jealous. And I hated her for it." Confusion choked the ease of her expression and she paused, looking up at him. "Why am I even telling you all this anyway?"

Rafe captured her chin and stroked her jaw with his thumb. Need crawled in his veins as Fallon's golden eyes smoldered, swirls of amber beckoning him. "Because I asked," he said gently. "Why'd you hate her?"

Blinking, she sighed and shook her head, releasing from his grasp, clearing away the intoxicating moment between them. "Because I thought she belonged to the world I spent so much time trying to break free from, only to have it ripped away from me instead." She lowered her head so he was no longer able to read the contradicting emotions on her face. "She reminded me of the very people I hate, the same people who broke me when they turned their backs on me. But she's nothing like them." Fallon cleared her throat. "Long story short, we talked, she took me back to the club, set me up in the apartment above the office, gave me a job, and a few years later the club's mine."

Rafe knew that small window had been closed. Whatever had happened in her past, she was doing her best to keep it repressed.

"So the club's yours?" he repeated.

"Yes," Fallon said, making her way to the bathroom door. "Camille's husband was Denver's very own Hugh Hefner and he left me the club when he died two years ago."

"Let me get this straight. Camille's husband left *you* the club?"

She laughed once. "He left it to both of us. He knew how much I loved it, and Camille wanted to open another one in New York City. So she's there and I'm here. We co-own both clubs together."

His hand found its way to the small of her back as they stepped out of the bathroom. She didn't flinch or step away this time, so he pressed a little more firmly. He molded his palm into the small dip in her back, absorbing the soft, thin fabric against his skin.

Fallon took her spot back at the bar and sipped her Diet Coke. She looked so damn out of place sitting there, yet at the same time she was comfortable. The straps of her red dress hung off her shoulder and the neckline scooped low, giving a subtle show of cleavage, but not enough. Her dress formed against her body, shaping over every curve and hitting just below midthigh. She showed enough to make you look, but not enough to allow you to see. Everything about her was tempting him.

"So what about you there, Rocky? Do you make a habit of beating up politicians?"

Rafe rolled his head back on his neck. "Fuuck, that asshole was a politician?" Dammit, the last thing he needed was for word about his fight to get back to his company.

She nodded. "He was one of my headliners. Not sure exactly who he was, though. Don't worry—they're not going to know who you are. But you didn't answer me. Is this a thing for you?"

"No."

She cocked an eyebrow, unconvinced. And she was spot-on. Rafe had been in his fair share of fights over the years.

"It's not a story I care to divulge right now," he replied.

Nodding again, she took another small sip of her Diet Coke, but the way she seemed dubious—hesitant of his intentions—rubbed him the wrong way.

"You think a man has a right to put his hands on a woman when she doesn't want him to?" he rebuked. "You may allow guys to grope your ass whenever—"

Her hand dropped from her glass and she twisted her body to face him so quickly he damn near missed it. "Men don't touch me," she snapped, the champagne color of her eyes deepening as her lids lowered into slits. She leaned forward a little as if her thin body could withstand a hurricane. "Ever. That's not how my club works. That's not how burlesque works. No touching, no private dances, no full nudity. I sell seduction. Temptation, fantasy. I don't sell my girls. And I sure as hell don't sell myself."

She was pissed. He could see it in the light flare of her nostrils as she leveled her eyes on his, unwavering. "That's not what I meant."

Seemingly calming down now that her tirade was out of her system, she propped her elbow up on the bar, recrossed her legs, and repositioned herself against the wood. "That might not be what you meant, but that's what you thought. There's a fine line—I know this. We push the boundaries of seduction at Velour, just slightly. But I just want to get one thing straight with you. That's my club. Those are my rules."

"Yes, ma'am," he said with a smirk. She was even sexier when she was pissed.

She raised her eyebrows at him. He enjoyed watching her little retort. Face flushed with the remnants of her agitation, she pursed her lips and folded her arms beneath her chest. "I also don't leave with random assholes who have a taste for blood and are drowning themselves in women and liquor," she jested.

"Oh yeah—and I suppose that's how you're pinning me?"

"Yes, handsome, that's exactly how I see you. I've seen every single walk of man come into my club, and they all want the same thing: a distraction. Whether they need to get away from their boring sex life with their prude wife, unwind from work, or are drinking themselves away from heartache, they all want a distraction."

Rafe nodded at Pete, who was talking to a guy on the

other end of the bar. Pete took the cue and nodded back, repeating his routine of wiping out a glass and pouring whiskey. "So if you don't leave with random assholes, then where does that leave me?" He pulled a cigarette from the pack he kept in his pocket and lit the end, inhaling deeply as he watched Fallon out of the corner of his eye.

Her lips parted and a shallow dimple formed. "Lucky."

Running his thumb around the rim of the glass of whiskey Pete had just put in front of him, Rafe asked, "How so?"

She could play this little game of banter. The severity of his mood had morphed, amusement folding in the creases around his eyes, his mouth curling as he regarded her response. "I make the rules. Therefore I can break them."

His smile extended upward, uneven on the side where his scar ran deep. She diverted her eyes, protecting herself from the vulnerability she felt from his jovial expression as he watched her.

Putting his cigarette to his lips, he inhaled, then let the smoke out slowly. "You know, I'm struggling to figure you out," he said.

She narrowed her eyes, sipping her drink. The chilled carbonation soothed and tingled her throat as she swallowed. "And why's that?"

He pressed his glass to his lips and sucked in a leisurely sip of whiskey. She watched as his Adam's apple rose, then fell as he swallowed; then she shifted her eyes back to his when he set the glass down.

This undeniable physical attraction she felt toward him was new for her. It was uncontrollable. Her traitorous body scorched with a need she wasn't sure she was ready to give into yet. The last eight years had been nothing but calculated decisions made to keep people at arm's length. Sexual relationships formed from want . . . not need. She'd never had the impulse—felt the need—to lean over, rest her hands on a man's thighs, lick his neck . . .

Rafe's tongue snaked across his bottom lip, lapping the lingering whiskey. "You don't strike me as a woman who breaks the rules often. At least not her own rules." His voice compelled her thoughts to retreat from the temptation she was feeling.

"I've followed and broken my fair share of *rules*. But you're right—the only ones I'm concerned with following are my own."

Mischief gleamed in his eyes. "And you're breaking your rules for me?"

"Don't get cocky. You needed a distraction, and I gave it to you. Besides, my bartender had called the cops and you were about ready to turn an ass kicking into involuntary manslaughter. I can't be having an investigation at my club because you decided to play the hero."

"He wasn't that bad."

She arched her brows. If that wasn't denial, she didn't know what was.

He laughed, tilting his head back toward the ceiling. "Well, he had it coming."

"You want to tell me about her?" Fallon asked as he looked back down at her.

"Who?"

She crossed her arms. He knew exactly who she was talking about. Not too many reasons a man like him is the way he is, and a woman was undoubtedly the reason. "The one who flipped you inside out. The woman you're attempting to forget at the bottom of your glass."

"No." The volume of his voice lowered and the finality of his tone told her that little topic of conversation wasn't up for discussion.

"Ah, the suffer-in-silence type. Sexy," she said, trying to ease some of the sudden tension that hardened his expression.

Standing up from his chair, he picked up his glass and drank the remaining liquor, the glass clanking against the wood bar as he set it back down.

She studied him curiously as his demeanor transformed again. Anger, heartache, guilt—all whirring mutely through his posture.

Capturing her gaze, Rafe took a step toward her, and she swallowed hard. His intensity returned and she willingly shrank beneath it, reveling in the way his masculine stance made her feel crazed and delicate at the same time. His hand fell to her knee and she swore a fire lit on the surface of her skin and ricocheted all the way down to her toes. Long fingers curled around her knees as he pulled her legs apart, pushing his thighs between hers. Her legs instantly closed, the insides of her thighs pressing against the outside of his. Arching her back, she leaned away to look at him, but he only advanced into her, preventing distance from growing between them.

God, he smelled so good. She wanted to coil her fingers into his shirt and pull him to her face so she could inhale. But she was frozen. Motionless by the sheer power of his focus as his velvety dark eyes inched closer to her own.

"You mentioned a distraction," he whispered, lips lowering to the sensitive skin below her ear, waiting for her to answer.

"Yes," she replied softly. His hand dropped down and his palm flattened against her hip—and if she hadn't been so determined not to, she would've shuddered.

His fingers grazed up her side until the tip of his thumb brushed beneath her breast. "You're right. I do need one." Warm breath bathed the side of her neck, causing her to involuntarily close her eyes. "And I want you to be that distraction for me tonight."

With his right hand on her side and his left hand latched onto the edge of her barstool, she was trapped between his powerful arms. Arms she imagined would feel incredible wrapped around her.

She wanted to be that distraction for him, which was probably reason enough to say no. She didn't have flings or random one-night stands. When she was with a man, it was planned and on her terms. It kept her in control. Sex that was brought on by intense sexual tension, desire, and pure wanton need was way too risky. Sex that was planned and initiated for raw, unadulterated pleasure with no other emotions attached was what she liked. Not spontaneous lust.

Yet that was exactly what this was. Lust.

She was helpless against her body's response to him, imprisoned by his eyes.

Curiosity and an unfamiliar longing swayed her, impulse overruling her. She would give him the distraction he needed. Just this once.

CHAPTER SEVEN

The fresh air whipped across his face as Rafe stepped out of the bar, once again leading Fallon by the small of her back. Her steps were slower now, and he wondered if she was reconsidering his proposition. Fuck, he hoped not. When he'd watched her eyes close as his mouth lingered above her skin, he about fucking lost it. It took all the restraint he could muster to refrain from showing her the other ways he could make her feel—show her the other reactions he could set off with his mouth alone.

Fallon pressed the unlock button on the key fob as they reached her car, but before she had an opportunity to open the door, he pinned her to it. His body collapsed against hers, her ass nestling against him as her chest pressed into the car. Inhaling deeply, he breathed her in as he leaned his lips down to the curve of her shoulder.

Moving his hands to the car on either side of her, his hips pressed against her, wanting her to feel what her body was doing to his. She did. And she moaned.

"I've wanted to touch you since the second I saw you

step onto that stage tonight. And not for the reasons you're thinking." Scattering featherlight kisses over her shoulder, he rocked into her again, obtaining yet another gratifying sigh from her mouth.

Her head tipped back and he obeyed her silent request, skirting his lips up the side of her long, delicate neck. Her legs swayed slightly and he moved a hand to her hip, securing her body in place.

"And what were your reasons?" she asked breathlessly, barely audible. Dammit, she was wearing down his self-control. It was already paper thin.

"You weren't just sexy. There was a sincerity in the way you moved," he started, shifting his hand from her hip to her stomach so he could press her tightly against his chest. "Confidence." His hand continued its journey up her body, cupping firmly as he reached the underside of her breast.

Watching her dance had turned him on, and just re-playing that image of her onstage in his mind was getting him worked up. Watching her dance had been like watching a woman pleasure herself. A woman knowing what she liked, secure and assertive enough to give herself the plea-sure she needed and deserved along with the unabashed confidence to allow him to watch—there was nothing sex-ier. And that's exactly how he felt seeing her on that stage: as if she was allowing him a peek into her intimate desires. Desires that only she knew, but ones he desperately wanted to learn.

"I want to feel you move against me. I want to see that graceful body need my touch the way I need to touch you," he said, brushing his thumb across her nipple, feeling it harden under the fabric of her dress.

She squirmed, arching into his hand. "Rafe," she pleaded, her ass pressing against his hard-on. It was as if she couldn't decide whether she wanted to rub against him or wiggle from his grasp. "Get in the car."

His mouth stilled against her flesh at her command, desperately fighting the urge to smile. Fuck, he wanted to get in that car. His body ached with the anticipation her words held. But he liked this game, her fight for control. And he was going to enjoy watching it siphon away beneath his touch.

Her hand moved to the door handle and she lifted, but their bodies were still pressed against the door, preventing it from opening. "Now," she whispered with an authority that made his dick jerk.

Cupping her breast more firmly, he grinded into her from behind. Her head rolled back in satisfaction and a soft moan unfurled from her parted lips. "Ask me nicely," he demanded.

She laughed once, her sweet voice taking on the shrill of a vixen. "Please," she answered.

Ah, hell. That word mewling from her lips whispered against his senses and did things to his accelerating pulse that he was damn near ashamed to admit. He fucking loved hearing it, and he knew then and there hearing her beg would be his undoing.

The warning rang sharp in his ear, like a quick whip of lightning. Since when did Rafe Murano let the breathy pleas of a woman unravel his strategically contrived approach to sex? He'd already severed any possible link he possessed that would tether his dick to anything outside of immediate gratification.

Fastening his lips on her neck, he sucked gently. He was overthinking this. She'd offered him exactly what he wanted— a temporary remedy to his lascivious ailment. And he was going to take her up on it.

Quickly grabbing on to her hips, he pulled her into him once more, enjoying the way she felt settled against him. He forced his hands to let go and walked around the back of the car, once again cramming his body into the tight confines of the passenger seat. The second his door shut, she crawled onto his lap. His eyes widened and he lost the ability to think. Her dress hiked up around her waist as she straddled him and Rafe took the open opportunity to run his hands along her bare thighs. Her flesh was smooth underneath his fingers until chill bumps bloomed beneath them, further confirming his dexterity. Wanting to strip her from her clothing and trail his fingers along every plane of exposed skin had him digging his fingertips into her thighs to prevent him from doing just that. It'd been so long since he'd felt a hunger for a woman's body in the way he did for Fallon's. He didn't just want to have her; he wanted to explore her, satisfy her, bring her to a numbing orgasm by his fingers alone. He couldn't process the reasons for his abrupt, curious greed. But he wouldn't be appeased until he had it. Until he felt her convulse and quake above him.

Goddamn. What the fuck was wrong with him?

"For the record," she muttered, pressing her warm mouth to his neck, shifting his attention to his growing erection from the feel of her lips alone. Damn. What would those soft lips feel like wrapped around him? His head rolled back against the headrest. "I never have spontaneous sex with strange men in my car."

Lifting an eyebrow, he cocked his head to the side. "Is that you telling me you don't want me to fuck you?" Coasting his fingers up the inside of her thighs, he stroked his thumb along the folds of her pussy, careful not to touch her clit. He wanted to tease her, not make her come. And judging by the way her breath halted midgasp, he'd say she wasn't too far from it.

Fallon's head shook, and he grinned as she rocked against his thumb. "No. I'm already breaking my rules—I figured a few more wouldn't hurt."

Threading his fingers through her hair at the nape of her neck, he yanked back, exposing her throat to him. "It'll only hurt if you want it to," he promised. The tip of his tongue darted out and thrashed against the hollow between her collarbones.

"Ahh." She breathed, and her approval only intensified his grip as he trailed his tongue up the center of her throat. When he reached her chin, he nipped it gently, then released his hold on her hair. She tasted so fucking good, and his dick agreed, straining painfully against his zipper.

"You wanted to feel me need your touch?" she asked, nimble fingers frantically clawing at his shirt, making quick work of undoing the rest of the buttons. "Well, I need it," she confessed with bated breath. "I need you to touch me, now, Rafe."

Her admittance avalanched over him with hot, trundling desire. His body hadn't craved a woman the way his was thirsting for Fallon since the vacancy inhabited his chest.

His fingers skimmed underneath the hem of her dress, drifting softly up her sides. But then her fingers left his chest and wrapped around his wrists, pulling his hands from her body. "However," she began, placing his hands on the seat next to his thighs, "right now *you* need the distraction." A stream of chills coursed over his skin as she raked her long nails down his bare chest. It wasn't just pleasure he was feeling as her touch fanned his body; it was eager anticipation. Her emphatic desire shocked him, and so did the way he responded to it.

Her fingers reached his jeans and she popped the button, then slid the zipper down. Lifting from his lap, she rose to her knees and gave his jeans and boxers a quick tug, then rested back down on top of him. The warmth from her center seeped into his skin, intensifying the blood flow throughout his body. "Jesus, you're—"

"Shh," she hushed, leaning down so her tits were pressed against his chest and her mouth was lingering above his. He inhaled sweet, hot breath from her mouth, and if she didn't let him taste her soon, he was going to take matters into his own hands.

Her hips rolled forward and a carnal groan hummed in his throat when the thin, wet lace between her thighs made contact with his cock. It had been a long time since a woman pushed him, made him crave her so fucking bad that he thought he was going to explode, but that's exactly what Fallon was doing. She was stringing him along, breaking him down, and turning him on. He wanted to touch her, wanted to glide his fingers around the lace and feel the fabric absorb her sweet arousal. He wanted to lean forward and latch onto her plump cherry red lips and suck them until they were swollen and numb. He wanted to make her moan and feel her body quake around him.

Goddamn. He wanted to please her.

The aphrodisiacal sound that vibrated against her as she leaned into him caused her own blissful moan to crawl into her throat. His hands found their way to her ass and he held her to him. Fallon felt his hard cock nestle between her thighs, and as tempting and easy as it would be to slip her panties to the side and sink down on top of him, she wanted to make him delirious first.

She smiled.

He wasn't too far from it already.

The pads of her fingertips skimmed across his chest, down the deep ridges of his stomach; then she reversed her previous path and did it all over again. Every time her fingers descended, the muscles beneath them would tighten in anticipation. Rocking against him again, she used her mouth to push his head to the side, then proceeded to tend to every delicious inch of his neck, paying close attention to his ear.

He groaned. "Are you trying to distract me or torture me?" he asked, his voice low and strained.

The struggle her body experienced, the out-of-control need that blistered inside her was worth this: the strength she gained from seeing that same struggle mirrored back at her. Pulling away from his neck, she smiled. "It's such a fine line, isn't it?"

Strong fingers latched onto her hips, digging into her flesh while he thrust his cock against her. "I'm walking that line right now, gorgeous. Don't tease me."

She didn't know whether to laugh at the pained struggle in his voice or shiver at the threat.

His hips thrust again, his thick erection coaxing a silent moan from her throat as it ran deliciously along her sensitive clit. "I didn't plan on teasing you, but if it evokes this kind of response from—"

Her words caught as he jerked beneath her, pinning her hips in place as he skillfully abraded her through her panties while dark eyes homed in on hers. "And if *this*," he said, rubbing against her once more, causing her to latch onto his biceps for support, "evokes this kind of response from you, just think what I'll do to you while I'm fucking you."

He shifted beneath her, the tight space of her coupe not particularly conducive to passenger-seat foreplay. Reaching down, he fumbled in the pocket of his jeans, which were bunched around his knees, and pulled a condom from his wallet.

His hand curled around the side of her neck, his thumb brushing over her lips. There was a gentleness in his touch that formed a small butterfly in the pit of her stomach. Rafe was apparently gifted in awakening cravings her body had never felt before. And butterflies from a tender touch was definitely one of them.

"You want this?" he asked, his gentle tone taking her by surprise as he continued stroking her lips.

She kissed the cushion of his thumb. "Do I look like a woman who does something she doesn't want? Yes, I want this." She leaned back into him, her mouth grazing his jaw before she tugged on his lip with her teeth.

"Mmm." He groaned. She heard the foil packet tear and felt his hands slide between their bodies, then working their way around her to her butt, lifting her slightly. Sucking in a sharp breath, she was pleasantly exultant at the way her body melted into him as she felt the rough pads of his fingers slip beneath the edge of her lace thong, caressing her silken, needy opening. She wasn't typically this responsive. But she wasn't just physically aroused. Nerves and thrill and confusion clustered in her chest and stomach. That one tiny butterfly she'd felt moments earlier suddenly transformed into an entire swarm of warm, fluttery, covetous butterflies, greedy with the longing his touch exemplified.

"So wet," he praised as he moved the lace to the side and dipped his long finger into her.

Her head automatically fell back. The feel of his careful touch deep inside her hit nerves that undulated a pleasure she had yet to experience from a man. She enjoyed sex very much, but she'd never been brought to that place of euphoria; she'd never shattered around a man before. The only full release of pleasure she experienced was when she occasionally gave it to herself. But this—the way Rafe's imperfect lips danced over her heated flesh, the way his cock brushed against her swollen clit, the way his fingers leisurely massaged that aching spot that caused her to clench tightly around him—was sublime.

She shuddered when he withdrew from her, but within the next few breaths, she lowered onto him. She sighed in relief as her body took all of him, her insides expanding around him as he filled her.

The narrow space of the seat drew her legs in close to him, forcing her body to tighten as the insides of her thighs molded against his hips.

Resting her palms on his chest for support, she rolled against him. "Ohhh," she cried, dropping her head between her shoulders.

"No, no, gorgeous. I want to see your eyes. I want to watch you while you come."

His voice alone tipped her closer. The honesty he admitted in his words felt like it was wringing her body, coercing her to comply. She lifted her head and her eyes immediately focused in on his shadowy stare.

His hand firmly grasped her hip, the other securing against the small of her back as she moved of her own motivation above him. "That's it," he encouraged, the corner of his mouth lifting into a perplexed grin. "Fuck me. Let me watch your beautiful body come undone."

A quickening began to frenzy inside her, spiraling wildly, threatening to combust. Her head fell to his shoulder and she latched on with her teeth, moaning into him as their bodies connected hungrily, chasing release.

It was so good, she wasn't ready, not yet. She wanted to drag it out, savor the maddening sensations he was giving her.

"Look at me," he demanded, the raw power in his voice forcing her from his shoulder and back to his eyes.

He slipped his fingers back into her hair. "You're holding back."

"I'm not—"

He tugged gently, exposing her throat to him once again. "Let go, gorgeous. Give it to me. Give me your pleasure." His warm, wet tongue slicked up the center of her throat, slowly and deliberately. She felt the sensation from his mouth ripple across her skin and she moaned.

"God, I want it. Come for me," he whispered. He pulled back on her hair a little harder and fastened his lips on the soft skin below her chin. She cried out, a breathy, pleading sigh that met her own ears with a seductive ring. She felt the uneven lift to his lips as he smiled a smug grin against her skin, plunging hard and deep inside her. "Give it to me," he implored, his voice husky and low.

She was never a believer in the orgasm on demand, like the ones she'd heard stories about or read about in sexy romance novels, but she'd never been with a man like this either. Demanding her pleasure, begging for her release. It was titillating. It was sexy. And the words caressed that tiny little soft spot, giving her just enough to send her over . . .

And for the first time ever, she did.

She gave him her release, shattering around him with a

force that made her entire body tremble in the most delectable way.

Sitting straight up in his seat, he folded his arms around her tightly, her entire body running against his. The heat from his bare chest soaked through her thin dress, detonating tiny electric jolts to prick her already sensitive skin.

"Oh, hell," he mumbled, then caught her lips with his, crushing his mouth against hers. Sealing his heady moan in the depths of her mouth, she imbibed his satisfaction as he thrust his hips upward one last time. But his kiss didn't stop. Instead, he cupped her face and plunged his tongue inside, tangling around hers. He tasted like whiskey and sex—like man.

Her lips sank to his, brushing over the deep scar. His kiss only intensified. She became light-headed and dizzy and she didn't want it to stop.

"Mmm." He moaned into her mouth again, and the sound vibrated against her lips, numbing them and warming them at the same time. "I needed to taste you," he whispered, his lips still lingering over hers. "Had I known you would taste this good, feel this good, I would have kissed you the moment you were in my reach." Then he kissed her again.

"I'm flying out to Philadelphia tomorrow, so I got a room at the Hyatt downtown if you want to keep me company," Rafe said. They were sitting in her car in the dimly lit parking garage next to Rafe's Jeep.

Fallon shifted toward him in her seat. Even the slow, casual movement of turning her body to face him had a beautiful fluidity. She smiled. "As much as I'm now positive I would enjoy keeping you company, I don't participate in sleepovers. But thanks for the offer."

A heavy, disappointed sigh pivoted through his chest. Once wasn't enough. He'd only sampled her, and it left him craving more. He needed to taste her body, drink in the sight of her naked beneath him. "I'd love the opportunity to change your mind," he suggested, running his fingers over the bare skin of her knee.

Her breath staggered when his fingers toured the soft, supple flesh inside her thigh.

Deftly lifting her gaze from his proficient touch, she chortled quietly, as if embarrassed. "I appreciate your commitment to persuade me, but that's one rule I don't intend on breaking tonight."

She might not break her rule tonight, but he'd have her begging again soon enough.

Another alarm fired off in his mind. He hadn't wanted to pursue a woman more than once since Bridgette. Repeat offenses didn't interest him. But Fallon? Goddamn, he had to have her again. It wasn't just the sex that was addictive; she was the only person who'd given him full relief from the agony still residing in his chest. She was a remedy that didn't numb him.

His palm flattened on the inside of her thigh, and she shut her eyes. Leaning over the seat, he buried his face in the curve of her neck. "Next time I'm inside you"—he paused, closing his lips around her skin, using the flat of his tongue to prepare the designated spot for the small assault his mouth was about to inflict, then he sucked firmly as he pulled away—"I want you flat on your back, naked, so I can appreciate this sweet, beautiful body."

He felt her skin break out in small, smooth chill bumps as his breath bounced over her neck.

Her eyes opened. "And you're sure there'll be a next time?" she asked breathlessly. He smiled at the irony. The small touch of his hand and the nearness of his lips on her skin caused the air in her lungs to stumble from her mouth. Yet she was questioning his certainty?

"Yes, gorgeous. I'm sure," he answered. Then, slowly removing his hand from her thigh, he clasped his fingers around her chin, holding her eyes to his. Then he kissed her once. "Until next time."

Rafe started his Jeep and waited for Fallon to safely pull onto the road before he left the parking garage. He was tempted to follow her home to ensure that she arrived safely, but he had to remind himself that she'd driven herself home late at night long before he'd spent a good portion of the night fucking her in her car.

The tires of his Jeep squealed as he turned the sharp corner out of the parking garage and headed toward his hotel. He was flying out of Denver early to visit his family, and the morning was going to come way too quickly. With the sound of Fallon's moans and the feel of her body coming undone around him still fresh in his memory, he was going to need another drink if he planned on getting any sleep tonight.

The light on his phone flashed from the passenger seat. Three missed calls. Two from his buddy Wright, and one from Graham.

Just as he was about to call Wright back, his phone lit up again, Wright's number appearing on the screen.

"What's up, Wright?"

"Murano? It's Stella." It was Wright's wife, her voice panicked. He could practically hear the tears raining down her face.

"Stella, what's wrong?"

"He . . . he . . . I don't know what to do. He just snapped . . ."

"Try to calm down. Tell me what happened." Rafe's intuition thrummed loudly in his ears. He hadn't known Wright long before they'd deployed, but he was a damn good man, good soldier, and Rafe never imagined he was a ticking bomb. Wright was one of the silent ones, the ones you never anticipated to go off. But Rafe just knew. Something must have triggered him.

She didn't answer.

His eyes flashed to the rearview mirror; then he swerved across the intersection, swinging his Jeep back around. "Where's he at, Stella?" His foot locked down on the accelerator, gaining speed as he headed back toward the interstate.

A quiet sob muffled into the phone. "Stella!"

"He's in the garage."

Relief crept through him, but it was chilled, icy, not at all the comfort he was hoping for. "Are you okay?"

There was a moment of pause; then she inhaled. "Yes." Her answer was unsure, scared, and the hiccup induced by her tears only intensified his concern.

"The boys, where are they?"

"The twins are asleep in their cribs, but I sent Michael home with the babysitter. I didn't want him to see—"

Fucking panic slammed him in the gut. "See *what*?"

"He was with us one moment and then . . ."

Goddammit. "I'm on my way."

"Murano?"

"Yeah?"

"Hurry."

CHAPTER EIGHT

Rafe made the hour-and-a-half drive from Denver back to Fort Carson in fifty minutes. Every second of every minute ticked away with a loud threat, his pulse joining rhythm with the silent, foreboding click of passing time.

He had relocated to Fort Carson only a few months before they'd deployed, but in that short amount of time Wright and his wife treated Rafe like part of their family. Bonds were formed quickly in this world, forged together by duty, strengthened by family, trusted with blood. But pasts were rarely shared.

Shadows consumed everyone, every soldier. They all had parts that cloaked the good. Soldiers didn't come back from the hell they'd been through unscathed, without earning war-inflicted darkness. Fuck, Rafe had more than he'd like to admit. But Wright, he was supposed to be one of the rare ones, awarded with peace of mind, free from the shit that threatened to haunt him.

Dammit.

The front door threw open and Stella rushed outside as Rafe pulled into the drive. Eyes strained and swollen, worry creasing her mouth, she threw her arms around his neck as he stepped out of his Jeep. Tears flooded, dripping onto his shirt as he hugged her.

"I'm sorry. I didn't know who else to call. Graham is on his way here too."

"Fuck, Stella, what's goin' on?"

Sniffling, she wrapped her short fingers around his hand and led him toward the house. "He just . . . hollered." She stopped inside the door, her breath catching in violent, jagged hiccups. "We . . . fed . . . the boys . . . dinner . . . and went to a . . . late movie . . . just to get out of the house . . . just the two of us," she cried, her words broken by the sobs convulsing through her.

"Stella, what happened?"

Stella swallowed hard, fingers trembling as she wrapped her arms around herself. She tried to force the tears away, her face flashing with worry and pain. "He was driving . . . we were on our way home. The car in front of us swerved . . . on and off the shoulder, losing control . . . Then suddenly it had a blowout. We heard the tire pop. Tommy jerked, yanking the car into the other lane. We were so lucky there was no oncoming traffic."

"Damn." Rafe latched onto her elbow, pulling her into his arms. "You okay?" he soothed, smothering her in his embrace.

"Yes, I'm fine," she whimpered. "But, Rafe, Tommy's not. It's like he just snapped. Gone. There's nothing but emptiness in his eyes. Pain. I don't know what to do, I've never—"

"Shhh." His grip tightened as she shook against him. "It'll be fine," he whispered, shifting her away from his shoulder so he could look into her eyes. "I've got him."

Leaving Stella inside, Rafe walked into the garage. Darkness swallowed the space, the only light coming from the narrow crack in the door that led back into the house. The outline of the SUV stood isolated in the middle of the cold concrete. Rafe's eyes adjusted and he saw Wright's silhouette sitting behind the steering wheel, motionless in the dark.

This wasn't the Wright he'd grown to know. This was a shell of the man. Even through the black, he could see. Wright wasn't here. He was no longer home, no longer sitting in his garage in his car. He was back *there*.

The trouble wasn't bringing him back. Rafe had been down this road with some of his men before, walked this path of hell himself when he returned home from his first deployment in Iraq. Getting him back, that he could do. It was finding him *there*, finding him in the depths of his torment, his broken memory, that presented a challenge. Wright had been in the army for nearly as long as Rafe, found his way through the pits of hell more times than any one soldier should. Locating the room in purgatory that imprisoned his mind . . . Rafe didn't even know where to start.

Opening the passenger-side door, Rafe slid across the leather, easing the door shut behind him. Wright's face was devoid of emotion, staring blankly ahead of him.

Rafe sat still and quiet for a few heartbeats, watching his friend relive the unimaginable. "Where we at, Sergeant?" he asked carefully, unsure, trying to garner a response.

Nothing.

"Sergeant Wright, I'm going to need confirmation on your location."

Silence.

Goddammit.

"Location, Sergeant. Now!" he barked, guilt choking him as the words sputtered from his mouth.

More countless moments passed, deafening, soundless minutes that only sent Wright further into the recesses of his memory. Then his fists unclenched and Rafe watched as his eyes closed. "En route to Ghazni, First Sergeant. Highway 1, twenty miles outside Kabul."

Rafe sagged against the seat. Fuck. He was *there.* Rafe knew exactly where he was. Because they had been there only three months ago.

Light filtered into the vehicle, the door to the house opening up as Graham stepped into the garage. Shaking his head, Rafe raised his palm for Graham to stop. He nodded, backing into the house, leaving the door ajar.

"Wright," Rafe said softly, trying to bring him back, away from the war taking place in his mind.

Wright's shoulders hardened, jaw clenched, every muscle in his body tensing. Then he started shaking. "It's an ambush."

"I know."

He knew because he'd been there too. Watched as an IED turned the armored vehicle in front of them into shambles, killing three of their guys, sending Rafe's vehicle—Wright's vehicle—headfirst into a blazing ambush, an ambush that would leave another two of their men dead.

"I can smell it, Murano."

Relief sliced Rafe open. He was back . . .

"I can smell them burning. I can hear it, the fucking thunder of the bomb hitting their vehicle. The goddamn bullet popping through Moore's Kevlar . . ." Pressing fingers to his forehead, he turned to Rafe. "This has never happened before, brother. Never. That car's tire blew out in front of us and it just sent me back . . . *Shit*. Where's Stella?"

"She's in the house. She's fine. Twins are asleep, Michael went home with the babysitter."

The car door jerked open and Wright scrambled out. Rafe threw himself out of the SUV after him.

"Stella, baby?" Wright hollered as they stormed inside.

Rounding the corner from the kitchen, Stella lunged at her husband, collapsing against him as he wrapped her up in his arms. Another set of tears surged down her cheeks.

"I'm so sorry, Stella."

"Shhh. Don't. I'm just glad you're back."

Rafe followed Graham down the hallway to the front door—those two had a lot to talk about. Stella was a damn good woman. But Rafe knew Wright wouldn't burden her with the hell of his past. Fuck, Rafe wouldn't either if it was him. Some shit in your past just had to stay there.

But Wright needed to see someone about his flashback, and Rafe would make sure he did.

"Murano," Wright called from behind him.

Turning back around, Rafe nodded, lack of sleep and the residual effect of the whiskey finally catching up to him. "Thanks."

"Look at these," Jade squealed, picking up a pair of pink strappy Valentino Garavani sling-back pumps.

"Try them on," Fallon answered as she browsed through the handbags. This was Jade's favorite boutique in Cherry Creek and Fallon had hoped it would cheer her up a little. She hadn't been acting herself since the club last night, and Fallon had a sneaking suspicion that Dexter was the root of her bad mood. But Fallon wasn't one to pry. She was the queen of privacy, and if anyone understood the need to bury the bad and move on, it was Fallon.

"I think I'm going to get them," she said, her voice a little leery.

"So get them."

Jade smoothed her fingers over the pointed toe as if giving it a parting caress before saying her good-byes. "They're eight hundred and sixty dollars," she whined, looking longingly at the shoes before setting them back down on the table.

Fallon reached in front of Jade and picked them up,

handing them back to her. "Okay, and I sign your paychecks. I'm pretty sure you can afford them."

Leveling her eyes at Fallon, she put the pumps back down. "That's not the point. Just because I can afford them doesn't mean they're not out of my league." Her face twisted with frustration; then she spun around and dashed toward the entrance.

Rushing after her, Fallon waved good-bye to the woman behind the counter and stepped out onto the sidewalk, squinting from the afternoon sun. "All right, I wasn't going to say anything, but you're as much of a shoe whore as I am, so now I'm starting to worry."

Whipping around, Jade snapped, her eyes pooling heavy with tears she was pleading wouldn't fall. "I went to Dexter's last night and things were off with us. Dammit, Fallon." She choked, pressing her finger beneath her eyes to catch the tears that escaped. "I didn't want to talk about it because I knew I'd get emotional."

"Okay, fair enough. How about some food?"

Pulling her purse into the crook of her arm, Jade inhaled a refining breath and aligned her shoulders. Composure sifted through the mangled emotions she wanted to suppress. She was so much like Fallon sometimes, it was scary. Showing emotion and letting your weaknesses seep to the surface was just terrifying—for both of them. It was one of the reasons Fallon got along with her so well. She didn't need to worry about having margarita Mondays or weekend spa trips where women divulged their deepest, darkest secrets to each other. That wasn't their thing. *Thank god.*

Naomi, on the other hand, would, and had attempted to drag them to those "girl time" events on more than one occasion.

"Food. Yes, please," Jade replied gratefully.

"Pizza? Chinese? Or there's that new burger place that just opened in LoDo by the Wynkoop Brewery." Fallon might have liked her designer shoes, but when it came to food, she was easy to please. She'd take a burger and fries any day.

She'd missed out on anything having a high calorie count growing up. Ballerinas were slender, willowy, and beautiful. Junk food was poison to the body, forbidden by her mother along with everything else she desperately wanted to try. Their cook, Ann, would make her children chocolate chip cookies and sneak Fallon some in her lunch when she was in elementary school. She loved when Ann packed her lunch. Until her mom found out, and Ann was fired. You didn't defy her mother without consequences.

"Burgers and beer sounds perfect," Jade said, sliding into Fallon's car.

*F*orty minutes later, they were both stuffed. Sitting outside at one of the sidewalk tables, Jade was about to finish off her beer when her phone vibrated against the glass table. She picked it up, smiled, and then strained her neck, looking side to side.

"What are you doing?" Fallon asked, turning her head over her shoulder, following Jade's roaming eyes.

"George is somewhere close—he just texted me that he liked my boobs in this shirt." She laughed.

Leave it to George to be the creep lurking in the shadows sending scandalous text messages to women on the sidewalk. He was the perviest gay man she'd ever known.

"Hey," Fallon heard from behind her, and she turned over her shoulder to see George in all his beauty standing behind her.

"Hey, stalker." Jade smiled. "We're just finishing, but sit with us a minute."

George had been with Fallon for the last two years. When she'd taken over the club, she'd made a few changes. One being the asshole bouncer who thought one of his job benefits was sleeping with her girls. *Wrong.* Gay men with no aspiration to screw her half-naked employees seemed the safest way to go. Even if he was verbally slutty.

"What are you two beautiful ladies up to this afternoon?" The chair scraped along the brick pavers as he pulled it out, taking a seat between her and Jade.

Jade sipped her beer. "Just shopping and indulging in burgers and pale ale."

"Did Dex ever show up last night?" George asked innocently, unaware that the trouble in paradise had now formed a lethal tsunami. Fallon shook her head infinitesimally and nudged him under the table with her foot. Fallon and Jade had the "don't pry" understanding, but that concept was lost on George.

"You're good friends with him—if you want to see him, call him," Jade snapped.

And here she was doing so well . . .

"Okay, I'm sorry." He shifted in his chair and pointed his curiously annoying eyes at Fallon. "So, Miss Run Off with Sexy Bad Boy, care to fill me in on what the hell you were thinking? And fair warning, Simone was ready to hunt you down and kill you herself after the cops left. What the hell happened to you?"

The club was closed on Sundays, so Fallon had luckily been able to avoid the questions she knew her staff would want answered. "George, *dear*, thank you for your concern for my well-being leaving with 'Sexy Bad Boy,' but I knew what I was doing."

"And what *were* you doing?"

"Getting him out of there before the cops came. He was doing what *you* should have done, George," she accused, raising her brows and pursing her lips at him. "He was defending Amelia."

"That was my fault," Jade cut in, lowering her eyes to the table. "I was having another pity party moment and George and Graham were talking me through it."

Fallon sighed. "Who's Graham? Never mind—it's all in the past now anyway. I cleared things with the cops this morning, informed a groveling senator that his friend was no longer welcome in my club and that if another incident occurred while he and his entourage were visiting, they would no longer be welcome either."

"Look at you, badass boss lady," Jade quipped.

Leaning back in his chair, George crossed his ankle over his knee and grabbed Jade's beer mug. "Okay, so what about Sexy Bad Boy?" he asked, then took a long pull from the frothy mug, finishing it off.

"What about him?" Fallon asked nonchalantly. Cutting her eyes to him, she did her best to send him a look that would warn him he was traveling down the wrong road.

His lips curled and he nodded.

CHAPTER NINE

Rafe was exhausted. Relying on the prospect of sleep crammed in the tight space of the airplane, with no legroom and an unhappy toddler behind him, was naive. He hadn't gotten a bit of sleep.

"I'm here," he hollered as he walked in the front door of his dad's house in Philly. It smelled the same, like fresh-baked bread and cinnamon. It'd been over a year since he'd been back home. He hadn't seen his dad or his brothers since before his deployment and the familiar surroundings were comforting.

"Where the fuck is everyone?" he yelled. Luca was there, with his vintage 1965 Cobra rebuild sitting in the driveway, and considering the house smelled of baked goods, it meant Marco was there as well. Marco ran their mom's bakery. He was the only one in the family who knew the secret to her pignoli cookies, so it just worked out that he was the one to take over the business. Whether his youngest brother, Leo, was there or not he had no idea. That one had been pulling a lot of stupid shit lately.

"Rafael?" a sweet, familiar voice hollered from the kitchen. The boards creaked beneath his shoes as he crossed the worn hardwood floors of the living room. He pushed through the swinging door that led to the kitchen that was the center of almost every childhood memory he had of his mother.

An elated squeal reached his ears before his eyes landed on Tilly, who was kneading a loaf of bread at the kitchen table. "I can't believe you're here!" she shouted, standing up and throwing her arms around his neck.

"Damn, Till," he mumbled into her shoulder as he hugged her tightly. "I've missed you." After kissing the top of her head, he pulled back so he could see her.

"You look fuckin' beautiful," he admired, taking a good, hard look at the woman he'd known since pigtails, sneakers, and bloody Band-Aids were part of her daily attire. Her curly blond hair was still unruly and her deep chocolate eyes were still rich and carefree, but her ivory skin was flushed pink and her once slender body was now round. "Beautiful" didn't even begin to come close to describing her.

Folding his hand over her stomach, he rubbed slow circles. "How many more months do you have, Till?"

"Three."

"And you're naming him Rafael, right? The little dude needs a studly name, ya know. Don't let Luca talk you into using his name. And hell, definitely don't let Dad talk you into using his."

She snorted, engulfing oxygen between a fit of laughter.

"What if it's a girl, huh?" Her apparent hopefulness was engraved in her eyes.

He sighed. "You know it's a boy, Till. Just get used to the idea now. There hasn't been a woman born into the Murano family in seven generations. A baby girl's not in your cards, sweetheart."

Rafe's mom always would say that God knew better than to put a baby girl into the Murano family. She wouldn't stand a chance against the men in his family. She'd be so damn spoiled and protected that she would never need to leave the house, and if she did, she would have generations of Murano men breathing down her neck.

If there's one thing my Murano men know how to do, it's love, his mom would say. *My boys love deep; it's in their blood.*

"I don't know," Tilly sang. "I kinda got a feeling."

Rafe looked over her shoulder when the screen door thudded against the wood frame. "Feeling about what?" Luca asked, walking into the kitchen. Rafe nodded his head in greeting at his older brother but Luca was too besotted by his wife to even notice him. Wrapping his arms around Tilly from behind, he kissed her neck.

She giggled. "Just that you're going to be a daddy to a sweet baby girl here very soon."

"I know you want a little girl, Till. But, baby, I don't think it's gonna happen," he said, laughing as he pressed a kiss to her pouting lips.

"I'd be just as happy with a boy," she assured, giving in to him as she sat back down at the small round table next to the window.

Luca locked an arm around Rafe's neck. "As long as he doesn't favor his uncle Rafe, right?" he jabbed, patting his back. "Good to see you, brother."

"Where is everyone?" Rafe asked.

"Out back. Marco and Dad are talking business—well, Marco is talking business and Dad is drinking beer."

"Where's Leo?"

Tilly shifted her eyes to Luca, widening them slightly in that shut-the-hell-up kind of way that women seem to be known for.

Everyone always wanted to protect the baby of the family, cut him slack, pacify his problems. Rafe didn't. Till might keep her mouth shut, but Luca always struggled hiding things from him. "Luca?"

"Leo's taking care of some things at the garage today," he finally said, but he didn't look Rafe in the eyes when he said it. He was a piss-poor liar.

"Bullshit," Rafe barked, shouldering past Luca as he stomped through the kitchen to the screen door leading out back. Rafe loved his baby brother, but they butted heads more than anyone else in the family. Leo was twenty-two and heading nowhere fast, and it pissed Rafe off. They'd all had it hard since their mom died, and Lord knows Rafe went through his own shit when he was younger. But Leo, it was one fucking thing after another with him. He just never learned. Drugs, vandalism, fights—he was spiraling.

And he was just like Rafe.

Which is exactly why Rafe was so damn hard on him. Luca was a straightlaced CEO worth more than Rafe could

even count. Marco was smart. He was a damn good busi-
nessman, and a master in the kitchen and with the ladies.
Then there was Leo—the baby of the family, and the royal
fuckup. Rafe got it. The two of them were made differently
than their other brothers. They didn't thrive on intellectual
growth or desire career success the way Marco and Luca
did. They earned their gratification by the sweat on their
brows and the burn in their muscles.

Rafe had his soldiers; he had his dedication to his country
to keep his head afloat. But Leo struggled to find that one
thing to keep his ass out of trouble. Nothing mattered enough
to him. He worked at a restoration garage, rebuilding old cars
and selling them to rich suckers like Luca. And he was good
at it too—really good. But he was going to piss it all away if he
didn't pull his head from his ass and wake the fuck up. Whatever he had going on, he needed to figure it out—soon.

The screen door screeched, banging against the house
as Rafe flung it open and stepped out into the chilly autumn
air. "Rafael!" his dad exclaimed, standing up from his chair
next to the fire pit. His dad opened his arms and Rafe returned an enthusiastic hug. He missed his old man, and regardless of the foul mood Leo's absence had put him in, he
was going to try his hardest not to take it out on his dad.

"Good to see you, Dad," he said as he pulled away.
"Where's Leo?"

"Ah, you know your brother . . . He's out enjoying his
youth."

"Yeah, so that's your way of saying he's into trouble
again, isn't it? When're you going to stop making excuses for

him, Dad? When are you going to realize he's sliding off the fuckin' edge?"

So much for trying . . .

His dad dropped his lids and tilted his head slightly lower, his expression morphing into one Rafe didn't see very often. "I don't know who you think you are talking to, son, but you will not disrespect me like that in my home—in your mother's home—again. And before you go running around here snapping at your family who hasn't seen you in over a year, you might want to think about the fact that you've not been here. You don't know what's going on with your brother, and you spitting out accusations when you don't know what you're talking about is a load of shit. Now say hello to Marco, then grab us a couple beers and sit the hell down." He patted Rafe on the shoulder, squeezing it firmly. "I'm glad you're home, son."

That was the end of that conversation, and Rafe knew better than to bring it up with his dad again. But he knew one thing was for sure: Leo was in trouble.

It was getting late, well after the garage's closing time, but Rafe had yet to see his little brother since he'd been back. Not surprisingly, the owner was still there, but he said that Leo hadn't even shown up for work in a few days, nor had he been able to get ahold of him.

Leo was fucking pissing it all away.

"That was a complete waste of time," Rafe muttered, slamming the door shut to Marco's car. It was Rafe's last night before he flew back to Colorado and Leo was still blowing him off.

"I'm sorry, man." Marco turned the key in the ignition and pulled out of the parking lot. "You wanna go grab a beer, or do you just want to head back to the house?"

"Nah, let's just go back to the house. I wanna say bye to Tilly before they head home."

Marco nodded and shifted his glasses up on his nose. Out of all his brothers, Marco and Rafe had the least in common. They enjoyed different types of women, listened to different music, and drank different beer. But Marco was probably the easiest to get along with. Not much bothered him—he was easygoing and rolled things off his shoulders. And the majority of the time, he just fucking *got* it.

When they pulled into their dad's small gravel driveway, Luca was leading Tilly to her car.

Smiling, Rafe got out of the car. "You leaving?" he asked, crossing the lawn to where Luca had parked Tilly's SUV on the road in front of the house.

"Yes," she answered, smiling her smile he'd loved since she was a little girl. Tilly's mom had grown up with his mom, so there wasn't one moment in his life when he couldn't remember her in it. "Come here and give your fat sister-in-law a hug—" She choked as unshed tears filled her warm eyes. "God, Rafe. I've missed you so much. Your brothers and dad miss you too. Try to come home more, okay?" she asked, her hand wrapping around the back of his neck, squeezing him tightly.

"I will, Till. You call me when my nephew is about to make his appearance and I'll be on the first flight out."

She sniffed. "Promise?"

Winking, he smiled his sincerity and nodded, then kissed her on the forehead.

The back of her hand thumped against his chest. "And don't worry about Leo. He's a lot like you, ya know?"

"That's what I'm worried about."

She never broke eye contact as she challenged him. "If I remember correctly, you ran into your fair share of trouble when we were younger, and you turned out just fine."

"I don't know about that, Till." He was still nursing a broken heart with bottles of whiskey, fucking away the heartache Bridgette implanted.

"I do." She stepped closer to him and rose up onto her tiptoes, her pregnant belly making it difficult to reach him, so he leaned his head down to meet hers. Leaning into his ear, she whispered, "And I can tell your heart's broken. Don't try to tell me it's not, Rafe. I know you too well." She kissed him on the cheek. "It'll get easier. Just don't let me find out who she is or I'll be forced to show her just how dangerous and pissed off a pregnant woman can be."

It didn't surprise him that Tilly knew his secret; he just hoped she never figured out the whole of it. He had no intention of disappointing her. And that's exactly what would happen if she knew the truth.

Rafe laughed. "Love you, Till."

"Love you too, Rafael."

Opening the door, Luca held out his hand to help her in. "And I'm telling all you stubborn men, I have a feeling it's a girl."

Marco joined Luca and Rafe next to the car and they all laughed.

"For you, baby, I hope it *is* a little girl," Luca said, leaning in and kissing her once on the lips. "The world could use another version of you."

"Kiss-ass," Marco jabbed, shoving Luca aside so he could lean in and hug Tilly good-bye as well.

Rafe and Marco watched as they pulled away until the red of their taillights disappeared. "Come on, I'm sure Dad's got some of that watered-down beer that tastes like piss," Marco said, walking up the front steps.

Rafe's phone vibrated in his pocket. Stepping into the house and shutting the door behind him, he reached in and pulled it out. He didn't recognize the number. The first thought that skirted through his mind was that it might be Fallon. Then the second thought questioned why in the fuck he got excited with the possibility that it could be her.

Probably because the idea of touching that soft body of hers and making her moan into his shoulder again kept replaying in his mind . . .

He pressed the phone to his ear as he walked into the kitchen, where Marco was grabbing a few beers from the fridge. "Hello?"

There was a pause.

His brows furrowed as he sat down at the small round kitchen table. "Hello?" he repeated.

"Rafe?"

The familiar voice rattled in his bones and set his heart in a rhythm that was threatening the strength of his ribs.

He felt the table beneath his fingers but was unaware of the intensity of his grip until he lowered his eyes and saw that his knuckles had gone white.

"Rafe," her soft voice repeated through the phone. "It's Bridgette."

Agonizing fire detonated in his chest. More than a year. That's how long it had been since he'd heard her voice, but he'd never fucking forget it. "I know who this is," he spat.

Marco's posture stooped as he rounded the table and focused his concerned eyes on Rafe. He placed a beer down in front of him, then took the opposite seat.

Sliding the ashtray his dad kept on the table next to the window in front of him, Rafe lifted a cigarette between his lips. Reaching in his pocket for his lighter, he asked, "What do you want?" The cigarette dangled from his mouth as he spoke.

"I heard you were back in the States. I thought we could talk."

He laughed, his anger bubbling into a menacing sound that rolled from his mouth in a cloud of smoke. "Don't you have a husband you could do that with?"

"Rafe . . ."

"No, Bridgette. You don't want to talk. You want to fuck with me. You want to slice me open and wedge yourself back in just so you can fuckin' wring me inside out all over again."

"Rafe, I'm sorry you're hurt. I want to see you, plea—"

"Good-bye, Bridgette," he interrupted, pulling the phone away from his ear. He couldn't listen to her bullshit.

It would be the same load of shit she'd given him time and time again. He'd always crawled back, but not anymore.

"No, Rafe—wait, I'm . . ." he heard her say through the phone seconds before he threw it across the fucking room, taking a nice chunk out of the wall before it landed with a *CRACK* as it hit the linoleum floor.

She wanted to see him. Of *course* she fucking did. She wanted to tighten the noose around his neck before she kicked the stool out from under him. Again.

He'd met Bridgette back when he was stationed at Fort Benning in Georgia, long before he moved to Fort Carson. She'd walked into the gym as he was finishing up the last few laps of his run. Rafe usually ran outside on the trails on post, but it was smoldering hot that day—even with the thunderstorm that had crept in. Long story short, they met, she bashfully flirted, and he had her in his bed a few hours later.

Biggest mistake of his fucking life.

She was married.

He was fully aware of how stupid he was. It was wrong. Fucking around with another man's woman was not something he did. That was a line he didn't cross. In his family, women were put on a pedestal. Marriage was sacred; it was forever. And you didn't screw with that.

In his defense, though, he hadn't known she was married when he first met her. She didn't lie and tell him she was single, but she didn't volunteer the information that she had a husband either. The signs were there. Spending all the time at his place, going on dates to her "favorite" restaurants that were out of town. Most of their time spent together had been in his bed, and he couldn't see straight when she was naked beneath him. She was so damn shy—innocent, almost. Her eyes wielded erogenous powers and she took no prisoners when she let those big browns loose. She was evasive, tricky. And he turned a blind eye, ignored what was in front of him. That was his first mistake right there.

The second was falling in love with her. He should have known he was in for it then. But he was suckered in like a pussy-whipped idiot.

Her long legs had been dangled across his lap on his couch while he rubbed deep circles into her thighs, calves, feet. She was drifting, her eyes fluttering closed. She'd never stayed over, never allowed him to hold her while she slept, and he was soaking up every damn minute of her relaxing beneath his touch.

Until her phone rang.

Goddamn. She'd jolted upright, dropping her legs off the couch, digging for her phone in her pocket. He remembered the way her long, slender finger quickly pressed to her lips, silencing him as she hurriedly sprang from the couch and darted into his bedroom.

He'd followed her and overheard the affectionate tone her voice carried and the profession of love she gave before hanging up the phone. It sliced him raw.

She was fucking married.

He had never felt like such a douche bag in his entire life. He'd foolishly ignored his intuition and allowed her to sneak that one past him. He'd fucked another man's wife.

So he'd called it quits.

Told her to leave.

But then she stopped by his house a few nights later, and no matter what his conscience was screaming at him, he didn't let her leave. Not until he had her in his bed again. Twice.

It became a thing. He learned the routine of when she was with her husband and when he was capable of seeing her. She would sneak over to his house during his lunch breaks, and make quick visits while her daughters were at softball practice or gymnastics. Yeah, she had kids too. Which only eroded away a completely new layer from the man he thought he was. He was invading a family, but it was like he was a fucking addict. Every time he stopped, he'd get a small sample of her—she'd call or stop by—and he could never tell her no. He was spiraling down an immoral tunnel and couldn't crawl his way back out.

Then, before he knew it, he was counting down the minutes until he could see her again. Savoring every god-damn second he had her body against his. He was spending his moments without her thinking of her, and his moments with her thinking about how much he dreaded the moments she was gone.

He loved her.

Why? That was a question he asked himself every day. She was charismatic, gentle, and most of the time shy. She had an unusual sense of humor that was contagious, and he would find himself laughing at the most ridiculous things because *she* found it hysterical. He loved how she was laid-back and unworried with him. And when he got her naked, she challenged him.

He'd liked to see her blush. He'd liked to see her nervous. And he'd loved to see her need him.

But then she left. After their affair consumed him for nearly a year, she left him high and dry without so much as a warning. Just a phone call late one night, telling him that she and her family were leaving Fort Benning and relocating to Fort Campbell, Kentucky. The army had already packed and loaded up their shit, and they were leaving Georgia the next morning. That was her good-bye. She wasn't his. She'd never been his.

And he never expected her to come back to him. But she did.

She'd visited him when she was able to get away and sometimes they would meet for a long weekend somewhere. And that was almost torture. He'd grown accustomed to seeing her damn near every day. Touching her, tasting her, feeling her. Then, in the span of a heartbeat, daily turned to every other month, then every few months—then it was over.

She ended it.

And it broke his fucking heart.

Rafe scrubbed his hands down his face. Just the sound of her voice filled him with a yearning he had hoped he would never feel again. But along with that aching desire to see the face that had haunted him for the last three years was an anger and resentment that now inhabited every nerve in his body.

She had stolen a piece of him—took the piece of his heart that she never gave in return. He knew she'd never intended to leave her husband to be with him. She'd never planned on being his.

And what pissed him off was that she turned him into someone he hated.

Being with her had made him fight every natural attribute he possessed. Rafe didn't share his woman. He made her his and only his. He took care of her, loved her, cherished her, protected her. It was branded in his bones. It's what his father's blood had encrypted in his soul. What he and his brothers held in their hearts. They loved their women hard. Fiercely. Passionately. Profoundly.

But Bridgette was never his to love in the first place.

The handle of the door recoiled into the wall as Rafe shoved through his bedroom doorway. The room he'd shared with Luca growing up looked the same as it always had and the small familiarity of his childhood, of growing up in that house with his mom and his dad—with his family—boiled a guilt inside him. His fist collided into his closet door. *Fuck.*

If Luca ever screwed around on Tilly, he would have one fewer brother after Rafe finished with him. And the repulsive knowledge that he allowed himself to turn into that man, the type of man he despised, made him repentant.

He felt Marco watching him from the doorway. "What do ya need?" Rafe stammered, tossing his duffel onto his small twin-sized bed. Flinging the clothes Tilly had unnecessarily washed and folded for him back into his bag, he faced Marco.

Clearing his throat, Marco asked, "You all right?"

"I had an affair with a married woman who managed to break my fucking heart, so no, I'm not all right. And, yes, I realize I fucking deserve it."

Marco exhaled a weighted breath. "Damn. If you were a chick I'd bake your ass a cassata rum cake."

Rafe laughed, surprised he wasn't dodging well-justified blows to the jaw. "How about just the rum?"

Marco nodded. "Follow me."

CHAPTER TEN

To say that Rafe felt like shit was an understatement. Staying up and polishing off a fifth of Captain Morgan with Marco the night before his flight wasn't the best idea he'd ever had.

Setting his duffel down next to the couch, Rafe staggered into his kitchen, rummaged through his almost empty fridge, and took a bottle of Gatorade from the bottom shelf.

Yanking his T-shirt over his head, he deposited it in the laundry room as he shuffled down the hall to his bedroom. Sleep was going to be the only thing to cure the dull throb that still lingered in his head—an annoying reminder of the voice he'd heard on the other end of the phone. After not speaking to Bridgette for more than a year, the simple innocent sound of his name spoken from her lips found a way to submerge that tiny little yearning into the alcove of his memory.

Then, plunging back to the forefront of his mind, was anger. Thrusting open the door with his shoulder, Rafe stepped into his bedroom. The bed still remained unkempt from the night of entertainment those two blondes had provided between the sheets the previous weekend. He stared mindlessly at the disheveled comforter at the foot of the bed and the empty beer bottles that still littered the nightstand. He'd found a way to dissipate the raw, merciless anger that flushed a constant heat through his body. He'd found a way to numb the maddening agony that burned in his chest. And he planned to do it again.

Turning on his sock-clad feet, Rafe traipsed into the bathroom and started the shower. Downing a couple of aspirin, he yanked his closet door open, fingering through the uniforms and jeans until he found the only other dress shirt and tie he owned.

He needed a distraction.

And he knew exactly where to get it.

S mall beads of sweat formed along her hairline as Fallon stared into the mirror and counted out her movements in her head. She'd been wanting to choreograph a provocative burlesque number to this sexy jazz song when she'd heard it a few weeks ago and she was finally getting around to it. She'd originally thought she would choreograph it for the new solo Naomi had been asking for, but now that she was watching her body move to the unsteady beat of the drum and the fast exuberant tempo of the saxophone, she knew it had to be a group number. All her girls needed to perform it together. It conjured sex and carefree fun that her clientele would fully appreciate with more than one body onstage.

Chairs. It needed chairs.

Turning around to pull one of the folding chairs from the prop closet, Fallon damn near ran straight into a panicked Naomi. Throwing her hand over her heart, she shut her eyes and huffed a relieved breath. "Holy shit, Na. You scared the crap out of me."

"I'm sorry." Her words were rushed, breathless. She was wearing only a beaded bra and panties, so Fallon could see her chest rise and fall quickly as she sucked air into her lungs. Obvious signs that she'd just come from the stage. "Have you seen Jade anywhere?" Naomi asked.

Confused, Fallon frowned, the skin around her eyes wrinkling. "No. Wasn't she supposed to be at the beginning of the lineup tonight?"

"Yes, but she missed the opening group number and she just missed her solo. It's fine—I went on instead—but we need to find her. My solo was supposed to be next and I know I'm good, but I think our fellas might get a little annoyed seeing the same thing twice in a row. I'm not that damn good."

Fallon reached down, picking up her thin cashmere sweater from the floor and pulling it over her sports bra and down over her butt. "Okay," she said, slipping her flats onto her bare feet. "Go call her. If she doesn't answer, check the loft apartment. I'm gonna go change real quick."

Naomi followed her up the basement steps that led back into the hallway across from her office. "What if we can't find her?" Na asked, and the worried tone to her voice spiked Fallon's own concern.

"We'll find her. Tell Molly to put her big-girl panties on because she's taking the next solo."

Naomi laughed. "You know she is going to have a fit, right? Molly's been here, what, two months? She's not ready for her solo."

"Well, ready or not, if she wants to keep her job, she's dancing. Tell her to get ready. And make sure she wears the pink lipstick—I don't like the way the red looks with her solo costume."

Fallon crossed the hall and stepped into her office as Naomi hurried toward the backstage dressing room.

A few minutes later, in Olympic gold medalist record time, Fallon was dressed in a simple black dress and nude stiletto pumps. As she swiftly continued down the hall that led backstage, the blended voices coming from the other end began to sound unnerved. She stumbled over her own feet as her pace quickened and she held her breath as her heartbeat started to race in her chest, constricting the amount of oxygen she was able to take into her lungs. She'd always felt that strong pull of intuition, that knowing tic that tapped along her bones as the unidentified fear she knew she was approaching came to a head. Then exploded.

She heard glass ricocheting across the floor, splintering in hundreds of pieces and scattering in every direction. Turning the corner, she stepped backstage, her eyes immediately finding Jade's motionless body on the floor next to her vanity.

And her heart stopped.

. . .

The deafening cluster of voices penetrated the room with their drunken conversations and it beat against Rafe's head as if someone were taking a chisel to his temple and slowly and torturously nicking away the bone encasing his brain. It was much more crowded in the club this weekend compared with last, and last weekend the place was damn near full.

The tables were all occupied and the standing room around the bar was pressed shoulder to shoulder. Rafe wedged himself next to a table of young women. They flashed appreciative smiles, welcoming his proximity, and whereas usually a smile from a group of beautiful women like them would have challenged him, tonight it only annoyed him.

"Hey, man," he heard from behind him. He turned to see the bouncer from the other night. "You're Graham's friend, right?"

"Yeah. George?"

"Yeah. Good to see you, man. Graham and Dexter with you?"

"No, it's just me."

George nodded his head back, as if what Rafe had just said pieced some invisible puzzle together. "Keep your fists to yourself tonight," he warned, then slapped him on the shoulder and walked off.

Rafe continued scanning the club for her, waiting to see

Fallon climb up on that stage. But every time he would hear the sound of heels click across the wood floor, just before the lights came on, he got uneasy. As badly as he wanted to see her, a larger part of him didn't want to see her up on that stage. He didn't want to see her taking her clothes off in front of every fucking suit in that place. He'd seen the way that body could move against him, and he'd felt that beautiful body beneath his fingertips and around him as she came. He imagined that every douche bag in that room would envision her while they jacked off that night. Yeah, he'd been with her only the one time, but that shit was definitely not sitting well with him.

Given the incident from the last time he was there, it was probably best if he just left. His fuse was cut short; he was annoyed and the throb in his head only intensified his irritation.

Shouldering past the hefty guy next to him, he started for the door. But out of his peripheral vision, he saw a woman rushing down the narrow aisle between tables. He knew without needing to shift his eyes that it was Fallon. No other woman could possibly be so deft in the fuck-me heels she wore.

He turned to face her and time halted. Fear controlled her eyes, pained her expression. Even from across the room, he could tell her breathing was labored.

Rafe shoved his way through the crowd, but the bodies were compacted around him. He strained his neck to the side as she collided to a stop in front of George. George's eyes widened as she spoke and his mouth set in a tight line, his entire demeanor shifting in the span of a second.

As Fallon pivoted around, their eyes found each other's in the midst of mingling, exuberant bodies. He felt her sigh from across the room. He couldn't tear his eyes away from her.

She blinked, a new emotion shedding from her eyes, then rushed back toward the stairs leading backstage. He didn't have a damn clue what was going on, but he knew that look that covered the bouncer's face. A look of fear mixed with undeniable anger. And the emotion embedded in Fallon's eyes was one he never wanted to see again. It was tortured, torn, scared.

Propelling himself through the crowd, he barreled after them. He didn't know what to expect, but he was ready for a fight.

"Watch her head," Fallon barked as George picked up Jade and carefully laid her down on the chaise longue next to the wardrobe racks. Sweat clammed thick on Jade's body, the costume for the group number sodding, clinging tightly to her body with wet suction. Some of the sequins had fallen off a loose thread and the small black circles were sticking to her arms, highlighting the fresh puncture to the inside of her forearm. A small red pinprick already forming the early stages of a bruise.

"I've got her," George assured quietly. But Fallon heard the waver in his voice, his concern.

Naomi worked her way around the chaise and squatted next to Jade's legs, the rest of her girls huddled close by.

"She just stumbled out of the bathroom." Na choked. "She latched onto the mirror and then she just fell. Should . . . should I call an ambulance?"

"No," Fallon said quickly, running her hand over Jade's sweaty, matted hair, peeling it from her sticky face. She'd seen Jade like this before. Once, shortly after Jade had moved into the apartment. "Check her to make sure she didn't get cut when the mirror fell," she ordered. She spoke to no one in particular; she just needed to claim the control of the situation. She needed to *feel* in control.

"What happened?"

The voice that carried through the small room backstage rained over her in a mist of concern. His voice was hard and stern, willing the answer he was seeking with the rich depth of his tone and the pure control in his volume. She felt the tension in the room shift to him, as if he were absorbing the panic from her dancers. She didn't need to look at him to know his posture embodied security, protection. Because she *felt* it—even with her back to him she felt it.

Which made him more dangerous to her than she could possibly even realize.

She kept her eyes on Jade, squatting next to her, watching the slow, steady rise and fall of her chest. The hairs on the back of Fallon's neck pricked when Rafe's leg brushed against her side as he approached.

"She's high," he stated.

Baring her teeth, she narrowed her sights on him. "I know, dammit!" She stood up and took a step away from the chaise. Jade had promised she'd never pull this stunt again. She'd been clean for nearly two years. When Fallon had found her strung out and on the streets, she'd offered her the apartment, offered her a job. And she'd told Jade she wouldn't put up with this shit. She'd be out on her ass.

But as she looked down at her, sweaty and still and silent on the couch, Fallon's heart broke. She wouldn't turn her back on Jade just because she'd fucked up. She couldn't. Not then, not now.

Spinning around so she was facing the wall—away from the waiting eyes of her girls—she drew in a deep breath and smoothed her hands down the front of her dress. Anger chased her, hot and enflamed, like a raw, swelling welt on her heart.

A hand tucked firmly against the small of her back and she allowed her posture to lean into it, allowed him to absorb some of the fury coursing through her body. His other hand secured around her elbow, fingers curling into her skin as he pressed his chest into her side.

"What was her preference?" he whispered. She appreciated his discreetness.

"Heroin."

"*Fuck*. Okay," he started, spinning her around to face him. "Do you know what to look for?"

She shook her head. She'd seen her days of teenage rebellion, but she'd never slipped deep enough to familiarize herself with hard drugs like heroin. But she could probably figure it out.

"It's a honey-colored powder, most likely in a small clear

bag. Find it and flush it. Look in obvious places," Rafe said, his fingers digging into her arms gently so he didn't hurt her, but just hard enough to encourage her to respond.

She nodded, trancelike. How could this happen? Right under her nose? In *her* club? She'd let Jade down—she should have noticed she was using again. *Was* she using again?

Her body trembled, palpitated by defeat and guilt.

"Hey." Rafe's fingers lifted to her chin, forcing her to meet his waiting gaze. She knew what was waiting for her in those eyes, and she couldn't afford to get lost right now. She needed to remove the fog, not get swallowed by it.

"Fallon, babe, you got to pull it together. I'm right here. I'll stay right here." He released his hold on her, his hands expelling the trance she fell into.

She stepped to the side, making sure her girls could see the authority she forced back into her expression. "Molly, your time to shine, baby. Get your ass onstage. Na, go tell Simone to call Ace and tell him to get here, *now*. Keep the lineup the same, just alter it without Jade. It should be no big deal."

Silently, Molly and Naomi nodded and stepped from the circle of bodies that still swarmed around Jade.

"The rest of you, please go prepare for the lineup. I need you to go," she said, aware of the desperate plea in her voice.

They all scurried like frightened kittens as Fallon approached the chaise again. "George, can you take her to your place and let her sleep this off?"

"Sure, no problem."

"I'll help you get her to your car," Rafe said, stepping next to Fallon. He reached down, preparing to slide his arm beneath Jade's head when George's hand reached out and stopped him.

"I'll get her."

After finding the discarded needle and flushing the plastic bag with heroin remnants, she dragged a trash can to Jade's vanity and started picking up the larger shards of glass from the floor.

As her hands held the jagged pieces, her mind replayed back to the fear that had strangled her when she saw Jade lying on the floor surrounded by splinters of glass.

But the moment she'd spotted Rafe in the crowd, her fear had loosened its grip a little. It was like the night she first saw him. She was drawn to him, finding him in a moment when her mind was elsewhere. Distracting her from the present.

Fallon had mastered the art of keeping her feelings hidden, but when her body relaxed and the panic eased in her chest the moment his hand pressed against her, she knew he was dangerous. This man was a complete stranger. A complete stranger who had the ability to drain the control from her body and claim it for himself. Her body had become her source of power, yet it was defenseless when it ran along his. Even with just the simple touch of his hand.

He was a confusing, compelling contradiction. He absorbed her hidden emotions yet at the same time made her *feel*. He was dangerous, yet his nearness alone gave her a sense of security she'd never experienced. He was a stranger.

A beautiful distraction.

The cool air brushed through the room as the back door opened, then sucked shut. She lifted her head to look at Rafe, then stood.

"She's gonna be fine. She'll be hurting tomorrow, but she'll be okay. I gave George my number in case he needed me. Can I help? Do anything? Call anyone? Do you want me to drive you home?"

"I'm fine."

"I know, but I can tell you're upset and—"

"Rafe, I'm fine," she snapped. "Just go." She needed him to add significant space between them before she ended up throwing herself in his arms, clinging onto him just so she could feel the comfort she knew his touch would provide.

Arm's length had been her motto, but at this moment, even arm's length was too close.

"Fallon, I will take you—"

"No," she interrupted. "I've got stuff to take care of here."

"That's fine. I'll help you, then make sure you get home all right."

"Goddammit, Rafe! I don't want you here! I don't need you to hold my hand and make sure I'm okay. I can deal with this just fine on my own. And I'm perfectly capable of getting myself home in one piece. I've been taking care of myself for a long damn time. Go!"

His eyes remained impassive, never hardening or darkening as she'd expected them to. He just studied her for another heartbeat. He didn't say anything, didn't nod or smile or give any other reaction. Then he crossed backstage and descended the stairs out of the club.

CHAPTER ELEVEN

Fallon sat in her car and waited for the headlights to appear in her rearview mirror. She'd seen the black Jeep pull out behind her as she left the parking lot of the club and she'd watched as it followed her all the way to her house. Her car was off but the music still hummed softly through the speakers as she waited at the front of her dark driveway.

When two small lights appeared in her mirror, she stepped out of the car, the motion-sensored lights on her house flickering on, casting a spotlight on her in the darkness. Her hands rested on her hips as she fixed her eyes on the Jeep, beckoning him to turn into her drive.

And he did.

The Jeep's tires spun slowly over the smooth cement as he traveled the long, winding path to her house. Parking behind her car, he stepped out of the Jeep.

"You caught me?" he asked, but he looked only amused, not guilty.

"You weren't necessarily subtle. You need to work on your undercover abilities."

His stride was long, his legs closing a large portion of the distance that remained between them. Lowering his treacherously dark eyes, he focused on her mouth. It made her nervous knowing his gaze was set on her lips, and she instinctively sank her teeth into the corner of her bottom lip.

His lids shut briefly and she was almost positive a growl rattled in his throat before he opened them again and took another step in her direction, the space between them nearly nonexistent now. "I wanted to make sure you got home okay," he admitted, but there was no hint of an apology in his tone.

"And I told you I didn't need you to."

"And I never agreed to listen to you."

She sighed. "So you waited till the club closed and followed me home?" She dropped her hands from their defensive position on her hips down to her sides. "That's kind of creepy, you know." She paused as his sable stare skirted back to her eyes. "You should scare me."

His hand reached out and flattened against the side of her neck, drawing her body the remaining way to him. "Are you scared?"

"No," she answered promptly. She stayed cemented to his hand, letting the hypnotic warmth from his palm spread across her skin, easing the muscles beneath. She wasn't afraid of him. Not in the way he was referring to. But was she afraid of the way his touch soothed her? Of the way his voice calmed her? Of the way his eyes claimed her? Absolutely.

She didn't want to admit it, but she couldn't deny that she was glad he was there. She shouldn't be—she didn't know a thing about him, other than the passionate way his hands were able to scorch her body. But still, she was glad.

"So do you always ignore what women ask you to do and do what you want anyway?"

His fingers curled gently into her skin, kneading her tight muscles. "I'm not going to apologize for following you to make sure you were okay. I told you back at the club that I was there, that I'd stay there . . . for you. And I meant it. Hate to break it to you, but bitchiness doesn't scare me off, gorgeous." His thumb moved to her jaw, tracing the delicate line. "You okay?"

She exhaled and nodded. "Yes."

Rafe's other hand cupped her nape, softly holding her head with both hands. It was comforting in a way she was unfamiliar with, in a way that was pure, genuine. "Is *she* okay?" he asked.

"George said she woke up for a minute or so. She's still sleeping it off."

"Good." He lowered his hands to the outside of her arms.

Standing in front of her, he was still, steady. She felt compelled to lean into him. She couldn't remember ever having that desire, ever craving the comfort another person offered. She'd been on her own for so long that she'd become accustomed to leaning only on herself, on needing no one.

And even before she'd been disowned from her prestigious family, she'd still never felt comfort or safety. She'd never felt cared for. Not in the way a person needs to be cared for. She had the best of everything: the best schools, the best ballet instructors, designer clothes, anything and everything money could provide her with. But when she'd lost the lead role in *Sleeping Beauty*, she never had anyone to comfort her; her mother had only scowled at her, telling her to practice harder. When she'd had the chicken pox when she was six, she was never comforted; she was merely threatened not to scratch and scar her skin. She was simply her parents' shiny trophy, and one that was easily discarded.

The men she'd known were no different.

This was exactly why the few relationships she'd had with men were more like a partnership—like a formal business partnership. A strictly physical relationship. No friendship, no talking, no cuddling, no phone calls or spontaneous pop-overs. When a woman included those things, it got personal—she'd end up letting him in. And if she let him in, she'd be giving him the chance of letting her down.

Alone was easier.

Even if it was lonely . . .

Rafe's hand coasted lower on her arm until he reached her fingers and laced his through hers. "Do you feel that?" he asked, lifting their joined hands to her chest. Her pulse quickened and her heart thudded rapidly against her chest, the beat colliding against their hands. "My touch does this to you."

"It does." She couldn't deny it. She wanted to, she wanted to retreat back into her comfort zone, secured and safe. But she couldn't. Not when his touch thawed her insides and ignited flames on her skin at the same time.

Lifting her hand to his mouth, he carefully and slowly brushed his lips against the inside of her wrist, undulating a shiver that coursed through her entire body. It was as if that thin spot had a direct line to every sensitive, feminine part of her that was begging to come alive.

"I can do this for you too. I can be your distraction."

The sweet, determined sway of his words melted a piece of her resolve that she'd been determined to withhold. Her body was her force of strength—her power. It gave her freedom and control, but when she was near him, her body became her weakness. The ascendancy her body had taught her to claim shattered beneath his touch.

And it was frightening. And redemptive.

Commanding her muscles to solidify, she drew in a breath of the cool autumn air into her lungs. Her hand was still next to his beautifully flawed mouth, and the smooth tip of his tongue flitted across the same patch of skin his lips had just caressed. "Just say the word." He breathed against her skin as his lips traveled to the cushion of her palm, securing a warm, wet kiss. "Just tell me yes, gorgeous, and I'll steal your thoughts from you and give you nothing but complete, numbing pleasure."

She trembled against him. He leaned back slightly and

her body followed as if tethered to him. "Yes," she whispered, unable to find strength in her voice the same way her body was unable to resist his touch.

And he smiled.

*T*he restraint he maintained while walking through her house and into her bedroom to not shred her dress from her body brought Rafe to an all new record of willpower exertion.

He kicked out of his shoes and socks, then grabbed the neck of his shirt and peeled it off, leaving a trail of clothes behind him. His lips remained sealed onto some part of her body: the back of her neck, the curve of her shoulder, the dip of her spine—anywhere his mouth could reach as they stumbled through her house and to her room.

Soft goose bumps chilled across her arms as his fingers tenderly descended a path from her shoulders to her wrists. Tilting his head down, his lips tentatively brushed over the smooth, sensitive spot near her collarbone he knew would make her shudder—and she did. Her hands flew to his biceps as her head rolled back onto her shoulders, allowing his mouth the opportunity to raid her neck.

Coiling the hem of her dress in his hands, he lifted it from her thighs and pulled it up over her head, discarding it somewhere behind him on the floor; then, gliding his fingers down her spine, he skillfully unhooked her bra. She dropped her hands from his biceps and the lace fell to the floor at their feet. His vigilant eyes raked over every part of her nearly naked body, learning and committing to memory every smooth line of her slender thighs, every slight curve of her hips, each heavy swell of her flawless breasts.

He'd seen her body stripped of virtually all its clothing while she was up onstage at Velour. But seeing her respond to his close proximity as he praised her body with palpable desire in his eyes was like nothing he'd seen before. The power she wielded while she was on that stage was sexy. Confidence was a seductive quality in a woman. It was an unspoken challenge, and he loved her ability to push him with her body, claiming the control as her own. But watching her submit that control over to him as her gaze coyly lowered from his stare, feeling her body softly tremble beneath his fingertips as he pressed them against the small of her back, as she leaned her weight against him for support—it was fucking beautiful.

"Lay down," he urged, stepping into her, forcing her body to retreat onto the bed behind her.

His fingers slid beneath the threadlike lace strap that covered each side of her hips, pulling them down enough so he could bend over her and pepper the flare of her hip with moist kisses. She writhed beneath him and he continued to kiss her, moving his lips over the flat, velvety skin below her belly button.

He felt her chest expand as she sucked air between her teeth when his hands effortlessly tore the lace from her body in one swift tug.

He enjoyed that little breath she took; he enjoyed feeling and hearing her attentive response to him. So without stopping, his mouth fell to the supple folds of her slick pussy. She was silken and wet.

"You need this?" he taunted, barely flicking his tongue over her swollen bud. It was everything he had in him not to plunge his tongue into the depths of her pussy and lap at her warm arousal that was coating her, preparing her body for him to fill her with his own.

She moaned her response, but he wanted more from her. He wanted her to tell him, he wanted to hear her composed voice quake with her request. "Tell me," he coaxed, watching as he pushed his thumb into her, her pussy drawing him in tightly as she clenched around his finger. *Fuck.*

"I need it," she murmured almost incoherently.

He grinned.

"What is it that you need from me, babe?" he replied, again taunting the response he wanted from her body as he pushed his other thumb inside her.

She bowed off the bed and her hips grinded against his hand, trying desperately to find the release she was searching for.

"Your mouth. I need your mouth on me," she pleaded.

Fuck yeah, she did.

His mouth feverishly descended to her, swirling rapid, hot thrashes of his tongue over her clit as he palmed the flesh below her ass, raising her slightly from the bed to allow him easier access.

His name staggered from her mouth in a desperate rasp that only intensified his hunger for her. His mouth sought out her release, needing to feel every muscle in her body convulse as his face was buried between her thighs, fucking her with his tongue.

Her hips rolled in rhythm with his tongue and he used his hands to anchor her to the bed, preventing her from aiding in her release. He wanted this all to himself. He wanted the gratification of making her give it to him. He wanted to claim her orgasm as his own.

She arched and bucked against his grip, trying desperately to find her release. She was there. So close. So close for him.

He dragged his teeth over her clit and latched on softly, then sucked her into his mouth. She cried out and he knew he had her. Thrusting two fingers inside her eager pussy, easily finding that smooth, round spot to hook into, he ravaged her clit with the forceful tip of his tongue. And she came. But he wasn't going to let her come back down.

Making quick work of unbuttoning his jeans, he stepped out of them and opened the condom packet he'd managed to set aside on the bed.

He watched her eyes widen in appreciation as she followed his hand as it stroked up and down his hard cock. Her teeth sank into her bottom lip and her thighs fell to the side.

Her glistening pussy, slick and swollen from the orgasm that was still ricocheting through her body, beckoned him when she moaned at the sight of him hard and ready for her.

Positioning himself between her thighs, he sank balls deep into her in one effortless thrust. She was so tight, but so incredibly ready for him. She tightened around him, her body writhing as the ripples of her lingering orgasm undulated a fresh wave of pleasure.

He stilled inside her, relishing in the sweet way her pussy drew him deeply into her. Brushing his thumb across her lips once, he leaned down and kissed her. She opened up for him and he gently dove into the warmth of her mouth. The luscious taste of her lips mixed with the succulent taste of her arousal that remained on his tongue was intoxicating.

"I'm gonna fuck you slowly, gorgeous," he warned as he pulled away from her kiss. She was breathless and eager as she lifted her hooded eyes to his.

"No . . . Rafe . . . I need it . . . uhn . . . I need it hard . . . now," she moaned as he started his relentless pursuit.

Rotating his hips slowly, he withdrew from her, loving the way her body clung to him. "No, babe," he said, pushing the tip of his cock back inside her. "I'm gonna fuck you slowly. I'm gonna fuck you softly. I'm gonna fuck you until you shatter around me, and then I'm gonna bring you down so slowly you'll shatter all over again."

*I*f Fallon had known how to form words, she would have. But Rafe had stolen her thoughts.

His cock moved tortuously inside her. Their sweat-glistened bodies glided fluently against each other as he kept up his slow, tenacious tempo, thrusting and circling and pumping in and out of her.

The buildup of pleasure was unyielding and constant.

She was riding a continuous surge of blissful release. She didn't feel as if she could get any higher—it was as if she'd reached the numbing peak of pleasure and there was nowhere to go but back down. But then it happened again. It was unexpected and overwhelming and absolutely incredible.

She shattered.

Just as he'd promised. Her release splintered in imperceptible bursts of pleasure that ignited every nerve, tightened every muscle, stole every breath, fulfilled every desire. She shattered completely until she was positive there was no known way to reassemble the fragments of her elated body. But he did.

"Look at me, gorgeous," he demanded, slinking his cock back, then gently plunging back inside. Her body arched, the sensations almost too much. "Babe," he implored.

The strain in his voice penetrated through the hazy plane she was still floating on and she lifted her lids. The velvet in his eyes smoothed over her, the black flecks drinking her in as he held her gaze. He rose to his knees and she winced as his cock slid from her sensitive sex, but the emptiness was only momentary. He lifted her, then positioned her back onto him as he sat on the bed.

She cried out. Even if she'd wanted to reel in the sharp, pleasure-induced moan that unwound from her throat, she wouldn't have had the strength.

"That's it, gorgeous," he encouraged as she started rolling her hips against him.

The fragments of her body started to mend as his cock

stayed buried deep inside her. It was impossible. There was no way to feel this much—so much pleasure, so much desire. Fatigue was ripping through her as her spent muscle ached and her sensitive sex throbbed. But she couldn't get enough.

"Slowly, babe. I want to feel every tremble you have to offer me." His hands guided her above him, keeping his desired tempo, lifting her and rolling her onto him. "Fuck. Yeah, babe. Goddamn, you feel so perfect."

His hot mouth scattered light kisses over her shoulder, his strong hands pinning her body flush against his as she moved above him.

The leisure friction that abraded her deep inside tightened as Rafe's teeth sank into the pad of her shoulder. He groaned, and the satisfaction she received from that deep, heady rasp reached all the way to her toes. She slipped away as Rafe's own release sent her blindly over the edge once more. She'd reached a new nirvana and she was lost to the sensations that pulled her in and held her imprisoned. She stilled, Rafe stilled. Unable to move a single muscle, she stayed wrapped around him, her forehead resting against his shoulder as his lips tended to the heated flesh of her neck.

It was seconds, minutes, hours, days, eternity before she felt her body lowered against the mattress. She was present, awake, in the same realm of existence as him, yet she couldn't find a way to pull herself from the depths of euphoria to reach him.

The soft flutter of a single kiss brushed gently over each

of her eyelids, then one on her lips, before she felt the heavy warmth of Rafe's body close around her from behind. His arm sheathed her stomach and pulled her in closely to him. Secured in his arms, tucked tightly against him, she sighed and slipped that last little bit over the edge.

CHAPTER TWELVE

*F*allon was a bed hog. A selfish sleeper. A kicker, a moaner, sometimes a talker, apparently a snorer, and most definitely a cover stealer. In her defense, she'd never shared a bed with anyone. Never. No man had shut his eyes and drifted into dreamland on her watch. She wouldn't let them.

So, needless to say, when she flailed her leg out to the side and attempted to roll herself up in her comforter sometime before dawn, she was more than startled to feel a hard body beneath her leg preventing her from reaching the other half of the comforter. Then she panicked. But only because the sight of Rafe asleep in her bed pricked a flutter in her chest that made her smile.

She wanted him there. As alarming as that should have been, it was comforting.

Slowly, so she didn't wake him, she lifted her leg from the dip in his back and straightened the cover that was barely covering his naked rear as he lay spread out on his stomach, thick arms bent above his head and his face buried into the pillow.

It was still dark, but the privacy of her property allowed her the ability to enjoy the large panel windows that lined every outside wall of her second-story bedroom without the protection of blinds or curtains. The moon fluttered over the mountains and sprinkled a haze of light into her room— almost as if drawn to Rafe the same way she was. The moonlight found all of his contours, all the ridges and dips in his muscles, and highlighted them perfectly, permitting the shadows to dance around them, refining the beauty the light was creating over his back and shoulders.

Lifting her hand, she gently skimmed her finger along the outline of the large angel wings that spanned the width of his back and reached all the way down past his hips. It was beautiful. A kneeling man with his head hung between his shoulders was in the center of his back, the wings protruding from his back. It was so beautifully crafted that it appeared that the wings belonged to both Rafe and the man. She continued to trace the intricate feathers, but as she glided the tip of her finger over his spine, he stirred. And she froze.

A sleep-induced rasp staggered from his parted mouth as he rolled onto his back, the comforter falling lower on his hips. The sharp cut that pointed toward his manhood was narrow and defined. The muscles of his stomach were ones a woman would be thankful for and the curves of his pectorals were simply delicious. Just as she'd imagined, his arms were fully covered from wrist to shoulder in a mix of beautifully designed and skilled works of art. His arms were quickly becoming her absolute favorite physical feature of his. Arms that held power and security and strength. All things she was realizing she enjoyed wrapped around her.

She blinked and shifted her gaze to his scruffy face. His buzzed head was sexy and the way his eyes fluttered beneath his lids as he slept was adorable. If she hadn't been worried about waking him, she would've leaned in to press her mouth to the deep valley in his lip and cascade her mouth over his jaw and down his neck, following the length of his scar.

He looked rough, and she smiled to herself. If only her mom and dad could see her now. Taking her clothes off for money and sleeping with a man who looked like he could kill with his bare hands, rob a bank, front a rock band, and give a woman an orgasm with his eyes. Wouldn't they be proud?

He inhaled deeply through his nose and stretched his body, slowly opening his eyes. The ebony color seemed to reach a new depth of dark in his sleepy daze—a depth that was endless and capturing, like quicksand.

Turning his head, he pressed a single light kiss to the inside of her palm where her hand was resting near his pillow. The stubble on his jaw grated against her skin in the most heavenly way, leaving a wavering sensation in its absence. He smiled when he saw her watching him, his scar making his bottom lip curve slightly lopsided in a way that was beginning to make her melt. She began to reconsider her favorite part of his body—no, not his arms; that imperfect mouth of his just took its place.

Reaching out, she ran her thumb across the scar and he pressed his lips together and kissed it.

"Hey," he said cheekily, the roughness of his voice leaving behind the same pleasant sensation on her skin that his scruffy jaw had. "Why are you awake?"

"Honestly? Because you were in my bed."

His brows danced across his forehead. "I'm capable of distracting you even as you sleep? I'd say that's damn good talent, wouldn't you?" he teased.

She rolled her eyes. "If you were distracting me, yes. But I'm just not used to having someone in my bed. Like I said, I don't participate in sleepovers. And that includes hosting them."

"Not so bad, right? I've been told I'm a great cuddler."

"I wouldn't know—you were too busy stealing my covers."

Parting his mouth, he laughed once, a low, arrogant chuckle. Then he hooked his arm around her waist and pulled her naked body to his.

"How about now—good?"

The feeling of his arms around her deserved a more adequate word than "good." Good felt mediocre, subpar—just . . . good. But the contact of his skin and the strength of his arms followed by the heat from his body—that was better than good. She just couldn't come up with a word that expressed it any better at the moment.

She returned his smile. "Yes," she answered, then rested her head next to his on the pillow, their mouths breathing the same breath of air. "So, tell me the story behind this beauty." Lifting her finger back to his lip, she traced his scar again.

He readjusted and pulled Fallon tighter against him. "That's my very first battle scar." He winked, attempting to lighten the mood. "It was my first deployment. May 2004."

"Deployment?" she asked, and he laughed.

"Yes, gorgeous. You've crawled in bed with a soldier."

She was aware how little she knew about him; it hadn't occurred to her how much he'd surprise her. She'd never have pictured him as a soldier. Tattoo artist, MMA fighter, president of some deathly motorcycle club—sure. All-American soldier serving his country—that she didn't see coming. But now that she knew, she could see it. His determination, his strength, his concern, his protectiveness— he depicted the ideal qualities of a soldier. And his physical attributes were an added bonus. Oh, and the uniform . . . She'd like to see him in the uniform . . .

"Does that surprise you?" he asked.

Her mouth curled at the image she'd conjured in her mind. "Yeah. But it fits you."

His grin morphed into a wry tilt and she assumed he had an idea what she was thinking.

"The first time I deployed, I was part of Bravo Company, 20th Engineers, 1st Cavalry Division out of Fort Hood, Texas. I was young, fresh to the army, and eager to get in on the action. My unit was part of the forces assigned to the Iraqi government to take down the power of the insurgent Mahdi Army in Sadr City. It was one of the most intense missions out of all my deployments." He cleared his throat and shifted his eyes to the ceiling before returning them to her, his memory working. Tension crawled through his muscles beneath her as he continued to hold her against him. She held her breath, waiting for him to release it, but he never did. It only grew, tightening his jaw, laboring his breath.

"It was early in the morning and we were out on Route Predator doing a presence patrol after a recent firefight with Mahdi rebels. Fucking ball-bearing IED went off thirty feet from where my squad and I were standing. And I only walked away with this scar."

"Only?"

He nodded. "The rest of them weren't so lucky. I at least had my life." He paused as if he was allowing the memory to silently sift through his thoughts before he continued. "This baby"—he lifted his arm above his head, exposing his rib cage to her—"I got only a few months ago while in Afghanistan. Fucking ambush on two of my unit's combat vehicles that ended in a lot of blood."

Straining his neck to the side, trying to work through the tightness, he ended his explanation. He wanted to keep that part of him locked away. She respected that. Some things in your past you just don't want to talk about. Talking about them is like admitting that they really happened. Of confirming your pain.

She touched the raised pink scar that made a diagonal down his side. "How many times have you deployed?" she asked, meeting his eyes in the darkness.

"I've been deployed four times in the last eleven years."

Her brows furrowed as she took in the smile that crept onto his face. "And you love it?"

"And I love it. I hate the fuckin' layers of darkness that seem to hover, a constant fuckin' reminder of the men I've lost. But it's who I am. I'm a soldier. Take the good with the bad and keep on going. I love it.

"After that first deployment, me and some of the guys in Barracuda went to Austin and got some ink. I learned a lot from those guys. Some of the best men I've ever met." His stare gravitated toward the ceiling, an apparent shift splintering through his memory again. Tilting his head back to her, he smiled. "That's when I got the tattoo on my back."

She propped up on her elbow and rested her head on her hand as she listened.

"This wickedly talented chick, Ronnie, did it for me. She made me feel like a complete pansy the one and only time I asked her for a cigarette break. It took her seven hours, and she only stopped once." He shook his head in disbelief. "Pansy, my ass."

"Well, she did an amazing job," Fallon said, approving of the angelic wings that rippled across his sculpted back. "What's its meaning?"

"It represents how when a soldier dies for his country— for his brother, sisters, friends—he gives his life up for another, to protect another, and to give them their freedom. Now they watch over us as they walk with the only other man who was ever willing to sacrifice himself for us.

"This one"—he pointed to a tribal symbol on his bicep—"was my first tattoo and has absolutely no meaning.

I don't regret a single one, though I could have probably done without this one. I was seventeen, piss-ass drunk, and more than likely high."

She laughed and dropped her head back to the pillow.

"I like that."

"What?"

"When you laugh. You should do it more often." His fingers brushed away the rogue hair that fell across her face. "What about you? Any ink?"

She snickered at his ability to fluently shift from topic to topic in the same breath.

Flattening her hands on the mattress, she pushed herself up into a sitting position. The cover fell when she straightened, exposing her bare breasts as she leaned into the pillows propped against her headboard. Modesty and physical insecurities weren't things she dwelled upon. She was confident in her skin, proud of her body, and content with the beauty and self-worth she possessed. She was a dancer—her body was her canvas and there was never room for insecurities in her art. Ballet and burlesque alike.

But as the cover fell from her body and the casual but intimate appreciation in Rafe's eyes skirted over her naked skin, she felt a slight tenseness in her muscles and a heaviness in her stomach. She felt vulnerable.

Pulling her right leg from the covers, she lifted her foot slightly off the bed and pointed her toes. "My very first tattoo. It was also my very first act of rebellion. I got it when I was sixteen after my first lead role, as Titania in *A Midsummer Night's Dream*."

Sitting up next to her, Rafe grabbed her foot between his hands, causing her to pull in a sharp breath from the surprise as he spun her body by her foot and pulled her to him.

Now that she was facing him, she was open to him, exposed in his direct line of vision. Her vulnerability kicked up a notch, which only made the compromising position she was in even hotter.

He lifted her foot closer to him, inspecting the small, feminine script that ran along her instep from toe to heel: *The Pointe of Life Can Be Found on Your Toes.*

He read the words aloud, running his finger over each word as he said it. She thought she moaned—she couldn't be completely sure, because he was still touching her, turning her mind to slush.

His hands skimmed their way from the inside of her foot to her calves, slowly torturing her as his skilled fingers kneaded the muscles of her thighs. When he reached her hips, he tugged her forward until she was no longer touching the silky cotton of her sheets but instead the warmth of his body as he situated her on his lap.

Drifting his hands up her sides, he tickled her skin with his rough touch. It felt so good, so relaxing, she had to stifle a moan.

"What about this one?" he asked when his fingers reached her wrists.

Once again, his fingers fluttered across her tattoo as he read the word aloud: *Unconditional.*

She felt a suffocating tightening in her chest as her mind

wandered to the one and only time she'd ever felt the brief bliss of unconditional love. It was beautiful. And it was gone before she had a chance to truly soak the feeling into her veins.

Rafe's voice rang through the deafness that fell over her as he gripped her wrist tightly in his hand and kissed the delicate script. She didn't know what he'd said, but it didn't matter. His touch alone pulled her back to him.

"It's to remind me how love should be. How love should feel."

"But love *is* conditional, don't you think?" he asked, his eyes piercing hers with their depth. She knew his heart was severed. She knew he harbored some guilt that he didn't want to share—she got that. But the anger that flashed in his eyes pulled against her own heart. She didn't understand it, didn't know how to even start comprehending it. But seeing that anger masking something deep inside him trickled *longing*, a longing to take it away from him. Distract him . . .

"Yes. Love is conditional. But not the true kind. Not the kind that matters." She paused, inhaling and releasing a deep breath. "My parents loved me conditionally," she confessed, unsure why the verbal floodgates were opening. Rafe's eyes encouraged her, enveloping her in her own safe haven. So she continued. "They loved me when their prima ballerina was the beautiful focal point of conversation at their elegant dinner parties. They loved me when I was their puppet."

Cupping her cheek, he stroked her jaw. "I can't see that. I can't see you doing something just to appease others."

Laughing, she turned her head and kissed the inside of his hand. "I don't. Not anymore. Everything was a show for my parents. They were members of the elite clubs, part of the inner circles of powerful families, and I was expected to fit. And I did—and I hated it. But I think I only hated it because it's what they wanted. So, like any pissed-off teenager, I rebelled. Partied, got a tattoo, snuck out of the house, and ran around with people they didn't approve of. I started skipping ballet rehearsals just to make them mad. I loved ballet, but I loved defying them even more. And my boyfriend at the time was reaping the benefits of my newfound adolescent rebellion."

"And you just left?"

"They didn't give me a choice."

Rafe could sense she didn't enjoy trudging through her past. There was more, so much more to this woman than he could even begin to discover, but he wasn't going to push her.

"How about you? Did you luck out in the family department or are you a product of screwed-up parents as well?"

He frowned, wishing he could take away some of the bitterness from her tone. "Well, my family was on quite the opposite social spectrum of yours. My parents were dirt-ass poor when they got married. But they were great. They loved us and loved each other. The true kind.

"My mom wanted to open a bakery, and although my dad couldn't even heat up an oven, he worked twice as hard every damn day so he could make her dream come true. Her dream was his dream. And he made it come true for her. My dad still has the bakery, but my brother runs it now. It's not making them rich by any means, but they love it."

Rafe didn't think it would matter if it was a money pit and his dad had to pay to keep it open—that had been his mom's dream, and as long as his dad was alive, her dream would be alive.

"So does that mean you know how to bake? I do believe I may have fallen in bed with the perfect man if that's the case. And I'd be happy to show you where my kitchen is."

He laughed. "I can bake a few things. I spent a lot of time with my mom at the bakery when I was a kid, and she taught me a few of her secrets. But my brother Marco, that's his gig."

"Mmm. Now a man who can bake is even better than a man who can cook."

Rafe shook his head. "No wonder women love him. Had I known baked goods were the key to a woman's heart, I might've asked Mom to teach me a few more secrets before she died."

Fallon's mouth pulled into a frown. "I'm sorry," she said.

"Don't be. I was thirteen—it was a long time ago." He shifted on the bed, Fallon still tucked on his lap. He lay back against the pillows, pulling her down on top of him so her skin ran along his.

"It hurt my family like hell when she died. We all took it pretty hard. My dad—she was his everything. But like I said, it was a long time ago."

He and his brothers felt cheated, as if they didn't get to say good-bye, as if they didn't have a chance to protect her. She died of a brain aneurism in her sleep and they'd wished every goddamn day that they would have known so they could have done something about it. But his dad made them realize that they were lucky. They'd never worried about it—she'd never worried. She wasn't scared or sad before she died—she was just her normal self. Happy, content with her family around her, asleep in the arms of the man she loved. He couldn't imagine a more peaceful departure from the world.

Rafe's fingers trailed up and down the smooth skin of Fallon's back, gently pressing against the ridges of her spine, enjoying the way her body seemed to soften into him from his touch. She remained still, her head tucked beneath his chin, silent. He was afraid he'd crossed some line. Rafe was, for the most part, an open book. But Fallon, she was like a journal, full of stories that only she could tell, stories only she knew.

The light seeping in through the window was transforming into the pale blue hues of dawn. He'd spent many mornings of late waking up in bed with different women, but never once had he woken up wanting to fall back asleep just so he'd have the privilege of opening his eyes to her again. "Do you want to curl back up and sleep in?" he asked, kissing the top of her head. "Or breakfast?"

She rested her chin on his chest. "If it's chocolate cake and coffee, yes."

"I was thinking more along the lines of you."

CHAPTER THIRTEEN

"Come on, gorgeous. I need food. You've managed to deplete all my energy," Rafe accused as he stretched out on the bed a few hours later, Fallon's lean, naked body curled up next to him.

"Food—yes, please," she muttered in response, and he laughed at her exaggerated exhaustion.

His feet hit the floor and he stood up, lifting his arms above his head. He stepped into his jeans and pulled them up over his ass with one hand while he threw his button-down shirt at Fallon.

She pulled it on and padded across her room to the door. "Come on. You can show me your cooking skills."

After spending the good portion of the morning in bed with Fallon, he was fully prepared to spend the day, and if he was lucky the evening, there again. Three fucking days. Three days. That's all the time he'd spent with her and that was all the time she apparently needed to make him addicted. But addicted to what? Dammit, everything. She was a distraction, and a good one too. Because since the moment he'd sampled her skin, he wasn't thinking about anything other than tasting her again. But there was more. No fucking question about it. Touching her, the sound of her laugh, the scent of her hair—he just needed to be near her. It was as if he was feening—for her.

Following her down the stairs, he marveled at the way his shirt just barely covered her ass, showing off her long legs. Legs that just moments ago were wrapped around him while he was buried inside her.

When Rafe stepped off the enclosed staircase, he stepped into a large, open foyer. He expected elegance and sophistication from Fallon, but he'd quickly learned that she was full of surprises.

Her home was large to say the least. She led him through a formal living room to a formal dining room. But when he crossed the space into the kitchen, he saw an entirely different atmosphere. It went from open and white and almost sterile to warm and inviting. The great room included an immaculate open kitchen that looked into a living room. A large TV hung on the wall in front of an overstuffed couch. A kitchen table littered with mail and a laptop sat in the center of the dining room, and the kitchen was clean but looked used. Pasta containers on the counter, canisters of sugar and flour and tea bags. There were a few glasses in her sink, and an empty coffee mug on the island. It felt like a home. He wasn't quite sure why, but that surprised him. Fallon was all those things, warm and inviting. He was just so used to seeing her through the lens of the confidence and sophistication she exuded at the club, and he assumed her place would be much the same. But instead, it was understated—devoid of elegance and sophistication—displaying simple comfort.

He quickly made himself at home in her kitchen, shifting through her near empty refrigerator looking for something to make. "What sounds good?"

Ducking under his arm resting on the open fridge door, she reached around him and grabbed a can of Diet Coke. "Hmm, I think I'll make a jalapeño grilled cheese sandwich."

He turned his head over his shoulder and glanced at the clock on the stove. "It's nine in the morning," he pointed out.

"I know."

"And you want a grilled cheese sandwich?"

"With jalapeños," she stated, pulling a pan out of the cabinet beneath the island.

He raised his brows. "With jalapeños?"

That sweet laugh of hers, which he now realized was a rare occurrence, seeped into the space between them. "Have you tried it?"

"Can't say that I have. That's just strange, woman."

"No, it's delicious."

"I'll take your word for it."

She strutted around the kitchen, making herself brush against him as she got the butter out of the fridge. "What about you?" she asked, turning the stove on and buttering a slice of bread. "I can make you some eggs or pancakes or something."

He loved the sight of a woman in a kitchen. It wasn't a chauvinistic thing. Not at all. It just reminded him of good. It reminded him of love. Everyone had stupid shit that reminded them of a way they felt at a particular time, and a woman in a kitchen reminded him of early mornings as a kid. Waking up for school and moping down the hallway into the kitchen and seeing his dad drinking his coffee as he hovered behind his mom, helping her make breakfast. It was one of the sappy memories that portrayed what should be. The small, everyday kind of love.

It would probably void his man card and make him a pussy for admitting this, but he wanted that love. The kind that had a man wrapped around a woman's finger at the sight of her messy hair and the red sleep marks indented into her cheek when she woke up. The kind of love that made a man call in sick to work so he could throw her back in his bed. The kind of love that could turn a man on just by watching her walk around in his shirt. The kind of love that could make a man drop to his knees.

He'd thought he had it. He'd thought he'd felt it with Bridgette. But it was a damn lie. He'd never watched her cooking in his shirt. He'd never seen her messy morning hair or called into work to get her back in his bed. He didn't have her mornings. He'd had her in-betweens—and even those weren't his to have.

Brushing Fallon's disheveled hair to the side of her neck, Rafe ran his nose along the short fine hairs that curled at her nape. His lips pursed and he tapped them to her skin. Her soft sigh that creased along the line of a giggle wafted to his ears and he smiled at her sweet reaction. This was what it was supposed to be like—what it was supposed to feel like. Mornings, with a beautiful woman.

"Got cereal?" he asked, pressing another kiss to the back of her head as he linked his arms around her stomach.

"Yes. In the pantry. But I have the eating habits of a twelve-year-old, so you're going to have to make do with Cap'n Crunch or Cocoa Pebbles."

Crossing the cold marbled tile, he opened the pantry and pulled the box of Cocoa Pebbles from the shelf.

He sat on one of the barstools at the island and watched as she finished preparing her sandwich.

"Can I make you some coffee?" she asked, setting her plate down on the island next to him.

Looking at her, he took in her messy hair and sex-induced glow. Goddamn. Three fucking days.

"No, gorgeous. I'm good."

Walking around the island, she hopped up onto the counter, her legs dangling over the edge. "What?" she asked as he looked at her, amused.

"Nothing."

She grinned at him and took a bite of her sandwich, watching as he sloppily filled his mouth with chocolate cereal. It was adorable.

A few thoughts were running on repeat inside Fallon's mind and she would've done anything at that moment to shut them off. She wanted to enjoy the company Rafe was offering her. She'd never cooked in her kitchen or had breakfast with anyone in her home before. It was strangely comforting. But the same thought kept rearing its ugly head. *Arm's length.*

Rafe took another bite, then, holding his bowl in one hand, he grabbed the top of her thigh, pulling her to him until her butt was on the edge of the counter. He settled between her legs, her knees pressing against his bare sides. "There are definite advantages to this counter-sitting thing," he said, the amusement in his voice making her smile before that pesky thought swung back around full circle one last time.

She squirmed under his touch, his fingers steadily applying pressure to her thighs. It wasn't hard, but it was enough to make her tighten her legs around him. His eyes lifted, looking at her as he skillfully parted his mouth in what she was sure was some sort of swooning mechanism. Because that's exactly what happened. She had that little "ahhh" moment where she wanted to tilt her head and sigh at the sight of him. His wry, arrogant grin had just enough pull on the corners that made it irresistibly sexy, but annoyingly adorable at the same time.

She jerked when he rested the cold cereal bowl on her thigh. "Are one of these advantages using me as a table?" she teased, taking another bite of delicious, cheesy jalapeño goodness.

"That, among others . . ." he suggested, and it didn't take a genius to know where he was going with that.

Setting her half-eaten sandwich on the counter, she took a few sips of her Diet Coke. Rafe lifted the bowl from her leg and brought it to his lips as he spooned another large bite into his mouth. Resting her palms on the edge of the counter, she slinked her body down on top of him.

He smirked around a mouthful of cereal when her legs wrapped around him, and although a surprised chuckle curled over his lips, his eyes darkened. The glints of light that were creating a velvety texture to his eyes seemed to vanish . . . and then smolder.

Her heart stalled when his eyes connected with hers. It was intense in a way that was almost frightening. But she wasn't the least bit scared.

His jaw moved slowly as he chewed; then she watched as he swallowed. A small, glistening bead of milk rolled over his bottom lip, then fell onto his chest. Her gaze seemed to transfix on that small drop of milk as it slowly rolled between his pectorals.

She couldn't help herself. The prospect of running her tongue over his hard chest and lapping up the single drop that had previously been on his lips was too appealing. She lowered her head and parted her mouth, catching the bead between her lips, pressing the tip of her tongue to his warm skin.

She heard the bowl clank against the counter at the same time her lips vibrated from the deep, silent growl in his chest. His hands melted against her skin, snaking them over the top of her thigh, under the hem of the shirt, until they reached the curve that ran into her hips. He latched onto her and rolled her hips forward. The rough texture of the denim grated against her bare center, and had her head not already been lowered to his chest, she didn't think she'd have been able to support it on her neck. His touch made her feel like putty. Soft and warm in all the right places.

This newfound nirvana he was able to create for her was coaxing her into a rare form of addiction. She couldn't get enough. Enough touch.

She'd been missing it. Missing the effect a touch, a caress, an embrace could give. She'd been limiting her body's contact, carefully safeguarding it. But the complete honesty his body gave to her penetrated her previously indestructible barriers. Rafe's touch was treacherous, though. Frenzied and chaotic in a way that was simplistic and easy. She knew the dangers that lay ahead with every flame that flickered between their connecting bodies. She'd constructed her walls to keep those dangers away, to protect herself. But she felt them shifting, weakening beneath his touch alone. Just his touch.

And she needed it.

His lips molded onto her neck, his tongue wet and cold as he swirled it leisurely, then sucked gently. Lifting her head, she unfastened the buttons of his shirt she was wearing and it parted, draping open.

"Perfection," he whispered, raking his penetrating eyes over her bare breasts and pantyless body.

His mouth dipped back down, focusing its attention to the thin skin at the hollow at the base of her neck. He was gentle as he fluttered kisses across her collarbone and up the center of her throat. Winding her hands around his neck, she swept them over his buzzed hair, the friction numbing the pads of her fingers.

She was lost in the sensation of his lips and hands smoothing over her body, so when his grip on her waist tightened and he lifted her back onto the counter, her eyes blinked open in surprise.

"What have you done to me?" he asked, his torturous mouth once again hovering over her body, breathing warm, tantalizing breath over her sensitive skin. She didn't have an opportunity to process his question before he lowered her back against the counter and started dragging those perilous lips lower and lower.

She rose to her elbows. "Rafe." She breathed.

His head lifted, his eyes finding hers in that one single instant. And he grinned. It was mischievous and taunting and sexy as sin, and whatever thought was processing in her already clouded mind, it left her.

Her muscles ached in exhaustion as they tightened and clenched under his deft caress and she moaned when his tongue soothed the throb between her thighs.

It had never been this good. Felt this good.

She'd never craved or needed the affection he was providing her body.

But he'd made her desirous for him. And the consequences were teetering along terrifying. If she wanted him like this—this much, this quickly—then she was already in trouble.

Rafe could feel Fallon's familiar tics indicating her sweet release was close. In the few times she'd come with him, he'd memorized the way her legs elongated and her toes pointed moments before she would wind tightly. He memorized the way her breathing deepened, lengthening as she inhaled.

"I need you to give it to me, babe," he whispered, then flicked his tongue over her clit once more, causing her to writhe on top of the island.

He rose from her and smiled when her brows pulled into a frown and she whimpered. "Ohhh," she moaned, running her hands over her tits and along her sides as if willing the sensations of pleasure to follow her touch. "Rafe," she moaned.

"Yeah, gorgeous?" he answered, but he didn't expect a response and didn't receive one. "I need inside you again." Pulling a foil packet from his back pocket, he unzipped his jeans and pulled them from his hips, letting them drop around his ankles, then stepped out of them.

"Yes—now."

Her urgency satisfied his masculine instinct. He loved that she was nearly begging.

Digging into her hips, he pulled her from the counter, her beautiful naked ass slipping across the marble as if draped in silk. She wrapped her legs around him and he lifted her, sliding her down his body until he felt her wet and warm against his cock.

Planting a single kiss to her mouth, he nipped her lip with his teeth. "Ask me nicely."

Her lids fluttered open and she challenged him with her eyes. "Please."

"Please what, babe?"

"You know what," she flouted, and pressed her hips against him. He withheld the fucking groan that was building in his chest as her smooth pussy cradled his cock, a breath away from encasing him.

"Say it." He lowered his voice and moved his lips to the freckle on her shoulder and attempted to lull his fervor to slide inside her with the taste of her skin.

Her head rolled back as his tongue sampled the round of her shoulder.

"Please," she implored, once again using the strength of her thighs that were clinging to his waist to roll her hips onto him.

This time the groan escaped. His eyes were fixated on hers, and she smiled. A smile that said just how much she knew his resolve was thinning out.

"Rafe," she whispered as her mouth danced to his. "Fuck me. Now. Please."

That word spoken from her lips put a whole new spin on talking dirty, and it was the sexiest sound he'd heard.

Without replying, he peeled her body from his, lowered her feet to the floor, and spun her around. He placed her hands on the island, then pulled her hips back . . . right . . . where . . . he . . . wanted . . . them. Then thrust inside her.

She gasped in satisfaction and he felt her tighten around him.

"Fuuck, baby."

"Harder, Rafe—please."

She didn't need to beg nicely now. Her sweet little body

was so close to release that he had no control. He had to give it to her—he needed it just as desperately as she did.

His name labored from her mouth in a jagged cry and the beauty of the noise triggered his own release.

Spent and elated, they sank to the tile and she liquefied in his arms. Lacing his fingers through hers, he brought her hand to his lips and kissed the inside of her wrist. And she shivered.

Fuck.

"What have you done to me, gorgeous?"

She tilted her chin upward and lifted her lips into a tired smile. "I believe I should be asking you the same question," she teased.

If only they were talking about the same thing. The sex was addictive, distracting, amazing. But feeling her body melt into his, shivering, needing . . . he was a fucking goner. He craved her response to him; he craved the way that little response relieved the anger. Replaced it with something else entirely.

He kissed her forehead and leaned his head back against the cabinet. "What are you doing the rest of the day?"

"Why?" she asked curiously.

"One of my friends in my unit is having a cookout tonight. Good beer, good food, good company. What do ya think? Wanna come?"

"I don't know, Rafe," she mumbled into his chest.

Yeah, it was probably better she didn't come. He didn't have a fucking clue why he even suggested it. No, that was a lie. He asked her because he wanted her there with him.

Fallon, the first woman he'd wanted to be with outside of the bedroom in nearly two years.

Kissing his arm that was tangled around her, she lifted her eyes back to him and smirked bashfully. But he knew she was playing him. This woman wasn't bashful—that he knew for damn sure. "Maybe if you asked me nicely."

Damn woman.

He laughed. "Please?"

CHAPTER FOURTEEN

*A*fter spending twenty minutes on the phone with George getting the full report on Jade, Fallon was relieved to hear that she was up and moving and back at the loft.

Rafe pulled his car into the club's parking lot. Unbuckling her seat belt and opening the door, Fallon asked, "Do you mind waiting here?"

"No. Go on."

She didn't want Rafe to go into the apartment because she didn't want Jade to be seen like that again. That wasn't her. Not anymore. But when you hit bottom, you don't want anyone to see you there. At least, that's how Fallon felt when she curled into the lowest low of her life and felt like there was no way to stand back up. Vulnerability and pride were equal counterparts in Fallon's perspective. And Jade's and Fallon's minds turned in the same direction. She figured Jade wouldn't want anyone to see her that way either.

She smiled gratefully at Rafe and stepped out of the Jeep. As the door clicked shut, she heard an identical sound echo it. Rafe had stepped out of the car and was walking toward her. "I thought you—"

"I'm not going in," he assured, then nodded toward the thick metal door that led backstage. "That's my friend Graham." He started walking toward him and Fallon followed. *Graham?* She knew the name from somewhere; she just couldn't recall where.

"Hey," Rafe said as he approached his friend. The guy spun around to face them, a surprised flick in his eyes when he saw Rafe.

"Rafe, what're you doing here?" he asked. He looked worried, anxious.

"I'm here with Fallon. What are you doing here?"

When Rafe said her name, Graham finally looked at her, as if he hadn't even realized she was standing there. He reached out his hand to her. "Hi, Fallon. I'm Graham," he said formally, but slightly irritated at the untimeliness of their arrival. But then recognition registered. "Fallon, I saw you the other week. You dance here, right?"

She nodded. "I'm the owner."

Graham's eyes rolled shut briefly and he sighed. "Thank fuck. I'm trying to get ahold of Jade. She's not answering her phone and George called me this morning and told me what happened and— Fuck . . . can you open the door?"

That's where she knew the name from. Jade had mentioned him.

Fallon raised her palms in the air. "Okay, first of all, slow down," she soothed, attempting to calm his frantic rambling. He scrubbed his hands over his face and shifted in a circle before facing her again. "I'm going up to check on her now. She more than likely knows exactly why you're blowing up her phone, which means she probably doesn't want to talk to you about it. Let me go talk to her first."

Nodding his defeat, he exhaled. "Yeah, okay. But you'll tell her I'm here? Tell her I just want to make sure she's okay."

The poor guy looked beaten with worry. It was apparent he cared for Jade, which in turn made Fallon Team Graham. "I'll tell her," she reassured him.

"Thanks."

*F*allon knocked once to give Jade the heads-up that she was there, then opened the door. The blinds were drawn shut and the dim haze that seeped through the cracks bathed the dark room with narrow beams of light. Dust particles danced in the spaces of light as Fallon walked into the living room.

Jade was curled on the couch, her eyes shut, wrapped tightly in a blanket.

"Jade," Fallon whispered.

Her lids lifted and a watery sheen glistened in them. "Hi." Her weak voice cracked.

Walking to the kitchen, Fallon pulled a coffee mug from the cabinet, filled it with water, and stuck it in the microwave. Uncomfortable silence stretched between them, the only sound filling the room the soft hum of the microwave before it dinged.

Dunking a tea bag into the hot water, she carried the cup to Jade.

"Here," she offered.

Jade sat up slowly. "Thanks."

Fallon didn't know where to start exactly, so she straightened the pillows at the foot of the couch and sat down. How was she supposed to bring up what happened last night with a level head? Now, seeing Jade in her coherent state, she wanted to scream at her until her vocal cords were raw and hoarse. But at the same time she wanted to throw her arms around her and tell her how glad she was that she was okay.

"Holy shit. Has hell frozen over?" Jade muttered between her failed attempt at a smile. "Fallon Kelly's in a pair of jeans."

She rolled her eyes. "I'm going to a cookout."

"Hell has indeed frozen over," Jade replied, bringing the steaming mug to her cracked lips.

Friendly banter and wisecracks weren't on the morning's agenda. Fallon was pissed and worried, and all Jade could do was joke? "Is this really how we're going to do this? Just pretend that you didn't shoot up last night? In my club? You scared the shit out of everyone. Na was a mess, all the girls were worried. Seriously, Jade. What in the hell were you thinking? Two years. You've been clean almost two years! Why?"

She shrank into the couch, her thin body diminishing beneath her blanket. Fallon watched as she swallowed hard and shook her head. "I slipped up."

"That's not a good enough answer for me, Jade. Why?"

"Dexter's been fucking around on me," she admitted.

The volume of her voice rose along with her anger. "Hence the whole not showing up and the whole distance thing. I went to his house yesterday. I wanted to surprise him, take him to breakfast, spend the afternoon together before I had to come back here for work. Well, I ended up the one being surprised when I walked into his house and found him curled up in bed with another woman."

Fallon sighed and puckered her bottom lip in sympathy. Heartbreak sucked no matter what way you looked at it. Caring about someone put you at a high risk for being let down. And Fallon could understand that kind of hurt even if she couldn't understand Jade's reaction. But then, everyone dealt with pain a little differently. Everyone had different ways to distract themselves. It was harder for some than for others. And Jade had decided to find her distraction with a needle to the vein.

"Who'd you call, Jade?" Fallon asked, wanting to rip apart whoever had provided her with her Kryptonite.

"My old dealer," she mumbled, averting her eyes to her hands. "I didn't think he'd still have the same number after two years. I just needed to go through the motions, ya know? But when he answered, the idea of just forgetting, even if just for a minute, won out."

Biting her teeth together, Fallon stared at the wall, shifting through the words that were jumbled in her head, attempting to unscramble them so she could speak.

"If you can just give me a few days—three max—I'll be gone."

Fallon snapped her head to Jade, her brows pulling down between her eyes. "You're not leaving, Jade."

"But you said—"

"I know what I said. But I'm not going to kick you out because you screwed up." That wouldn't solve a damn thing. It would just leave Jade alone, and scared, left to deal with her mistakes by herself. She would never do that to her. She would never abandon Jade the way her parents did her.

Jade's eye glossed over with unshed tears. "I don't know what to say."

"You could start with 'I'm sorry' and end with 'I'll never scare you like that again.'"

She nodded. "I knew you loved me," she teased. "And if I was a hugger, I would hug you."

Fallon laughed, grateful for that little piece of Jade to slip back into the shell she was staring at. "Are you going to be okay?" she asked.

"Yeah, I will be."

"Promise?"

"Promise."

"And no more drugs—I mean it, Jade."

Making an X over her chest with her finger, she said, "Cross my heart."

"And Graham's here?" Fallon questioned, still unsure as to what part Graham played in Jade's life.

Jade perked up and wiped at the black dried flakes beneath her eyes. "He is?"

"Yeah, and apparently he and 'Bad Boy' are friends."

Her interest sparked. "Wait, is *he* here too?"

"His name is Rafe, and yes, he's here with me. Do you

want me to let Graham up or not?" she asked. She wasn't ready to answer the question she knew Jade would have asked if she divulged any more information. Fallon didn't have any answers anyway.

"Yeah, send him up."

CHAPTER FIFTEEN

"Dammit," Rafe said, swiping his finger across the red ignore button on his phone before he tossed it into the cup holder between the seats. He'd just exited off of I-25 and pulled onto Bijou Street toward Wright's house when his phone rang, waking Fallon up, who was sleeping in the seat next to him.

She stirred and stretched, dropping her feet from the dashboard. "What's with all the hostility?" She yawned, straightening up against the seat.

"Just someone from my past trying to fucking slip through the cracks," he muttered before he realized he was opening up the proverbial can of worms.

"The someone you're trying to forget," she stated as she looked out the window.

"Pretty much."

He saw her head shift back to him from the corner of his eye, the light from the window illuminating the golden streaks in her hair as it tumbled over her shoulder. "What'd she do?" she asked simply, as if asking him what his favorite football team was.

Rafe laughed. If only the answer were that fucking simple. It was a question with so many different layers of answers he couldn't even begin to peel them away from the messed-up situation that lay beneath. But he said the very first one that sprang to the front of his mind. The one that obviously made him the angriest. His jaw clenched tight as he pushed the words through his clamped teeth: "She turned me into the type of man I never thought I'd be."

He glanced at Fallon and watched as sympathy crossed her face, but her eyes still squinted in confusion.

"For what it's worth"—she smiled at him—"and please don't make me regret saying this, but, from what little I've seen of the type of man you are, I'd say you just might be one of the good ones. Arrogant, and maybe a little bit intimidating. But I see the good. And I've seen a lot of the bad to recognize when I see the good."

Rafe's knuckles whitened above his grip on the steering wheel. He definitely wasn't one of the good ones. "She's married," he said, noticing the coldness that had crept into his voice.

He felt the tangible tension that worked into Fallon's body, and her silence drove it home. He'd already made her regret what she said . . .

"It was a long time ago, back when I was stationed at Fort Benning in Georgia. She lives in Kentucky with her family. She's not a part of my life now—she's not someone I'm proud to admit anything about."

"Are you telling me this so I don't spill the secret to your friends that you had an affair with a married woman?"

Ouch. Her words bit into his flesh, stinging deep. "No, I'm telling you because you're right. She's the one I've been trying to forget." Reaching over, he peeled her hand from her lap, pressing a kiss to her wrist. But she didn't shiver. "And I think I finally have."

Which wasn't to say that the thought of her didn't bring on the phantom pain lurking in his chest, but she wasn't the one on his mind anymore.

Fear flashed across Fallon's face and she gently pulled from his grasp. After a few moments of silence, she lifted her gaze back to him and finally spoke. "Do you love her?"

He shifted his eyes from the road and nodded, although admitting it to Fallon made his repulsion deepen. He hadn't just had an affair with another man's wife; he'd fucking fallen in *love* with her. "I did. But not the true kind," he answered, setting his sights on the stretch of asphalt in front of him.

Pulling her legs beneath her on the seat, she faced the window again. "I'm not saying what you did was okay, because we both know it wasn't, but we all make mistakes that we regret, Rafe. The heart is sneaky and manipulative, and more often than not it hurts even worse when we let ourselves down." She looked at him again, and he returned her glance, her understanding creating a crater in his chest. He reached across the seat and grabbed her small, delicate hand in his, bringing it to his mouth and kissing the inside of her wrist.

"You sound like you speak from experience." He looked

at her briefly, but she quickly shifted her gaze back to the blurring landscape—but not before the phantom pain she tried to conceal reached the bursts of light in her eyes, dimming the fire in her just enough for him to notice.

"I didn't just let myself down, Rafe," she whispered.

Her parents. Rafe wanted to wring their necks for making her feel that she wasn't worthy of their love. He'd been around her three goddamn days and already knew she was worth that and more. She wielded strength and compassion regardless of what their fucked-up perception of success was, and anyone would be lucky to love a woman like her.

Fallon's fingers tightened around his and her determination was palpable in the grip of her petite hand. "You just tuck it away and keep it close to remind you of the way you never want to feel again." Her spine straightened against the seat, releasing the strength she used as her crutch as the grip she had on his hand relaxed against his fingers. She stared ahead at the road in front of them, the volume of her voice rising as she spoke confidently. "And then you make sure you don't." But he was unsure whether she spoke the words for him or for herself.

Fallon stood in the kitchen holding a store-bought pie while Rafe loaded his beer into the refrigerator. For the first time since . . . ever, Fallon was nervous being in a crowd. She knew how to act, how to blend, what to say and when to say it, and could easily claim this shindig if she needed to. But the swarm of angry butterflies in her stomach was apparently going to challenge her ability to do so with ease. This was the first time she'd gone on—what was this even? A date? Did a cookout at a friend's house classify as a date? The nerves she was unfamiliar with feeling might as well have been a Magic 8 Ball because that little sign pointed to yes.

"Here, I'll take that." Rafe shut the refrigerator door and took the pie from Fallon's hands, setting it down on the counter next to the rest of the sweets. "What can I get you to drink?"

She absentmindedly chewed her bottom lip. Her mouth was a little dry all of a sudden. "I'll have a diet soda if there's any."

Rafe winked and opened the fridge back up and pulled out a Diet Coke, pouring it in a Solo cup with ice. Then he added a small handful of cherries to the glass.

It felt like her smile was slicing open the corners of her eyes. Only a few, rare people knew the way she liked to drink her soda. "Thank you," she said, taking the cup from him. "How'd you know?"

"I notice things, gorgeous." He grinned. One that said just how proud he was of his acute ability to observe. "I saw Pete dump a few in your soda last weekend. Come on—let me introduce you to everyone." His fingers brushed down her spine before finding their familiar place on the small of her back, the woven fabric of her sweater rasping against her skin from the pressure of his palm. He led her to the back door, his hand on her and the nearness of his body her very own haven. She was her own beacon of protection. But there was no denying the way that small touch calmed the foreign fluttering in her chest.

She smoothed her hands over her sweater and ran her fingers through her loose waves before stepping out onto the back patio.

"Rafe's here," a short, stocky man hollered out from behind a smoking grill. He was mildly handsome in that cute, domestic way that would make you think of family outings in an RV.

Rafe's hand clamped down on the man's shoulder. "You doing good, brother?"

He nodded, a moment passing between them that made Fallon feel she was intruding. Rafe nodded and slapped the man's back before pulling him into a hug. She was lost on the outskirts of the emotions surrounding the two guys, and it was heartbreaking. There was nothing to pinpoint the pain that unfurled from their embrace, but it cinched her heart. A heart that was a stranger to feeling. But she did.

Rafe did that to her . . .

His tall frame towered over her as he grabbed her hand and pulled her to him. Her knee-high boots clicked against the concrete patio as they walked to a cluster of people sitting around a long glass table. As introductions were made, Fallon felt her confidence return to her, and she began questioning why she'd been so damn nervous in the first place.

Then she remembered as Rafe pressed a kiss to her neck, pulling her onto his lap as he sat down. Affection—let alone a public display of affection—was as foreign to her as tennis shoes. She was more comfortable in heels. . . .

"Uh-uh. Fallon, doll, come sit over here with us. You're bound to be subject to army talk and deployment stories if you stay over there with the men," the woman Rafe had introduced as Stella said, waving Fallon over to the far side of the patio, where she and a bottle blond were sitting around another table.

Stella was right. The men had already jumped in to stories from their recent deployment to Afghanistan, but Fallon was actually interested in hearing them. Of course, the other women had probably already heard them time and time again, but Fallon had learned Rafe was a soldier only that morning. She was intrigued with this man, and despite her desire to stay firmly curled in his lap, her well-instilled manners won out and she joined the women at the far side of the patio.

"So, Rafe's never brought a woman around," Stella stated with a Jersey accent and a smile on her face as Fallon took the empty seat next to her. Fallon was a pretty good judge of character, and she liked Stella from the start.

"How are we supposed to meet them when he has a different woman every night?" the woman named Claire interjected with a tinge of hostility that made Fallon smirk. Claire didn't like Fallon, and she didn't like that Fallon was there with Rafe—it didn't take a mind reader to reach that little conclusion. But unfortunately for Claire, her words were meaningless to Fallon. Fallon already knew Rafe's secret—hell, she'd found him neck deep in the aftermath. His need for women wasn't news to her.

"Yeah, I'm one of the lucky ones. But I'm sure if you ask

him, he'll be happy to introduce you to the woman he screws tomorrow night."

Claire's eyeballs bugged from her head. Fallon simply crossed her legs and took a sip of her soda.

Stella laughed. "I do believe I like this chick."

"I do too," a tall, beautiful woman with a thick German accent agreed as she approached the table and sat down next to Fallon. Claire's face tightened up.

Fallon searched for the apologetic smile stored away on reserve and brushed the dust and cobwebs off it. "I'm sorry, Claire—you made that one too easy for me."

Claire only furrowed her dark brows even more. "So, how did you meet Rafe anyway?" she asked. Fallon didn't get into it with women. She didn't care to indulge in the petty bullshit that women appeared to thrive off of. But the accusation in Claire's words seemed to scratch at a layer of her resolve.

This time when she reached in, she looked for the smile that her mother had taught her. The one that inflicted a false sincerity of kindness. She was a lady after all. "I only met him last weekend."

Claire nodded and leaned back against her chair. "Oh." She sipped her white wine. "So you're one of the two girls he took home from the bar last Friday that Carter told me about."

Stella thudded Claire's arm with the back of her hand. "Damn, Claire, what the hell's your problem?"

Fallon shook her head, dismissing Stella's attempt at shutting Claire up. "Actually," she started, and all the women around the table shifted their eyes from Claire's to hers, "I didn't meet Rafe until Saturday night, so sorry to disappoint you, but I was unfortunately not one of the two women he took home Friday. However, I have to admit I'm a little upset that I missed out on all the fun."

Stella and the German woman snickered to themselves as Claire sulked. Fallon didn't have the desire to entertain women who enjoyed getting a rise out of others, but for some reason she thoroughly enjoyed getting a rise out of Claire.

Two hands rested on top of Fallon's shoulders the second before damaged lips pressed a tight kiss to her head. "Hey, gorgeous, I'm gonna go grab another beer. Do you need anything?"

Turning her head over her shoulder, she smiled up at Rafe when she met his dark eyes. "I'm fine. Thank you, though." He leaned down and whispered a kiss over her mouth, letting his lips linger a little longer than necessary for such a chaste kiss—yet she didn't think any kiss with him could be chaste. Even just the simple tug of her bottom lip as he pulled away was sexy and intimate. "Ladies, can I get you anything?"

"No, we're fine," Stella assured, grinning at Fallon. Her hand had a brief spasm in front of her face as she fanned herself the second Rafe was inside. "Mmm, honey, that man is sexy. I've always adored Rafe, but I'll tell you right now, that was hot."

Smiling, Fallon felt heat reach the surface of her cheeks. She'd just blushed. Maybe Jade was right. Maybe hell had actually frozen over.

Fallon stood. "Excuse me." She never much understood the women who felt the need to cling to their dates, and she wasn't clinging. She was simply following her body's instincts as she trailed Rafe.

She made her way inside and came to a stop next to him as he was getting into a pile of brownies on the counter. His jaw worked around a mouthful and she rolled her eyes when he noticed her and smiled. His arm snaked out to the side and wrapped around her waist, pulling him in front of her. A surprised squeal caught in the back of her throat.

"What are you doing?" she asked as he pushed her back into the ledge of the counter.

"This." His mouth pressed a wet kiss to her jaw, then scattered up to her lips. His tongue wasted no time pushing its way into her mouth, devouring her, and the taste of chocolate and beer mixed with the luscious taste of his mouth was piquant. Her legs softened and she latched onto the counter for support. Blushing and melting and swooning. Hell had frozen over all right.

He gripped her tightly and she swore she heard a soft chuckle rumble low in his throat. "I've got you," he whispered, then continued his brazen assault to her lips, her neck, and her jaw. His plundering kisses left her breathless beneath him as she tried to keep up.

Her head began to cloud with desire as her body responded to his touch in every way a body could. Her breathing quickened, her pulse accelerated, her chest tightened, her muscles weakened, and the ache between her thighs throbbed.

She sighed. "Rafe," she mumbled incoherently as he skillfully tended to the skin below her ear, her head involuntarily rolling to the side, opening up for him. "I think you should—"

"You think I should what?" he interrupted, concealing her body with his as he brushed his thumb firmly across her nipple. It tightened and peaked beneath his touch as the lace of her bra abraded her tender skin. Her body was still sensitive and reeling from the nirvana he'd sent her to that morning—twice—and the friction he was creating rippled across her skin, igniting a fire low in her stomach.

An impish grin fanned against her neck and she imagined the delectable way it pulled to one side. "You were saying?" he jested, applying pressure to her body with his hips, revealing his own body's desires. The way his cock beckoned her through their clothing was only a testament to how quickly he had turned the switch and turned her on. And also how incredibly hard he was for her . . .

She moaned.

And he chuckled.

"Do you plan on having your way with me right here in the middle of the kitchen, because if not, I would appreciate it if you stopped teasing me." She sighed inwardly, relieved at her capability to form an articulate sentence while his mouth still levitated above her skin.

Dropping his head to her shoulder, he groaned in frustration, then lifted her up onto the counter and pulled her center against him. "If only you were wearing one of those sweet dresses you like, I could've already had you trembling." His warm, moist lips danced along the curve of her shoulder. She might have done just about anything at that moment to feel his deft fingers press inside her.

Lifting her legs around his waist, she writhed against him at the vivid thought. His head lowered back to her shoulder in defeat and he nibbled on her collarbone, then dotted a quick kiss on her neck. "Come on. I need to get your ass back outside before I strip you down and bury my face between your thighs."

She took his offered hand and popped off the counter, landing a bit shakily. "See, I fail to see the problem in that little scenario," she teased, already making her way through the kitchen to the back door. Before she was able to gain another step, Rafe tugged back on her hand, pulling her against his chest. His hands drifted down her arms, resting firmly on her elbows.

She lifted her chin to look at him and was swallowed by the intensity in his molten eyes. The raw, wanton passion in them overwhelmed her in their near proximity, so she tried to create a breath of space between them. But he only held her closer.

Pulling away was an option, but it wasn't one she wanted to entertain. She was drowning in his intensity, consumed by his scent. Her heart crashed against her chest, extinguishing what little resolve she was clinging to. She wanted this . . . him. His overpowering body, his considerate touch, his dangerous kiss. She wanted him and what he made her feel.

Delicate. Vulnerable.

Cherished.

. . .

"*I* wasn't kidding, babe," Rafe said, trying to inflict as much gentleness into his words as physically possible. He'd love nothing more than to peel the jeans from her legs and glide his tongue along her pussy until her legs convulsed around his neck, and he was more tempted than she could possibly even realize. He needed to get her outside before he perverted Wright's kitchen and allowed everyone there to know the way Fallon sounded when he brought her over the edge. And the idea of his jackass buddies outside hearing the sweet, heady sounds that mewled from Fallon's lips when she came was reason enough to cease and desist.

She softened under his hold, a physical offering of herself. And it made him harder. He saw a layer melt away in her eyes, felt a shift in her stance.

His hands left her arms and palmed the sides of her neck, his thumbs tracing the lines of her jaw. "Would it be rude to grab that plate of brownies and take off so I can get you in my bed?"

Her shoulders relaxed even more and she lifted her lips into a smile. "Yes, it'd be very rude."

"All right, then get your ass outside."

*R*afe handed Carter another log to add to the fire pit while the women were finishing up taking the leftover food back into the house. There was plenty left over, even with the multiple burgers each of the men had ingested.

Stella was a go-big-or-go-home kind of woman, and that included her menu for the cookout. She'd made enough food to feed his entire company.

"So are you going to divulge any information on the chick you brought or what?" Carter finally asked, taking his seat along the built-in brick bench that surrounded half of the fire pit that was built up from the patio.

"Information?" he asked, playing dumb. He knew these jackasses just wanted to know why in the hell he'd brought a woman with him. Especially given his recent binge of different women, and especially since they'd never known him to be any other way. They didn't know the Rafe that existed before Bridgette shredded him, gutted him, and hung him out to dry. They only saw the man she'd unknowingly turned him into. Seeing Rafe with a woman who wasn't making her way to his car after initial introductions was new for them. Fuck, it was new for him too. But he didn't want to be that man anymore.

Carter nodded. "Yeah, information. Other than her name and the fact that she is way too hot for your ugly ass, we don't know anything about her."

"I'm still learning." And he wanted to learn everything.

"Bullshit. You can give us something better than that load of crap. Rafe Murano doesn't arrive with women—he leaves with women," Carter said, dragging a few extra camping chairs around the fire in the center of the patio.

"Yeah, and I intend on leaving with Fallon as well," he barked.

Carter laughed from across the fire, then tipped back

his beer. Rafe had already narrowed his eyes at him, so when Carter lowered his head he was greeted with a look Carter was all too familiar with. "Damn, Murano. Getting a little defensive? A little territorial?" he asked, which apparently meant Carter had a death wish. He was a good guy, but he didn't know when to shut the hell up.

Rafe leaned back in his chair and watched the flames pop and crack. "I like her," Wright said, handing Rafe a beer before taking the seat next to him. "She fits you."

This time Rafe laughed. Only Wright could pull off saying something like that. The dude was one of those hopeless romantics that women try to mold men into. Rafe liked to think he had a romantic side, that he knew how to woo and pander to a woman's amorous needs. But Wright—he was one of those sensitive, corny, sentimental fucks who men like Rafe took notes from. "Care to elaborate?"

"I don't know, man. She complements you. She's beauty, you're the beast. Don't fucking know—you just fit."

"Okay, thank you for that. Should I start calling you my fairy godmother?"

Carter joined Rafe in a laugh. Wright just shook his head and took a drink from his beer. "You two laugh . . ." he said, as if warning them.

"What are you goons laughing about?"

Rafe turned his head over his shoulder at the sound of Stella's voice before she came into his peripheral vision and walked to Wright.

"Just trying to enlighten them on the ways of a woman, baby," Wright answered as Stella leaned down and kissed him.

Fallon came to a stop behind him, and he reached his hand back for her. "Come here."

She smiled knowingly and took his hand, and he pulled her around and onto his lap. Wright was right. She just fit. Her body contoured against his and it just felt right.

Three goddamn days. He'd been around her *three* days.

A warning signal was blaring in his ear, ricocheting off his eardrum and thwarting his mind. The last time he jumped headfirst he fell hard.

And he crashed.

But denying the way she felt in his arms was impossible. The sun had started setting behind the mountains and the evening chill skirted over them, causing Fallon to curl her legs over his thighs as she tucked herself in tighter on his lap. Her head nestled into the crook of his shoulder and his arms easily encased her. Yeah, there was no fucking denying it.

Fallon's body shook above his as she laughed at something Stella said. He wasn't paying attention; his thoughts were trying to shuffle through the reasons he should stand up and take Fallon home. The reasons he should chalk up their few nights together as a well-needed distraction and leave it at that. But he couldn't find one. He couldn't find one reason good enough to remove her soft body from his and end the night alone in his bed. And he'd be a fucking liar if he said he wanted to.

Christ.

"Oh, we'll see about that. Right, Rafe?"

He regained attention with the sound of his name and

blinked his eyes into focus. "Huh?" he asked Stella, who was obviously irritated by the looks of the scowl wrinkling her face.

Fallon huffed, feigning annoyance. "Apparently, she's being dragged to a military redeployment ball and she's mistaken her fondness for my company with the idea that I'll be attending said ball."

"Oh no, you're going even if I have to find some young, eager private to take you."

Rolling her eyes, Fallon shook her head.

"Looks like I better ask you to the ball before someone else beats me to it."

"I don't really think a military ball is my thing."

"Well, it's mandatory that I attend, and it would be a hell of a lot better if you were on my arm. I promise to make it worth your time. Plus, I look damn good in my dress uniform."

"I don't doubt that for one second." Her eyes glassed over with a need he was becoming eager to fulfill.

"Then go with me. It's in a few weeks."

"You'd better go," Stella threatened.

Rafe shook his head. That woman was something else. "You don't have to tell me now, but just let it be known that I will persuade you in my favor."

"Is that so?"

"Yes."

He pulled her in tight and kissed the top of her head as the gate in the fence opened up.

"Bridgette."

CHAPTER SIXTEEN

allon felt the muscles in Rafe's arms stiffen around her. His breathing expanded his shoulders as he inhaled deep, steady breaths. Lifting her chin, she looked up at him. His square jaw with a sexy amount of stubble was now twitching above the tight muscles beneath. His flawed mouth was pressed in a firm line, and his glossy, inky eyes had dulled and hardened.

The crackling of the fire seemed to pop along with the quickening beat of Rafe's heart. The palpable tension he was emitting had seeped into her skin. No one else seemed to be witnessing the man beneath her struggling to keep his emotions controlled, but then again, Fallon was an expert at the task. She was privy to the signs. Spending her entire life grappling beneath the emotions she suppressed, keeping a controlled facade for everyone, gave her an extensive amount of practice reading them. When she followed his gaze, she saw a beautiful woman who looked as though the air had been sucked from her lungs. Her eyes were wide and it was easy to see the hurt and jealousy that rolled through them like thunder. Then realization slashed Fallon's flesh like the sting from an icy palm. And she knew—it was *her*. The one Rafe was trying to forget.

She didn't need verbal confirmation from him. She could see it in the way the woman returned his intimately guarded stare, shifting her worried eyes over to Fallon. The woman looked surprised and nervous in the same hesitant expression.

Pushing off his chest, Fallon made a move to stand up and give Rafe the space she assumed he needed, when his hand clamped down on her thigh. She knew he would inevitably have to speak to the woman across from them who'd managed to suck the color from his face in the matter of seconds since she'd arrived. But relief coursed through her muscles when Rafe prevented her from getting up from his lap. Had she had a moment to process the unexpected reaction of her emotions, she'd have peeled herself from his hold and separated her body from his piercing touch. But she looked at him, his eyes once again capturing her in their depths, almost pleading with her.

This was the woman Rafe wanted to forget, the woman who broke his heart. And when their moment of reckoning came, Fallon would be there to distract his heart from her. As terrifying as it was, she was up to the task. She wanted to be there for him.

The ambience around them morphed and twisted. Everyone around the fire was now shifting their eyes, looking for the cause of the evident tension.

"Rafe," Fallon whispered so only he could hear. His eyes left the other woman and returned to hers. "You okay?"

"I don't know."

Fallon sucked in a breath at the way his voice had taken on a menacing volume and a broken rasp. His honesty tore at her even more. She wasn't supposed to care. Until now she'd been successful at keeping herself protected from caring . . . feeling.

She didn't want to care. But she did. And feeling his vulnerability, feeling the way his hands rubbed soothing circles on the inside of her thigh—trying to comfort *her* as *he* was falling apart—only chipped away another section of the emotional wall she'd built. And anger seeped out.

Fallon's eyes were drawn away from Rafe when the clank of the gate shutting echoed through the yard again.

"You've got to be kidding me," Fallon muttered. The second the words left her mouth Rafe's entire demeanor shifted.

"What?"

She nodded toward the man who'd just walked through the gate carrying a case of beer in his hands and a bottle of white wine in the other. "God, I didn't even put it together."

"All right, you're going to have to stop talking in shorthand and fill me in."

"Your friend from earlier today—Graham—he's friends with George and he knew Jade and you know Graham. I didn't even connect the dots."

"Again, not following, sweetheart."

"Dexter," she said spitting venom from her mouth as she narrowed her sights on the asshole. "That's Dexter."

He looked the same as she remembered him. Tall, lean,

sculpted body—pretty. Dressed in dark-wash jeans and an ivory sweater that clung to his arms and fell just below his waist. His ash blond hair was styled short, but the front swirled up in a faux-hawk. He was good-looking and had that air about him that told her he knew just how good-looking he truly was. He looked like the type of man a woman would brag to her parents about—but not the type of man that made your heart beat a little wildly. Point-blank, he looked like a well-groomed prick. And he was.

"And Jade is his . . . ?" Rafe asked as he started piecing the puzzle together himself.

"Yep."

Around that same time, bottle blond Claire bound from her chair and greeted "the woman" with a schoolgirl squeal and one of those rocking-back-and-forth hugs. If Fallon needed further motive not to like this woman, the fact that she was a squealer sealed the deal.

"Bridgette, I told you to call me when you got here!" Claire squealed again.

The big picture opened up and Fallon started to see the players in the game. No one else here knew about Bridgette, but Claire did—which meant they were friends. Fallon didn't know the why or the how, but it all made sense. Claire didn't like Fallon because she knew the secret about Bridgette and Rafe, and Fallon was walking on her territory.

"Sorry. I got in town a little early and met your boyfriend at your house—he was getting ready to head this way. We thought it'd be fun to surprise you."

"Okay, but did you think this was the best way to let

Rafe know you were here? You were supposed to wait," Claire whispered. It just so happened one of the perks of working in a loud burlesque club was that Fallon had become an expert at reading lips.

"I wanted to surprise him too. Why didn't you tell me he was here with someone?"

Claire stole a glance their way. "Because I didn't know. And because you were supposed to meet me later at my house."

Fallon readjusted on Rafe's lap, physically offering him a chance to talk to Bridgette and maybe settle some of the obvious tension. Fallon and Rafe seemed to be trapped in a suffocating bubble with Bridgette and Claire, as everyone else around them just stared in confusion.

"I don't run away from confrontation, Rafe. But if you want to talk to her—"

His fingers bit into the flesh of her hips, prisoning her body to his. "I want you right where you are, gorgeous." His voice dropped low, grazing her skin with his command, all the while veiling his undeniable plea as he moved his mouth to her shoulder.

That shouldn't have made her smile, but it did. Being needed, truly needed, for more than someone's vainglorious reason, spurred open something raw inside her. She could handle whatever shitstorm was silently brewing between Rafe and this Bridgette woman, but she wasn't confident in her ability to handle the sudden elation she felt from Rafe's confession. He wanted her with him right now, with so many conflicting emotions clearly tormenting him. And as vulnerable as that made him, it made her defenseless too, heedlessly exposed to him.

An uncharted electric current was crackling between them. She could feel her heart stutter unevenly against her chest while his eyes caressed hers with an unspoken profession that she didn't understand. But she was powerless to look away from him. She was aware of the isolated moment they were spelled under, and she was aware of the tangible tension penetrating from everyone around them, but Rafe didn't seem to care. He didn't seem to mind the attention he'd silently drawn to himself; as if Fallon was the only one of importance at that moment.

She tried to breathe as gracefully as possible, but it was useless. She was suffocating, confused by the desperation in Rafe's eyes. Confused because, even while she was incapable of looking away from him, she didn't want to.

His hand lifted slowly, as if she were a feral cat he was trying to capture, as if his movements would startle her. Brushing his thumb over her bottom lip, he smiled. That one dexterous touch melted her. Her body warmed from the inside out.

"I want *you*," he whispered, his voice dripping with a desirous hunger as his lips tenderly swept over her jaw. When he raised his head back to look at her, his velvet eyes swam with a heady lust that forced every nerve, every sense to sharpen and bind to him. "Okay?" She helplessly nodded. Whatever hypnotic force had just overcome her, she welcomed it. Rafe chuckled quietly, the vibrations seeping into her as he shook against her. "Good."

His words reassured her. The look in his eyes told her everything she didn't know she needed to hear.

The fire crackled and popped, she blinked, and the amorous moment between them receded.

"Fallon?" Dexter said, surprised to see her.

Her teeth ground together at the sound of his voice and she lifted her ireful eyes. "Dexter," she hissed.

Hearing Dexter and Fallon greet each other, Claire looked at them and frowned. "You know her, baby?" she asked, moving to Dexter's side and winding her arm around his waist in a hug.

Dexter's eyes shifted between them and he dipped his chin to his chest, but he didn't respond.

"Dex?" she asked again.

"Yeah . . . uh . . . I . . . um . . . uh . . . She works with Jade," he finally mumbled. Had Fallon not been so pissed off, she would have enjoyed his obvious discomfort a little more.

The sound that spilled from Claire's mouth met her ears like two metal forks rubbing together, causing her muscles to coil. "The stripper? So Fallon's a stripper too?" She smirked.

Her little attempt at an insult rolled completely over Fallon in one swift gust. If she thought she'd ruffle Fallon's feathers, she was sadly mistaken. Fallon didn't need, nor did she want, any sort of approval from that woman.

And if they were going to get down to the nitty-gritty, Fallon made more money than anyone at the cookout could even dream about. She co-owned the most elite club in

Denver and was co-owner of the club taking off in New York City. Insulted, no. Proud, definitely. And did her girls strip? Yes. Were they strippers? No. And did she see the necessity in spelling out the difference to the squealer? Hell no.

Rafe sucked the air around them in between his teeth, his fingers digging into her thighs, and her head snapped back to him. His eyes were piercing Dexter and his body had gone tense, as if ready to lunge. "Watch it, Claire," he warned.

"You're defending the stripper? How sweet of you."

Fallon felt the muscles of Rafe's body tense beneath her as he cut his eyes to Claire.

And it threw her.

Was he ashamed of her? Was he embarrassed by her?

"So let me get this straight. You took two sluts home from that shit bar last Friday, then took home this stripper Saturday? What's next, Rafe?"

Tension worked through Rafe and his body infinitesimally jerked forward. He was trying desperately, and nearly failing, to keep his temper in check. Unfortunately for Claire, Fallon didn't need to harbor the same restraint as Rafe, and she was more than happy to give her something to chew on.

Fallon lifted his hands from her thighs and hopped off his lap. "You crawled into bed with a man who was claimed by someone else," she said, surprisingly calm as she slowly stalked toward her until they were almost chest to surgically enhanced chest. "So does that make you any better than the two 'sluts' Rafe screwed? Or does that just make you a slut?"

Claire's blue eyes rolled to the back of her head. "Oh, please. Like Dex was ever serious with her. She's nothing but a pathetic, strung-out stripper."

Fallon had never hit anyone in her entire life. So when her palm rose behind her head and landed hard on the side of Claire's face, she gasped. It was an involuntary reaction. She hadn't planned on slapping her, but that didn't mean she regretted it either.

"You don't know the first thing about her," Fallon snapped as Claire stood wide-eyed and stunned with her head now leaning into Dexter's armpit for support.

"And you—" she barked, pointing her finger at Dexter. "You're a stupid asshole. If you even step one foot onto the sidewalk in front of my club, I'll have George on your ass before you can blink."

She whipped to the side. "And, Bridgette, is it?" Fallon said, continuing her little rant as she turned toward the small woman next to Claire. She was older than Fallon, but not by much. She couldn't be more than thirty. And she was beautiful in a simple way. Plain and natural and simple. An innocent kind of beautiful. But Fallon knew better than to believe that facade. "You don't deserve him. You didn't before and you sure as hell don't now."

"And I suppose you believe you deserve him?" Bridgette retorted. "You don't know a damn thing about what I deserve, little girl." Ahh, *there* was the fire she had to possess in order to cheat on her husband and string along another man without blinking an eye.

Fallon's hand still stung from the contact it'd made with

Claire's cheek and she balled it into a fist at her side. "I know you deserve to feel every ounce of heartbreak that you inflicted on the people who cared about you when you were too fucking selfish to care for them back. Yes, I know your dirty little secret. Rafe should have never touched you, but you're the one who's married. And I hope for his sake he breaks your heart right here and now."

She turned quickly and faced Stella, shock and worry and confusion flinching across her face. "I'm so sorry to make a scene at your home," she apologized. "It was good to meet you."

Stella winked. "You've got nothing to worry about. You come visit me anytime. I'm always up for a little entertainment."

Fallon returned her smile.

Rafe's protective hands skirted down her arms from behind; then he embedded a gentle kiss on the side of her neck. The calm his touch imbued her with slowed her breathing, only making her blood boil more. She tried to pull away from him but his hands tightened and he spun her around.

"Babe?"

Looking up at him, she focused on the spatter of moisture that had accumulated near his hairline and the tight pinch in his black eyebrows. She didn't look in his eyes. She knew if she did she wouldn't be able to look away. "Say what you need to say to her. Then take me back to my house." She yanked her arms from his hold and stormed off.

. . .

Rafe stood for a couple of heartbeats too long before understanding hit him like a fist to the gut and it registered that Fallon was pissed . . . at him. Women could be the most complicated creatures, but, goddammit, they were worth the crazy. Most of them.

Rafe's feet moved quickly after her but they froze midstep as Bridgette's hand shot out and grabbed his arm.

His eyes immediately shifted to her hand, to her touch that he had been fucking craving since he'd seen her last, two years ago. Then they lifted, and he saw in her eyes the same innocent, beautiful look that had branded him the first damn time he'd looked in them.

And he hesitated.

The woman who had filled the space of his mind and soothed the ache in his heart for the last few days was walking away from him. He'd done something. He hadn't figured it out yet, but whatever it was he would fix it.

But the woman who was holding on to him now stole his thoughts for a brief moment. A brief, hesitant moment he should have spent running after Fallon.

"Rafe, wait a minute!" she shouted as he jerked his arm away and stalked toward the gate. "Please!"

"What, Bridge?" Fuck, even his words were used to the familiarity of her. "What the hell could you possibly have to say to me?"

"I miss you," she said softly.

The words slammed against him, and for a second he thought the air was going to heave from his chest.

Then he turned on his heels and ran after Fallon.

Heavy footsteps followed her out the gate, but Fallon didn't turn around. She wasn't going to indulge in providing everyone with any more outbursts. She didn't expect Rafe to follow her either. She wanted him to stay and talk to Bridgette, and hopefully tell her to forget he existed. Because she didn't even deserve the memories. Fallon had experienced his tenderness, his passion. She'd felt his strength and crumbled at his control. She didn't have many memories, but she knew and understood just how much those memories could mean.

"Fallon, shit. Wait up!" Rafe bellowed, closing in behind her. She didn't stop until she reached the passenger side of his Jeep. "Why'd you run off?"

"Take it from me—if you have something to say to her, say it now. I felt the way you reacted to her, Rafe. She hurt you. Fucking tell her—or hell, go grovel at her cheap-boot-wearing feet and beg her to fall back into your bed. Just do it and get it over with so you can take me home."

"What the fuck?"

She laughed. "No, there will be no fucking. Either go talk to her or take me home."

A snarl rumbled in his chest and he jerked open the door and threw himself inside. Fallon got in and he thrust the Jeep into drive before the sound of her door clicked shut. She leaned her head against the back of the seat and shut her eyes, trying to ignore the fury of the man next to her. It couldn't have been more than ten minutes before she felt the Jeep roll to a stop. Rafe yanked the keys from the ignition and got out.

She blinked her eyes open and looked around. They were in a driveway in a small, older, quiet neighborhood. Groaning, she shoved her door open and followed Rafe to the front of the car. "What are you doing?" she nearly shouted.

"Cut the shit, Fallon. What the hell's the problem?"

His tone surprised her. She could feel his temper rising. His chest was heaving with frustrated, labored breaths and his muscular arm lifted to scrub his hand behind his head.

What was the point in dwelling on the fact that Rafe had gotten worked up like some territorial canine when Claire was spouting out her crap about Fallon being a stripper? It wasn't the first time she'd been called that and it sure as hell wouldn't be the last time. It didn't matter what name you put on it, it didn't change anything. She wasn't ashamed of it. But for the first time in a long time, she wanted someone's acceptance. She wanted *his* acceptance. She didn't know whether he could give it to her or not, but the simple fact of the matter was, she wanted it. And that realization meant he was no longer arm's length away. She'd let him get too close, gave him the power to make her care—gave him the power to let her down, to break her. And she was about to remedy that situation.

"The problem is this." She flailed her arms out, gesturing between them. "I'm good at distractions. It's what I do. It's what being a 'stripper' is all about. But this? Meeting the friends and cuddling on your lap, telling off your ex? I don't want this! It's not me. It's not who I am."

With one stride, he slammed his body to hers, pushing her against the hood of the Jeep, gripping her face between his hands, and forcing her to meet his eyes. "You feel that, babe?" he growled. "You feel the way your heart just crashed into your chest when you felt my body against you? Don't tell me you don't fucking want this! You can't tell me my hands on your body don't make you feel!"

No, she couldn't tell him that. And that was the problem.

He dropped his hands and ran them down the sides of her neck until his thumbs softly touched her collarbone. He looked at her lips and her teeth sank into the bottom corner of her mouth. He groaned, then lifted his eyes to hers. They had softened, and the anger she expected to see in them was absent. His voice dropped and trembled through her body all the way to her toes.

"Because I can feel every muscle in your body soften when I touch you," he said slowly, deliberately. "I can feel your breath elongate and deepen. I can see need fill your eyes when you look at me. So please, gorgeous, tell me if I'm wrong, but this *is* you. Right here, right now. When I touch you, I'm touching *you*," he whispered, skimming his fingertips down her arms, then around her back, pressing her strongly against him.

Her head tipped back when she felt him hard and ready

against her stomach. Then he lowered his head to her throat and flicked the flat of his tongue against her skin before gently sucking. And her body betrayed her once again, shivering against him.

"When I taste you, I'm tasting *you*. I'm not chasing some fucking distraction. This"—he moved his lips to hers—"*is* you. And goddammit, Fallon, I want *you*."

She wanted to weep. She wanted to scream.

Then he kissed her.

And she crumbled.

It wasn't just a kiss. It was hungry and powerful and consuming. His lips crushed hers and moved strongly and quickly above them. She couldn't get enough. Her lips matched the fervent rhythm he set as his tongue explored her, tasted her, claimed her. Her hands lifted and her fingers coiled into his shirt, fisting the thin material in her hands as she tried to pull him even closer to her. But it wasn't close enough. At that moment, nothing would ever be close enough.

A carnal growl reverberated through him and his fingers bit into her ass, lifting her as he continued to steal the breath from her lungs. Wrapping her legs around him, his cock settled between her thighs and the pure anticipation of feeling him warm and hard against her bare sex made her cry out.

Her back rolled on top of the hood of his Jeep as he leaned her down, his hands moving to her stomach, up her sweater, and finding her breasts. His fingers roughly teased her nipples and they grew taut and sensitive beneath his touch as he continued to ravage her mouth with his perfectly damaged lips. Yes, she needed this. His touch, his intensity.

Arching her back, she squeezed him with her thighs and he responded to her eagerness by grinding his hips forward, rolling him against her, the friction of her jeans provoking her to strip them from her body so his hands could touch her.

More. She needed more.

His mouth left hers and moved to her neck, searing hot, intoxicating kisses over every inch of skin on her neckline that was visible to him.

"Tell me," he rasped, reaching behind him and peeling her hands from where they were clawing at his back, trying desperately to get more of him. He pinned her hands above her head on the hood and dragged his bottom lip up the center of her throat. "Tell me what you feel when I touch you," he said, his teeth tugging gently on her chin.

Scared.

He pressed his hips into her and she moaned quietly. "Tell me," he whispered across her lips, lightly brushing them to hers. "I want to know what you feel when I touch you," he whispered across her skin.

And she needed this too . . . his tenderness.

She willed her confidence to form her words. "Scared," she admitted, her voice just barely above a whisper.

He stilled and released her hands. With his mouth still hovering over her neck, his warm breath bathed her as he spoke slowly and evenly. "I scare you," he repeated. It wasn't a question, but she nodded nonetheless.

When he started to pull away, she wound her arms around his shoulders and brought him back down to her, tightening her thighs above his waist. "When you touch me," she started, searching for his eyes in the darkness, trying to read the black ink in them, "I'm scared of the way it makes me feel . . . just *feel*.

"Your touch makes me *feel*, Rafe."

The power in his stare shifted to her and he relaxed above her as his head dropped to her shoulder. "Fuck, babe. What have you done to me?" he mumbled into the curve of her shoulder. Then he caught her lips with his own before she could ask him the very same question.

*R*afe stared through the dark at the ceiling of his bedroom listening to Fallon softly snoring, her head nestled in the crook of his shoulder as he stroked her hair. Her eyes were fluttering rapidly beneath her lids and she whimpered softly in her sleep.

Pulling her naked body in tightly along his, he kissed her forehead and closed his eyes.

Then he fucking saw Bridgette. Her soft, dark hair pulled away from her face, her big round eyes, those goddamn lips. And he saw the hurt that had molded into her expression when she saw Fallon tucked tightly on his lap.

Fallon was right. He should have said something to her. But what would he have said? Seeing her dragged up every emotion he had attempted to drink and fuck away. And there they were, front and center in his line of vision when he closed his eyes.

He blinked them open and looked at the woman in his arms. Her kiss-swollen, heart-shaped lips were parted slightly, her warm, sweet breath spreading over his chest as she exhaled, her leg flung over top of his, and her arm draped across his stomach. She sighed contentedly in her sleep, and Bridgette disappeared.

He already knew he was looking at a woman worth staying in bed all day for. A woman who easily could—and quite possibly had—become more than just a good distraction. A woman who could fuck him up something bad.

CHAPTER SEVENTEEN

*F*allon was sitting in her office filing—or, actually, attempting to file—some of her disorganized paperwork that seemed to accumulate at warp speed. Procrastinating was not one of her finer attributes. She needed to put in the liquor order Simone had given her, but also needed to go home and pack. She was flying to New York City at an extremely unfortunate time the next morning, which meant she actually needed to crawl into bed before three a.m.

She'd been so busy getting everything worked out before she left, between juggling things for the club and finishing up the chair routine so the girls could practice it while she was gone, that she barely had enough time to choreograph an audition number for the New York City girls.

Camille had already cut eighty women down to a whopping thirty-two, and after the group audition number Fallon was teaching them this weekend, hopefully they could get it narrowed down to fourteen. The club was opening in only a few short months, which meant that Fallon needed to help her hire not only dancers, but also a new choreographer. Camille was a stunning dancer, but she didn't have the vision for choreography.

Knock-knock.

Fallon set the liquor order paperwork down on her desk and swiveled her chair toward the door as Jade stepped inside.

"Well, don't you look fancy," Fallon praised, looking at Jade's curve-hugging black dress and stunning aqua stilettos. "Where are you heading off to?"

Fallon had given Jade the week off to just wallow. Eat ice cream and chocolate and indulge in *Sex and the City* reruns. She needed to mope in usual female breakup fashion. They both knew that Jade needed new methods of coping, and Fallon happily gave her the week to figure it out. But come next Tuesday, her skinny butt would be back in the lineup. Jade was too good a dancer to keep her out.

Fallon never told Jade about the run-in with the evil bitch Claire. She should have; she knew that. But she couldn't see the point in hurting Jade for no apparent reason. There was nothing beneficial to her knowing. She knew Dex was a cheating piece of shit, and the details about how horrible the woman was he cheated on her with were irrelevant.

"Graham is driving down. We're gonna go eat and maybe have a drink or two."

"Graham?"

"He's been a really good friend." She fidgeted with her

hands and looked down at her shoes. "Anyway, just wanted to tell you bye. Have a safe flight."

"Thanks." Fallon's phone vibrated on her desk as the heavy metal door shut behind Jade.

Hey gorgeous

Hey sergeant

Can I see you?

She smiled. That was quick and to the point.

Sorry. I'll be out of town this weekend.

Damn, I forgot. NYC right?

You're telling me. I hate to fly. HATE it. And yes, NYC. My flight leaves at seven a.m.

Noticing that she was staring at the screen on her phone, waiting for a tiny little message box to pop up, she quickly shoved her phone into her purse and stood. Since when did Fallon turn into *that* woman? She'd never been that woman. The one to get excited over text message conversations.

She hadn't seen Rafe since he'd dropped her back off at

her house Monday morning after the cookout, and she missed him. It was an unfamiliar and uncomfortable truth, but she missed him. After admitting to him, and to herself, that she was scared of the way he made her feel, she couldn't stop feeling. Excitement, disappointment, fear, lust, longing . . . she felt them all.

But it was still so new, and so overwhelming. Other than a bunch of text messages, they hadn't talked. She refused to admit that she was disappointed by the lack of conversation. But realizing that she was refusing to admit it was almost the same as admitting it. So she'd accepted it: she was disappointed.

Twice. She'd participated in sleepovers twice now. Both times with Rafe. Both times amazing. Mornings and Fallon usually weren't on the best of terms. She didn't particularly care for them, and they surely didn't care for her. But mornings with Rafe—that was an entirely different category.

She enjoyed watching him stretch when he first woke up. He'd make a small grunting noise, deep and raspy, as he raised his arms above his pillow and rolled onto his back. And his hard body in the mornings, warm and inviting as he would untangle the covers from around her and pull her against him—perfect. She'd never imagined enjoying those small things. But then again, she'd never experienced those small things.

Mornings. There was definitely something to be said about them when they included Rafe.

Looking at the clock on the wall, Fallon slipped her feet back into her purple Prada pumps. It was one thirty. She would just call in the liquor order tomorrow when she got to Camille's. Tomorrow morning was approaching entirely too fast, and without a certain someone to wake up to, she predicted her early morning would be as unbearably unpleasant as they usually were.

With his army duffel flung over his shoulder, Rafe wandered into the B terminal after clearing security. Fallon was sitting in one of the hard blue plastic chairs nearby. A cheesy-ass smile took over his face. Her hair was a mess, twisted on top of her head in some sort of ball, and stray waves had fallen loose around that delicate nape of hers he enjoyed pressing his lips to.

Her body was covered in a long gray dress, her arms tucked in a thin white cardigan. Her knees were pulled against her chest, her feet propped up on the edge of her chair. She looked young, sweet. Which she was. But she looked nothing like the woman he was used to seeing. She seemed tired and nervous. Fragile.

"Hey, gorgeous," he said as he approached.

She lifted her head from her knees and blinked up at him in surprise. "Rafe, what are you doing here?"

Ah, hell. The amazed expression that flashed across her face turned him into a weak fucking man. And there was something else etched in her faint smile, smoothing her eyes—relief. God, what he'd do to see that look cross her face every time she saw him. She was happy, grateful . . . . Beautiful.

"You hate flying." He shrugged.

He wanted to laugh when her champagne eyes squinted in confusion and she pursed her lips. It had been almost a week since he'd seen her, and now that he had, he was finding it difficult keeping himself from leaning down to catch her lips with his and kiss her. And before long, he would.

She gauged his response, watching him, her head tilting to the side like a curious puppy. "Yeah? So?" she finally said.

Dropping his duffel to the ground, he sat down next to her. "So here I am. My family lives in Philly, so I thought I'd fly to the city with you for moral support and then go visit my dad again."

This trip was all about her. She was the only reason he'd paid an unfathomable amount of money for a ticket last night. But he was also hoping he could get ahold of Leo's ass. He was worried about him.

"You bought a plane ticket to New York City just so I didn't have to fly alone?" Her eyes grew wide in surprise. Was it really that hard to believe? Goddamn, he'd do a hell of a lot more for her than buy a fucking plane ticket.

"Yeah, babe. I did."

Lowering her feet from the seat, she crossed her legs toward him—in a challenge, almost. Apparently it *was* that hard to believe. "Why?"

"Because," he said, pushing a strand of hair away from her face. "There's a part of me that couldn't fuckin' stand the idea of you being afraid and me not being there. Crazy, I know." He brushed his thumb across her bottom lip briefly, then dropped his hand. "So I'm here."

Her smile lifted slowly, her evident appreciation wrinkling around her eyes as it grew wide until she was nothing but teeth. "I don't know whether to hug you or file a restraining order."

He laughed, lifting his arm around her shoulders and pulling her against his side. "Can't say I blame you there."

Her body relaxed into him, and she sighed as she lowered her head into the crook of his shoulder and burrowed in. "Thanks, Rafe," she said softly, sleepily.

"Anytime, gorgeous. Anytime."

"You're awful fidgety, babe," he said, his eyes shut, his head resting against the back of the seat.

She grinned as she looked at him. Sitting there with his eyes closed and a faint, amused smile lifting his lips, he exemplified everything a man should be. Strong, sexy, safe. And staying true to the way this man contradicted every way she felt about him, he was intimidating. The way his square, stubbled jaw absentmindedly flexed, the way his powerful arms crossed in front of him, and the way his legs were parted open—it was intimidating. He didn't look like an approachable man, a man someone would want to disturb. But in the same glance, he looked like comfort. His broad shoulders, his thick thighs, his beautiful mouth. The need to crawl onto his lap and feel his arms secured around her pulsed. But she wasn't there yet. She wanted to be, but he'd stripped her bare, made her vulnerable, and she couldn't.

The way he'd held her and caressed her at Stella's house was the most affection she'd ever experienced. It was different from the way he touched her while their bodies slid naked against each other. It was tender, thoughtful. Claiming.

She needed it.

And she wanted it. Right now. She wanted to lift his arm and cradle into him.

But she couldn't, she didn't quite know how to get there yet.

They'd been in the air for maybe thirty minutes, and having Rafe with her actually helped. Was she still shocked by his sudden decision to buy a plane ticket and fly to New York City with her—just for her? Yes.

It was hard for her to wrap her head around the idea of someone being there for her. Someone being there for her in a way different from Jade, or George, or anyone at the club. Because they would—she knew that. But Rafe's intentions were different. Whatever was starting to grow between them was undeniably different.

Rafe put her first. She'd never been first.

Folding her legs up onto the seat, she pulled her dress over her bare toes, her elbow bumping into Rafe's arm. His eyes opened and he shifted them to the side to look at her. "Sorry. I'm cold," she explained when he continued to smile at her squirming around. "I knew to bring a blanket but I forgot and they never have enough of those flimsy little blankets they hand out." She pulled her thin white cardigan closed, wrapping it around her torso tightly.

Rafe's hand shot out as one of the flight attendants walked by, stopping him. "Sir, could we have a blanket, please?"

The man barely acknowledged him. "Sorry, we're out."

"I would appreciate it if you'd check, please." His voice had lowered with evident demand and the flight attendant finally looked at him.

"We're out, sir."

Rafe's signs of an approaching temper were becoming more and more readable every time she was around him. His hard body contorted from relaxed to tense, his posture leaning forward in his seat. "Maybe you're not understanding me. My girl's cold. I know for a fact that you've got a storage compartment in first class where you keep a stash of extra blankets and those scratchy-ass pillows. Now I'd appreciate it if you'd go check," he said, teeth clenched. He wasn't giving the man an option.

He nodded. "I'll check, sir."

"How do you know they keep extra blankets?" Fallon asked once the man had made his way down the narrow aisle.

"Some old man gave up his first-class seat for me on my way home for R&R on my last deployment. I saw the flight attendants go in and out of that storage compartment twenty damn times getting extra blankets for people. They've got 'em. This douche bag is just being lazy."

In a surprisingly timely manner, the attendant was back in front of them—handing Rafe a blanket.

"Thanks," Rafe snapped, glaring at the attendant, who only turned and walked away. Unfolding the tiny square, he draped it over Fallon, tucking it behind her shoulders to keep it from falling down.

"Better?"

"Much."

Turbulence rocked the plane, the seats vibrating beneath her. It was over as suddenly as it came, but Fallon's heart had already lodged into the pit of her stomach. She'd absentmindedly latched onto his thigh, digging her fingernails into the denim of his worn jeans. He chuckled and shook his head, but she didn't care. "No laughing. I hate flying, remember?"

"Babe, you don't need a reason to hold on to me. You can hold on to me anytime you need to."

Sable eyes softened, smoldered, morphing with a gentleness, a sincerity that stole her breath. His gaze never broke, never waned, as his long fingers threaded through her hair, curling around her nape. She needed to look away, but she couldn't—she didn't want to, but Rafe didn't let her either. He carefully pinioned her head in place, stealing her eyes, forcing her gaze to remain on him. It was unbearably raw, in the middle of an airplane, hovering thousands of feet above the earth. Intimacy swirled hot and heady around them.

Eyes honing, he leaned in slowly. She braced for his gentle assault, nearly begging for it, but he paused. Fingers bit into her nape, and he shifted her head back. He nuzzled her, his nose burrowing below her chin—and she froze, needing to lift her hands, to cling to him, to clutch him against her. But her limbs had liquefied, turned to mush from the pressure of his lips along her neck.

"This is fuckin' insane, babe. God, I know it is." His teeth nibbled her chin, then her bottom lip, before he lowered her head back down to look at her. "But I'm here. You, me—I don't know what the hell this is. But I'm here. You need me, you name it, I'm here. You know that, right?"

She nodded helplessly, unsure what she was agreeing to. She'd lost all semblance of coherent thinking. What was he offering her? Himself?

She opened her mouth to speak, but his lips descended upon hers, desperate and hot. Teeth hit teeth, tongues fought for control, lips crushed painfully.

On an airplane, gliding through clouds, she experienced the most earth-shattering kiss of her existence. She broke a little. She didn't understand it, the heavy shift in her chest—she just knew it was Rafe. It was him finding his way in.

Breaking their kiss, Rafe pulled away. He smiled, his lips glistening with the passion their kiss consumed. Lifting his arm, she fell easily into the crook of his shoulder and he sheathed around her as she tucked in tight.

She sighed.

He laughed.

"Go to sleep, gorgeous."

"Rafe?"

"Yeah, babe."

"Thanks for being ridiculous and buying a plane ticket so I didn't have to fly alone. No one's ever been thoughtful like that toward me before. No one's ever taken it upon themselves to make sure I felt safe." She tilted her chin up again and looked into those damn quicksand eyes. "But I always feel safe when I'm with you. So thanks."

He didn't respond. He just smiled and leaned his head back against the seat again and she curled into him as much as the narrow seats would allow.

Mornings with Rafe were definitely better.

CHAPTER EIGHTEEN

alking outside of the baggage claim at LaGuardia Airport, following behind Fallon, who was pulling an excessively large suitcase for only a weekend trip, Rafe forgetfully reached into his jeans pockets only to realize he didn't have any cigarettes on him.

Dammit.

"Your friend is picking you up?" he asked.

"Yeah, she texted me a few minutes ago and said she was almost here."

Rafe noticed Marco's SUV slowly making its way to them. People were crowding everywhere, waiting in line for cabs and buses, so he lifted his arm to signal where he was.

"That's my brother," he told her when Marco pulled up.

Marco met Rafe at the back of the car. Giving him a quick hug and patting him on the back, Rafe threw his duffel in the back. "Marco, this is Fallon. Fallon, my little brother Marco."

Fallon stepped forward, her feet covered in a pair of flat sandals, which was the first time he'd seen her in a pair of shoes that didn't have a lethally high heel on them. She looked even shorter next to Marco's tall frame when he stepped onto the curb to greet her. "Nice to meet you, Fallon."

"Likewise," she said formally, then, still holding his hand in hers, she cocked up a brow. "Are you the little brother who bakes?"

Marco laughed and shook his head. "Women. They only care about me for my cake-making abilities."

Rafe shook his head, knowing damn well Marco used his "cake-making abilities" to his advantage to impress women. Seriously, what the hell was it about a man who could bake a damn cupcake?

Fallon dropped his hand and joined in on his laughter. "I'm sure women care about more than just your cake-making abilities."

Marco smirked. "Thank you, Fallon. I'd like to think my abilities go way above and beyond making cakes." His eyebrows danced. Fuckin' flirt. But Fallon wasn't taking his bait.

"I agree. There are breads, and pies, and cookies. You have a lot of desirable options."

Rafe laughed. This woman just stuck it to his brother.

A heat that Rafe was sure he'd never seen on his brother before fanned across his cheeks. "This little lady's got jokes, huh?" He laughed. "You comin' to Sunday dinner? Dad would get a kick outta you. And I'm sure Tilly would appreciate another female in the house."

"Tilly?"

"Our sister-in-law," Rafe answered. "Yeah, babe. Why don't you come?"

"Oh, no. Thank you, though."

Marco smirked, and Rafe knew he was about to get his way. Marco usually did. "No, little lady. I wasn't actually giving you an option. You see, Rafe here hasn't brought a woman home since that chick he snuck into the house, stoned outta his mind, after his junior prom. So Rafe's due to bring a pretty new face to dinner. And Tilly is making Mom's salmon ravioli. It's fantastic. And I'm baking a chocolate cake with orange buttercream and ganache. What do ya say?"

Something about the way Fallon's smile flitted sweetly across her face melted away his controlled demeanor. It sliced a possessive urge through him, one that made him want to grab her hand, pull her against him, and kiss her until neither one of them could breathe. She was beautiful, and she'd given him a small glimpse in that sweet smile of hers to a Fallon he wanted to see more of. She was always so poised, so polished, but that smile she'd just had was light-hearted and easy. Carefree.

"I'd say you had me at chocolate cake," she said.

Marco clapped his hands together in a loud, approving slap, then reached over and gripped Rafe's shoulder. "It's always the cake, big brother. I'm telling ya, the cake gets 'em every time."

An expensive-as-hell sleek blue Jaguar convertible pulled up in front of them.

"Damn," Rafe muttered, appreciating the muscled beauty that had just parked along the curb.

A long-legged redhead stepped gracefully from the driver's side. She was in a pair of shoes Rafe was sure were unsafe for operating a moving vehicle and wearing a long-sleeved dress that hit just above her knees and was tied with a belt below her tits. Tits that, might he add, were nicely accentuated by the slightly low neckline. He knew before she spoke that she was Camille. She was as sophisticated and beautiful as Fallon had made her seem, but she didn't even come close to comparing to Fallon.

"Hi, sweets," Camille said, pulling Fallon into a hug. "Who are these handsome men?"

Smiling, Fallon lifted her hand in introduction. "Cam, this is Rafe and this"—she gestured to Marco—"is Rafe's brother Marco. He just managed to talk me into Sunday dinner by bribing me with cake."

Camille laughed. "Smart man right there."

"There'll be plenty. Why don't you come with her?" Marco suggested, his eyes admiring her discreetly.

"Oh no—I've got thirty-two girls to pick from, a bartender and four cocktail waitresses to train, and routines to learn. Sorry, baby. I wish I could, but I don't have time."

Fallon wheeled her luggage to Camille's car and Rafe helped her load it. "So send me Camille's address and I will come pick you up Sunday morning," he said, brushing away a stray tuft of hair that kept falling down in front of her eyes.

"That's okay. I'll borrow one of Cam's cars and come to

you. That'll save Marco from having to bring you back to the airport on Monday anyway."

Gripping her waist, he pulled her against him, loving the way she sucked in a breath when her body softly collided with his. "As long as I get a chance to get you alone," he murmured. Her body leaned into him as his hand pressed against her lower back, liquefying under his touch. It was going to be damn near unbearable to wait till Sunday to get her beneath him.

*F*ollowing behind Camille, Fallon stepped out of the elevator and into her lavish apartment. It was perched high atop a co-op building across from Central Park. Fallon wouldn't have expected anything other than elaborate from Cam. Not a single frame was out of place, not a single cup was littering the countertops, not a single article of clothing was draped across a piece of furniture. It was breathtakingly beautiful with its clean lines and marble counters, parquet floors, and stunning accent lighting. But it didn't feel like a home. It didn't feel lived in. Actually, it didn't even look lived in.

Fallon's attention was fixed on the lushly planted wraparound terrace that connected to a glass solarium. The view of Central Park and the reservoir backdropped by the city skyline was extraordinary. Opening the glass door to the solarium, Fallon stepped inside and made her way to the terrace.

She turned around when she heard the familiar click of Cam's heels on the concrete. "Here you go, sweets," she said, handing Fallon a glass of Diet Coke complete with cherries. "And I believe I've waited long enough for you to volunteer information on your sexy piece of man."

Rolling her eyes, Fallon took a sip. "He's not mine, Cam," she said.

Laughing, Cam took a seat on the lounge chair against the wall. "He could be, baby. I saw the way he looked at you. And you looked at him the same way. What happened to arm's length?"

She shrugged. "Arm's length wasn't far enough. I don't know, Cam." And she didn't. She'd never experienced anything like him before.

Cam's thick copper eyebrows darted upward. "Are you seeing him?"

"If by seeing him you mean sleeping with him, yes," Fallon answered, sitting down in the chair next to her.

"What about your rules? I didn't think trips to the city and family visits would apply," she egged on, knowing good and well the extent Fallon went to in order to keep her rules, and also knowing good and well that she had already broken them.

That little prying thing that Fallon and Jade had an unspoken understanding about? Well, Camille didn't play by unspoken guidelines, and she usually didn't play by spoken ones either. And when it came to Fallon, Camille's favorite pastime was meddling.

"None of my rules apply to him," she snapped, frustrated at Camille for bringing up everything Fallon already knew. She knew Rafe had found a way to slip through the cracks, causing her to break her well-constructed rules—and it worried her. "He's found a way to break them, Cam. He slept over, took me to a cookout, and somehow managed to get me to spend the night in his bed."

A pleased grin curled on Camille's red lips. "Good. You needed someone to break your damn rules. I never liked your rule book anyway. You need a little fun and attention from a man."

"Since when have you known me to need anything from anyone?" she challenged.

Camille leaned forward in her seat and sharpened her eyes on Fallon. "That's exactly the problem, Fallon. Everyone needs something—someone. It's time you let yourself love. Or hell, at least let yourself want. You need this. And it's time you let someone need *you*."

Let someone need her? She'd need to let someone in, completely in. Not just within arm's length. She'd have to break down the remaining walls that were still holding her together. And she just couldn't do that.

"So what time are auditions?" she asked, changing the subject. But Camille was used to her antics.

Cam shook her head in mock defeat and rolled her eyes. It looked like Fallon was off the hook, at least for now. The one thing she had playing in her favor was that, like Fallon, Camille didn't mess around when it came to the clubs. "Auditions start this afternoon at three. You'll teach the girls the group number; then they'll audition it as a whole tomorrow morning. Then your talented butt is going to hire my choreographer. I've got three lined up for auditions tomorrow after the girls perform their solo routines for you."

"You're making them do their solo numbers again?" she asked.

"Yep. I want your opinion. These girls here are no joke, sweets. They remind me a lot of you. They're talented. We can take Velour to a whole new level here." She beamed. Her excitement was tangible and Fallon couldn't help but reciprocate it.

Standing up, Camille made her way to the solarium. "Come on, sweets. Go get ready for auditions and we'll grab lunch before we go to the club."

Typical Cam, always on the go. That woman didn't stop or slow down for anyone. More than likely the reason her apartment looked like a showroom instead of a home.

"And, Fallon," she said, her steps halting as she spun back around to face her. "We've both become experts on the way a man looks when he wants something. But Rafe, baby—that man didn't just look at you like he wanted you right then and there in the middle of the road in every delicious way a man could want a woman. He looked at you like he needed you. In the way a woman wants to be needed. In the way a woman deserves to be needed. And, baby, I'd say that man is exactly what *you* need."

CHAPTER NINETEEN

Stubbing out the cherry of his cigarette in the ashtray on the small wicker table, Rafe leaned back in the old wooden rocking chair on the front porch and crossed his ankle over his knee. He'd finally talked to Leo that morning, and the guy sounded rough. Rafe didn't know what was going on with him, and he was pretty positive that Leo wouldn't tell him either. And that shit didn't sit well with him.

"Hey, kid," his dad said, pushing through the screen door.

Lifting his head, he nodded. "Hey, old man."

He handed Rafe a beer. "You waiting on that woman of yours?" He grunted as he sat down in the rocking chair on the other side of the wicker table and pulled a Marlboro Red from the front pocket of his T-shirt.

"Eh, I'm just thinking."

"Not a whole lotta good thinking does for a man, Rafael."

He inhaled a fortifying breath and blew it out. His dad

was right. Unless Leo wanted to talk to him about whatever the fuck was going on, there was nothing Rafe could do. His brother was a grown man. And thinking about what he could or couldn't do to help him wouldn't do him any good.

"You're a wise man when you want to be, Pop."

His dad took a long drag from his cigarette, the cherry quickly burning the paper closer to his fingers. "I'm a wise man all the time—you shits just have selective hearing."

Laughing, Rafe nodded in agreement.

"So you gonna tell me about this woman you and your brother bribed into coming here?"

"What do you want to know? Because I don't know a whole lot," he admitted. Of course, that wasn't completely true. He knew the way her body looked astride him, the way her mouth tasted, and the breathy sounds she made when his face was between her thighs. He also knew that whatever was between them was heavy; it was insane, and fast, and uncontrollably real.

It didn't take him long to realize he was a goner; he knew the first morning he woke up next to her. He just hadn't realized how far and how fast he'd go when it came to her. His dad sat there for a second, inhaling another long drag and slowly blowing it out before he finally answered. "She pretty?"

Rafe laughed. Of all the things his dad could possibly ask, he wanted to know whether she was pretty. *Perverted old man.* "Yeah, Dad. She's fucking beautiful."

"Can she cook?"

"She cooks," he said, thinking back to the grilled cheese

she'd made herself the first morning he spent with her. Whether she could cook a real meal or not he didn't know.

"She let you hold her while everyone's lookin'?"

He thought for a moment, back to when he'd pulled her onto his lap when they'd arrived at the cookout. Her body was stiff and he could tell she was uncomfortable. But soon she'd relaxed and curled up against him, holding on tight even when his old wounds were being splintered open by another woman.

And the way she clung to him on the plane today . . . .

"Yeah, Pop. She lets me hold her while everyone's lookin'."

"Those are probably the three most important things you can find in a woman."

His dad's logic was usually questionable—he was a romantic. "How ya figure?"

"Every man needs to eat. And there ain't nothing better than a woman who can cook."

Rafe shook his head. He could think of a few things that were better than a woman who could cook . . . Like a woman who moaned his name while she bit into his shoulder . . . yeah, that was better. And a whole lot sweeter.

"And she ain't gotta be pretty, son, but it sure doesn't hurt. But if she lets you hold her while everyone's watchin', you know she'll love you even when everyone's gone."

"Yeah? How you figure?"

"There are women, women like your momma, who give their heart freely. She loved in those small moments when everyone was gone, when it was just the two of us. And she loved for everyone to see. But then there are women who guard their heart, women like Tilly. They make a man fight for it, want to make sure he deserves it, can keep it safe. Those women hide their love, protect it themselves. But if she lets you hold her for everyone to see, she's giving you the chance to earn her love, to protect her heart. You get that, son, she'll love you in those small moments." He paused, nodding at Rafe, then continued, "You find a woman who'll let you hold her when *you* need her, and you've struck gold."

"Ways of a woman, huh, Pop?"

"Damn right. But you listen here." He lowered his head and lifted his brows to drive home the importance. "You make sure you hold her when she needs you to. Don't let that moment come when your arms aren't around her when she needs them."

Rafe nodded and remained silent as he watched his dad's eyes go distant, just as they always did when he was about to talk about his wife.

"You know this already, son. But as hard as it was for me to wake up that morning to your mother"—he paused, clearing his throat from his swelling heartache—"to see her life gone, I knew I was there when she needed me, even if I didn't realize she did. I was holding my sweetheart. I was holding her in my arms."

Rafe missed her, always missed her, but it was in these moments when he watched her essence live on in his father's memory, when he witnessed his father's permanent sorrow living without the love of his life—that's when he missed her the most.

Rafe looked at his dad and waited for him to return from his memory before he said, simply, "I know."

His dad leaned back into his chair, causing it to rock unsteadily, and took a drink from his beer.

"Hey, boys."

Rafe and his dad both looked up at Tilly, who was standing at the door holding a mug of hot tea.

"Hey, Till." Rafe smiled.

Tilly waddled to Rafe's dad and sat down on his lap. "You know who the Giants play today, right?"

"Ah, Till. Please tell me you're not still cheering on those cheese-head Packers." Rafe groaned.

"Yep! And all my boys will be here to watch me cheer them on and watch the Packers kick some Giant ass!" she exclaimed way too enthusiastically.

"Watch it—you get too excited, you'll be having my nephew tonight."

She rolled her eyes at him. "All right," she said, slapping Pop's knee, using it as leverage to heave herself up from his lap. "I'm gonna go see if Marco is done making that cake. You boys need anything?"

"No, sweetheart. And you take it easy in there. Don't be standing on those feet too long."

"I'm fine, Pop," she assured, kissing him on the top of his head of thick gray hair, then nodded toward the street. "That must be Fallon."

Whipping his head to the driveway, Rafe watched as Fallon pulled the blue Jaguar into the driveway.

"Come on, Pop. I'll sneak you some salmon if you keep

me company while I cook," Tilly said, holding the screen door to the house open.

Pop stood up. "Lead the way, darlin'."

*F*allon turned the ignition off and glanced at herself in the rearview mirror. Tired eyes stared back at her, and her hair had lost some of its volume from when she'd blown it out smooth and full that morning. Gently she bit her bottom lip in hopes of adding a little color to them. She'd fluff her hair, pinch her cheeks, and smack on some lipstick, but she could feel Rafe watching her from the porch.

Normally she wouldn't feel so self-conscious. But she wasn't just seeing Rafe again.

She was meeting his *family*.

Her mouth went dry at the sudden realization and nausea crept into her stomach. She'd known him only a couple of weeks and could count on her fingers the number of days she'd spent with him.

This was fast—too fast. Plus, she wasn't good with families—it wasn't exactly as if hers had been an ideal model.

Sucking air into her lungs, she pulled her shoulders back and looked at Rafe, his eyes glued to hers. She couldn't turn back now.

Heat blazed low, fast, hard. The need to be with him fluttered along her skin. When it came to Rafe, her body never gave her a choice.

Opening the car door, she stepped out and looked up at

Rafe, who was leaning against the short wooden railing that lined the porch. From what she understood, Rafe had all brothers and one sister-in-law. Men she could handle. It was the sister-in-law that she was slightly concerned about. The only woman in a family full of men was bound to give another woman hell.

She smiled at him and he returned that lopsided, perfectly unperfect grin that made her do that whole swoon thing again.

He was in a T-shirt and jeans, his tattooed arms hanging loosely at his sides, hands shoved in his pockets. The jeans were worn and tattered, as if he'd owned them forever, thinned out and softened from years of use. His feet were crossed at the ankles and he just stood there against the rail watching her, taking in the sight of her just as she was him.

"Hey, gorgeous," he said as she finally climbed the few steps to meet him on the porch.

"Hey."

"I take it you found the house okay?" he asked, straightening himself from the railing.

"GPS is a wonderful invention."

His hand reached out, wrapped around her nape, and before she knew it he had pulled her into his arms. His scent smothered her, encased her. It was delicious, smelled so good. Like Rafe. Like nicotine and an earthy soap. A spicy, heady aroma just barely noticeable on his skin.

She leaned her face into his shoulder and inhaled, breathing him into her lungs, then lifted her head and kissed the side of his neck. The way her lips pressed along his warm skin startled her for a moment. Her body, her lips, her hands were moving of their own volition, leaving her mind and her defenses to play catch-up.

His fingers clasped around her chin and he pulled her face up to look at him, dipping his head down to hers. "I'm glad you're here." His breath bathed her, fusing the intoxicating warmth of his mouth with the comforting scent of his skin.

She hummed in satisfaction. "Me too."

And he smiled. It was genuine. Not one of those he used to use when attempting to weaken her resolve. She'd realized he'd figured out that little trick by the second day she'd spent with him.

But the smile on his face now was rewarding, because she knew she'd put it there.

She was waiting for it, anticipating it, but even then, when his lips finally closed the small space between them, she sighed. His mouth moved tenderly, softly, sensually. He hadn't kissed her this way before. Almost careful, and it was over way too quickly.

"Come on, babe," he said, running his hands up and down her arms, adding heat to her chilled body. "Let me introduce you to everyone."

"Okay," she replied, and his hand coasted around to its secured spot on the small of her back. She smiled at him and he winked, leading her into the house.

A groan mewled from her lips, helplessly softening by the warm aroma that hit her face when she stepped inside into the living room. "Oh my god—is that the chocolate cake?"

She hadn't seen Marco lying on the couch until he paused the football game on the TV and popped his head up. "Sure the hell is, little lady. My cakes have been known to make a woman orgasm on the spot. Fair warning," he jested.

"Babe, you remember Marco?"

"Yesss," she hissed playfully, keeping a cautious eye on him. "And do we get to eat cake before dinner?" she teased.

"Little lady's eager, huh? I like this one, Rafe."

Rafe ignored his brother's jab and leaned into her, planting his mouth just below her ear. A path of goose bumps ricocheted across her skin as his hot breath danced over her flesh. "If you want an orgasm before dinner, I'd be happy to make that happen for you, gorgeous."

An unfamiliar heat reached the surface of her cheeks and she glanced over her shoulder at Rafe. She was looking for the playfulness in his eyes, the teasing pull of his lips, or the sound of a chuckle—something. But his eyes were clouded, his lips slack and slightly parted, and the only sound coming from his mouth was the silenced pants from his quickened breath. His gaze seared her and the heat on her cheeks inflamed and scorched her entire body. The intimate way his eyes fixated on her lips had her going soft beneath his palm on her back.

She would've given in. She would've let him toss her over the back of the couch or slam her against the floor or whisk her away to some forbidden faraway land—

But she was jarred from the moment when a larger, older version of Rafe walked into the room.

"Dad," Rafe said. "This is Fallon. Fallon, this is Sergio."

She gaped at him. He was gorgeous. Tall and broad. His dark hair was speckled with gray, especially around his temples, and the dark, coarse hair of his trimmed beard was nearly completely taken over by gray. His eyes were blue, just like Marco's, but whereas Marco was tall with lean, sculpted muscles, Sergio was bulkily defined, like Rafe.

Realizing she was staring, she shot her hand out in front of her and Sergio's swallowed hers in his firm grip. "Nice to meet you, Sergio."

"My son wasn't lying when he said you were beautiful," he complimented. "And call me Pop. Everyone does. No one calls me Sergio, 'less I did somethin' wrong—which, come to think of it, happens too damn often."

She smiled. She'd call him Pop because he asked, but it made her a bit uncomfortable. She hadn't even used parental titles with her own parents when she was growing up. She'd always called them by their first names. It was impersonal—not to mention unusual—but she hadn't known anything different.

"Marco Valente Murano! Get your butt in here and ice this cake. Preggo here is having a craving, seeing it cooling on the damn counter," a very beautiful and very pregnant blonde said as she emerged from the swinging door that led to the kitchen.

"You got it, Till." Marco laughed, shooting up from the couch and kissing her on the cheek before dashing into the kitchen.

She was laughing at him when her eyes met Fallon's.

Yep, in the 2.5 seconds she had seen this woman, Fallon had confirmed her suspicions that she had these men wrapped around her pinky finger. *No pressure . . .*

But any fear of impressing the sister-in-law was wiped from Fallon's mind when Tilly's smile widened. "Fallon," she said warmly, quickly crossing the living room. Fallon, surprised, hesitated as Tilly pulled her into a hug; then she returned the squeezing embrace. "I'm so glad to meet you."

The sincerity in her words tugged at Fallon's unused heartstrings a little. "You too."

Tilly slapped Sergio's chest with the back of her hand. "Gosh, look at her." She lifted her eyes to Rafe. "She's gorgeous." Then shifted to look at Fallon. "And those shoes! I'd break my neck if I tried to walk in those. Luca!"

Barging through the swinging kitchen door, a man came into the living room, beer in one hand and a sandwich in the other. "Yeah, babe?"

Fallon pushed back the snicker that erupted in her throat. He sounded just like Rafe.

"Get your handsome butt in here and meet Fallon."

Handing Tilly his sandwich, he wiped his hand on his jeans, then stuck it out to her. "'Bout time my little brother brought home a woman. Nice to meet you."

"You too."

Tilly laughed, curling her small fingers around Fallon's hand. "You've met the guys—now come on, let's go confiscate Marco's cake!"

She liked this woman already.

CHAPTER TWENTY

The Giants were down by one and the Packers were on the offensive thirty-yard line, first down with eighteen seconds left on the clock in the fourth quarter. Tilly was perched on the end of the couch cheering next to a sulking Luca. Apparently they'd made some stupid domestic bet and Luca was obviously on the losing side.

Fallon was curled up next to Rafe, nestled into her designated spot in the crook of his shoulder. She'd only just drifted off, content to sleep in his arms in the same room with his loud, obnoxious brothers and his dad. They were more than a case of beer in between the four of them.

She just *fit*.

His dad walked out of the kitchen carrying the plate of leftover cold ravioli, and looked their way. Setting his plate down on his ratty old leather recliner, he picked up a throw blanket from the back of his chair and draped it over Fallon's legs.

"Thanks, Pop," Rafe whispered. His dad winked.

"Wahoo!" Tilly cheered as the fourth-quarter buzzer

went off. Rafe and Sergio both shushed her. "Sorry," she mouthed, looking at Fallon, who was out cold.

"All right, boys," she said quietly, standing up from the couch. "Will you help me with dishes? Rafe, you're off the hook."

"Good win, babe," Luca said, kissing the back of her head, then leaned down to whisper something in her ear that made her already rosy cheeks darken a shade before following her into the kitchen.

Rafe slowly lowered himself into the corner of the couch and lifted Fallon up onto his chest so he could slide his leg beneath her and rest her between his thighs. She stirred slightly, then pressed her cheek into his chest and sighed contentedly in her sleep.

Encasing her in his arms, he leaned his head against the armrest of the couch and closed his eyes.

She just fucking fit.

"Who the fuck drives a brand-new Jaguar?"

The front door banged against the wall as it thrust open, jerking Rafe from the half-awake, half-asleep limbo he'd fallen into. Fallon jolted up, startled, and Rafe leaned up, looking back toward the front door.

"Shit, Leo," he barked. The living room had darkened and the light seeping in through the open front door was dim from the light blue of the night sky.

"Sorry, brother," he slurred, staggering in and sitting down on the chair across from the couch.

"You're fucking trashed."

"Guilty," he mumbled, lighting one of the cigarettes their dad had left on the side table.

Rafe's little brother seemed to have the detonator switch with a direct line to piss Rafe the fuck off.

"Hey," Fallon said, placing her hand on his knee. "I'm gonna go see where everyone went to and try to sneak some cake from Tilly." Her plump, heart-shaped lips lifted into a confident smile. Rafe pulled her hand from his leg and pressed a light kiss to the inside of her palm.

"Thanks, babe."

The smile still on her face, she moved the blanket from her legs. Her bare feet hit the cool hardwood floor and she stood.

"*Da'am*. That your Jag in the drive, baby?" Leo asked, pulling a drag from his cigarette.

Fallon nodded slowly, unaffected by Leo's drunken antics and piss-poor flirting. "So you're the baby of the family, huh?" she asked as she stepped in front of him. "Leo, right?"

He nodded his head back, the alcohol in his blood slowing his body down. "Yeah, baby. What's your name?"

Rafe watched as Fallon's demeanor shifted. Her spine straightened and her hip swung expertly out to the side, her curve-hugging, navy knit dress showing off her beautiful body—the control and dominance she possessed resurfacing.

She reached her hand out but remained far enough away so that Leo would have to stand in order to reach her—making him come to her. He slowly stumbled to his feet and stood uneasily in front of her, taking her hand in his.

She held his large hand firmly and met his eyes, as if prepared to strike.

"I'm Fallon." She stepped toward him just enough to make Rafe tense, but not close enough that they were touching. "You know what a woman loves in a man, Leo? Confidence. But it walks a fine line with arrogance. And, *baby*, judging by the way you look right now, you've already crossed that line and moved on to asshole." She dropped his hand. "Whatever woman is the reason for this"—she gestured at him with her hand—"just start with 'sorry.' It doesn't hurt throwing in a compliment or two either."

Leo stood gaping openmouthed as Fallon made her way through the living room and through the kitchen door. "Damn, Rafe. Did your woman seriously just call my ass out like that?"

Rafe nodded, slightly proud, slightly shocked, and slightly hard. "Yeah, she did. Better her than me because I would've drawn blood. Is that's what's going on with you, brother? This about a woman?"

Leo fell back into the chair, sagging against the worn cushion. "She like a mind reader or some shit?"

"Something like that. Leo, is that what this shit's about?" he repeated, his patience growing even thinner. "Is a woman the reason you're acting like a prick?"

Leo pulled another cigarette from the pack on the table and lit it, then tossed the pack to Rafe. "It's always a woman, isn't it?"

Rafe lit a cigarette, then nodded as he sucked in, the red burn of the paper beaming like a laser pointer in the

KELSIE LEVERICH

dim in the dark room. "I should've known. You're a lot more like my sorry ass than I like to admit."

Sighing heavily, Leo dropped his half-smoked cigarette into the beer can on the side table. "I don't know what to fucking do," he confessed, scrubbing his hands over his face.

"You love her?"

"Hell." He sighed. "Fuck yeah, I love her. But she deserves a lot better than me."

"I'll be the first one to tell you love sucks."

"She deserves the fuckin' world, Rafe." His head rolled back onto his shoulders and the pain that was eating him away from the inside out was one Rafe was all too familiar with. It killed him to see his brother like that. But when it came to the woman you loved, nothing would make that pain subside but her. Nothing.

He inhaled deeply, holding the smoke in his lungs, then slowly released it. "All I know, little brother, is if you want to give her the world, first you've gotta find your place in it."

Holding a glass of milk in one hand and a plate with a piece of cake in the other, Fallon nudged the back door open and walked out into the backyard, where the guys and Tilly were sitting around a fire pit. She'd been around more fire pits in the last two weekends than she had in her entire life. But with the cold nip of an October night in Pennsylvania, she was grateful for the warmth.

"You get a good catnap?" Sergio asked.

"Yesss," she said, dragging out the word as she sat down next to Tilly. "I'm sorry I fell asleep."

"No sense in apologizing, darlin'. You just make yourself at home here."

Darlin'. She liked that. Sergio's genuineness was admirable. He reminded her of a big gray teddy bear. Warm, cuddly. The type of man she imagined good fathers were made from.

She smiled, but it was forced. Sergio was wonderful; they were all wonderful. But it saddened her. Jealousy was an evil, sneaky creature. It latched on at the most unwelcome, unpredictable moments. She was grateful being welcomed by this family. But she was jealous she never had anything like this. She never shared simple moments like this.

Fallon handed Tilly a fork. "I'm counting on you to eat most of this for me. I've had two pieces already. I seriously can't seem to get enough."

Marco's brows danced on his forehead. "That's what they tell me."

"Oh, shut up," Tilly spat, forking a large piece of cake.

Luca's hand was rubbing soft circles on Tilly's back as she sat snuggled up on his lap. "Where's Rafe?" he asked after taking a sip of his beer.

Fallon swallowed her bite of cake, then said, "Inside, talking to Leo."

"Leo?" Marco stood up from his chair. "Fuck, he drunk?"

She blinked up at him. "Yes," she said warily.

Luca lifted Tilly off his lap and started toward the house with Marco and Sergio not far behind. "Twenty bucks says Leo took the first swing but Rafe knocked his ass out cold."

"Just get in there," Sergio ordered as he pushed them through the door.

"Um, did I miss something?" Fallon asked once the guys were inside.

"No." Tilly laughed, taking another bite of cake. "Rafe and Leo are two of a kind, so they butt heads . . . usually with their fists. But they love each other."

"I'm noticing Rafe likes to lead with his fists."

He was a hothead; she'd already witnessed as much. In only a couple of weeks, she'd learned his tics, the subtle signs of his approaching temper. She'd heard his tone change with a single breath, and watched as uncontrollable rage exploded from inside him. She had no doubt that he was a good man—that much she knew. But his warnings, his worry suddenly splintered her thoughts. He was always so worried that she was scared of him, always so concerned with the fear he inflicted.

Should she be worried?

Cutting her eyes to Fallon, Tilly cocked her head, disapproving. It was the first glimpse she had of the woman Fallon expected to meet. The woman who guarded these big, strong men who became giant teddy bears around her. "Yes, he does lead with his fists. But only with good intentions, Fallon."

Fallon nodded, still uncertain.

Sensing her skepticism, Tilly glared, eyes narrowing

tightly. "He's a good man," she snapped defensively. "If it wasn't for him, I'm pretty positive I wouldn't be alive."

What? Fallon's brows bunched together in a frown. "What do you mean?"

"I've known the Muranos since I was a little girl. Our mothers were best friends as children and Rafe and I were born only a few weeks apart.

"I grew up following Rafe around everywhere, and of course Luca didn't go anywhere without Rafe tagging along. The three of us were inseparable. I loved them. And of course, when Marco and Leo were born, I loved them too. But as I got older, my love for Luca changed. That's a whole other story, though."

So her bond didn't just stem from her marriage to Luca; she was raised with this family, grew up with the very men who adore her now. She wasn't just a sister-in-law; she was a sister.

Jealousy found its way back in. Tilly had them all. Sergio, Luca, Marco, Leo . . . and Rafe. She had more love dangling from these men than Fallon could even comprehend. Oxygen chilled her lungs as she inhaled. She forced her jealously back to where it came from as Tilly continued.

"Rafe and I were seniors in high school and it was Luca's first year in college at NYC. I didn't have a lot of girlfriends. Mostly because I was always with the Murano boys—and mostly because I was always with Luca. So the few girlfriends that I did have didn't stick around long after Luca and I got serious. They didn't understand how I would want to be with someone all the time, but it was just that kind of love. I never wanted to be without him." Light illuminated her smile. "And I still don't."

"You're lucky, to have that."

"To have Luca? I know."

"To have it all. To have that kind of love. The endless, romantic, fairy-tale kind of love. I never thought it existed. You're lucky."

"Luck's got nothing to do with it, sweetie. I love a Murano. It's part of the package. Endless, soul-crushing love is what you sign up for when you love a Murano." She laughed. "You're falling in love with him, aren't you?"

The erratic beats of her heart stalled. She didn't know what to say; words wouldn't form. Tilly graciously let her off the hook, switching the conversation back to her story.

"It was Luca's first weekend at college and I met up with some of the girls I used to hang around. We went to a house party, and like typical teenage girls we drank and danced and were having a great time. The party had died down, and two of the girls I was with were passed out, and the other one was happily locked away in one of the bedrooms with the guy she'd been crushing on since we were freshmen. I'd just called Rafe to come pick me up . . ."

Her trembling fingers balled into fists in her lap. She swallowed. "One of the guys I'd danced with earlier tried to kiss me. Looking back on it, it was a harmless kiss. A harmless kiss that included shoving his tongue down my throat, but . . ."

Fear coiled in Fallon's stomach and her hand lifted to her mouth. She knew. The tears obscuring Tilly's blue eyes said it all. "You don't have to tell me this," she said, shaking her head vigorously, desperately trying to ward off the fear. *She knew . . .*

"Actually, I do," she continued, offering a sad smile. "I'm not the biggest person, and I was even smaller back then. The asshole outweighed me by a hundred pounds, easy. There wasn't much I could do to get him off me, so I kneed him in the balls."

Pride swelled, expanding, pushing the fear away slightly.

"He went down fast," Tilly said, pausing, breathing. "But he came up even faster. He beat me."

Heat burned the back of Fallon's throat. "Oh my god, Tilly."

"And when my body could no longer move from the pain fusing to every nerve, every muscle . . . he raped me."

Fallon's hand flew to her mouth. *No. No.*

"No one was around to help. He'd tucked me by the back door. And if there had been anyone around, they were in no coherent state to help me anyway."

Fallon's eyes widened but she remained silent.

"Rafe found me."

Oh my god.

"I could barely move, barely keep my eyes open. I felt like nothing but mushed flesh and throbbing muscles. My insides ripped open, bleeding from a heart that hurt too much to beat.

"Fallon, I'll never forget the way Rafe looked at me. I saw every fraction of his soul shatter. And I saw him flip the switch. I'll never forget the hatred deep in his eyes. He was so scared . . . scared for me . . . and it made him murderous."

"He didn't ki—"

"No," she said, shaking her head. "But he tried. I won't lie to you. It wasn't hard for him to find the man who raped me—my blood covered him. And when he did, he was ready to end his life." Tears rained down her face, streaking her ivory skin. They weren't tears for herself; they were tears for Rafe.

Guilt slammed Fallon in the gut for ever feeling jealous of her. Tilly loved Rafe—they were bonded by more than time and family. They were bonded by blood. "I screamed," she whispered. "I was horrified. He was going to kill him, and nothing I did could stop him."

"What did stop him?"

"I don't know. Maybe some part of him knew where the line was and he stopped when he began to tiptoe along it. I don't really know. But he spent our senior year in juvenile detention because of it. Got out, and joined the army.

"His love runs strong and deep, Fallon. So does his anger. But they go hand in hand. The only thing that triggers his hatred is his love. He's a passionate man. He's a loyal man. A protective man. He doesn't give his love out easily. But when he does, it's intense."

She'd seen the depth of his protectiveness, the intensity of his anger. His rough, intimidating, masculine demeanor was structured by love.

"So yeah," Tilly continued. "He leads with his fists. But he's a good man, Fallon. He feels the need to protect everyone, to bear the weight and harbor the guilt.

"He's a Murano. He'll love you so fiercely that you'll

question every other love you've felt before him, and no other love will ever compare after him. I promise you. You're a lucky woman to have him, Fallon. Family is everything to these men. Fists and all."

Fallon sighed heavily, needing to cry or laugh or curse—something. She was so confused. "It's all so new. I'm not sure I want . . . I don't know . . . I don't *have* him."

"You do, honey. And I'll admit I was a little surprised, because just a few weeks ago he was sporting a broken heart and a bad attitude. When Marco told me Rafe was bringing a woman to dinner, I was worried I'd be leading with *my* fists."

Fallon smirked knowingly. "No worries. I gave that woman a piece of my mind last weekend."

"See, I knew I liked you. It's nice havin' another woman around."

Fallon shrugged. "Men are easy. And the way I see it, you have these men wrapped around your finger."

She giggled sweetly. "Not for long."

Fallon cocked her head to the side and raised her eyebrows.

"Can I tell you a secret?"

"I don't know . . ." Fallon said, slightly uncomfortable. Secrets weren't quite Fallon's thing.

"I haven't told anyone this, but if I don't I'll go crazy," she whispered, ever so slightly approaching squeal level, but coming from Tilly, it didn't make Fallon cringe like it usually did.

Fallon smiled, this time amused. "Okay, my lips are sealed."

An enthusiastic grin curved over Tilly's pregnancy-flushed glow. "I'm having a girl!" she whisper-yelled. "I found out a few weeks ago. The guys swear up and down it's a boy, and I want to tell them so bad! But even if I did, they wouldn't believe it until they saw her. I can't wait to see the look on Luca's face when he holds his baby girl for the first time."

Fallon's eyes swelled with the image. She'd known Luca only a few hours, but the love he had for his wife and for his unborn child was breathtaking. Tilly was the lucky one.

"Your secret's safe with me." Then Fallon did something that surprised herself. She leaned over and pulled Tilly into a hug. The cloth camping chairs they were sitting in leaned off-balance as they maneuvered their weight to the side to reach each other and embrace. It was heart consuming, a simple gesture that meant more than any words possibly could. "She is going to be one lucky little girl," Fallon assured her.

Tilly laughed. "Can you imagine? This little girl is going to have it rough with these men. I've seen the way they love the women in their lives. I can't even begin to fathom the love they'll feel for her."

A tear skidded down Fallon's cheek. She hadn't cried in years.

"Hey, babe."

Walking into his old bedroom, Rafe pulled his shirt off over his head and stepped out of his jeans. He felt like shit for ignoring Fallon for the last hour while he and his brothers talked with Leo, but he was glad he did. And he hoped like hell Leo would take their advice.

He grinned. *Little brother's in love. Son of a bitch.*

"Hey," Fallon replied sleepily as she rolled over away from the wall to face him.

Rafe pulled off his socks and stood at the side of the bed. "Scoot over. I'm comin' in."

She laughed and pushed herself back, making a small wedge of space for him to slide into on the old twin bed.

"This bed is too small for the both of us." She laughed again. "It's too small for you even without me in it. There's another one on the other side of the room, ya know," she teased as she took it upon herself to lift his arm and curl her body up against his side.

"Babe, you're fuckin' crazy if you think I'm sleeping in this room with you without your body next to me."

He felt her lips tighten into a smile on his chest as she wiggled her body, adjusting herself next to him until she was comfortable.

"So Leo's okay?" she asked through a yawn.

"He'll be okay once he fixes things with his girl." Rafe encased her in his arms and started running circles with his thumb over her shoulder. "You and Tilly have a good time?"

"Yeah, she's pretty wonderful."

That was the damn truth—she'd have to be to put up with all of their crazy asses for all those years.

"She told me what you did for her," she whispered. Rafe's arms tensed around her. It wasn't something he was proud of. Nor did he regret it—not for one single moment. He only regretted that Tilly witnessed it.

He knew he'd gone too far. But he didn't stop because he'd almost killed the man. It was because if he would have killed him, the guilt would have eaten Tilly alive.

Seeing Tilly fear him, hearing her screams penetrate the dense roar that hummed inside his head, tortured him. He never wanted to see her look at him that way. Never wanted to see any woman look at him that way. The rage that was like a dormant beast lurking inside him had taken over, and it nearly ruined him.

Fallon pressed a light kiss to his chest and he relaxed. "He deserved it," he whispered. "And I'd do it all over again if I had to."

"I know. I'm not afraid of you, Rafe. Your heart's in the right place, always."

Grasping her chin between his fingers, he lifted her face to his so he could look into those honey-colored eyes, still vivid in the darkness. "I'm glad you came."

"Me too." She sighed. "But another part of me wishes I'd never met your family."

Frowning, he weaved his fingers through her soft hair, sliding and tugging gently on the tufts of waves. "What? Why?"

"Because they're amazing, Rafe. Because it makes me realize everything I already knew I never had," she admitted. "You're lucky to have them. To have a broken little brother who drinks away his heartache like another man I know"—her shoulder softly rolled into his accusingly—"and to have an entire family who's there for him when he shows up wasted. You have a sister-in-law who loves you men like nothing I've ever seen, and a pretty amazing dad to top it off.

"I'm an only child. No siblings. It was just me and my parents. No relatives. Just us. My family was devoid of emotion. It never felt like this, Rafe. Like a family should. Love and joy. Playfulness and even fighting.

"*I've* never felt like this."

Kissing the top of her head, Rafe pulled her in a little tighter.

"Every time I'm around you, you make me feel," she continued. She kissed his chest again and scooted her body up so her face burrowed into the side of his neck. "I promised myself I would never give anyone the power to hurt me. I forged these walls to—"

"Keep people out?"

She shook her head. "No, to keep me from feeling. I wanted to retreat into the void I'd always run from. I didn't want to hurt."

"I'm not going to hurt you, baby. That won't fuckin' happen."

"You can't promise that."

"I can try like hell."

Her lips curled against his neck, smiling quickly before she kissed him, her mouth brushing over his jaw. "You make me feel, Rafe. And being here with you makes me feel a little more."

Damn.

There it was, that little tightening in his chest that re-minded him he was a fucking goner.

"A little more?" he asked.

She lifted her head and narrowed her eyes at him. "Don't play coy. It doesn't suit you."

His mouth twitched with an emerging smile and he softly ran the pad of his thumb across her bottom lip. "What if I told you I feel a little more too? That I think I might be falling in love with you?" he asked, the apparent need and sincerity in his own voice taking him by surprise.

She held his eyes in the darkness and he could feel fear skirt through them. "I'd tell you that you shouldn't."

"Why?"

"Because I don't know how to love you back."

He knew she believed that. But she was wrong—he'd seen it. He'd seen her love when she cared for Jade. She knew how to love. He just needed to remind her.

CHAPTER TWENTY-ONE

Wrapping her wet hair up in a towel, Fallon walked out of her bathroom and started pulling clothes out of her closet and tossing them onto her bed. She needed to get to the club a little earlier than normal today so she could play catch-up on the payroll paperwork for her accountant. Plus, she missed it. She'd been spending a lot less time at the club lately and more time at her house, and after her trip to New York a couple of weeks ago, she'd been spending a lot of that time with Rafe.

"How do you expect me to watch you walk around your room, naked and wet, and not touch you?" Rafe said from behind her as his fingertips carefully trailed up her spine to her nape.

"Willpower."

"Babe," he whispered, his lips fluttering over the wet skin of her hairline. Goose bumps pricked her skin from his warm breath and she absentmindedly rolled her head back onto his shoulder. "I'm learning I have no willpower when it comes to you."

His deft fingers skidded around her stomach and he pressed her back against him, his bare, hard cock nestling against her butt.

"I've gotta get ready for work," she whimpered, his fingers disappearing between her thighs.

She wiggled from his touch, her body protesting as his fingers withdrew from her sex when she pulled away, backing up against the wall next to her closet.

His dark eyes sparked with an unspoken challenge and she pressed her lips tightly together to keep from smiling. Any other time, she would have reached into her stockpile and pulled out her go-to-hell smile that was one of her favorites to use on a man. But Rafe, she only wanted him. Any way and anywhere she could possible get him.

But he was challenging her. And Fallon was always up for a challenge.

Raking her lustful eyes over his naked body, she shuddered as his arms braced against the wall on either side of her head, imprisoning her between them. Warm, hard body was pressed in close to hers and she yearned to arch her back away from the wall to smooth her breasts against his firm chest.

But she didn't.

She just smiled and tried like hell not to melt into a sopping puddle on the floor. His eyes alone could have done it. They were her weakness, her undoing. They had been since she first looked into them.

Slowly, deliberately, and unequivocally arrogantly, Rafe pulled the imperfect corner of his lips up slightly. Just enough to cause an instinctive reaction from her body. Clamping her thighs together, she sunk her teeth into her bottom lip.

"Fuck, gorgeous," he muttered; then he had her wrapped around his waist and pinned to the wall before she could release her lip from her teeth.

"Okay, now I really have to get ready for work," she warned, peeling herself from his arms and standing up from the floor. "When's your leave over?"

"I sign in Sunday at midnight," he said, situating himself on the bed, pulling his jeans up over his hips. "But I'm gonna check in at headquarters this afternoon, make sure my guys on leave haven't gotten into any trouble. Then I'll head to the club tonight."

Smoothing her dress over her hips, Fallon lifted her eyes to him. "You can't come to the club anymore," she said simply. It made complete sense to her, but she could see from the confused and slightly angry expression on Rafe's face that that was not the case for him.

"Why?"

Sighing heavily, she answered, "Because I don't know what this is between us, but regardless, I don't need you there. It's part of the rules. Boyfriends, husbands, lovers— whatever you want to call them—are not allowed at the club."

She watched as the muscles beneath his jaw started flexing and an acute awareness spread over her. He was pissed. "You're still dancing?" he asked.

She laughed. "What do you mean, am I still dancing? Of course I am."

Sliding his shirt over his head, he reached for his black boots and pulled them on. "I'm not okay with that." His voice had lowered, trying to inflict some sort of control that he was going to learn real quickly he did not have over her.

Trying to keep her composure, she focused her sights on the shelves of shoes that lined her closet wall. "I'm sorry," she replied, noticing the derisive tone that had crept into her voice. "I don't remember asking your permission."

"I don't share my women, Fallon. I don't want anyone to see your body but me. I don't want you taking off your clothes for anyone but me."

Was he serious?

Stepping out of her closet, she moved toward him so she was in his line of vision, so he could see the sincerity in her expression.

"First of all, I'm not yours. Second of all, you knew I danced before you knew my name. Velour is my club, Rafe. These last few weeks didn't change that. Sleeping with me didn't change that. And whatever this is"—she gestured between them—"doesn't change that. And I will let you in on a little secret: it's not going to change either."

Feel.

He made her feel. And at that very moment he was making her feel enraged.

"Fallon," he warned as he stalked slowly toward her, his eyes boring holes into her. She swallowed, frustrated with herself for the sudden quickening of her pulse at the sight of his powerful, tempting body closing in on her. "I'm not okay with this."

"God, Rafe," she said, backing away. "This is me! This is my life. It may not be acceptable for you, but I don't need your acceptance. I don't need anyone's. Every girl who works for me has her reasons for this job. I get it. Taking your clothes off and dancing is not something people are usually proud to discuss. Molly, she's in med school. Cliché, right? Dancer working her way through med school."

"Fallon—" He tried to interrupt, but the cathartic feeling she was getting only fueled her fire.

"And Na, she works full-time as a physical therapist. She works for me at night to save money for her mission's yearly trip to Guam. With her church! Ironic, right? Then you have Jade. The former junkie who dances because no one else would give her a chance!"

Strong hands captured her face, his forehead lowering to hers. Her breathing was quick, heart thudding painfully against her chest. And he just held her eyes, the molten heat in them melting away the ice that had seeped into her veins. Seemingly satisfied, he pulled his head from hers, but he remained holding on to her. And she hated that she was grateful for that. She needed his touch at that very moment, even if she didn't want to.

"You've heard them all before," she said quietly. "We all have. But not me. I didn't dance with the idea of fast cash at the end of the night. I came to Velour because I wanted to be on that stage. I was at a point in my life where I had given up everything that wasn't already taken from me. Everything. I needed to feel that feeling again. I was suppressing every other damn feeling I could possibly feel, but that feeling—the feeling of being on the stage in front of an audience . . . it was seductive. So I did it. And I loved it. Dance has always liberated me, Rafe. Now it empowers me. And I'm sorry, but I won't give that up. This is me. Take it or leave it. Here's your chance to turn your back on me like everyone else. And there's the door."

She pulled away from his hold and pinned him with a look she never thought she'd be able to possess. But she was hurting. Hurting because she was so angry. And she was angry because . . . "Actually, you know what? Leave. Just leave! You were more right than you realized. Love *is* pretty fucking conditional."

The piercing sound of the doorbell rang through Rafe's alcohol-blurred mind as he sat and stared mindlessly at the TV in front of him. It had been four days since he'd left Fallon's house pissed all to hell that she was still going to take her fucking clothes off for the asshole suits that attended her club. But he was even more pissed off with himself for actually leaving. He should have just stayed there, fought it out with her, let her scream and yell and get pissed at him. Then he should have pinned her to the bed and kissed every part of her body until she gave in to him.

But that was the whiskey talking and his dick responding because he knew the likeliness of that scenario playing out would have been slim.

Stumbling from the glass of whiskey he'd just finished, Rafe shuffled to his feet and ambled to the front door. And if anything could have sobered him up and ruined his pity buzz, it was the face on the other side.

"Hi, Rafe."

Using the door for stability, Rafe staggered, then caught himself. "Bridgette," he slurred.

"Yeah, baby," she said, lifting her hand to the side of his face. "God, Rafe. You're drunk."

Her touch burned him, like ice over salted flesh, and he jerked away. "What do you want?"

His response time was a little off and Bridgette took advantage of his sluggish body and slipped into his house before he had the chance to slam the door in her face.

"Again, what the hell do you want, Bridgette?"

"You look like shit, baby. Have you even eaten today?" she asked, walking straight into his kitchen as if she'd been there a hundred times before doing that exact thing.

He hadn't eaten—shit, he couldn't even remember the last thing he put in his mouth that didn't come out of a bottle.

He stood and stared after her, thinking for a minute that maybe he had passed out and was having some sick nightmare. Because this could not possibly be happening.

Stalking as quickly into the kitchen as his impaired limbs would carry him, he stopped behind her as she stood in front of the pantry.

"What. Do. You. Want?" he asked again.

"Dammit, Rafe. Do you really need to ask that question? I'm standing in front of you, in your home miles and miles and miles away from my husband and my children, and you still feel the need to ask me that question?"

She spun around to face him, the familiarity of her closeness invading him like a stony virus, spreading quickly and irreversibly through his veins until his entire body was infected.

Her hands lifted to his face and she rose to her toes and pressed a single kiss to his lips. "I want *you*, baby," she whispered. Then her mouth came crashing back down to his. His hands moved of their own accord to her waist and pulled her petite body hard against his as his mouth hurtled over hers.

Her eager hands tore at his shirt, peeling it over his head, before they journeyed to the button on his jeans. He palmed her breasts as he forced her body into the wall behind her, filling his intoxicated mind with her moans and the taste of her mouth.

Her taste . . .

She tasted the same as he'd always fucking known her to taste. Like vanilla and mint. But it soured on his tongue and settled uneasily in his stomach.

He wanted cherries. He wanted to taste the coolness of soda and the sweetness of cherries on his tongue after a kiss.

Fallon.

He jerked away quicker than his body was ready for and it left his fuzzy head swimming with the aftershocks as he latched onto the counter, sucking air into his lungs.

"What the fuck, Bridge?" he finally asked when his mind and his body came to.

She stepped in front of him cautiously. "Don't pull away from me," she begged.

And he laughed. "Don't come here spouting off your bullshit to me. I'm over it."

"I left him," she quavered, her voice growing weak as she ducked down to try to peer up at his face, which was lowered to the floor. "I did. I left my husband."

He lifted his eyes to hers and they widened when he saw the truth behind her words etched into the lines around her tearing eyes. "And what do you want me to do with that information now, huh? You want me to fall at your feet and thank you for finally giving a shit about him and leavin' him and for giving a shit about me and runnin' back here? What, Bridge?"

"I want you to want me. I want you to hold me, Rafe."

He shook his head. "I wanted you for too long. I craved holding you in my arms, longed for the day you would tell me you were mine—"

"Okay," she said placing her hands on his chest. "I'm here now. That day's today, baby. I'm yours, all yours."

His fingers wrapped around her wrists and pulled her palms from his chest. "But I'm not yours."

Bridgette's eyes widened as she sucked a sharp intake of air into her lungs. "So you choose her?" she quivered, the apparent hurt in her voice for once not sparking his usual need to comfort her.

He nodded. "Fuck yeah, I choose her."

"I heard that you were in town," Fallon purred as she rounded the table and stood beside her new favorite headliner, Jake Murphy, Oakland Raiders star QB and also Fallon's closest friend from high school.

"Damn, Lynn," he said, calling her by her old nickname.

"It's Fallon now, Jake," she corrected politely.

"Well, Fallon, you look absolutely stunning."

"And you're absolutely as flirty as you were back in high school. I imagine the ladies still flock to you with the single sweep of your eye, don't they?" she teased.

He smiled, his thin lips arching into the bashful smile she knew he would provide her. Jake Murphy was as far from a ladies' man as they came and could blush upon eye contact. It appeared that his fame and fortune in the NFL hadn't changed that about him. And she wasn't sure why, but she admired that.

"So this is where you've been all these years, huh? I'd heard you owned a club in Denver. Just never realized you'd taken your talent for dance and turned it into a success like this. I'm proud of you, Lynn . . . Fallon."

"And I never realized my favorite dance partner who danced the part of Oberon would turn into some big football star."

He shrugged. "You still keep in touch with anyone? You ever talk to Curt? I haven't heard from him since he left for West Point after high school."

"No," she said coldly, then readjusted her weight in her stilettos and smiled. "You're the first person I've seen from back home in eight years. And to be honest, Jake, I don't care to ever see anyone else."

"Whatever happened to you, Lynn?" Concern filled his eyes. He was her friend, and she'd just upped and left without any explanation. "You were just gone one day, and no one liked to talk about it."

"It's a long story, Jake. Definitely not one to put a damper on your Saturday night with." She patted him on the shoulder and waved Amelia over. Jake was a good guy, but he could use a little Amelia to spice up his evening and she could use a little Amelia to distract him.

Not disappointing, Amelia approached wearing her signature smile and a subtle sway to her hips. "Amelia, this is my friend Jake. His drinks are on the house tonight." She winked at him. "Jake, Amelia will take great care of you, but let me know if you—"

"Fallon," Jade interrupted, strutting quickly toward the table.

"Excuse me, Jake. It was good to see you. Good luck at your game on Monday. Don't tell anyone, but I hope you kick the Broncos' asses." She winked again.

Jade's lips tucked into her mouth as she came to a stop in front of Fallon, a hesitant expression on her face.

"All right, don't skirt around it. What's wrong?" Fallon asked.

Jade sighed. "George wanted me to let you know that someone's trying to get in who's out of dress code."

Bullshit. George would never ask for her if someone was out of dress code. He just wouldn't allow them in. Simple as that.

Fallon knew exactly what this meant. And who.

Two things wafted through her mind as she descended the stairs toward the entrance. The first and obvious question running rabid was why, after exact instructions not to allow Rafe back into the club, was George even flirting with the idea of allowing him in? She didn't need George to play matchmaker. And the second thought was, Why was he here? But she knew why. He was here to see her. And the reaction that conclusion gave her body was reason enough for her to just turn the other direction and go to her office.

But she didn't.

That would've been too easy, too smart.

As she stepped from the spiral staircase and into the main part of the club, her eyes found him instantly. He was leaning against the door with his strong, tattooed arms folded across his chest. Those butterflies that had made their first appearance their first night together returned with a vengeance. The undeniable increase in her heart rate made her breath come in quick, short pants. He was breathtakingly sexy. Sexy in that rough-around-the-edges, arms-that-could-make-her-whimper, eyes-that-could-make-her-lose-her-breath kind of way. But also in that angry way. In a way that his jaw was clenched, his beautiful, imperfect mouth set in a tight line, and his stone eyes like cold, black glass.

He was sexy when he was smiling or laughing—anything to do with that damaged mouth of his was sexy. But seeing him like this—mad—did something else to her completely.

It fueled her.

Anticipation licked up her spine. That intensity, the overwhelming power found in his posture, his body language, his eyes—it seared her open and welcomed hot, raw need. But she couldn't.

Rafe patted George on the shoulder and stepped into the club. Her appreciation for a well-dressed, well-groomed man took a back burner to the way Rafe looked right now. His black T-shirt hung just below the waist of his perfectly worn-in jeans, which fell straight and loose over his black boots. The sleeves of his T-shirt gripped the delectable cut in his biceps. She wanted to feel his sturdy hand press into the small of her back, flattening her body against his, and she wanted to lean her head against his chest and kiss his arm as it wrapped around her. His face was rough with a few days of stubble, and his eyes were thirsty—for her. She felt the need to quench her own thirst as she stood before him, a short distance away from touching him. . . .

But those were thoughts she had no business thinking right now.

Continuing her way around tables clustered with people, she neared him until they were face-to-face. Rafe disregarded any semblance of personal space and stepped even closer, until their bodies were touching. For once, she couldn't find words to spit at him. And she was ready to cave, ready to tell her pride to take a hike and allow herself the fulfillment this man had given her in the short time she'd known him.

She was ready to cave . . .

"Hey, gorgeous." He breathed, wasting no time pressing his open mouth to the side of her neck, dotting a single moist kiss to the skin below her ear. She begged her body not to tremble from the nearness of his lips, but it was almost impossible when they moved to her mouth and dusted a swift, gentle kiss across her lips. Caving. She was caving . . .

She missed him. An ache so painful it burned had lived inside her for the last four days. Longing dripped heady, carnal need into her body, drowning her resolve.

Gentle fingers held her elbow, his other hand pinning her by the small of her back. Caving . . .

"Don't dance, babe," he pleaded, pressing another kiss to her lips before she pulled away.

And just like that, the weakness this man was capable of instilling in her left her with his words.

She laughed. "Rafe, you came to me—you came to my club—my burlesque club—to ask me not to dance?"

"Dammit, Fallon. Don't you get it? Don't you realize how fuckin' bad I want you? How much it's killing me right now not to push you up against the wall and show you just how bad I want you?"

Wanting her didn't have a damn thing to do with this. She thrust her palms against his chest and pushed out of his embrace. Grabbing on to his hand, she led him quickly through the club and up the stairs that led backstage. Naomi's and Jade's eyes darted to her as she stormed past them and down the hall to her office.

She slammed the door behind him. "You're fucking drunk," she spat. "What were you thinking, coming here and causing a scene in my club?"

Rafe's hands scrubbed over his face a few times, over his head, then latched onto the back of his neck as he looked up at the ceiling.

"Back to your old habits, huh?" she accused, the volume of her voice pulling his eyes to level on hers. "Finding your distraction at the bottom of a bottle?" she yelled.

She meant her words to hurt him. But all they did was hurt *her*.

His arms opened up, flailing out to his sides. "Just drinking away my heartache," he confessed, spitting her words back at her. His hand fisted, punching his chest hard over his heart. "Drinking away the fucking hole where you used to be."

Shaking her head, she opened her mouth to tell him to go to hell, but he didn't give her the chance.

His steps were quick and his strides long. His body crashed into hers with a force that would have sent her flying onto her rear had his arms not secured around her waist at the exact moment their bodies collided. She could feel the hot stream of air leave his mouth and bounce off her lips. "What am I supposed to do? You were my distraction, babe. You were the only one who was capable of shifting my focus until all I could see was you! So you tell me. What the fuck am I supposed to distract myself with when all I can think about is you?"

The second the words left his mouth, his hands flew to the sides of her face and he slammed his mouth to hers. She had no choice but to reciprocate his forcible lips and kiss him with the ferocity and passion that had been swelling up inside her since the moment she saw him at the door.

His hands dug painfully into her hips, her fingernails biting into the back of his neck, each trying to get closer to the other, only to fail and try again.

Rafe walked forward, forcing her steps backward until her back collided with her desk. Hoisting her onto the desk, Rafe plunged his tongue into her mouth, crazed and frenzied and hungry. Wrapping her legs around him, she threaded her arms around his back, pulling her closer to him. She couldn't get enough. Never enough.

"Don't dance, babe," he mumbled against her lips—and she pulled away.

Their breathing was jagged, their chests heaving vigorously.

"What?" she said.

His hands found their way back to her face, holding her in place as he looked into her eyes as if she were the only thing keeping him together. She broke a little more.

"I'll go to jail if I see those fuckers out there looking at this body that belongs to me. Please." His voice, only seconds before ireful and hard, had softened into a plea. And it tore at her. It tore at every single shred of her heart.

She wanted to do it for him. She wanted to ease his anger and steal his thoughts. But this was her. He needed to accept her.

"I'm dancing, Rafe," she said calmly.

"Babe." His dangerous eyes narrowed, stubbled jaw tightened, nostrils flared. His breathing became labored and heavy. A warning . . .

She held his smoldering gaze. "I'm dancing," she repeated.

Disappointment crossed his face, and it crushed her. He

shook his head and, spinning around, flung her heavy metal door open. It slammed into the wall.

Fallon released her breath and slid down from her desk.

Her fingers fluttered to her lips, her lipstick smeared across her face from Rafe's kiss, feeling the lingering sensations his flawed mouth had left there.

Pulling her straps down her shoulders, she let her dress fall to the floor. She was dancing. This was part of her. If he didn't want to see, then he sure as hell didn't have to stay.

Opening her wardrobe, she pulled out a costume she very rarely wore. It was for a routine that she very rarely performed, one she hadn't done in the two years since she'd taken over the club and rechoreographed most of the numbers. It was grittier, dirtier, and a hell of a lot sexier.

Rafe couldn't accept her choices? Fine. Wouldn't be the first time someone turned their back on her.

But she hoped he would enjoy the show—because she was going to give him a good one.

Rafe was watching her, fighting back the urge seething inside him to take a swing at every man in the club. He wanted to drag her beautiful ass off that stage.

The last time he'd watched her dance, it was different. God, yeah, it was sexy as hell, but the way she danced now—she was trying to prove a point. But the only point she was proving was that she knew how to work his last nerve. She wanted to get to him? Mission accomplished. He was worked up, in more ways than one. And he was thoroughly pissed.

"Hey, handsome." Amelia approached him where he was sitting at the bar. She eyed the empty glass next to him on the counter. "Whiskey, right? Simone! Get this gentleman another shot."

His lips closed around his cigarette, pulling much-needed nicotine into his lungs. Then he quickly smiled, nodding his thanks. Then went back to watching Fallon.

Amelia stood next to him for a second longer and he had the pressing suspicion that she wanted to say something more. But she didn't. And Rafe was wound up so tightly at the moment that he couldn't find it in him to care enough to ask.

God, how many minutes had she been up there?

Picking up the shot Simone had just slid next to him, he knocked it back, the glass clanking against the bar as he slammed it down and skidded it back across to Simone for another.

Thank fuck, the music finally ended and Fallon was leaving the stage. *'Bout damn time.*

"She's hot, huh, bro?"

Slowly, looking for the calm that was submerged somewhere inside him, Rafe turned his head and glared at the douche bag suit next to him.

"She doesn't get onstage often, but damn. Too fucking bad she doesn't take it all off, huh?"

Rafe couldn't understand for the life of him why this

guy was running his mouth when it was obvious he was about one second from losing it.

His barstool flew back and landed on its side as he jerked from his seat and stalked toward the stage. That beautiful body of hers was his. He knew it and she knew. She just needed a little reminder.

$\mathcal{S}$hutting the door to her office, Fallon leaned against it and rolled her eyes closed. Her skin was heated and slicked with sweat and the cold steel felt good. She didn't know how long she stood there, inhaling slow breaths of much-needed oxygen into her lungs, but when she finally pushed away, her pulse had returned to normal.

Reaching behind her, she unhooked the sheer bustier covering her feminine parts with bronze and gold crystals. It was a beautiful costume, sexy and scandalous.

There were so many eyes on her tonight—just like every night she danced. She felt the intense heat of their eyes grate across her body at every move. But unlike every other time she was on that stage, tonight the power her body had given her and the control she'd yielded was gone. The liberation she felt on that stage was suppressed by the opaque, sable stare that never left her.

Her body was hyperaware of him—of his eyes, of the tension wringing his body, of the wanton need that was cloaked with anger tightening in the flex of his jaw.

And it distracted her.

He distracted her.

Her mind, usually lost in the movements of her routine, had been prominently and irreversibly fixated on the only man that had ever stolen her control.

But it wasn't stealing when she gave it willingly, when she craved his eyes on her, claiming her, needing her.

Pulling the crystal-embellished briefs down her legs, she whipped her head around as the sound of her door slamming shut met her ears.

Her fingers opened, dropping the thin costume to the floor. Her eyes widened—but she was not surprised.

"You're still here."

Rafe's chest expanded with his deep breaths, his taut arms hanging at his sides. "Yeah. I'm still here."

She was naked, completely exposed to him, but his eyes never once left hers.

"Did you enjoy the show?" she sneered, forcing her body to take a step away from him.

His eyes hardened as he moved into her office. He was unhurried as he took deliberate steps toward her.

The backs of her knees hit the couch and she reached down to grab the armrest for support as Rafe continued his leisurely advance. When he reached her, his hand slowly wound around her back and scooped her naked body into his arm, pulling her flush against him. She could feel the quick thud of his heart against his chest as her body soaked into him.

"Babe," he implored, the ink spattering in his eyes morphing with raw need.

She flattened her palms on his chest, trying to force a sliver of space between their bodies. "Rafe, you're drunk. I'll have Simone call you a cab. You need to go home."

His large hands skillfully traced up her arms as he lowered his head to hers. She could smell the whiskey mixed with the aroma that was Rafe and Rafe alone—the mere scent could inebriate her.

"Babe, the only thing I need right now is inside you. I just watched a roomful of men watch you bare this beautiful body to them." A hand moved to her nape, tilting her head back to look at him while the other kneaded her breast with the pad of his thumb, causing her to melt against him. "This is mine, gorgeous," he growled. "I need to be inside you."

He was demanding her at the same time he was begging her. The command, the plea . . . They were both tangled together so tightly that they became one, and she had no choice but to give it to him. She'd be lying if she tried to convince herself that her body wasn't his. It belonged to him since the first moment she saw him.

"Babe," he growled, the strain in his voice almost agony.

Holding his quicksand eyes, she removed his hand from her breast and placed it between her thighs. A jagged, raw groan vibrated in his throat as he sank his touch into the heated depths of her sex.

Her knees liquefied beneath her and Rafe used the force of his body pressing against her to keep her upright.

She didn't realize how much she needed his touch until that very moment. A satiated sigh escaped her throat and rolled over her lips and she dropped her head to his shoulder.

"That's it, gorgeous," he said, steadily stroking her with his fingers, bringing her to the place that only he'd been able to reach. "It's mine, babe. This. Is. Mine. Give it to me," he coaxed as his mouth lingered below her ear. The warm flat of his tongue lapped at the moisture still clinging to her skin. She shivered.

Her hands flew to his biceps and she clung to him, needing the strength he was offering her, as a current of pleasure tore through her core. Her teeth sank into his shoulder. "Rafe . . ." She moaned, her body shuddering against him as he sent her cascading into the depths of his touch.

He withdrew his fingers from her, too quickly, and the sudden absence undulated a whimper from her lips. She lifted her head, her eyes searching the ones staring back at her, looking for something that would solidify the way his touch had just made her feel, looking for something that would confirm the emotion that was abrading her, wearing her down bit by delicious bit. Breaking her.

She was his. He'd claimed her body, and even with the bricks she'd laid, he'd claimed her heart. He'd broken her. He'd loved so hard he'd broken her impenetrable barriers and taken the love she didn't even know she possessed.

His lips lowered to hers, gently, carefully, and the sensations numbed her. His tongue parted her lips and slipped into her mouth, swirling and tasting and consuming her with his kiss.

She was lost, unable to move. Her body was still shivering from his touch, and his mouth, his kiss, had stolen her thoughts. She was consumed in him once again, just as he always managed to do. His intensity swallowed her, burrowing her within his warmth.

But his mouth hardened above hers and a tortured groan hummed against her naked body through the thin material of his T-shirt. She felt it, the shift in his kiss, the hesitance in his warmth.

Then he pulled away.

The cold air slammed into her, nearly knocking her over.

He closed his eyes briefly and licked his lips. "Cherries," he whispered, then dropped his hands from her face and turned toward the door.

"Rafe?"

His head turned over his shoulder, his intoxicated stare slicing her open—raw. Her skin pricked from the look in his eyes, a physical pain to go along with the excruciating heartbreak she was about to endure.

She shook her head, pleading. Take her control! She didn't want it! She wanted to feel carried by his strength, suffocated, smothered in his intensity. Everything he'd given her, she wanted it back. Yet the words never left her mouth.

But his did.

"I can't, babe. I can't do this."

Then he left.

"To what do I owe this pleasure?" Pete asked as Fallon sat down in one of the many empty barstools at the bar.

"I need something hard and something strong."

His brows furrowed as he leaned his forearms onto the bar. "You wanna talk 'bout it?"

She smiled. Pete didn't comfort; he poured. Which was exactly why she was there. How could she possibly talk about something she didn't even understand? Rafe was a complicated contradiction who'd barreled through her well-contrived world and shattered every barrier she relied on.

"No. Thanks, though." She winked. "Hard and strong." She was beginning to realize the appeal of finding your distraction at the bottom of a bottle. Quick and easy. A few shots and she'd be numb again.

"No cherries tonight, sweetheart?"

She met Pete's worried eyes and forced a smile onto her face. "Nope. No cherries."

CHAPTER TWENTY-TWO

The pain wasn't what surprised me; it was the fear. I didn't realize I would be so afraid. But I was alone. I had no one to depend on to get through this but myself. But then again, that's all I needed.

Climbing out of bed, I grabbed my bag that had been packed for a few nights now. It didn't contain much; I didn't own much.

The room was full of sleeping women and children, and I tried desperately not to wake anyone as I padded across the cold linoleum floor. Sleep was a rarity in this place. It wasn't always quiet, it was usually never comfortable, and it was always lonely. But that was just my opinion. I knew there were plenty of women who loved and appreciated the shelter. It was better than the streets—hell, even I could appreciate that. But the erratic flow of people in and out kept me on edge, and the lack of privacy was draining.

As I reached the steps that led downstairs, I held on tightly to the railing as another wave of pain clamped down inside me, knocking the air from my lungs and pricking tears at the back of my eyes. It was like nothing I'd ever experienced before. When the pain started to subside, I slowly continued my way down to the bottom level of the house. It was so quiet tonight.

I knocked on the house mother's door and sighed with relief when Rachel appeared on the other side. Out of all the women who volunteered at the shelter, I liked Rachel the best. She didn't ask a lot of questions. She just let me be. I was grateful for that.

Rachel's sleep-deprived eyes widened slightly when she looked at me, but without saying a single word she spun around, slipped on her thick green robe and shoes, and grabbed her purse off her dresser.

The car ride was bittersweet. It was almost over. I could try to get back to normal; I could try to move on and start my life over again. Maybe I could even start dancing again. But at the same time . . . it was almost over. And deep down, I knew I could never go back to normal, and I didn't know how I would ever move on from this.

Six hours later, the pain I felt was gone and the memory of the pain I'd endured was like a dream you couldn't remember. All I could feel was every single emotion that I'd been trying so hard to keep submerged somewhere I wouldn't have to feel them, somewhere I could ignore them. Where I could be numb. But they were at the surface now. Anger, pain, hate, sorrow, guilt, fear, hope, joy . . . they were all floating around in a tight pocket of air that was suffocating me. I couldn't breathe. All I could do was feel.

But one feeling was so strong, it was like oxygen to my burning lungs . . . It was unconditional love. It was a feeling I'd never seen, never felt, never known. But as I held my baby girl in my arms and looked down at her beautiful, perfect little face and held her tiny little hand, the feeling overwhelmed me.

I'd never known anything to feel so wonderful and so unbelievable, and to hurt so excruciatingly. And it was beautiful.

This tiny life loved me. She'd been in this world for only minutes, but my daughter loved me. She was born knowing nothing other than the feel of my heartbeat and the sound of my voice—and she loved me. She didn't know anything other than that. And I loved her back with a ferocity that claimed my entire being.

As I ran the back of my finger down the side of her flushed cheek, I finally knew how love was supposed to feel. For the first time that I could remember, I understood what loving someone felt like. In that small amount of time that my daughter was in this world, I knew without question that I would do anything for her. I knew I would always love her.

The muffled, animated voices from out in the hall became louder and I forced my eyes to look at the clock that hung on the wall opposite my bed. Another hour had gone by and a soft knock on the hospital door confirmed my fears—it was time.

The small, average woman and the tall, scrawny man that I'd met with and talked to over the last few months slowly walked into the room. The woman, Renee, was carrying a bouquet of mixed flowers and a stuffed elephant. Her narrow, simple features were elated and her thin lips were beaming with a smile. Tears streamed silently down her face as she looked at her husband with such happiness, such wonder, that my own tears became heavy and quick.

"Fallon," she admired. "She's beautiful. She's absolutely perfect." Moving closer to me, Renee leaned down and softly ran her hand over the dark, downy hair on my daughter's head.

I wanted to scream. I wanted to shield my daughter from their touch and tell them to get the hell out, to leave. It was caught in the back of my throat, strangling me, suffocating me and ripping away every single muscle and every single nerve that was holding my fragile heart together, keeping me alive.

This wasn't their baby. This was my baby. This was my daughter. I loved her. Jesus, I never knew I would feel this way, but I did.

"I love you," Renee whispered as she stared in awe at the little life in my arms.

I felt as if I were dying, losing my heart, losing my soul. But even though every fiber of my existence was now intertwined in the little life I held in my arms, and even though I loved her more than anything—because I loved her more than anything—I pressed a single kiss to her forehead and ran my finger down the side of her sleeping face, then lifted her up and placed her in Renee's arms.

The undeniable love and joy that filled her eyes broke my heart all over again. This woman looked at my daughter like a mother who was looking into the heart of her child for the first time—the way I had looked at her only an hour ago.

Renee loved her. She was her mother now.

"Here," she whispered, reaching out and placing a small pendant necklace in my hand. It was a dainty gold chain holding a tiny gold elephant charm. Her eyes flitted lovingly over the baby, then back down to me. "Elephants are my favorite animal. We've decorated the nursery in grays and whites with a beautiful elephant mobile." She paused and glanced back at her husband as her tears became more constant and her voice became strangled with emotion. "Elephants represent strength, and you, Fallon, have such strength. I can't imagine the strength you have inside you, and I admire you for it. But elephants also represent memory. And I want you to know that I will never, ever forget the love you have for this little girl, and I will always remember the sacrifice you've made. And I promise to love her with every breath I take."

I could only nod. What words was I supposed to form that would convey the utter agony I was feeling inside me? The words I wanted to say I knew I couldn't. I wanted to tell them she was mine, that I loved her, that I wanted her. But what could I possibly give her? I had no family, no home, no money. She deserved so much more than the life I could provide her. She deserved the world.

I watched silently as they left the room, taking with

them the only person I had ever loved. The only person I knew how to love.

I felt the shield go up around me as I lay curled into myself, broken and alone in a hospital bed. Then I rolled to my side and cried until I was empty.

Hot tears flooded down the sides of Fallon's cheeks. "Shh. I'm here, babe. *Fuck.* I'm here."

Her eyes shot open, startled by the heavy feel of arms around her. She was still on the couch in her living room, where she'd fallen asleep, still in her dress from work, after she'd stupidly driven home from Pete's. Her mouth was dry, evidence of the Patrón she'd had. And the tears wouldn't stop.

Another sob raked down her back as Rafe pulled her against him, cradling her in his arms as he picked her up like a toddler and carried her through her house to her room. How did he get in? When? Why was he here?

Her mind tried to keep up, but it only made the world spin around her. She didn't have the energy to attempt to contemplate him. Nor did she want to. He was here. And right now, that's all she needed.

Laying her down gently in bed, Rafe slowly unzipped the zipper along the side of her dress and lowered it from her body. He peeled the covers down and she crawled beneath them as he stripped from his T-shirt and jeans.

Her eyes stayed fixed on him, like an anchor holding her in place, preventing her from receding back into the deep crevice of her mind where her memory haunted her. She was mad, and hurt, and scared—all because this beautiful man in front of her had made her feel. He melted her defenses with just his simple touch, and she felt.

He sank to the bed next to her and gathered her limp body in his arms, his rough hands rubbing circles on her back as he held her against him.

"Rafe," she sobbed.

He pressed a tender kiss to her forehead, which only made her crumble more. "Yeah, babe."

Lifting her chin from his chest, she found his beautiful, imperfect mouth and smoothed her lips over his. "Make love to me," she pleaded. "Please."

He tensed around her as a heavy, anguished groan rumbled deep in his chest and vibrated against her skin.

"Steal my thoughts. Please, Rafe."

"Fuck, gorgeous." He sighed, and his mouth fell back to hers.

Not knowing the reason for her tears was clawing away at Rafe's insides. Dammit, he was a goddamned idiot. He'd been pissed and drunk as fuck—and he'd walked away from her.

The sound of his name unfurling from her lips as he'd turned his back on her had replayed on constant repeat in his mind all night. She'd needed him—he'd heard it in the pained inflection of her voice—but he'd walked away anyway.

But not anymore.

He'd driven to the nearest motel and sat in his car, trying to talk himself into getting out, getting a room, and sleeping off the whiskey and the image of Fallon's face as he'd fucking walked away from her. But he couldn't. She was there, ingrained behind his lids—every time he blinked, he saw her.

He'd come back for her. He'd promised her he'd be there. He'd promised he wouldn't hurt her. He'd fucked it all up. Now he was going to fix it.

His hand flattened on her back, drawing her as close to him as physically possible, but even then it wasn't close enough. His mouth moved over hers carefully, slowly, trying to emit what he was feeling for this woman as she softened against him.

Her delicate hand cupped his face, her thumb running along the hideous scar that extended over his jaw and down his neck as he continued to kiss her.

The sweet taste of cherries was absent from her mouth, replaced by the residual flavor of tequila mixed with the salt from her tears. She'd been drinking, and Fallon didn't drink.

Dammit.

He'd fucked up.

His fingers found the clasp of her bra and unhooked it, removing it from her body, revealing her supple breasts that peaked with taut pink nipples.

Breaking their kiss, Rafe moved his mouth to her breast, swirling his tongue around her hardened peak, coaxing it into his mouth. Fallon's back bowed, pressing her chest into him as she silently requested more. And he happily obliged.

Squirming her body against him, she wound her hands around his back, eagerly pulling on him as she shifted beneath him. His weight urged her slim body into the comfort of the mattress and he propped himself up on his forearms, his mouth still worshipping the perfection of her breast. Cradling his hips with her thighs, Fallon writhed beneath him, grinding her hot pussy against his erection, searching for the release her body was begging for.

Lifting his head from her, he placed a hand on her hip, holding her still against him. "Let me take care of you, gorgeous," he promised. "Let me do this for you."

Her teeth sank into the corner of her bottom lip and she nodded, the gold bursts in her eyes brightening as she watched his mouth slowly descend to her sinuous hips. He nipped the thin strap of fabric that covered her hip with his teeth, rubbing his thumb over the damp satin covering her pussy.

Sliding the small scrap of fabric that covered the beauty between her thighs down her legs, Rafe wasted no time lapping up the arousal that glistened over her tight opening.

"Mmm." She moaned, her hips rotating against him. "Rafe."

So responsive, so ready.

"Yeah, babe," he answered, sliding a single finger into her, applying pressure exactly where she needed it.

"Please?"

"I love when you ask me nicely, gorgeous."

He withdrew his finger from her, watching as her eyes widened with arousal when he licked his finger clean of her. "So sweet," he praised.

. . .

She could feel the phantom sensations of Rafe's hard cock buried inside of her as she watched him hold his erection in his hands. His balls were drawn tight, his shaft hard and long as he rolled the condom down. Her body clenched, tightening in anticipation for the way she knew he would make her feel.

"Please, Rafe," she begged again, trailing her hands down her breast, over her stomach, and delving her fingers into the wet warmth between her folds. The silkiness in his deep sable eyes became coarse and darkened as he watched her squirm from her own touch.

"Fucking beautiful."

The bed dipped from his weight as he positioned himself in front of her and grasped on to her knees, prying her legs open. She let them fall to the sides as she continued to caress her body, not only for her own pleasure, but for his visual satisfaction.

His gaze smoldered while he dragged the rough pad of his thumb across her sensitive clit and she cried out.

"That's it, gorgeous. I want to know how your own touch makes you feel."

His words seared a heat through her body and she pushed herself deeper into the depths of her craving sex, searching for the spot that would unravel her. Then she felt her body stretch as Rafe's strong finger pushed inside her, joining in on her exploration.

Oh god.

Too much, it was too much. His desirous stare was boring through her, his finger gliding smoothly alongside her own, and she begin to shudder. But she didn't want it this way. She wanted to feel Rafe inside her as she lost herself. She wanted him to bring her there—just him. No one else. Never anyone else.

Her head pressed into the mattress, her back arching off the bed as the building pleasure intensified. "Rafe."

"I know, babe. I'll take care of you."

She inhaled a breath as he pulled his finger from her, withdrawing hers along with it. He brought her hand to his mouth and softly kissed the inside of her wrist before sucking the wetness from her finger.

She trembled.

"Come here," she beckoned.

Rafe's lips lifted unevenly as he lowered himself, his cock plummeting inside her before he stilled, holding his weight above her.

"I love you, gorgeous." His head dropped to the curve of her shoulder and she mindlessly wrapped her arms around his neck.

His words ruined her, broke her, sent her into unimaginable peril while cleansing her soul. They were beautifully detrimental words, healing her and scarring her. She wanted to cry, she wanted to laugh . . . she wanted to scream.

But instead she crawled into the expansive haven those words constructed and burrowed in deep. If only just for tonight.

Brushing his lips over her skin, he singed kisses up the

side of her neck. Slowly, torturously, he withdrew from her. She clenched him tightly, summoning him with a roll of her hips. His languid thrusts produced slow, agonizingly delicious tingles that pulsed almost numbingly inside her.

"God, what have you done to me?" he whispered against her ear. "I love you."

Turning his face to her, he crushed his lips to hers softly, intimately. They molded against hers perfectly as he dipped into her mouth with a passion that was defeating her—breaking her down and smoothing away her hesitance. She needed this man—right now—in every way a woman needed a man. She needed him to care for her, to claim her, to protect her, and to love her. If only for this moment.

Her breathing quickened and her lips began to move feverously against his and he complied with her demands, matching the pace of her kiss with the increasing beat of her heart and the rhythm of his thrusts. His tongue lashed over hers, his lips sucking hers between his. Nibbling, pulling, kissing, sucking. Their bodies were in sync, fine-tuned to each other's moans and sighs, and their simultaneous breaths that expanded between them.

She couldn't get enough.

It had never felt like this. This all-consuming passion. And she knew it never would again.

The indescribable need to melt into him, to seep into his essence, just to get more, closer—just to feel *more*—was overwhelming her.

"Look at me, babe," he said, breaking their kiss.

But she knew what she'd be looking at if she opened her eyes . . .

His thrusts deepened and her body uncontrollably bowed as she tightened her legs around him and latched onto his biceps. Her release was so close.

"Babe, look at me. Let me see you give yourself to me."

She complied, Rafe's body not giving her any choice as he plunged deep inside her. Her eyes shot to his as the pleasure only he could give her caused her to convulse around him. She drew him to her and held on tight as he pumped his release deep inside her, his hips slowing, liquefying her from the inside out.

Lifting his head, he looked at her, holding her captive with the rich luxury in his eyes. Plowing his fingers into her hair, he brought his lips to hers. "I love you," he whispered, and the last sturdy barrier of her wall shifted beneath those three words, crumbling until she was left vulnerable, exposed, and terrified. But with their heartbeats syncing in rhythm as their bodies remained connected, she wouldn't have it any other way.

Although her breaths had become deep and long, he knew she wasn't asleep. Running his fingers through the lush waves around her face, Rafe tilted his head and kissed her eyelids. "I'm here, gorgeous."

Slowly, her eyes fluttered open.

Christ, he was a goner.

"I'm sorry," he started. "For walking away from you—dammit, babe, that won't fuckin' happen again. I swear."

She nodded and burrowed her head into the crook of his shoulder, and although holding her in his arms soothed some of the tension he was feeling, it wasn't enough.

"How did you get in?" she asked, lifting her swollen eyes to his.

"I could hear you crying through the front door, babe. I knocked, but nothing. You left your car in the driveway, unlocked, so I used the garage door opener and came in through the garage."

She nodded, seemingly satisfied, and tunneled back into his chest.

"Talk to me, babe. I can't fix it if you don't talk to me."

"You can't fix this, Rafe."

Like hell. He'd find a way. Whatever the hell it was, he would find a way to fix it for her. Grasping her chin, he lifted her face to his. "Let me try," he implored.

She shut her eyes, inhaling a deep breath and releasing through her mouth. Coaxing her strength. "When I was seventeen, I got pregnant."

Shit.

Of all the possible reasons for her tears that had trudged through his mind, this wasn't one of them.

"I was so afraid to tell my parents. I knew they would be furious. Their prim daughter—their prima ballerina—knocked up at seventeen. They wouldn't accept it. So I went to my boyfriend first, even though I was just as terrified to tell him. We were young, Rafe. And I'll admit I cared about

him, but never in the way that felt true. We were thrust together as kids. Basically married off while we were in dia-
pers by our families, whose ambitions in life were to join our
two prestigious families together after I graduated fine arts
school and after Curt graduated West Point. It was all
mapped out and going according to their well-designed
plan—until I got pregnant."

Rafe's newfound hatred for her parents was growing by
the second. Bringing the inside of her wrist to his lips, he
kissed her gently. He didn't know what else to do but be
there. No words he could give her right now would ease her
pain. So he listened.

"If I thought that Curt would've handled the news better than my parents, I was wrong—very wrong. He blamed
me, said I was trying to ruin his chance at West Point. I
forgot I was capable of creating a child on my own," she
seethed, her anger creeping into the volume of her words.

"But when it came down to it, I was the one carrying
the child. I was the girl ruining the hopes and dreams of
two families. Two families who wanted nothing to do with
me or the baby inside me. We threatened their names, their
reputations, and their positions, and they couldn't have that.
My parents, of course, sided with Curt's and I was out on
my ass before I could even comprehend the idea that I was
going to be a mother. A single mother, with no one. No family, no father for my baby, no money, no home . . ."

"Babe," Rafe whispered, tightening his arms around
her, kissing her lips, her jaw, her tear-streaked eyes. "God,
I'm so sorry."

"I gave her up, Rafe," she said, answering his unspoken question.

Fuck.

"I gave life to someone so small and so beautiful and so perfect. And I loved her more than I'd ever even known was possible—and then I gave her up."

What could a man say to a woman who was shattering in his arms? Rafe wanted to shield her from this pain that was eating away at her, but he couldn't. She was right—he couldn't fix this. And feeling the woman he loved hurting, and not being able to do a goddamn thing about it, ripped him open from the inside out. All he could do was hold her in his arms. But he knew even that wouldn't be enough.

"I wanted so badly to free myself from their world devoid of joy and love and life. I wanted to find love—experience what it felt to be wanted, needed. And I'd found it, wrapped up in my daughter, who wanted me, her mother. Who needed me, her mother. *She* loved me.

"I turned my back on her, Rafe. Just like they did to me. She needed me and I turned my back on her. I never wanted to be like them. Turned out, I already was."

I don't know how to love.

I don't know how to love you . . .

CHAPTER TWENTY-THREE

*M*ornings with Rafe were better. Always better.

But as the late-morning sun rolled in through the windows of her bedroom, Fallon wished it hadn't risen yet. That it was still night so she could stay tucked away in the safety of Rafe's strong arms for just a little longer.

She rolled over to face him, the weight of his arms tangled around her heavy and limp as his sleep-induced breaths continued to come in slow, even exhales.

She gently traced the scar on his lip with her thumb before kissing it lightly. He stirred and his arms tightened around her, pulling the front of her body flush against his naked chest. She absorbed the warmth of his skin as he held her, tucking her head into the crook of his arm.

She breathed him in and tried to memorize this moment, this feeling, because she knew it wouldn't last. It couldn't last. Too many variables lined up pitting the odds against them. He deserved someone who could love him the way he deserved to be loved, because she knew with every beat of her breaking heart that this man could love so hard it hurt. But it was the best possible pain. The soul-crushing pain that knew how to break you down and heal you in the same breath.

Tilly was right: no other love would compare, and Fallon knew undoubtedly that no other love ever would. He was the true kind.

And he deserved the true kind.

She just didn't know how to be that for him.

Dusting a soft kiss to his chest, she slinked out beneath his arms. He moaned in his sleep and she froze. After another heartbeat she rolled from the bed and, snatching her dress off the floor, tiptoed quietly from her room.

Making quick work of her feet, Fallon pulled her dress down over her head, zipping it up the side as she descended the stairs. She needed the security Velour would provide her, needed the numbing distraction of the cold basement studio and her worn pointe shoes.

"So that's it, babe?"

Her entire body stiffened, petrified by the sound of his voice echoing from the landing above her. Smoothing the wrinkled fabric of her dress down her thighs, she rolled her shoulders back, commanding her body to hold itself upright, because at that very moment she didn't think her legs would be able to support her.

She took another step before Rafe's voice sounded in the space right behind her. She could feel the heat from his naked chest pressing against her, and it took everything she had in her not to lean into him and allow his arms to secure around her.

She couldn't.

"You're just gonna walk away from me? Is that what you want?"

No.

"Yes," she whispered, fighting back the sob that was constricting her throat. Heat flamed behind her eyes, warning her that if she didn't leave soon, her tears would fall.

"I'm right here, Fallon." He turned her around, his eyes imprisoning her as his hands held her face.

Quicksand . . .

"I'm right here, gorgeous. I'm not going anywhere. I'm not going to turn my back on you."

This man in front of her, his eyes harboring sincerity in his concern, awakened that unknown feeling. The walls she built grew indestructible the day she gave her daughter up. It was also the last day she allowed herself to feel. But Rafe changed that. She should have known how dangerous he'd be. He broke her down. He broke her completely and he offered her what no one else was ever able to—to feel. And it hurt.

She watched his eyes follow the single tear that skidded down her cheek until it landed on his hand. Clenching his jaw, he tipped his head back to the ceiling.

"But you're still gonna walk away from me, aren't you?" he hissed between his teeth.

How could she respond? He already had his answer.

Grabbing her hand, he crushed it against her chest, above her heart thudding so hard, so quickly against her ribs that it felt like at any moment it was going to pierce through her skin. She couldn't breathe.

"You feel that, babe? You can't tell me you don't want this! I can feel it. My touch does this to you."

She swallowed hard as the burn in her throat expanded.

He moved their hands from her and pressed them to his chest. "You feel *this*? You own me, gorgeous. Every single beat of my heart belongs to you. *You* do this to me."

Silence. That's all she had for him. He deserved more. So much more.

When his hands left hers and raked over the top of his head, she turned from him and stepped down the last few steps and into the foyer.

And walked away.

CHAPTER TWENTY-FOUR

Sliding down onto his usual stool that had gone vacant these last few weeks, Rafe pulled the black ceramic ashtray over in front of him. Rolling the cigarette between his lips, he nodded at Trish, who was busy restocking beer bottles in the refrigerator below the back counter.

"Hey, baby. Haven't seen you 'round here in a while. Thought you mighta moved on, found someone else to pour your Envy."

He felt the familiar lift of his lips. A smile. He hadn't smiled in two goddamn weeks. He should've known Trish would be the one to shift his mood. "Nah, Trish. I only drink Angel's Envy with you, sweetheart."

Her back was to him but he knew her beautiful, haunting eyes were wrinkling with a smile. "Where're you heading tonight lookin' like that? I know you didn't get all dressed up to come visit me." Turning her head over her shoulder, she winked at him and flashed her teeth.

He pulled nicotine into his lungs, then exhaled a cloud of smoke. "Redeployment ball. Can I snag you as my date?"

Squatting down, Rafe heard the recognizable sound of glasses clanking together as Trish pulled her stash of Angel's Envy from below the bar. Pouring the gold liquid into the glasses, she shook her heard. "I don't think I'm the type of woman you want on your arm, baby."

"Yeah, well, the woman I wanted on my arm made it pretty fuckin' clear she didn't want to be there."

"You still hung up on that married woman?"

Rafe's surprised eyes shot to hers as he lowered his glass of whiskey from his lips.

Trish laughed. "Rafe, you'd been coming to my bar drinkin' yourself stupid for weeks. You didn't think I was gonna let one of those drunken nights go to waste without pumping you for information, did ya?" She arched her brows. "And I told you then, which I know you don't remember, so I'll tell you again. No woman who shares her heart with two men is worth it, baby. You want it all—not part. Wait till you find a woman who will give it all to you. So I don't want to see any more moping around about that two-timing slut."

Rafe cocked his head from side to side, popping his neck as he rolled his eyes. "Nah, I'm not moping about her."

"Then who? You've already managed to get your heart trampled on again? I'm not liking your taste in women, baby. I need to teach you how to pick 'em."

Rafe laughed. He knew for a fact that Trish would more than like Fallon. Fallon may not be Trish's preference of a blonde, but she had a body and an attitude that would drive Trish fucking crazy. "You'd have liked this one," he assured her.

"I don't think so. I tend to pick sides, and I'm always on yours. She broke your heart, she's on my shit list."

Rafe slid his glass across the slick bar. "Just one more and I gotta get goin'."

"I see how ya are. Come in my bar lookin' handsome as ever, drink my Envy, then leave me. I'll remember that the next time you stroll in here and try to take one of my blondes, which by the way you need your ass kicked for."

His head rolled back on his neck and he laughed. "Ah, Trish. I should've let you have 'em. They were good—don't get me wrong—but they enjoyed each other more than me. Besides, I'm done with that shit."

Shaking her head at him, Trish sighed heavily. "This one's messed you up something bad, hasn't she? Aw, baby. You love too much too fast. She's not worth it."

"She is, Trish. She's the true kind."

*K**nock-knock.*

Jade's brown head of curls popped through the crack in the office door. "Hey," she said.

"Hey, come in," Fallon replied, scooting up from where she was lying down on the velvet couch, wrapped in a blanket.

"I told you, you could sleep in the apartment and I'd gladly take over your house, seeing as you are back to sleeping at the club every night."

Which was true: Fallon hadn't slept at home since the night she'd made love to Rafe and woken up in his arms only to walk away from him. All these years she'd blamed the people in her life for turning their backs on her and her baby, for being the reason she felt so much hurt and betrayal, that she locked it up tight and threw away the key. But she was coming to find out that self-inflicted pain was much worse.

Choosing to walk away from her daughter, choosing to walk away from Rafe—those hurt more than when she had no choice at all.

Stepping into her office, Jade plopped down on the desk chair and swiveled around to face her. She looked beautiful. Her eyes were done smoky and sexy, lined heavily with charcoal liner and accented with subtle false lashes. Her lips were dusted a rosy pink that matched her cheeks and her—

"Wait a minute. Why aren't you dressed?" Fallon asked "The ball starts in an hour—it's gonna take you every bit of an hour to get to Fort Carson from here. Go. Get. Dressed."

"Oh, I've already told Graham I'm not going. He's gonna meet me here afterward," she lilted, her cheeks darkening a shade of pink. Fortunately for Jade, Dexter's cheating ass turned out to benefit her when she used Graham as the proverbial shoulder to cry on.

"Why not?"

"Because you're going instead. Graham is expecting you there in ninety minutes to walk you in, so you better hurry your butt up and get ready."

Leveling her sights, Fallon glared at Jade. "That is absolutely not happening," she snapped.

Pouting like a toddler instead of the grown woman she was, Jade folded her dainty arms over her chest and stuck her lips out in a pout. Pouty lips didn't work on Fallon. Not much could at this point.

"Why not?"

"I have more than enough reasons why I'm not going to a redeployment ball with your new boyfriend, where—"

"Rafe will be?" she interrupted.

Dammit.

Fallon sighed. "Exactly. I closed that door with no intention of opening it back up. I appreciate your attempt at whatever it was that you're strangely trying to attempt, but no."

"Well, that's too damn bad," she egged on.

Fallon took the bait, if for nothing else, just to appease her. "And why's that?" she asked.

Jade grinned. "I ordered that sexy little red Valentino dress we both love. You know the one that rests slightly off the shoulders with the plunging, ruffled neckline and the—"

"Slit up the center," Fallon finished, her eyes popping open wide. "You ordered it?"

"Yes. In your size. Call it a thank-you for, you know . . ." Clearing her throat, Jade jumped up from the chair. "But you only get it under the condition that you get your sexy ass to that ball and make nice with the handsome soldier."

"You're seriously bribing me with Valentino?"

A wry grin pulled across Jade's otherwise innocent expression. "Yes. I had to find your weakness."

Except, Rafe had become her weakness . . .

"I don't understand why it matters so much to you that I go to this thing," she said, feeling her resolve beginning to waver.

"Look, Fallon. You picked me up when I didn't think that was even a remote possibility anymore. You gave me a kick in the ass when no one else would. Consider this your kick, honey."

"Dammit! Go get the dress." She caved. She didn't know who she was trying to fool. Rafe was the second person in her entire life who she truly missed, and the thought of seeing him, if only for a moment, and if only for him to tell her to go to hell for walking away from him, made her burn with an ache . . . with desire.

The appeal of him in his dress uniform and her wearing a Valentino dress didn't hurt either.

Getting up from the couch, she sat down at her vanity and pulled the small gold chain from its designated spot. She ran her thumb across the delicate charm before clasping it around her neck.

She'd go and see Rafe. Hopefully it wouldn't break her heart any more than it already was.

CHAPTER TWENTY-FIVE

There was something to be said about a woman wearing Valentino. One of the very few things Fallon's mother instilled in her that she was actually grateful for was the knowledge that it didn't matter how beautiful you were, if you didn't feel beautiful, no one would believe it. *Confidence.* Her mother had given her confidence.

But there was so much truth to her mother's words that she didn't realize. A woman always felt better—prettier—after leaving the salon or after soaking in a pedicure chair or after finding a new lipstick she loved. The little things that made a woman *feel* beautiful.

When a woman feels beautiful, she exudes beauty.

And every woman should experience the way it feels to slide her body into a red Valentino dress.

"I do believe I just became the luckiest son of a bitch to walk into this place." Graham beamed, offering his elbow for Fallon to take.

Shifting her head to the side, she smiled at him, grateful

for the way he eased her nerves as she cupped his bicep with her hand, allowing him to lead her into the room.

Walking into the ball, she felt like she'd stepped into an adult version of the prom. Every set of eyes turned to her like some horrifying eighties movie. The staring didn't bother her, and much to her amusement it didn't seem to bother Graham either. If anything, she'd say he was enjoying his bout of attention.

But what bothered her was that she didn't feel the set of eyes on her that her body was craving. She didn't see the velvety depths finding her through the crowd the way they'd always had.

Rafe wasn't here.

She looked to Graham for some sort of explanation. He shrugged, thankfully understanding her indecipherable expression. "I don't know, Fallon. Not sure why he's not here yet. He better get here, though—cocktail hour is over and the company commander will be starting his speech and the awards soon."

Inhaling a breath, she nodded and straightened. Why was she so eager to see him? She'd be lucky if he'd talk to her, let alone listen to her apology. But at the end of it all, an apology wouldn't change anything between them. It couldn't.

Oh god.

Damn Valentino dress and Jade's uncanny ability of persuasion. What the hell had she been thinking, coming here? Apparently, she was a glutton for self-inflicted punishment. Because seeing him again was going to hurt.

Graham led Fallon around the room, weaving between large round tables covered in thick white tablecloths with beautiful centerpieces that apparently each represented a different unit of the company. For fear of sounding naive, she refrained from asking Graham what all this unit, brigade, platoon, company, division, squad stuff was that he was rambling about. It was a different world that she was getting a glimpse into, and as interested as she truly was, she was confused out of her mind. *Fake it till you make it.* Her motto to live by for the evening.

Leaning in and whispering into her ear, Graham filled her in. "I switched our seats around so we'd be sitting at Rafe's table, but unfortunately that has also landed us in the company of Dexter. I'm sorry."

Shaking her head, she nudged him with her shoulder and smiled. "I realize we don't know each other very well, Graham, but I don't scare easily when it comes to catty females and assholes. These seats are fine, thank you." She leaned in close so only he could hear her. "And for the record, I like you much better than Dexter." She winked.

He chuckled and a faint blush warmed his face. "Put in a good word for me, then?"

"I don't think you need one, but—done."

"Well, well. I wasn't sure I'd actually see you here."

Fallon turned around as they approached their table to see Stella with her hand on her hip and a smile on her face. She pulled Fallon into a hug and she awkwardly hugged her back.

"Damn, this dress is amazing. Beautiful, honey." She leaned over and kissed Graham on the cheek. "You're looking as handsome as ever, might I add. Where's that sweetie you've been spending all your time with lately? I was lookin' forward to seeing Dexter's jaw hit the ground when you walked in with her."

Fallon laughed under her breath. She remembered why she liked this woman.

"I brought this beauty tonight instead, but I'll see Jade later," Graham replied.

Stella's brows bunched and she pursed her lips. "Where's Rafe?"

Graham shrugged. "Haven't seen him yet. We've been wondering the same thing. Fallon, I'm gonna grab us something to drink at the bar. What would you like?"

"Diet Coke, three cherries, please."

"Stella?" he asked.

"I'm good."

As Fallon pulled out her chair and sat down next to Stella, the bottle blond's glare seemed to spit daggers in her direction. "Look, Claire," she started, deciding there was no way she was going to indulge in this woman's drama all evening. "I have absolutely no interest in this catty crap that you're obviously fond of and I have no desire to go a few rounds with you. However, I will. And I will win. So withdraw your claws and get your eyes back in your head, please, and let's just enjoy our evening."

Stella snickered, trying to reel it in as Claire's jaw hung open for a few moments before she snapped it shut and averted her eyes.

Graham came back with their drinks and sat down next to Fallon. She instantly could feel tension building between him and Dexter.

Catty women in horrible dresses, male testosterone pissing matches, alcohol, tacky music—definitely an adult version of prom.

The visuals were much better, though. Men in uniform compared with boys in tuxes won hands down.

Fallon sat politely at the table and included herself in the conversation at the appropriate times and nodded and smiled when needed, but beyond that, she couldn't keep her mind from wandering to Rafe, wondering where he was and hoping he would show up.

Dinner was served, then dessert, then champagne. Still no Rafe.

"I'm sorry, Fallon. I know I'm not the company you were hoping to have this evening. And believe me, I will be happy to kick Murano's ass when I finally see him."

"It's okay. You're good company," she assured him. "And he couldn't have had any idea I was going to be here anyway."

"You sure I can't get you anything stronger than a Diet Coke?" he asked, standing from his seat.

"No, thank you."

The mingling bodies started finding their way back to their seats as the room darkened and a slide show popped up on a screen overhead. Chatter and laughter filled the room as everyone watched the pictures of the company's most recent deployment to Afghanistan. It was a simple slide show of pictures put to music, but it was probably one of the most humbling things she'd ever watched.

She followed the news and tried to stay up-to-date on current events; she followed debates and participated in elections. Just like most people in the country. But she'd had the honor of stepping into their world for an evening, and it was humbling.

The pictures that flashed across the screen were of the very men and women sitting around her with their significant others at their sides. Pictures of them in combat uniform, with weapons strapped to their bodies. Some pictures were of missions, some were of the locals, and some were just of them smiling and making the best of the time away from their families as they fought for their country. She'd seen similar pictures before, but it gave her a whole new perspective seeing those same faces right in front of her, hearing their voices. *Humbled. Honored.* Those words felt insignificant compared with the joy she felt to be allowed a glimpse into this band of brothers and their families.

She smiled when she recognized the uneven smirk peeking from beneath a pair of goggles and a Kevlar in a few of the pictures. Even in full combat gear Rafe stood out to her—his confident, secure posture and his beautifully flawed smile. She imagined she could pick it out anywhere.

The music softened and slowed and the voices quieted as photos of soldiers emerged onto the screen. These images included their date of birth and date of death below.

It was a strange feeling for her to experience unequivocal sadness for these men and their families. Just as before, she'd seen images of fallen soldiers, but being around the men who fought next to them and the friends and loved ones who were there in their honor, mourning them—it was heartbreaking.

For a woman who was adamant about keeping people at arm's length, adamant about not caring—not feeling—she was feeling more than she had in a long time.

She heard Stella sniffle next to her and she looked at her and offered a small smile.

Stella nodded toward the screen. "He was in our men's unit—he was one of my husband's guys. Young kid, got married right before he left and was killed a few months before the tour was over."

Looking back at the screen, Fallon watched the picture fade away as she inhaled a deep breath. Most definitely humbling.

"Are you bored yet?" Graham asked.

"Not completely."

"You're a horrible liar, and I'd like to tell you that it will get better once this political part is over, but it usually doesn't. CO's getting ready to do his speech and then we can leave."

She nodded and watched as a tall, lean man approached the podium. Chants and hollers and a couple of "hooahs" echoed through the room, cheering their respect for their commanding officer.

Grabbing her phone from the table, she sent a quick text

to check in with George at the club and to tell him that she would be back before closing.

"Good evening, everyone," the man said, and Fallon's head snapped to him at the sound of his voice.

"Fallon, you okay?" Stella asked.

Crossing her legs beneath the table, she shifted her weight in her chair. "Uh, yeah. I'm fine," she assured, but every muscle in her body had gone stiff and her palms became sweaty. Would he recognize her? Did he know she was here?

She sat silently at the table, her eyes unable to look away from him as she listened to him talk about army values and duty and family. What a joke. If she was the type of woman to stand from her chair in the middle of a speech and laugh in his face, she would have.

And a large part of her wished like hell she was that type of woman. He was a fake and an asshole who couldn't care less about values and family. His aspiration for success and his ability to rise to the top stomped on those so-called values he preached about.

The commanding officer no sooner ended his speech and was stepping away from the microphone when Fallon stood, reaching for her purse to leave. She'd never wanted to bolt from a room more than that very moment.

Until she felt the air still around her.

Until she felt him. His hands on her arms. His mouth next to her ear. His breath heating her skin.

And everything else faded away.

The tightness in her chest loosened and was replaced with a flutter she hadn't realized she missed. His warm hands melted away the tension in her muscles, and the unbridled desire she had for his touch consumed her at the small contact. She needed more. Always more.

She stood there and allowed the steady beat of his heart thumping against his chest to vibrate over her back as his breath continued to bathe the side of her neck. It was taking every molecule of strength she had to keep her traitorous body from softening against his hard chest. She'd missed him, and the nearness of his body was morphing her longing into a torturous ache. This was harder than she thought . . .

She sucked in a sharp breath as his lips just barely swept over her neck. "Dance with me, gorgeous?"

Rafe didn't wait for her to answer him; he wasn't going to give her the opportunity to tell him no. His hands skirted down her arms until he felt her wrists beneath his fingers.

He'd never imagined he'd walk through those doors and see this woman sitting here. His steps stalled like a goddamned idiot when he noticed her. And he'd just stood there, watching her as if she were untouchable, unreachable—even when she was only steps from his reach. Her golden brown hair cascaded down her back in large, thick waves and he'd wanted to move his hands through the strands so he could push it over her shoulder and view her long, delicate neck.

She was here, and he had no doubt in his mind that she was here for him. And that fact alone had caused his feet to remain cemented to the floor—because it was going to take an act from the big man himself to keep him from laying her back on that table and sinking his cock balls-deep inside her.

But when she'd stood from her seat, his paralyzed limbs had found the mobility they needed the moment the tangible tension seeped from her body. He could see the stiffness in her shoulders and discomfort in the slight expansion of her back from her quickened breaths.

And he'd gone to her.

Spinning her around, he lifted her hand to his mouth and pressed a soft kiss to the inside of her wrist. He was expecting her sweet, subtle shiver from his touch, and she didn't disappoint.

"You look unbelievable," he said, barely able to shift his eyes from her pillowy red lips. Her forced smile might as well have punched him in the gut. Seeing that phony smile she was trying to pass off as real fuckin' stung.

"You look good too."

He pulled her through the room to the small dance floor in front of all the tables and pulled her into his arms— and she let him. The plunging back of her dress dipped low into a V, the point connecting just above her ass. And the scanty design allowed his fingers the pleasure of skimming down her spine from her nape to the sexy twin dimples above her ass.

She slinked into him, her arms wrapping around his neck as she softened against him, just the way he liked to feel her—affected and needy.

"So I'm not going to pretend that I wasn't surprised to see you sitting there, babe."

She didn't respond; she just burrowed her head into his neck. And dammit, she just fit.

"Did I tell you how fuckin' beautiful you look? Because from where I'm standing every man's eyes are on you right now, and I can't say that I'm not proud to be the one holding you."

She lifted her head and looked around. "They're looking because we're the only people on the dance floor."

"Think what you think, babe." He pulled her in tighter, moving her against him as they danced. "I've missed you," he whispered.

"Rafe, don't. Okay? Just dance with me."

"Then what're you doing here?" he asked, leaning back to look at her.

She met his eyes quickly, then returned her face to his neck. "I wanted to apologize. I shouldn't have danced while you were at the club. I did it because I knew you'd be watching, and I wanted to make you mad, and I'm sorry for that."

"That's what you wanted to apologize for? Babe, yeah, I was pissed. That tends to happen a lot. And I'm sure you'll piss me off a hell of a lot more."

Her body tensed in his arms. "Rafe, my coming here doesn't change anything."

Bullshit. It changed everything.

"Then why'd you come?"

She shrugged. "Jade bribed me with the dress."

He laughed. "Remind me to thank Jade."

His fingers grasped her chin and forced her to look at him, his thumb brushed over her bottom lip, and he watched her eyes liquefy into dripping honey. But then she turned her head away from his hold.

"By the end of the night, you'll want it. You'll want me to touch you."

"That's never been the problem, Rafe. I've always wanted your touch. I want it now."

He sucked oxygen into his lungs. Curling his hand around her nape, he arched her head back and dragged his bottom lip up the center of her throat. A breathy moan met his ears, swirling unrelenting passion through his body.

"You can't say things to me like that, gorgeous," he muttered against her skin. "Not when I'm struggling, not when I'm hangin' on by a fuckin' thread here trying to keep my hands in line." Moving to her ear, he whispered, "Not when all I can think about is the way I know you'd feel beneath this dress. The way it'd feel to run my fingers up your thighs . . ." He stepped into her, his thick leg pushing effortlessly between hers, causing the split in her dress to open up. The fabric of his pants rasped against the suddenly sensitive skin of her inner thigh and her legs softened slightly beneath the sensation. "Or the way it'd feel to bury myself inside you."

She was caving . . .

. . .

*S*he really shouldn't have come. She should've listened to her gut. Did she know it would hurt to see him? Did she know seeing him would ignite fire in her body like it always did? Yes.

But she didn't know that it would be so hard to keep herself upright. Hard to keep herself from latching onto the back of his head and yanking his mouth to hers. That damn flawed mouth that could inflict so much pleasure.

"Hey," she said, drawing his attention back to her eyes. "I'm gonna get going."

Once again he'd managed to steal her control. He owned her body—that she knew. It was her weakness.

"First Sergeant Murano?"

The voice that penetrated the safe haven Rafe had unknowingly created for her slimed across her skin.

His head popped up, looking to the man behind her. She shouldn't have come. She really shouldn't have come. "Yes, sir?"

"You want to introduce me to this beautiful lady you're with?"

Rafe's palm remained flattened on the small of her back as she turned around. "There's no need for false introductions here. Don't play games. I know you recognize me," she hissed.

She saw Rafe's face contort in confusion from the corner of her eye, but she kept her eyes on the man in front of her, holding his gaze with the strength she wished she possessed all those years ago.

"I almost didn't recognize you, Lynn. I had to do a double-take. You're all grown up now, aren't you? Can I cut in?"

"No. I was just leaving."

"Fallon? How do you know Captain Green?" Rafe asked, stepping closer to her.

Ignoring Rafe, she narrowed her eyes. "You're an officer, I see. I guess West Point worked out well for you."

"I see you've gotten a little sassy with age."

"Okay, I don't know what the fuck is going on here, but you're gonna want to watch the way you're talking to her."

"Rafe?" she asked, feeling the prominent tension forming in his muscles. "Can you give us a minute?"

His eyes flashed to hers in warning. "Babe," he said in a way that told her he didn't like that idea whatsoever. In a way that said there was no way in hell he was going to leave her.

"I just need a minute to talk to him," she insisted. But he didn't budge. Smoothing her hands along the fabric of her dress, she turned from his hands and walked toward the nearest empty table.

She knew the fluid, leisurely steps that followed behind her weren't Rafe's. They were nothing like his strong, determined steps.

She turned swiftly, her butt bumping against the table as he stood right behind her. Pulling oxygen into her lungs, she stared up at him.

Ever so slightly, he smiled. Her stomach churned. "So it really is you. Fallon Kelly. I'll be damned. It's been, what? Seven years?" Reaching out, he brushed his fingers down her arms, chafing her skin with his grating touch.

There was nowhere for her body to retreat to. He was so close, the coolness of his medals that hung proudly below the ribbons on his uniform chilled her. It was as if she were a scared seventeen-year-old again, standing in front of the person she was hoping would come to her rescue. And it infuriated her. How could he possibly think she would want to see him, talk to him, after everything that had happened between them? After he'd cowardly turned his back on her?

"Eight," she replied, forcing herself to meet his eyes.

"When I saw you walk onto that dance floor, I thought there was no way in hell you were my Fallon. But here you are."

"I was never 'your Fallon,' Curt. Let's face it, we were kids thrown together by our awful parents. I was never yours. I was merely a piece of their game until I changed the rules."

"You broke the rules, Fallon. Everything was right on track. I'd been accepted into West Point; you were starting your senior year in high school. But you stirred the pot. You knew I wouldn't get into West Point with legal obligations to a child. They would have pulled my acceptance, given someone else my spot. There was no other way. If you had stayed and I'd given up my parental rights to secure my spot at West Point, what would that have done to my name? I would've become the villain, the deadbeat. And if you'd stayed and lied, said it wasn't mine, think of what that would have done to your family's reputation. There was no other way, Fallon."

"I know, in your opinion, there was no other way. I get it."

"Good."

"I get that you're an asshole who thought of no one other than himself. You didn't for one minute think about how terrified I was, Curt. I was a kid! I was pregnant. I didn't care what people thought of me or my family or your precious reputation. I was scared and I needed my parents. I needed you. All I wanted was for someone to be there for me so I could figure it out. But no one was!"

"Fallon—"

"Can you for one second—just *one* second—think about what it was like for me? While you were off playing soldier, I was living in a women's home, growing *your* child inside my body. I had no one but myself. No home, no family, no money. Everything I'd ever known, ever had, was taken from me and I was left with nothing." She was seeing red. Her heart was beating so fast that her body shook as it slammed against her chest.

"Well, from what I understand, you're doing pretty well for yourself."

Sighing, she shook her head and turned away from him. She was done. She had nothing more to say other than a few choice words that would most definitely make a scene, and although she loved to claim a room, at that moment she just wanted to disappear.

"Wait a minute," he barked, grabbing her around her wrist as she bolted for the door. He spun her around to face him and she sliced her eyes at him.

"What?" she said with all the hatred she had buried inside her.

"You can at least tell me what you had. Tell me what you did. Did you keep it?"

A bloodcurdling scream formed and swelled at the base of her throat, burning with the need to escape. "You fucking asshole!" she seethed. "You have no right—*no right*—to ask me about her." Tears formed in her eyes, blurring her vision as she willed them away, silently begging them not to fall.

"Her? You had a little girl?" he asked, and the genuine curiosity in his tone sucked what little air she had left from her lungs. She couldn't breathe.

"Fuck you," she whispered, because if she would have released the scream that would have soothed her anger, the tears would've fallen. She would not let him see her cry. Jerking her arm, she tried to pull from his grasp. She needed to get out of there, she needed to get away from him.

"Let go, Curt."

"I want to know, Fallon," he said, tightening his grip on her wrist. "I have a right to know if you kept her, if you kept my daughter."

"You have no fucking right!"

She didn't think; she just reacted. Her palm lurched up and made contact with his face in a sharp slap that echoed through the room.

"Now let me go!"

She thought she'd said the words aloud, but she couldn't be sure. Because at that same moment, Rafe's fist barreled in the space between their bodies and rammed into Curt's jaw with the uneasy sound of bone meeting bone.

She waited for him to lose it, for his rage to consume him, for him to charge back into the fight.

But it was just the one blow. The one hit. And it knocked Curt to the ground.

His hands plowed through her hair, grabbing her firmly behind her head as he brought his inked eyes to her. "You okay?" His voice, his touch, his eyes brought her back—slowing the anger, the hurt that was gnawing at her insides.

"I'm fine."

"That's him, isn't it?" he asked, piecing it together.

"Yeah."

"You realize you just publicly assaulted your commanding officer," Curt bellowed as he shuffled to his feet.

Rafe's body straightened and his hands left her and in the same fluid movement he was in front of Curt again. Baring his teeth, he lowered his voice, threatening. "And I'd fucking do it all over again," he snarled.

Curt laughed, his smile menacing, looking around the room as if beckoning an audience to witness his authority. Always looking for the rise. "I'll have your rank, First Sergeant. You can guarantee it."

"Take it," he urged. His body moved infinitesimally closer to Curt so their chests were touching. Balling his hands into fists, he leveled his threatening eyes. "You think my diamond is more fuckin' important to me?"

Stepping back, Rafe reached into his pocket and pulled out a knife. Raising it to his bicep, he took the corner of a patch that was sewn onto the shoulder of his jacket and cut away the diamond that rested at the center.

He cut away his rank.

"It's not," he said, throwing the ragged scrap of patch at Curt's feet. "*She* is. Take my fuckin' rank, *sir*," he said mockingly. "I'm taking her."

CHAPTER TWENTY-SIX

*T*he desperation in her kiss was simply impossible to absorb. But he tried. He tried like hell to take it all from her.

Her fingernails dug into his scalp as he lowered onto the bed above her, her smooth, naked body contouring to every hard muscle of his.

She fucking fit.

His cock eased into her slick pussy and she instantly tightened around him. He sighed from the pure relief he felt sinking into her. She claimed him. Every fucking part of him. She had the power to destroy him, and he didn't care.

"Rafe," she pleaded. He knew what she wanted. He knew what this body of hers needed.

"Babe," he said, pulling his cock slowly from the depths that were clinging to him so tightly he thought he was going to lose it.

"I'm going to make love to you, slowly. I'm going to make love to you so slowly there won't be anything left for you to feel . . . nothing but me."

Her eyes blinked open, her lids hooding the light bursts that flecked her eyes when she was aroused. Her hips circled, coaxing him to move with her, and he carefully pushed back inside her. She moaned, her eyes drifting shut as her back arched off the bed, her breasts pushing against his chest.

When she was taking all of him, he brushed away the hair that had fallen over her face.

"I've only felt you," she whispered. Her eyes fluttered open and held him with a vise that was the very grip keeping his heart in his chest. Champagne eye softened, bursts of light absorbing him while her hand lifted to his face "You're the only person who's ever made me feel . . ."

Yeah, he was a fucking goner.

He lay on his stomach, his strong arm wrapped tightly around her waist, her legs tangled through his. They just lay their together, spent and elated, breathing the same air that smelled of sex and Rafe.

But she couldn't shake the fear that was crippling her. She wasn't afraid for her own heart. Rafe had broken down every indestructible wall and formed his own barrier around her heart, protecting it. She knew undoubtedly that this man loved her. That this man would love her like no one ever had and like no one ever could.

But she was scared.

He deserved a woman who would take his heart that he was offering and protect it the way he would protect hers.

He deserved a woman who knew how to love him in the fierce way he loved.

"What's going on in that beautiful mind of yours?" he asked, shifting their bodies so they were curled onto their sides, tucked into each other.

Her body melted into his and he lifted his arm for her to nestle into the crook of his shoulder. He swaddled her with his body. She felt so small folded against him, wrapped in his arms, his legs, his warmth. He was so much, always so much. Overwhelming, breathtaking.

She kissed his chest, his arms sweetly crushing her as her lips peppered his skin.

His breathing altered, no longer smooth, but deep and strained while he contracted his arms around her. "You're not thinking about walking away from me again, are you? Because, babe, I'm not letting that happen."

"Rafe." She sighed.

"No," he said, tightening his hold around her, not trapping her, but comforting her. He was safe, warm . . .

"I'm right here, babe. I'm not going anywhere."

"Until I have to dance?"

He flinched. "I can't tell you I accept that, Fallon. You're mine." His hand skirted over her, his finger trailing between her breasts, over her stomach, dipping between her thighs.

Heat scorched, burned, turned to flame as his fingers caressed deep, then withdrew.

Brushing her legs together to relieve the dull ache he'd put there, she lifted her chin to look at him.

"I can't see you on that stage if you're undressing. I can't fuckin' do it, Fallon. I don't want you to fuckin' do it."

The anger she thought would ascend never came. Knowing what she knew about him now . . . she understood, and she sympathized. This was Rafe, intense, protective, passionate.

"That's why I don't want you there," she said, stroking his cheek. "I can't say I would want other women looking at you if the roles were reversed." She lifted her brows, waiting for a smile to form, but nothing came.

"I can make you a deal. If I dance onstage, I'll give you your own private show afterward. Only I'll take my clothes all the way off."

A hard smile lifted his lips, unsure, struggling, but trying. "You're not going to cave on this, are you?"

She shook her head. "It's a part of me, Rafe."

His muscles moved beneath the stubble on his jaw, tense. "I don't like it, babe."

"I'm not asking you to like it."

He sighed. "I do, however, like the way this deal of yours sounds. Completely naked, dancing just for me?"

She nodded, her heart swelling. He was trying. His distress was lining his eyes, but he was trying, for her. "Yes. Completely naked, just for you. I'll even break my rules and allow touching."

He shook his head, his smile softening a little, lifting into the one she loved. "Bribery, huh?"

"Is it working?"

"Well, I'm not giving you up. So yeah, it's working. I still don't like it, babe. And I can't promise that will change."

She captured his face between her hands. "It doesn't have to. I don't dance often, only when I need that escape, that distraction."

Gripping her hips, he pulled her hard against him. "Let me be that for you. Let me give you the distraction you need. Don't you think I can be that for you?"

He already was . . .

"I know you're scared—"

She pulled her head back and tilted her chin up to look at him. "But that's just it, Rafe. You don't know me."

Hurt flashed through his expression, but he smiled through it, his lips curling in that uneven way that melted her. Every. Single. Time. And this time was no different. She felt out of her own skin, completely thawed against him.

His palm cupped her cheek, his touch calming her erratic pulse. "I know you," he whispered, the rough pad of his thumb caressing her bottom lip. "I know that your kiss tastes like cherries."

He picked up her hand, watching as his thumb now rubbed soft circles on her wrist. It was his spot, his direct link to every sensitive part in her body, including her heart. It squeezed, then picked up a gentle, thrumming, hypnotic pace in tune with his fingers as he continued to swirl feather-light patterns on her skin. "I know that the insides of your wrists make you shiver and are just as sensitive as the soles of your feet.

"I know the beautiful freckle on your shoulder and the

two on the small of your back. I know the color of your eyes when you're holding back tears and I know the sound of your laugh and the ease of your smile. I know you don't like to be touched while you sleep but that you love to press against me in the mornings. I know that you bite when you shatter, and I know the way you tremble when you do.

"I know you, babe. I've memorized you. And if you'd let me, I'd memorize your heart. I know how to make it beat a little faster. Just tell me how to make it mine."

"I don't know, Rafe. God, I want to let you. I want to love you the way you deserve to be loved. But I don't know how."

He smiled. "You don't need to know how. That's what you've got me for. Fuck, babe. I'm not going to let you walk away from me because you're scared. Let me love you until you don't know anything other than my love for you.

"You own me, gorgeous. My heart already belongs to you. You just need to give me yours."

Heat swelled behind her eyes, stinging; intruding hot tears filled above her lashes, wanting desperately to spill. Grabbing his hand, she laced her fingers through his and placed it on her chest over her heart. "It's been yours. You stole it a while ago."

That wasn't true. She'd given it to him, placed it inside his own chest, the very moment he gave her his. She just hadn't realized it.

His mouth connected with hers, slow and determined, and she felt his beautiful, damaged lips pull into a smile against hers. "I love you, gorgeous."

Stalling, the words caught in her mouth. If she did this, said this, there was no going back.

She was so completely broken because of him, surrounded by the shards of her walls, yet irreversibly mended.

He opened his eyes and she was lost. Lost in their depth, their honesty, their tenderness. But she was enslaved by their desire, imprisoned by their ferocity, their passion.

His lips smoothed against hers gently, almost careful, and she ached. He wasn't kissing her; he was loving her. Telling her with his mouth.

His taste assaulted her, his tongue tangling with hers, caressing the inside of her mouth. She felt it in her soul, her heart.

Brushing a single light kiss to her lips, he looked at her.

There was a quiet intensity in his eyes, an unspoken passion. A promise that didn't need words.

He licked his lips, tasting her, and she went weak. Everything changed in that one moment. She dove at him, her mouth sealing over his, quick and powerful. Gone was the hesitance he'd instilled in her when he stole her control, her heart.

A heavy growl, luscious and needy, vibrated from his mouth as he flipped her beneath him, pressing his body hard against her softness, sliding effortlessly inside her as her body welcomed him.

His arms tucked underneath her, wrapping her in his arms as he rocked into her, hard, claiming, controlling.

She couldn't get enough. She needed all of him.

"I love you," he mumbled, scattering kisses over the hollow in the dip of her throat.

"I love you too," she whispered. "The true kind."

He stilled inside her, his eyes flashing to hers, and he laughed once, a sweet, comforted laugh, then brought their hands to his mouth, brushing a featherlight kiss to the inside of her wrist.

She shivered.

And he smiled.

"Yeah, babe. The true kind."

EPILOGUE

Fallon was nervous. She'd never been more nervous for a performance in her entire life. She felt as if she were the one stepping on that stage for the very first time, the eager anticipation, the blinding lights, the waiting crowd.

She felt she might be sick. But then Rafe reached over the seat and grabbed her hand, intertwining their fingers, calming her and reassuring her with the gentle squeeze of his strong fingers.

The curtain opened and the dancers walked onstage. Her eyes fell to the center of the stage, to the lead ballerina. Fallon felt a tightening in her chest as she watched her lithe body move across the stage. It was beautiful. It was imperfect and messy and completely beautiful. Fallon knew she was one of those rare talents, that dance ran through her veins. That she was born to dance.

"You okay, babe?" Rafe asked as he leaned into her, his mouth close to her ear.

She nodded. She didn't know seeing a ballet would be

this hard on her. It was the first one she'd been to since leaving her family.

A single tear fell down her cheek and Rafe's lips kissed it away.

His head shifted back to the stage in front of them; then he looked back at her, grasped her chin, and tilted it back, kissing her sweetly. "She's a beautiful dancer, babe. Just like her mother."

She couldn't find any words, so she just nodded and looked back at the little girl with freckles and golden brown hair as she leaped across the stage.

Love encompassed her, filled her so completely. Rafe showed her time and time again how deep his love ran for her. But never more so than when he'd found her daughter. She didn't know how, only that Luca had helped. But the how didn't matter. That crevice in her heart that was saved for her daughter, it shallowed. It would forever be there, but seeing her happy took away some of the pain that crevice held.

Fallon watched from a distance, tears spilling silently down her face. She would never touch her daughter or hear her laugh or her little voice. She could only watch quietly from a distance. But she was okay with that.

Because Fallon had given her the world when she gave her up: a chance at a life that Fallon could never have given her at the time. She gave her unconditional love.

Turns out, she'd always had the ability to love. The true kind.

It just took this irritatingly sexy, mostly adorable, and completely overwhelming man to help her remember how. He'd held her close until she didn't feel anything but his love.

Until she had no other choice but to love.

ONE

Three more days and this hearts and flowers shit would be over. Three more days and the boxes of chocolates filled with things that should definitely not be paired with chocolate would be cleared from the shelves, the cheesy "Be Mine" balloons would deflate, and those damn stuffed gorillas, holding giant hearts, singing "Wild Thing," would be put to rest.

It was almost Valentine's Day in Watertown, New York, and the typical achromatic atmosphere at Fort Drum was replaced with shades of pinks and reds, complete with love banners and window decorations filled with hearts and chubby babies holding arrows. It was Ronnie Clark's personal week of hell.

Needless to say, Ronnie was not a fan of the lovey-dovey mushy shit; in fact, that was putting it graciously.

It was getting late, and Ronnie was listening to the soft

tick of the second hand on her watch as she softly pressed the needle dipped in black ink into the hip of some lovesick barracks brat who had finally landed herself a private. You would think these girls would learn, right? Soldiers are lonely, and, yes, they look damn good in uniform, but the young, single ones are dangerous. They fall hard and fast and pull you in with their puppy-love eyes and promises of forever. These girls know it too; they are looking for it, and once they find it, it's a ring on the finger, a judge-officiated ceremony, and more often than not, it's matching ink declaring their love for each other. Blah blah blah . . .

"All right, Kara, I'm almost done with this locket. Are you sure you want me to put Craig's name under it? Names are not fun to cover up and I charge double to do it. I'm giving you your chance now," she said as she wiped the ink on Kara's hip, smearing it across the Celtic locket. Branding was not Ronnie's thing, but in this town, she was lucky if she went an entire workweek without getting stuck doing at least one.

"Yes, I'm sure." She narrowed her eyes at Ronnie before she turned them to her eager new husband, who was holding her hand.

"Don't say I didn't warn you," Ronnie mumbled under her breath. Oh how she wished she could just slap some sense into this girl. Sure, Craig was every shade of hot, and even Ronnie had an image of him without his uniform on begging to be brought to the forefront of her mind, but he was not tattoo worthy. No man was. No man was that damn permanent.

"Your six thirty sketch consult is here," Harold said, popping his tiny-ass head into Ronnie's room.

Ronnie slathered some ointment on top of the freshly branded flesh. "Tell him I will be there in a few. I'm just finishing up this girl's latest mistake."

"Ronnie!" Harold admonished, but he knew good and well that Ronnie said and did what she wanted and even he couldn't stop her. She was too good an artist to let go anyway. She was the best he had ever seen.

Ronnie lifted her head and raised her eyebrows at Harold, challenging him. He just shook his head and walked away.

"All right, keep it clean, but don't mess with it too much." She covered the girl's tattoo with a nonstick bandage and taped it down before turning and cleaning up.

"Harold will check you out." She stood from her chair and headed out of the room without as much as looking back behind her.

Most would call her rude, but she liked to think of it more as "real." She didn't sugarcoat anything and she wasn't going to pretend to like you if she didn't.

Ronnie sashayed to the front of the tattoo shop. She had one last client tonight and then she could slip off her heels and go home. Sure, she was going home to nothing, and not because her fiancé was still deployed and overseas, but because her fiancé was now an ex-fiancé and her solo living arrangement was now irreversible. Apparently her fiancé had a problem keeping it in his pants while he was gone, and his squad's female medic just so happened to be the lucky one to help him with his little, and she did mean little, dilemma. Okay, maybe she was being a smidge too hard on him . . . nah.

The shitty thing about it all—well, other than her fiancé sleeping around on her—was that she found out from someone else. His best friend, who just so happened to be deployed with him, called and told her what was going on. That was not a phone call that she wanted to get, let alone from someone other than the piece-of-shit cheater himself. When she confronted her fiancé about it he didn't even deny it, just acted like she should forget about it. He was halfway across the world, how could she possibly think he could wait that long? Fucking prick.

"Kale Emerson?" Ronnie said, scanning the waiting room. There were only two people there: one was Harold's intern, who was waiting to do his nightly bitch work, and the other one was a fuckingly handsome Captain America impersonator. He was tall, broad, and his well-defined arms were bulging through the thin material of his shirt. His sandy brown hair was cut short, barely enough on top to run your hands through, and of course he had to have blue eyes that seemed to grab onto hers with a force that held her captive. And for the first time in a long time, she felt vulnerable.

Kale Emerson turned around as a melodic voice sang out his name. Standing next to the front counter was a brunette bombshell in the sexiest purple heels he had ever seen on a woman's feet, making her damn near as tall as he was. Her legs went on forever and her almost black hair hung down past her shoulders and curled at the ends. Kale would like to say he saw her deep brown eyes first, but lying wasn't his strong suit and so help him if those lips weren't the first thing on that gorgeous face that caught his attention. They were plump, full, and cherry red and they parted into a smile when his eyes finally locked on hers.

Kale sauntered up to the counter and outstretched his hand. "Hi, I'm Kale. I have an appointment with Ronnie." The woman looked at his hand but didn't make a move to place hers in his.

"You're looking at her," she said bluntly.

"You're Ronnie?"

"Guilty. Come on back. We can talk in the design room."

Kale followed Ronnie through the narrow hallway, lined with framed drawings of cryptic angels and dragons, among other things. The entire place smelled like antiseptic cleaner, but Kale could still smell the hint of vanilla and musk that lingered in the air as Ronnie passed through. She was wearing a tight black shirt that dipped low into a V in the back, showcasing a delicate dream-catcher tattoo that started at the base of her neck and ended at the curve in her spine. The entire tattoo was done in shades of black; the only color was the turquoise beads dangling from the dream catcher. It was stunning; he had to refrain from reaching out and tracing it with his finger.

"Right in here." Ronnie stopped in front of a door leading to a large room and gestured for him to go on in.

"Ladies first," he said, reaching his hand out toward the open space in the door.

Ronnie's thick black eyebrows arched up and her full lips curved in a sexy-ass smirk. "I'm no lady," she said, then turned toward the room and glided in.

Kale followed her past the black sofa and flat-screen TV to the back of the room where a large glass table with black leather desk chairs took up the back wall.

Ronnie sat down at the table, crossing her legs, and her shoe slipped off her heel, causing it to dangle from her toes. Fuck, those heels were hot. Kale had been home from Iraq for all of six days. He had yet to sleep with a woman and this one sitting in front of him was becoming tempting.

Kale lived alone. He had no family to go home to, so coming back to Fort Drum for R & R was the only option. If he had his way, he would have just stayed with his platoon and continued to lead his troops, but he didn't have his way and it was mandatory he took his leave. He told his commander that he wanted to wait until after the holidays. Why should the men with families and kids have to miss Christmas if they didn't have to? No, Kale wouldn't be missing out on spending Christmas and New Year's with anyone: he wanted his soldiers to have that chance, so he opted to take his leave now instead. Six days down, eight more to go. Then it's back to the sandpit and Kale couldn't wait.

One perk about getting the hell out of that country was the women. It had been eight months since he had been in the States, and it had been eight months since he had had sex. Casual sex was Kale's forte. He didn't do relationships or commitment, just sex. Kale didn't have time to worry about putting someone else ahead of him; hell, he didn't even have time to put himself ahead of him. His soldiers came first, they always had. He loved his country and he loved his job, and a woman just didn't quite fit into that equation. No woman he had ever been with had been able to change his opinion either, but that didn't stop him from needing a woman to get underneath him from time to time. Now was one of those times and he wanted Ronnie to be that woman.

"All right, let's get down to business," Ronnie said, sliding a sketch pad in front of her from the middle of the table. "What do you have in mind?"

Her voice broke through his mental slush pile and brought him back. "I want a memorial tattoo."

"Okay."

Kale leaned back in his chair. "I want a poem, a soldier's prayer. I want it tattooed on my back, and I want it to look like my skin is ripping, revealing the words."

Ronnie wrote notes on her sketch pad.

"And I want the names of my fallen brothers to be after the prayer."

Ronnie looked up at Kale and an emotion flashed across her face that he didn't quite understand. It wasn't pity; was it awe?

"That's beautiful," she said quietly. Kale didn't know the first thing about this woman, but he gathered she didn't throw out compliments much. "How does the prayer go?" she asked, her eyes returning to her sketch pad as she prepared to write.

Kale slowly recited the prayer, his eyes locked on Ronnie as she wrote the words that told of courage and strength, of sacrifice and devotion. "And may my fallen brothers walk with you now, Lord. Amen."

Kale cleared his throat after he finished the names of his fallen soldiers, and rubbed his hand over the back of his head. Their eyes met and Kale's mood shifted back. One look at her and he couldn't seem to think of anything but touching her. Yes, it apparently had been a long time because he felt like a twelve-year-old boy who just saw his first pair of boobs.

"I can have this ready for you tomorrow. When would you like to get started?" Ronnie asked as she closed her sketch pad and stood up. Kale stood up as well, his body leaning a little closer to her than he intended, and she took an immediate step back.

"Tomorrow will be fine." Kale shoved his hands in the pockets of his jeans to keep himself from grabbing her tiny waist and pulling her against him. That thought kept taunting him and he was damn ready to do it.

"Okay." She narrowed her big brown eyes at Kale, confusing the hell out of him. Ronnie walked back to the door and stopped, turning around with a hand on her hip. "You can stop fucking me in your mind now."

Kale's eyes came close to popping out of his head. "Excuse me?"

Ronnie rolled her eyes. "Let's get this straight, soldier. I'm not sleeping with you. You can get it out of your pretty little head, and I suggest you do so before I stick a needle in your skin." She turned back around, her sexy heels clicking out of the room.

*H*oly shit, he was sexy. And the way he was looking at her? He was threatening to make Ronnie come undone right there in the design room. She was used to having men gawk at her. She worked in a man's industry and had been subject to more than her fair share of pathetic one-liners and roaming eyeballs, but the way Kale looked at her was different; she didn't know what it was, but it was different. He was unashamed as he took her in, but he wasn't vulgar or offensive about it. He was just . . . hot. But he was a soldier and Ronnie sure as hell didn't do soldiers, not anymore.

"Since this is a large tattoo I need you to be my last appointment of the day. Can you be here tomorrow night at seven?" Ronnie asked as Kale finally emerged from the hallway.

"I will be here." He looked her in the eyes, unwavering and unaffected from the little threat she gave in the other room.

Before Kale walked around the reception desk, he stopped at the end of the hall and leaned in close to Ronnie. Her body jolted to attention the moment the heat from his breath hit her neck. She was about to spit out words to him that even her trailer-park, sailor-swearing momma would be embarrassed by when his hand touched the small of her back.

"For the record, sweetheart, I wasn't 'mind-fucking' you, but thank you for putting that image in my head." He pulled away, and his pretty-boy, clean-cut, "yes-sir" persona faltered a little bit. The corners of his mouth tilted just slightly into an imperative smile, but it didn't last long. "See you tomorrow night." His tone was now formal, like he hadn't just planted goose bumps along the side of her neck. Fuck, tomorrow was going to be interesting.

Kelsie Leverich is the *New York Times* bestselling author of *The Valentine's Arrangement* and *Feel the Rush*. She lives in Indiana with her husband and two children and their three pets. When she's not writing, you can usually find her out on the lake with friends and family or snuggling on the couch with her kids and a good book. She loves stories that sweep you off your feet, make you fall in love, break your heart, and heal your soul.

CONNECT ONLINE

kelsieleverich.com
facebook.com/kelsieleverich
twitter.com/kelsielev